Father's
Day

Father's Day

Day

John Calvin Batchelor

A Novel

Henry Holt and Company

New York

Henry Holt and Company, Inc.
Publishers since 1866
115 West 18th Street
New York, New York 10011

Henry Holt® is a registered
trademark of Henry Holt and Company, Inc.

Published in Canada by Fitzhenry & Whiteside Ltd.,
195 Allstate Parkway, Markham, Ontario L3R 4T8.

Library of Congress Cataloging-in-Publication Data
Batchelor, John Calvin.
Father's day: a novel / John Calvin Batchelor—1st ed.
p.   cm.
1. Twenty-first century—Fiction.   I. Title.
PS3552.A8268F38   1994
813'.54—dc20   94-14461
                                                          CIP

ISBN 0-8050-3266-5

Henry Holt books are available for special promotions and
premiums. For details contact: Director, Special Markets.

First Edition—1994

Designed by Paula R. Szafranski

Printed in the United States of America
All first editions are printed on acid-free paper.∞

3   5   7   9   10   8   6   4

My Anna Belle

"When the shooting starts, they always send for the sons of bitches."

—ADMIRAL ERNEST KING, 1941

Prologue

In the election of 2000, Governor Theodore G. Jay, Democrat of Michigan, was elected the forty-third president of the United States of America, and Senator T. E. Garland, Democrat of Texas, was elected vice president.

The Jay-Garland ticket carried forty-five states and won five hundred electoral votes.

Within two years, President Jay's approval rating had plunged to a post–Cold War low.

Then the president collapsed with a disability diagnosed as a major depressive episode.

Invoking the Twenty-fifth Amendment, "Presidential Vacancy, Disability, and Inability," President Jay temporarily transferred the duties of his office to the vice president.

Vice President Garland took the reins of power on January 7, 2003, as the nation watched and waited on its first ever acting president.

Part One

OPERATION FATHER'S DAY

---

1 Sunday Dawn, Arkansas

Red Schofield's plan for the assault on the president began with a solitary car alarm going off in the rental section of the parking lot across from the airport terminal.

It was morning in America, a cool half hour before the dawn, and Schofield could see his whole plan play out in his mind's eye just as it played out there on the field. It was a trick Schofield possessed, a trained power to see, hear, feel, touch, and even smell the events he had set in motion with his command.

Schofield could picture the president's plane beginning its descent from twenty-five thousand feet. Air Force One was due on the ground in twenty-five minutes. Schofield knew there would be no circling for other traffic, no delay whatsoever. The president was coming down in the same meticulous manner that attended all the preparations for his arrival. Schofield could

3

count the Secret Service agents already deployed in and around the terminal building—the thirteen special agents and four technical agents as well as six dozen local law enforcement officers from both the state police barracks and city police headquarters. He could hear them rocking on their heels; he could smell the coffee on their breath; he could even overhear them talking about their assignments—who was first in line for the motorcade, who had the whole wheat doughnuts, who was getting the breakfast receipts to pass on to the watch commander.

Schofield knew the car alarm would rattle everyone. Like a flat tire on a limousine, it would be an unacceptable break in the routine of prepping for the big boss. No one would have thought about such a surprise. Lone snipers, mad bombers, lightning strike, power failure, flash fire, aircraft trouble—all that was credible to the Secret Service Office of Protective Research, which studied and swept and certified each new presidential travel route; but a car alarm was not in the book.

Schofield knew that the agents of the advance team were in no better position to deal with such a turn than the book, yet it would be left to them, surely it would be. The local cops would hang back. Let the feds with the voices in their ears and the Uzis in the attaché cases take care of it, the cops would think; let the feds in their eight-hundred-dollar suits get their hands dirty looking under the hood.

Now there was a second car alarm. Schofield could just see two of the special agents at the terminal door glance at each other and wince. A mistake? No, those were Detroit-made car alarms, first from the Avis section in the parking lot and then from the Hertz section—both broadcasting a series of wails, whistles, honks, and Klaxon blasts that would not quit. For thirty seconds no one volunteered, no orders were given; but now there was a crackle in the earpieces, and the shrill voice of the special agent in charge demanding, "Shut it off!" The two agents at the door, male and female, moved reflexively, the hatless man in the trail and the trim-skirted woman on the point. "I guess it's up to us," the man said. The woman reported on her headset to the team leader, "We've got it."

The pedestrian gate was padlocked, so the agents had to skirt back around to the vehicle entrance. Above them to the right were the golden nightlights of a small four-story Hilton hotel. Now there was a third car alarm, and then a fourth, from the National and Budget sections, some of General Motors' most obnoxious noise screaming out like a dozen sirens.

The new alarms made the agents reach defensively for their ears. This was wrong, they were thinking, but how? All they could see behind them was the line of police cruisers and the presidential minivan at the terminal's curb. What else? This was a modest civil airport in the rolling wooded hills above the river—two major carriers, several maintenance hangars, and a lineup of parked private aircraft, one traveler's hotel. The two-story terminal building was redbrick rectangles topped by the squat inverted cone of a tower. The sky was charcoal. The air was moist ozone.

Where was the threat? The light was muted neon. The scent was pollen-laden springtime. The early ground-feeding birds were chirping as they darted over the tall grass.

So where was the threat? What was that faraway thumping sound? More car alarms?

It would take the two agents the time to make a few deep swallows, Schofield knew, for them to sort through all the contradictions and decide that they must act.

The male agent would say to the woman, "I don't like this." The female agent would gripe, "All of them at once isn't very likely."

The Hertz car alarm was in a Ford hatchback, maroon with Texas plates. It was the nearest to the agents, so they would try once more to reassure themselves by looking inside. And what would they see? This was a parking lot. Besides the three dozen rentals, there were at most ten private cars left long-term in an otherwise flat, vacant field of blacktop, and beyond that there was a two-lane road down from the bluff; there was a small bridge over a creek.

What was to see? What was to report, except four, then five, then six car alarms—a symphony of alert bawling out a threat-warning that everyone could hear but no one could understand?

Red Schofield understood the threat-warning. Lieutenant Colonel George M. "Red" Schofield was the threat. And he was coming at two hundred and fifty knots in command of an American light infantry task force that could not be stopped.

At that moment Schofield was ten kilometers to the north of the parking lot. He was belted into a starboard-side foldaway seat in the main cabin of a V-22 Osprey, and with a headset he was listening in to the four point-attack helicopters leading his assault. The pilots' voices were scratchy and taciturn. What Schofield cared about was that the point guy with the first glimpse of the parking lot and the terminal gave the green light signal.

"Sky King, this is Eye One," the lead pilot radioed. "Car Alarm. Repeat, Car Alarm. Roger. Over."

Schofield waited for confirmation from the wingman, and then he looked across to his executive officer to give a thumbs-up.

Schofield transmitted to his company commanders, "This is Sky King. All stations. We have Car Alarm. We have Car Alarm confirmed. Repeat, Car Alarm is a definite go. Everybody move now. Roger. Over."

The confirmation calls of "Roger, out" came back to Schofield's XO, Major Mario Cello, and Cello gave Schofield a thumbs-up for Brauchli's Able Company on the point; a thumbs-up for Incavagglia's Charlie on the flank; a thumbs-up for Engelmann's Baker in ready reserve at the staging area.

Schofield felt the Osprey bank forty-five degrees and then yaw to a roaring hover for the transition. During the wing-fold from the airplane to the helicopter mode, the integrated electronic cockpit took over the ship, and the pilot sat by, watching the six monitors and waiting to take the control column and swoop. What it felt like was flying sideways to nowhere. The Ospreys were coming in at shrub level anyway, so what was another few meters closer to failure? Schofield had told the flight leader to get them in under the power lines, and he didn't care if the guy aimed to go in under the telephone lines.

Transition done, the ship accelerated to one hundred knots. The green light flashed, and the Osprey's crew chief poked through the screen and waved at Schofield with four fingers: four minutes to contact.

Every soldier in the cabin saw the signal, and two squads of Schofield's streamlined headquarters company—twenty-five pathfinders, map carriers, medics, and technicians—snapped up their chinstraps and slapped down their body armor tabs: weapons tucked; feet planted; postures fixed for a crash landing. The crew chief popped the rear loading ramp/door a hair to test the hydraulic actuator.

The crew chief signaled his door gunners and then cried out over the whining roar, "Three minutes, Colonel!"

Schofield sucked air and tapped his RTO, Corporal Ky, to check the signal on the manpack transceiver one last time. Schofield never wanted to hit a landing zone again without that transceiver certified.

Schofield's headset crackled, and he listened in on the lead AH-6F Defender pilot. The ugly little bumblebee of a helicopter cleared the highway and darted for the Hilton. The pilot had night vision goggles, a thermal imager, and a laser rangefinder to lock on the line of police cruisers.

Did the special agents ever solve their confusion? Did they figure out that the car alarms had covered all those turboshaft and rotor system power plants coming in at zero meters?

The agents did manage to shout "No!" before they were taken down by the four-man fire team that came out of the rentals. Two more fire teams came out of the service entrance of the Hilton and leaped the chain-link fence, heading through the main terminal door. The police were paralyzed by the surging sound waves thrown before the closing Defenders. No one got a weapon free. The pod-mounted Chain Guns tore up the pavement like tank treads. Men and women were screaming and crying, "Hey!" and "Shit!" and looking to run into the brick walls.

Two Ospreys swept past the Defenders and heaved over the terminal superstructure to hammer onto the parking lot beside the rentals. All three squads of Able's second platoon were soon jumping over the waist-high fence and screaming at the paralyzed police, "Down! Down! Everyone down! This is Uncle Sugar, everyone down!"

Before he exchanged his headset for his helmet, Schofield got the report of Able's lead platoon hitting the parking lot. He knew the strike teams would be into the terminal building by now, targeting anyone that moved, and the very first foxtrot would be at the tower door entrance. Would the Secret Service figure it out in time? And do what? Return fire? Make a stand? With what—Uzis? Against frags and M16s and body armor?

The crew chief told Schofield, "Thirty seconds, Colonel!" and threw his hand up.

"Stand up!" cried the squad sergeants.

Schofield lowered his night vision goggles and stood up to brace himself. He pictured the main terminal secured of hostiles. It was as if he could inspect the inside of the control tower, could hear the two air traffic controllers talking to their supervisor, could feel the weapons lowered on the civilian personnel. The team leader told the air traffic controllers, "Routine, just routine, sirs," and then he got on the horn and called Able Company's CO, Brauchli, with the all-clear report.

Major Cello was listening in on the channel. Schofield waited for Cello's thumbs-up signal that the tower was secure before he took another deep breath. Air Force One's transponder was on a radar set he owned now. Not that he needed it for more than making sure he could control the talk to the flight deck. It was a useless radar scope for anything else, since a matter of fact was that if you don't turn on your transponder, you don't exist to modern aviation. Schofield's point-attack Defenders and two squadrons of Ospreys came in as black as stealth with the assault elements of a battalion.

The rear door swung down as the Osprey hit, and Schofield was out with his squads. One step, slide, two steps, slide, he moved by rote, his mind's eye everywhere on the field at once— with Charlie Company at the hangars and tank farm, with the strike teams in the terminal, with Able's Second with the prisoners. Once on the ground, he ran easily without looking where he was going. He took hold of the horn of the transceiver. *One check at a time,* he thought. He spoke in single words that conveyed prearranged instructions. His code name was Sky King. The go code was Car Alarm. The task force was named for the commander, Task Force Schofield.

Schofield's position was on the median strip along the northeast runway. He forced himself to come up out of his crouch, a six-foot man of weapons, camouflage, body armor, and fret. He pictured the two special-loaded Ospreys sweeping up from the river basin at the treetops. His RTO, Corporal Ky, was at his left, and Schofield handed back the horn. The footing was sloppy. It had rained last night, thunderstorms out of Oklahoma. He could smell the wet oil slicks and the evaporation.

Schofield told Ky, "Watch the ground. No bad ankles this time, Ky."

Ky exhaled in reply. Last time had been two weeks before, fifteen miles east of the Dniester River, with Black Cossack snipers like shadows trying for throat shots.

Schofield stopped Ky on the grass between the taxiway and the runway, and he signaled Cello's assistant to plant the commander bunker. The small headquarters company deployed along the lights in the declivity between the concrete: a security perimeter, an aid station, a command and control position, and most important the dolly with the portable unit of an early warning/ground control station that they'd brought along in case they lost the tower's help. Cello was airborne again in the unloaded Osprey, back to take a standby position with all the transports in hidey-hole holding patterns north of the field. In case of a disaster Cello was to supervise an extraction by Baker Company, covered by the Defenders and all the firepower in the remnant.

The two special-loaded Ospreys roared down out of the tree-line and released their cargoes with rubbery thuds on the tarmac.

All this was in a weak darkness, and the night vision goggles that turned everything a sick blue-green were beginning to fail Schofield. He was on the horn to Cello. "This is Sky King. Talk to me, Mario." He ripped up the goggles. "Cello, read me the numbers!"

Major Cello spoke convincingly. "Sky King, this is Cargo Primary. Your signal is Lima Charlie, sir. All right, sir. We're holding our position at Checkpoint Smith. It's just like you scripted it. Over."

"Tell me the shooters are in place," Schofield suggested.

"Sky King, the shooters are copacetic, sir," Cello returned. "All's gone exactly as you said it would. Roger. Over."

Cello's tin-tongued, he thought. "Give me the time," Schofield barked.

"Sky King—we're coming up on H plus twenty-four minutes," Cello replied. "It's a go. Car Alarm. Over."

Schofield signed off. "Roger. Over."

The special loads were Hummers that had been stripped down to carry, when deployed, what looked like twenty-six-foot-high lifeguard towers on their backs. After banging and crunching in blue light, the towers were ready. The strike teams mounted the equipment, four on a platform. The Hummers backed up a hundred meters to Schofield's command post and slowed at his side. Schofield walked close enough to smell the fuel. At the top the strike team leader, Master Sergeant Tom Owen, the Top of the battalion and the clear-eyed first dog soldier, spoke to his boss. "Coming up H plus twenty-nine minutes, sir."

Sergeant Childers on the other platform grunted, "It's cake for us, sir."

Schofield didn't reply. He wasn't the hard guy he was supposed to be. He got easier about details as the action got rougher, and he worried all the time. At forty-two, twenty-one years out of West Point, he had face lines enough for a sixty-year-old, and only a fringe of his red hair remained. Mario Cello and Tom Owen were trying to calm him down. He didn't want to calm down. When everything went according to plan, when every detail was a go, that still left him in a place where he had to carry out an unthinkable act.

Schofield looked up to Tom Owen. "Here's what I think about my plan. Who knows if the shooters can stop it? Who knows what happens when you set off charges? If it doesn't stop, we can do it from this end. It'll be messy, but we can do it. And good luck."

The Hummers veered off across the grass to their positions a mile up the runway. Schofield told himself, *They can do this, they could always do this, but can I do my part?*

"Ky," Schofield said, "what's our luck this morning?"

It was an old habit of a question—a fretful CO to his even-tempered RTO—and big-shouldered Ky returned his old habit of an answer, "Our luck is all green lights, sir, all green lights."

Schofield took the horn from Ky and called Cello. "Cargo, this is Sky King. Owen and Childers are away. I guess I'm pleased. Get the birds back another five clicks. And think up what you'll do about anything. Here we go, Mario. Roger. Over."

A dozen miles downrange, the hundred-meter-long extensively modified 747-200 jumbo jet designated VC-25A, known as Air Force One, continued its final approach.

On the flight deck the captain and cocaptain were listening to the air controller's routine recommendations. The 89th Military Airlift Wing ran its fourteen-year-old premier aircraft—there were actually two of them, 28000 and 29000—as though they were the best first-class commercial jetliners ever put in the air. Each item was double-checked to the point of numbness. The captain sighed like a patient father when he leaned forward to inspect the engines visually. What could go wrong? Gremlins on the wings? The cocaptain put on the Fasten Seat Belts sign. The captain called the special agent in charge of the president's living quarters.

"This is Major Bohr," the captain said. "We'll be on the ground in three minutes."

The special agent at the door of the living quarters acknowledged the captain on the same intercom. "Okay, everyone's mostly ready."

In the ample living quarters directly below the flight deck, in what would have been the first-class area of the plane, the president was licking at his second cup of coffee at his desk. He didn't use cream or sugar, and he liked it weak. He was dressed comfortably in loose jeans and a white pullover, with untied running shoes, like a tennis player who had decided to go fishing. Cradling a receiver in one hand and the coffee cup in the other, the president was looking down at notes he'd made. Across the aisle from the president's desk three aides were trying to act bright-eyed while a gaunt steward, after folding up the president's bed, was fetching the cups. The female aide was fixing her fair hair; the two young males were shifting papers in their hands. One said, "Guess we'd better buckle up for safety." The woman said, "God, it's early for it to be so early."

In this vast aircraft, four thousand square feet of an airborne bed-and-breakfast, there was room enough to feed and sleep a presidential staff of thirty, an air crew of twenty-five, and a press pool of forty. This presidential excursion was lightly attended, and the galley cooks had an easy time delivering up breakfast. The president had already eaten a double portion of pastry, and he grabbed an apple tart off the tray as the steward stored it in the cart. The president said, "I feel like a real breakfast when we get to the camp. Must be the short night. You guys hungry, too?"

Air Force One swept in over the perimeter fence and settled down inside the landing lights of the ten-thousand-foot southwest runway.

Fifteen hundred feet along, the tires hit once and stuck at one hundred and thirty knots.

Flaps down, engines racing, the speed dropped quickly. The pilot nodded to the copilot at the landing.

Sixty-five hundred feet along, the aircraft slowing to seventy knots, there were two puffs that splashed black smoke on a front tire.

Seven thousand feet along, the copilot took the ship

and began the easy turnoff to the taxiway at sixty knots.

A moment later the traffic controller called the flight deck to report that there was smoke showing on the front gear.

The captain muttered, "Fffff——," and ordered routine emergency shutdown. He was thinking, *A blown tire. No sweat. Park the bird here and let them tow me in.*

The jumbo jet slowed below sixty knots. The crew was suddenly very busy bringing two hundred tons to a convenient stop.

Underneath the aircraft, the two special Hummers were running at speed on opposite sides of the fuselage until they matched the velocity of the aircraft. The soldiers atop the siege towers were standing like wind surfers with their equipment slung over their shoulders.

As the aircraft slowed to thirty-five knots, as the Hummers reached the spots where the wings met the fuselage, the soldiers on both platforms leaped onto the wings. They made their way with large flat-footed steps, as if they were moonwalking on a truck bed.

Air Force One was at a sprinting pace now. The engines gave a low rushing roar. The troops on either wing reached the emergency exit doors over the wings. Air Force One was an enormous flying fortress, with hardened communications, shielded cable, and grounded metal screens covering the windows; only the emergency exits were necessarily constructed so they could be removed in a hurry.

Critically, the emergency exits had no warning lights on the flight deck.

The two fire teams worked as if they were mirror images of each other. Two sergeants gave hand signals, two sets of men pressed themselves flat against the fuselage with heads turned away from the hatchway. Two dull thuds sounded, *rump! rump!* as charges creased the emergency doors out and violated the seals. Tugs on two lines heaved the light metal hatches back, one giving way entirely to clang on the wing and then fall to the pavement twenty-six feet below.

Two teams were into the cabin like spelunkers. One hatchway was in the empty galley section portside; the other was in the long twin-seated staff section. Stepping over the stunned, choking passengers, the teams each had a goal: Childers's Red Team to the flight deck on the upper level; Tom Owen's Blue Team to the president's living quarters at the bow.

Amidship, Red Team overran two special agents and hardly slowed to flatten them as Childers reached the airstairs. He took three giant steps and touched the flight cabin door. He knocked once.

"Captain?" Childers called. The door cracked.

The engineer saw Childers's M16A4 first and coolly asked, "Is this a hijacking?"

Childers told the crew, "Routine, just routine, gentlemen. I'm Uncle Sugar like you," as he eased the engineer away from his panel.

"Stop her right here, sir," Childers suggested to the copilot.

Schofield had designed the assault so that Childers took the Mission Communications System room right after the flight deck. The tactical approach was first put out the eyes, then slit the throat. The MCS was on the upper level aft of the flight deck, and it was vital to secure it in such a way that there was no interruption in command and control. Childers breached the MCS room by just opening the unlocked door and stepping inside. The wall of microchip boxes and video screens lit the chamber like an arcade.

Schofield could picture the warrant officer on duty. The young man couldn't believe what he faced with Childers's flat expression and black weapon and unmistakable intention.

Childers said, "This is Uncle Sugar. Everybody real slow, look down at your hands real slow." The two female radio operators put their hands on the console and watched the weapons. Childers urged his RTO inside to slip into the warrant officer's chair.

"All is routine this morning, compadres," Childers said. "Routine."

On the main deck, at the door of the living quarters, the two agents answered the knock. Blue Team leader Tom Owen smashed back the door and kept going right through the conference room, past the lavatory to the president's office and then inside with a leap.

Tom Owen had to reach the president before he could dive for the survival capsule.

Gunfire was needless. The agents went down silently before the hurtling mass of the armored troops. In the president's office, the three aides couldn't clear their seat belts before they were pushed back down and warned.

This was the part Schofield wasn't sure of. Would the president put the receiver down and relax in his chair with his accustomed sense of invulnerability? Or would he start yelling orders and reach for his beige telephone?

Tom Owen would do his job, lowering his weapon and saluting. "Good morning, sir. I'm Master Sergeant Tom Owen of the First Battalion, Fourteenth Regiment, Tenth Mountain. My orders are to ask you to please remain seated, sir, until we get the situation sorted out."

Would the president comply, or would he argue back? Perhaps he would say, "I doubt that, Sergeant," or perhaps he would just try, "Who is your commander?"

In any event Schofield knew that no more than five minutes were gone from the blowing of the emergency exits to when all twenty-five crew members and thirty-two passengers were neutralized if not secured.

Schofield watched Air Force One roll to a full stop on the taxiway approximately half a mile from his position.

It was 0535 hours. First gray light was giving way to a surging rosy hue on the rolling eastern horizon as the stars vanished before the inevitable hot day.

Across the breadth of the airport, there was little to be heard other than four of GE's biggest engines shutting down with surly whimpers. Schofield's standing orders put a premium on silent skill, and the airport was now so completely in hand that, when the jumbo jet finally shut down, the single irregular sound was that the field was too quiet for all to be normal.

There was a popping noise as the forward staircase unfurled from the belly of the plane below the president's living quarters. Designed to accommodate a field that didn't have landing gates, the staircase provided quick access for the three additional fire teams that climbed into the aircraft to bind and secure all prisoners.

Schofield started running over the wet field. By the time he was standing at the foot of the belly staircase, he was talking to Cello on the horn. "Cargo, this is Sky King. I want our people out now, Mario. Get Charlie out first. It's over when we're out of here, and not before. Extract, now. Over."

Schofield's orthodox thinking was that you don't deploy five hundred and sixty soldiers and call it a success until you get them out of trouble as quickly as you got them in. "Tell me you understand me, Mario," Schofield demanded. "Tell me your people are coming lickety-split. Tell me we have uplink to the big birds. Tell me the brass is on its way."

The big birds were the C-17s that had airlifted the battalion into the staging area, Car Alarm One. Schofield wanted the Ospreys moving back to the LZ to extract the battalion. Cello acknowledged the orders and then told Schofield that the brass flight was approaching, ETA three minutes.

Schofield threw the horn to Ky and charged up into the aircraft. Three minutes gave him very little time to inspect how his plan had worked. He emerged in the presidential conference room—a boat-shaped board table, several padded swivel chairs, the trimmings of a hotel suite—and he didn't bother checking the prisoners. He just started up to Childers on the flight deck.

"All routine, sir," Childers reported on the stairwell. "No casualties either way. They've been good about it, like you said they would."

Schofield saw that Childers was not understating his success. The security on board Air Force One had been as by the book as Schofield had supposed. No one had anticipated landing on a hostile field. No one had figured a blown tire was because of two sharpshooters. No one had been prepared for a forced entry while still rolling. No one had been ready to start a firefight on the aircraft. No one in the MCS had been quick enough to send out an alert without orders. They'd all heard the double bangs of the charges. But what was an explosion in the landing of a behemoth?

Schofield bumped his elbow as he went down the stairs, and the pain made him pause to get his bearings. *Okay, George,* he told himself, *you got the easy part right, you took the beast. What about the next part?*

Schofield took a moment to duck into the galley to inspect one of the ripped-open emergency exits. The charges had been just enough to let the airlock fail on its own and blow out as designed. An unlocked back door without an alarm.

Schofield was half pleased all around. To pull three companies out of a battle zone, load them on C-17s at night, fly them around the world for a rendezvous with Ospreys, load up again, and then hit an unprepped LZ before dawn, and to have planned the whole operation on paper while they were orbiting for the last sixteen hours, and to do it on cold food and worse sleep—all such miracles were a credit to the battalion's readiness. The other credit was to the clever Hummer design Cello had worked up on a notepad and radioed ahead.

Back down the gangway, Schofield found Ky and some disorder he'd missed before. The chamber smelled like a Budapest bordello. Someone must have crushed a bottle of perfume in the passageway, and with the power down and air-conditioning off, the fumes were spinning out like CS gas. The generals wouldn't care about such a trifle, but it wasn't right to have that aroma in a combat zone. Maybe the stink of the charges would drift up here.

Schofield stopped himself. *Why worry about this? Leave it alone. You're stalling, get on with it.*

He pushed forward to the president's living quarters. Tom Owen was the lone guard on the president, and he came to quick alert.

The president looked at Schofield the scornful way a man might consider a disappointing messenger.

Tom Owen whispered sideways, "He's frigging mad as a treed cat, sir."

Schofield saluted and started, "Good morning, sir. I am Lieutenant Colonel Schofield, and this is my task force. I can understand that you're upset, but can't help you much just yet, sir. We are moving this along as fast as possible. No one's going to be more relieved when it's over than us, sir. Your people are well treated. There were no casualties on the aircraft other than some banged heads."

The president glanced at the American flag on Schofield's sleeve and the one on the side of his Kevlar helmet. He moved his tongue until he found his command voice. "You can't know how I feel, Colonel. I'm asking again, who is your commanding officer?"

Schofield's commanding officer was landing off the portside wing in an Osprey packed with the communications and power of a command and control vehicle suitable for observing military exercises. Schofield ducked to the window to watch the Osprey ramp/door lower.

Out trotted a half dozen large men in armor. The trailing soldiers were bodyguards; the two lead figures were outfitted the same as the others except that they carried no weapons and had stars on their helmets.

Schofield excused himself from the president and got down the gangway to the head of the staircase just in time to greet Generals Sensenbrenner and Breckenridge with a salute.

"Good morning, sir," Schofield said to Sensenbrenner. "All's secure. The president's waiting for you, sir, right through here." *Tell them he's mad.* "And he's hopping with questions."

Schofield had seen Sensenbrenner many times before, yet always from a respectful remove, and he'd not addressed the man until now. Sensenbrenner was as tall, coppery, beak-faced, and unreadable as his ceremonial appearances: a bronze statue of the Virginia tobacco farmer's boy inside himself, a man who had shed all the tics of character like excess pounds, so that what showed at fifty-six was no more than an official image: silver burr cut, safety goggle eyeglasses, tan-creased necklines, and gigantic hands—the farmer's hands of the nation's first soldier, chairman of the Joint Chiefs of Staff, General Lucius S. Sensenbrenner, U.S. Army.

Sensenbrenner blew out his cheeks and turned to his companion, his number-two guy, and said something about Schofield that was too soft to hear, something like, "Bull in a shop, Brick."

Sensenbrenner's big-shouldered colleague was the vice-chairman of the JCS and all-around super gyrine, Lt. Gen. William T. "Brick" Breckenridge, U.S. Marine Corps—whom Schofield did know personally from two years on his CENTCOM staff.

Breckenridge addressed Schofield. "Outstanding, Colonel. We liked what we saw coming in. No fires, no ancillary damage. How about command and control? No interruptions?"

"None that we detected from this end, sir," Schofield said. "Unless they have equipment we don't know about, like a silent alarm."

Breckenridge was a chipmunk-cheeked man who always seemed cheerier than he was, and he was about to add more upbeat remarks when Sensenbrenner interrupted by asking, "You have communication established with the White House, Colonel?"

Not waiting for answers, Sensenbrenner took his long strides through the conference room and walked in on the president. "Good morning, sir," Sensenbrenner said. "I know it's difficult for you to have us here like this, and we will be as quick about our business as possible."

"You don't know spit, General," said the president, "and I hope we have an amazing explanation coming for this outrage. General, are you responsible for this? I want communication with the White House right now—my chief of staff on the line—and I want these soldiers out of here and my Secret Service team returned."

Sensenbrenner replied, "We've already established communication with the White House. Before we get to that"—Sensenbrenner waved to Schofield that he wanted him to go around to the other side of the president's desk—"we have critical orders, sir."

The president demanded, "Damn it, what are you doing?"

This was the part of the plan Schofield hadn't figured out. He hadn't been able to imagine what it would feel like to be here: the colorless compartment; the reeking perfume; the towering Sensenbrenner and beaming Breckenridge; the angry president; and now orders to be obeyed. It felt like a nightmare.

Sensenbrenner put a single sheet of paper before the president. "Please sign this, sir. It is your resignation. I have no other comment at this time, sir."

"This isn't serious," the president said. He batted at the paper. "And if it is, you can go to hell, General."

The president was a long-limbed man, and he was leaning all the way forward from his executive chair, so that he rested on his elbows, with his forearms stretched out and hands squeezed together. He was about to get up.

Sensenbrenner spoke clearly to Schofield with the ultimate order, "Do your duty, Colonel."

Schofield drew the .22 pistol from his hip holster and in one motion shoved the barrel under the president's left armpit and fired a single round into the heart with a *tphut!*

Tom Owen yanked the man's arms forward so that his head fell heavily on the desk. Schofield fired a second round behind the left ear into the brain.

Simple, Schofield thought. He sucked in the nitrates and unwound enough to get his posture erect. *Be the good soldier. This is for keeps. You just executed the forty-third president of the United States.*

Sensenbrenner took up the phone receiver on the president's desk and spoke firmly. "This is Sensenbrenner in Air Force One. Good morning, Mr. Vice President. The president refused to sign. The president is dead. Congratulations, Mr. President," and then, with a flick of his right hand, Sensenbrenner ended the call and returned the receiver to the cradle.

Sensenbrenner backed away from the desk and studied details in the compartment: the dead president, the cloud of gunsmoke, the statues of Schofield and Owen, the unsigned paper.

"Very well," said Sensenbrenner to Breckenridge, "I'm satisfied, Brick. Change of mission. And get them out, get everyone moving." Sensenbrenner addressed Schofield: "Get your people moving, and then come back, I want to talk with you."

Schofield excused himself to hurry down the belly stairs to

Corporal Ky; at the same time the general's signal was passed to the command and control Osprey on the apron.

Across the airport everyone got up, the so-called Secret Service and state and city police and aircrew got up, the soldiers of the battalion got up, and finally the so-called president got up; all of them got up and moved out.

Throughout the complex at Fort Chaffee Military Reservation, the big and small details of the facility were put right again, and the men and women of Fort Chaffee's opposing force, OPFOR, as well as the soldiers of Task Force Schofield, set themselves to a change of mission.

There was a rich, precious Arkansas sunrise burning the soft green tree canopy in the bluffs and on the slopes.

The rehearsal for Schofield's plan, designator CAR ALARM, was at an end, and it was rated outstanding by the most powerful military officer in the armed forces, Sensenbrenner.

Schofield called Cello once more and verified that his company commanders had the battalion standing down. Change of mission coming. Prepare for the word.

Schofield handed off the horn to Ky and climbed hastily back up into the jumbo jet.

In the president's quarters, the two generals had not moved from their footprints.

"What I want you to do now," Sensenbrenner told Schofield, "is get your command back on board the big birds. We're bringing the C-17s down here. You just stand by and we'll get you loaded. And get you back to your laager. Occupied Moldova, right?"

"Sir," said Schofield, "Dniester River valley, sir. South of Bendery, sir, what they call the Left Bank."

Breckenridge provided the most recent detail. "They're out there with the NATO joint effort—the Indonesians and that Argentine contingent just deployed."

"Yes," Sensenbrenner said, his mind seizing on the facts. "I was on the Left Bank, late last year," he told Schofield. "At Slobozia. What's left of it. What I saw was gang warfare."

"It's touch-and-go with hostiles called the Black Sea Cossacks, sir," Schofield said. He was a little surprised the generals didn't know the exact details of his mission and bivouac, but then that was the purple suits at the Pentagon—they regarded their thirty-five combat brigades or regiments as interchangeable parts of one dynamo.

Sensenbrenner declared, "Moldova's not working out, is it, Colonel?"

This wasn't a question. Schofield thought, *They probably picked us at random. What kind of luck is this? Maybe we'll get some R and R out of this.*

Sensenbrenner jammed his hands in his pockets and leaned against the president's desk like a man who wanted to light a cigarette but had trained himself otherwise. This was a tobacco picker who'd grown up rough enough to expectorate four meters when he was eleven, and who owed his success to a scholarship from the R. J. Reynolds largesse that made him a poor boy who could go to West Point.

"We're shifting you to an outfit called EXCOM," Sensenbrenner explained, pronouncing it in the military way: X!-com. "You're reporting to General Breckenridge. You're dropped out of your chain of command. Not NATO, not some backwater Moldovan Ministry of Defense—and aren't they sweethearts?—none of the warlords is going to have you. Your chain of command begins and ends with EXCOM. And your orders are signed by General Breckenridge, understood?"

Brick Breckenridge, who as vice chairman ran the JCS staff at the Pentagon as a tight combat command, took up the explanation. "EXCOM is ours, Colonel. We've pulled you out of the NATO sandbox and brought you into the D Ring sandbox. As if you're attached to the Joint Staff. Got that? Orders from me or my chief of staff. His name's Johnny Jones, and he's your action officer. He's cutting your orders now. They will be on your bird. You know Johnny Jones, don't you? He's told me he kept you from the top ten percent of your class."

"Yes, sir," Schofield said, not correcting the general that it was he who had made the top ten percent, not Jones. "Colonel Jones and I worked together on your CENTCOM staff. Operations."

Breckenridge nodded, though he had no memory that Schofield had been on his operations staff once upon a time—just four years back—before the latest realignment, when Breckenridge had been a three-star marine and commander in chief of Central Command, and the hero of Walvis Bay.

"What's important," Breckenridge said, "is that Colonel Jones says you're a reliable, confident officer. And I see he's got that right."

"Yes, sir," Schofield said.

Sensenbrenner closed the briefing. "We're changing the designator for this operation from CAR ALARM to FATHER'S DAY. Don't think about it too hard. The go code is 'Happy Father's Day.' Understood?"

Schofield responded, "The designator is FATHER'S DAY. The go code is 'Happy Father's Day.'"

Sensenbrenner added, "We like what you've done here—straightforward and superior firepower to a fixed point. Overwhelming firepower. We don't see how any security arrangement could keep you out. Do you?"

"No, sir," Schofield said. "My XO figures it would take another battalion to stop us if we have the Ospreys. If we have to walk in, it'd hold us up some, but we'd get here."

"Yes," Sensenbrenner said. "Good. Change of mission, then."

Breckenridge contributed, "We have hot food coming out to

your people, so get them formed up. We're bringing the Seventeens in here. We want you back on the big birds inside three hours and back in Moldova in twelve."

"Yes, sir," Schofield answered. *No R and R,* he thought.

Sensenbrenner crossed his arms and straightened his straight spine to his six and a half feet. "You're locked down," he ordered. "The whole of it. No communications, no operations. Questions?"

Schofield had plenty of questions; however, he concentrated on the fact that his battalion had been now ordered locked down indefinitely. "We've been in the field for twenty weeks, sir. This trip was a breather in comparison. How long can we expect to stay on the ready-up, sir?"

Sensenbrenner held his hands apart to register uncertainty.

The rosy Breckenridge said, "No more than seven days," and then he looked to the dark-faced Sensenbrenner and added, "No less than four."

It was fate that the African American Breckenridge was fairer than the German American Sensenbrenner. They were salt and pepper in reverse—the burnished brown Sensenbrenner with the silvery white fringe, the bright beige Breckenridge with the charcoal curls.

"That sounds right," Sensenbrenner agreed. "Thursday the twelfth at the least, Sunday the fifteenth at the most."

Breckenridge sounded impatient when he asked, "Anything else, soldier?"

The way the generals were treating this briefing—at ease and informal but loaded with details of situation, mission, execution, service and support, signal, command—told Red Schofield that he was not to ask for any more information.

If he did, he knew he was not going to head back to Occupied Moldova with his battalion.

But what about the president? I just shot the president in here. What kind of exercise? What kind of outfit is EXCOM? What in God's name is going on?

"No more questions, sir," Schofield said; he saluted and withdrew.

What kind of exercise gets a go code after it's done? What kind of wiring diagram has the JCS running a locked-down battalion five thousand miles from the Pentagon?

Red Schofield was on the runway before he let his doubts spook him. The Ospreys were swirling around the airfield as if it were feeding time. His outfit was trotting off the runway at the double-time. The C-17s were coming down from orbit within three hours.

Why bring us to Chaffee and send us back to Moldova? Why lock us down for seven days? Why us?

Schofield took the horn from Ky and spoke to Cello. "Cargo, this is Sky King. Give them the bad news, Mario. The Seventeens are coming. We're out of here in three hours. Form up the battalion in the parking lot. We've got hot food coming out of the kitchens. Let's get them fed. Briefing for the officers and NCOs in ninety minutes." Schofield glanced at his wristwatch. "Briefing at 0800. Where shall we do the Operations briefing? Over."

"How about in the terminal?" Cello returned. "There might be a chair or something that doesn't hop around. Over."

"Make it so," Schofield said. "Roger. Over."

Cello's signal was loud and clear, since his Osprey was rumbling overhead. "Sir, since we're chowing down, how about I take a chance to get over to that big PX in this bird and load up all the oranges and ice cream I can get? Do we have a requisition order for that? Do we have time to go for it, sir?"

"Mario, grab whatever you can reach, and use my charge card, and your charge card, and Brauchli's, Inky's, and Engelmann's cards. We're airborne by 0930 and we aren't coming back. Roger. Out."

Schofield was inside the terminal building before he had a clear thought as to what he'd heard from Sensenbrenner and Breckenridge. The OPFOR was cleaning up the broken glass. His foxtrots from the terminal tower, still armored and cinched, were strolling over their handiwork with the cockiness of a winning baseball team. A sergeant saluted Schofield and urged his men to stop celebrating.

Soon as they get the word, Schofield thought, *there's not going to be a smile in five hundred and sixty.*

Schofield sauntered over to the Hertz desk. This was a real airport, down to the advertisements in the display cases, the long curved counters for American and Delta, the newspaper and card shops, the fast-food franchises. Before the realignment of the DoD, the Fort Chaffee Military Reservation, at the edge of Fort Smith, Arkansas, had been a sprawling monster of an army base—the center of the light infantry tactics training grounds— where the U.S. Army had trained for decades to fight the Red Army when it came barreling out of the Fulda Gap.

But now the Red Army was a corpse, and Fort Chaffee was a ghost town, and this air terminal was a mothballed hulk—as if a bomb had gone off that smoked the people and left the facility intact down to the digital clocks and the ringing telephones.

The telephone's ringing, Schofield thought.

He turned to Ky, who wasn't paying attention. The telephone at the Hertz counter was one of those old-fashioned multibutton desktop models, wired and stationary, manufactured by Ericsson. The ringing was hollow and throaty.

Schofield put his M16 down on the countertop, uncinched his flak jacket, and reached over to pick up the receiver.

"This is Schofield at the field," he said.

No one. Just a dial tone.

Schofield put the receiver down. They'd closed the base, downsized the force, obsolesced the facilities, but somehow they'd left the old telephone switching system intact.

He thought, *A dial tone.*

He thought, *Operation FATHER'S DAY.*

He thought, *A coup?*

He thought, *D Day minus seven days.*

He thought, *Area code two-zero-seven* . . .

Part Two

THE TWENTY-FIFTH
AMENDMENT

2 Sunday Morning, Mount Desert Island, Maine

Jack Longfellow was out in the shabby formal garden, working with his eldest daughter to clip the hedges before the summer growth.

Jean Motherwell was on the videophone in the summer kitchen, returning a conference call before more calls started coming in from Washington.

Here on Sargent Drive on Somes Sound on Mount Desert Island on the coast of Maine it was another bursting blue June day without rain, and for all the world to see, Jack and Jean Longfellow and their healthy family were enjoying another excellent Sunday morning after church. It would have been farfetched not to be happy on such a fine day with such a top-drawer house—a weather-beaten clapboard Federal stuffed with Colonial Revival bounty and enlarged by a summer kitchen and sleeping ell—on such a firm three-acre estate along the granite-built Downeast coast.

All happy families have their moods, and the Longfellows' contentment was only from the outside.

From the inside, Jack was muttering to himself about the godawful Democrats in his legislature who had never met a prohibition they didn't like or a tax they couldn't cozy up to. And how was he going to get a budget by July fourth if he couldn't get twelve more votes out of the state house and four more votes out of the state senate for a compromise package?

Jack's complaint had some common sense to it, since he was the very popular second-term Republican governor of Maine. This was John Gerry "Jack" Longfellow, Jr., forty-eight, as fleet at sail and sure of tongue as any man ever took the helm at Blaine House at Augusta.

At present his temperament for office was in some small doubt. It was Sunday, June 8, and with only three weeks to go before the mandated balanced state budget was due, and with an eleven percent gap between revenues and expenditures to close, there were only sloppy seas on the horizon and a mutinous crew in the fo'c'sle for the ship of state and her sturdy captain.

"For the kids of Washington County!" he'd rant to the air. "What's a pension system that can't protect our treasures!" he'd rave to the sea. Then he'd fire up the clippers and whack at another brown hedge branch.

Jack's eldest daughter Lilly's advice was measured: "Don't take it out on the shrubbery. This isn't the state retirement system, Dad. These things have to grow!"

"I'm inhibiting growth for the good of the whole, I'm not cutting back!" Jack yelled.

There were the four thigh-high concave hedges arranged around the Greek Revival birdbath at the center of the garden. "Don't cry to me if they die off by August!" Lilly yelled back.

A formal garden on the shore was an impractical vanity. The thick firs, pines, birches, and oaks of Acadia National Park, just up the ridge, were always a season's growth from taking back any cleared space. Jack's garden was more a stockade than a paradise, with hedgerows like fences; island mounds of delphinium, daisies, bellflowers, and poppies; and broad peninsulas of wildflowers like creeping phlox and baby's breath. At the center of this fortress was a tribe of chipped cast-iron furniture needing white paint. The whole quarter-acre-sized affair seemed a little more doomed each year that Jack waited until June to defend it.

At a pause in the buzzing Lilly replied with excellent rhetoric learned from her grandfather, " 'Inhibiting' is your word for scorched earth, Daddy. You're a cheapskate, face it."

Jack defended himself. "You sound like the damned Aging Committee and that scheming Bonnie Nash!"

Lilly returned her opinion with regard to the powerful Democratic Speaker of the state house, "It's no fault to be like Ms. Nash!"

"She's a demagogue!" Jack cried, and then he fired up the clippers.

It was more true than not, however, that Jack was tightfisted about taxpayers' money and long-winded about bleary-eyed subjects such as the untamed rivers and fields of fruited plain of Aroostook County. Jack Longfellow was the greenest-growing governor in America, lord of the primeval Acadia woods and the immovable Maine coastline.

More grandly, in this paramount political summer of 2003, Jack was one of the Republican Party's leading candidates for the nomination next year.

After five very successful years in Maine's governorship, Jack was held up by friend and foe at the Statehouse as a tireless combination of skinflint and nature lover, with a Puritan soul and genuine Abenaki bloodlines—a Maine Maritime Academy graduate, a veteran of twenty years in the Merchant Marine, a green giant of a sea captain tossed up on the beach.

Best of all, he was a war hero—veteran of Walvis Bay. This was the very same sitting governor who had parachuted into Walvis Bay in the summer of 1999 along with seventy-four other merchant marines. This was one of the forty-nine survivors who'd brought out the tanker fleet. This was the man who'd been nominated for vice president by acclamation from the floor of the Republican National Convention in Anaheim in 2000. This was jolting Jack Longfellow, the one they called Captain Maine.

And when Jack's nomination had been defeated by the old guard, and when the old guard had gone down to defeat once again in the presidential election—swamped by Teddy Jay's five hundred electoral votes—this was the Jack Longfellow who stood as the great sandy-haired hope of the Republican Party.

This was the soundest presidential timber out of New England since Webster. The last six months it was impossible to watch cable television and not see Jack reading speeches and hosting coffee hours from Manchester to Concord to Wolfeboro to show he had one foot in Maine's present and the other in New Hampshire's critical primary next February, 2004.

The other half of the Longfellow dynamo was not an inconsiderable presidential candidate on her own.

Jean Motherwell, fifty, on the videophone in her summer kitchen, was not only the governor's second wife—both married for the second time after losing their first spouses—she was also a handsome creature of the political class of the United States. Former federal prosecutor, former representative from Maine's Second District, the only child of the late Associate Justice of the U.S. Supreme Court Motherwell, and now, eight months into her second term, she was both the junior senator from Maine and the newly elected minority leader of the U.S. Senate.

At just this moment she wasn't getting much for her lifetime of public service but sturdy resistance from her two best friends in the Senate.

"What I'm saying is that the leadership agrees we're not opposing the White House," Jean told Sue Bueneventura, the liberal Republican junior senator from Florida. "I'm recommending to the members we vote with our heads, not our pride. There'll be no stonewall, not while I'm leader. Senator Stonewall is retired."

Jean's controversial subject was the upcoming Senate vote on Acting President Garland's tax-margin-slashing budget: a budget so procapital and antiregulation and profit-worshipping that it was threatening to reconstruct Garland's vast family feud of a Democratic Party into the Republicans with poor relatives.

Indeed Garland had been calling his budget "New Reconstruction" the last five months as he'd been selling it to an amazed media and public.

The larger subject wasn't the budget but rather Acting President T. E. "Shy" Garland—what a phony Democrat he was, how popular he was, what a horse thief he was, how he'd stolen all the good ideas in the Republican bakery and presented them as his own. Garland called his blueprint for the future New Reconstruction, but no one was fooled. It was really familiar old What's-Good-for-Garlandism, and you spoke it in Garlandese.

"He's surrounded us, Sue. He's going to cut taxes the way he wants to, and we'd look like fools to try to stop him. There's something in his budget everyone can love. He wrote it that way."

"We've got to fight," Nan Cannon contributed. "Not stonewall, Jeannie—slam him hard."

There were other Sunday faces on the teleconference call: Jean's legislative aide and Sue's legislative aide, both at the Hart Building on the Hill; and also the autocratic senior senator from Indiana, Nan "the Wabash Cannonball" Cannon.

Thanks to telecommunications genius, here sat three senators in nearly identical brushed Levi's and linen blouses and scuffed loafers casually doing the nation's business while drinking tea in their own kitchens on Mount Desert and in Jacksonville, Florida, and Fairfax County, Virginia—all projected in crisp quality above Jean's long kitchen table. It was a phenomenon of video conferencing that so many VIPs preferred to set up the equipment in their kitchens.

The formidable Nan Cannon stamped her imprint on the discussion. "You go along with Garland on this, Jean, he's going to treat you like an ex-wife."

Jean took Nan's crack in a good spirit, since Jean's lusty affair with Shy Garland—eight years before, when she was an unmerry widow in the House and he was a tireless rake in the Senate— was well-distributed capital dirt.

"He's Garland if you love him and he's Garland if you don't," Jean said, a loving trill in her alto. "For now, no showboating, no jawboning, no stonewalling. That old-boy game is out."

Sue protested, "But he's cut the muscle out of the EPA, and the Finance Committee just let it go. I'm not talking about regulation. I mean what it takes to stop them crapping up the Okefenokee."

Jean promised, "I'm sympathetic. We'll wait for conference on the EPA. A lot can happen between now and August recess."

"Like what?" Sue complained in her cypress swamp lilt. "Blackwater country can't wait for maybes."

"Maybe," Jean sighed. She had to offer some hope to Sue. What? Garland was going to win. After last year's election the Democrats held the House, 305 to 140, and the Senate, 68 to 32.

Jean tried, "Why don't we wait to see what the president says—I mean, what Garland says, after we send it to conference."

Sue picked up on the commonplace confusion between President Jay and Acting President Garland. "You know we wouldn't have this problem if the president was still in the White House. You know that the only chance the Okefenokee has is if the president comes back before August."

"Well," Jean said, trying to sound understanding, "anything's possible."

"You know something we don't?" Sue asked from Florida.

"Like what Connie knows?" Nan asked from Virginia.

Jean conceded her intuition that something was going on. "I know that Connie's coming for luncheon," she said of the First Lady.

Two C-SPAN–famous sighs of recognition joined together from Florida and Virginia.

Now the three senators were sky-sails-set on the true dirt of the day, the month, the year—the only dirt that any politician had wanted to talk about all year—the breakup of the First Family and the breakdown of the president.

For it so happened that Doctor Connie Jay had filed for separation from President Jay the autumn before and fled to Mount Desert Island to take shelter near her best friend and Holyoke '75 roommate, Senator Jean Motherwell.

And it so happened that Theodore G. "Teddy" Jay of Grand Rapids, Michigan, the forty-third president of the United States, had voluntarily hospitalized himself for depression the January before—invoking by letter to the House and Senate the Twenty-fifth Amendment, section three, that had made Vice President Garland of Houston, Texas, the acting president for the foreseeable future.

The future was here. The Friday before—just forty hours ago—President Jay's spokesperson had announced that the president would be making his first public appearance in five months this afternoon in Miami, Florida, at the invitation of the Florida governor and the Speaker of the House, at the dedication of the largest National Refugee Act Center so far constructed.

This was old news now. What Sue and Nan wanted to know

from Jean was the up-to-date news: what was the president going to say this afternoon?

Jean explained, "Connie's coming over, because she doesn't
have cable. She wants to see him. She's not seen him, you
know—that's how sorry it is."

Sue said, "What we've heard is true—five months and he
hasn't called her once?"

"He's communicated, all right," Jean said, "with his usual
go-betweens like Joe Friar. I don't think of a chief of staff the
same as a husband, and neither does Connie. Cards, long letters, presents on the kids' birthdays and the holidays, he's
communicated, and from what I know of the contents, it's
been painful stuff, the sort that comes out of heavy work with
therapists. But in all this time, no appearance, no personal
call—until last Sunday."

"Well, what?" Nan demanded.

"It was a private call," Jean said, deciding to tell more anyway. "I can tell you Connie was surprised. She said he sounded
calm and apologetic. He said he wanted to come see her and the
kids. As soon as possible."

"When?" Sue asked.

"They made a date for Father's Day," Jean said. "His idea,
next Sunday. Father's Day."

The divorced mother in the durable Nan Cannon sounded
peeved. "Men like that always like to use Father's Day on you,"
she said. "As if all the bunk can be pushed aside, like Father's
Day was a safe passage."

Jean didn't disagree. She'd thought Teddy Jay's tactic calcu-
lated, manipulative, dishonest.

Jean continued, "The twist is that this was all Connie knew
until the announcement Friday about today's speech. It's as if
he's coming out of his shell. Connie's had five months of face-
saving nothing while she sat up here, talking herself to sleep

when she could sleep. Otherwise she's been on the road for her book or volunteering at the clinic here or just generally being a fine lady while the press branded her a traitor. And now the president calls and wants to make it all up to her by coming up on Father's Day. And just when Connie was thinking that there was going to be some progress, just when she had reason to hope she could save her marriage—then out of nowhere she hears on television with the rest of us that Teddy's going off to make this speech in Miami. His first appearance isn't going to be for his wife and children, it's going to be with Rainey and the cameras."

Nan acknowledged, "What a tough thing. What a tough, tough thing—from First Lady to last to know."

Sue said, "What's your best guess, Jeannie? Is Jay quitting like they're saying on TV down here? He'll quit today and then fly home to Connie on Father's Day?"

"My first blush is no," Jean offered. "TV's repeating what TV's saying. They know more about earthquakes than they do about the president."

"What do we know?" Nan asked.

Jean answered with the sort of inductive logic she'd learned from her dad, Agassiz Motherwell, the supreme court justice—this was little Jeannie Motherwell of Portland and George-town—and from her deceased first husband, U.S. Attorney Will Seward.

"We know that there's not been a peep out of Garland's boys—especially nothing from Quinn Roosevelt—since Friday when Jay made the announcement. We know that if there was really something going on, Garland would not be at a baseball game in Chicago today and flying out to a banquet in Cincinnati tonight. We know that if Garland was about to become the president by oath, he would not miss the opportunity to rush to his stricken president's side and hold his hand while he passed the

torch. And we know that Garland so looks down on the president
that he would sooner put a pillow over the man's face than let
him get out of bed—"

"Jeannie!" burst Sue.

"You asked what we know," said Jean.

"We know a lot for a simple little old minority leader, don't
we?" Nan tried with her best woman-of-the-world charm, "What
do we know about what the president's going to say? Why is he
doing this?" Nan groaned in frustration. "Guess for me, Jeannie,
that's why we made you leader. Guess."

Jean tried to be firm: "If I could guess this one, I'd guess he is
going to walk across the stage and accept the grateful applause
of his people and take what strength he can from their love. And
I'd guess he is going to do exactly nothing. But that's what
bothers me—the president's not trustworthy enough to do anything so useful as to do nothing. He's a pitier, he always has
been. It's what made him, that power to pity on the spot, and it's
what might finish him. Pity is what he's got for energy, and if he
turns it on himself . . ."

"Tell me what you're thinking," Sue said.

"He quits today, is that the verdict?" Nan asked.

"He wants to quit," Jean said reluctantly. "He's empty. He
should quit, he wants to quit. But will he? No. Not today.
I've got too much respect for Garland's spy network to believe
that Jay could quit without Garland knowing about it and
tacking down the carpet for his own coronation. Not today.
More of the same. Teddy Jay, mental health patient, fighting
back."

"You could call El Presidente Cubano and find out more,"
Nan tried, again poking at another one of Jean's frisky passions—when she and the rising star of Rafael "Rafi" Ros-Rosario
were in the House. Now Rafi, as the very powerful governor of
Florida, was called El Presidente Cubano.

Jean let Nan's crack about Rafi go with a snort.

Sue covered the dissonance with, "You could call Jay for us, Jean. Just sort of ask him."

"It's not a bad idea," Jean teased, "and if I get the chance I'll just ask him over here for our family barbecue next Sunday and ask him. Mr. President, happy Father's Day, here's a pickle, and are you quitting or what?"

Jean ended the call before she said what she really thought about the now nine-month epic of presidential melodrama since Connie had taken the six children (biological and adopted) and walked out of the White House, and the president had sunk to baggy-eyed sullenness for three months and then, three weeks before the State of the Union address, had checked into Walter Reed.

What Jean really thought was that the president was every woman's nightmare of a successful husband who one day just sat down and said, "I'd prefer not to, dear" and quit trying—and that Connie Jay was every woman's fear of what would happen to her if she were ever honest about a manipulative, withholding spouse and just refused to hold a lousy union together.

What Jean really thought was that the Union was overflowing with lousy unions, and that the First Family was just more honest than most.

Then again, the Jays' honesty had delivered up the strange issue of Shy Garland—a man less truthful about love and more covetous of power than any manchild who'd operated in Washington since Lyndon Baines Johnson.

The unsurprising fact was that Shy Garland was actually a nephew of the late and feared thirty-sixth president. The unkind joke was that Shy Garland was one of old LBJ's Houston bastards—what LBJ would have looked and walked and talked like if first he'd gone to Harvard and then he'd gone into orbit (Garland was an ex-astronaut) and then he'd gone on the make:

Garland the once and future First Lover, who was on his third or fourth wife. It was hard to get the truth.

Jean's attention turned to her legislative aide on the video line from her Hart office, since her aide was also her tall, fair, and rosy twenty-four-year-old son, Tim Seward.

"Those are two agitated votes, Mom. They despise Garland, win or lose, and think you should, too."

"It won't work, and you know why," Jean argued. "Garland wants us to oppose him so he can divide and conquer us. You know that."

"I know, Mom," Tim said.

Jean relaxed. "We'll see what I should do in a couple of hours."

"The president's not gonna rock the boat, Mom," Tim said too quickly. "Look at the poll numbers out today. Garland's got a sixty-eight approval and a fifteen negative. Only fifteen! The guy's got box office as big as John Wayne! It says if he goes head to head with Keebler now, he's up forty-four to forty."

"Don't talk Keebler today," Jean said.

"Yeah, okay," Tim said.

Gus Keebler was America's latest political craze, another billionaire for Führer, and this one with a weekly cable cooking show: Julia Child meets Daddy Warbucks, the myth of Howard Hughes, the personality of a busy signal—and he was not only a native American but also the elected sheriff of Yuma County, Arizona.

"Old rule in love and war, Timmy," Jean said.

"I know, Mom: don't count the votes till they're in." Tim beamed just like his dead father, and Jean felt that old flame in her heart before she punched off and stood to stretch.

What did Jean really think about Jay's suddenly announced appearance at the dedication of the Four Freedoms Park in Miami this afternoon?

She thought that she wasn't sure of the president any longer. Her best friend's husband had turned into a stranger to everyone who knew him. And if Jean didn't know him at all, if he was just another politician who had achieved the White House, she would have said that any man who'd been savvy enough to capture the Michigan governorship two times, and take the Democratic nomination by defeating Shy Garland in the California primary, and then go on to sweep a presidential race, such a man was fox enough to do anything and was less dependable than dice.

Jean spent the next half hour dealing with several other wavering Republican senators supposedly in her pocket—Garland's budget vote was scheduled for Senate vote on Thursday—and also with the unwavering Moons.

The Moons were supposed to be the servants of the house. Instead Viola Moon ran the kitchen like the deck of the *Bounty*, and Froggy Moon ran the grounds like a warden. Worse, once a week, Viola's cousins, Edna and Erma, assaulted the twelve rooms with red hands and 7.5-horse vacuum cleaners, striving for the pristine perfection once achieved by Jack's acquisitive mother, Louisa, and enhanced by Jack's well-to-do first wife, Allison. It was easier for Jean to deal with the budget than it was with the Moons, who never stopped complaining about the needy house and the unpredictable residents.

For today's luncheon Viola started her disapproval with: "Nine for luncheon, Mrs. Longfellow?"

The clue to the disapproval here was that Viola called her Mrs. Longfellow instead of either Jean or Senator.

Jean responded, "At least nine. I thought a lobster stew and a fruit salad? Or perhaps a lobster bisque and a Caesar salad? What do you think? For watching TV."

"I'm sure I don't care, ma'am," from Viola.

Jean sighed, "And a lemon meringue tart with a good dining

wine. One of the California zinfandels. Forget that, just the good chardonnay. The Kistlers."

The devout Pentecostal urchin in Viola replied, "Someone else should get the wine, not me in that cellar on the good day."

Finally, Viola banging away on the stove in the background, Jean cleared the last of her calls (to the minority counsel on the Judiciary Committee about the four sticky federal bench nominees Garland had sent up in the last month) and had a chance to pee before her guests arrived, and maybe change her blouse.

There was never enough time to do more than just change. Jean was a long-limbed frosted blond who always felt a half minute short of being as well dressed as she wanted, and if not for her treasure box of good pearl strands and Maine gemstone earrings, she'd never have been satisfied with any of her last-moment decisions.

At the last there was some shepherding to do with regard to the reluctant Jack, who was acting out more and more since the New Year and Jean's election to minority leader. She'd expected some jealousy and disharmony, and she couldn't say he was wrong to feel left out. There were tabloid polls that said she should take the top of the family ticket next year.

Still, it bothered her that Jack was acting less like a loyal second husband of four years and more like a cranky first of forty. But then she didn't have time to worry about what she couldn't solve. Jack was a naval hero, was Jean's opinion of the man, and naval heroes either righted themselves or went down with the boat, nothing else to be done.

Jean called across the summer kitchen porch, "Jack, I want you cleaned up, pronto! Connie's bringing her houseguests, and one of them's a muckety-muck in the AMA! Lilly, get him moving, will you? Do it for the First Lady, please, Jack?"

3 Sunday Afternoon, Somes Sound

Sweaty Jack met Jean's order with mockery. "Oh, please, Jack, clean up your act for the First Lady," he muttered back at his wife from behind the hedgerow.

Lilly understood many of her father's moods. "It's okay, Dad, I want to shower first anyway. Give me five minutes' lead, and then the bathroom's yours."

"Thanks, Lil," he said. He gave it fifteen minutes. He didn't move from the garden until he saw the First Lady's distinctive power launch push off from the landing far catercorner across the narrow Sound.

The Longfellow house was along the eastern-side Sargent Drive. The First Lady was staying at the old Rockefeller place—a rambling, shingle-finished cottage—along the western-side Hall Quarry Road. On opposite sides of the vase-shaped Somes Sound, the old Rockefeller place was properly in Somesville at the head of the Sound while the Longfellow house was most of the way toward Northeast Harbor at the foot of the Sound. Yet both were understood as outposts on the steep pine-heavy banks of the only fjord on the East Coast of North America.

Jack didn't get serious about showering until he saw the power launch back its engines and land sloppily at his landing much too close to his Boston Whaler—since the Secret Service could not drive a shopping cart without banging something.

And Jack didn't finish dressing until long after the party had gathered in the front parlor below his room. Still he wasn't ready to go down, and he dawdled over phone calls.

First, he called his press secretary at Augusta, Cory Saltman, to tell her that he was flying down in the morning, not tonight, and that if he didn't make the first press call, to be sure to insist he was going to veto all three Democratic prohibition bills (the Democrats were opposing a new casino in Aroostook County, all 850cc or heavier motorcycles, and an expanded enterprise zone at Lewiston) and also to confirm his nine o'clock powwow with his budget staff and the numbers woman from the Speaker's office for a showdown over the porkpie of teacher retirement benefits. Jack wanted either to lay off fifteen of every one hundred school administrators or he must have a major giveback in the teacher benefits package—or both.

Second, he called his father at Georgetown, the notorious Long John Longfellow, former senator, former secretary of defense, in order to see if he could catch hold of his younger daughter, Louisa—and he got the E-mail, so he left a message.

"Beep me when you can, dear," Jack told Louisa by proxy. "Lilly's flying me to Augusta in the morning, and then I'm putting her on the hop into Boston. She'll make National by one, so remind Poppop to send a car. You send a car. You're more in charge than he is."

Finally he made a call that had been tempting him all morning in the hedgerow.

"Toni," he started to his lover's machine, "I know you're on the water with the kids. Just calling to say that I miss you. And I don't want to go back tonight. I want to see you. Call if it's impossible. I'll be at your window by ten. I love you."

Jack punched off with a growl. He was in love. He could tell. He was taking chances that he'd not taken since MMA. And the fact that the love was impossible, and the most carnal he'd ever experienced, made it all the more necessary. Her name was Antonia Albanese, of nearby Hancock Point, and he worshipped the sound of her name and the curve of her ankle; he worshipped everything about her, and that she needed him made his worship seem less sinful.

Downstairs, Jack traded shrugs with the special agents stationed in the hall like linebackers. He'd gotten friendly with the First Lady's team leader, Mike Calcavecchia, a bald Boston College alum who, on a weekend of liberty, had come along to crew for Jack on an overnight up the coast on *Louisa*.

Calcavecchia gave Jack the sign that Jean was peeved by running his finger across his throat. "Big-time, Governor," he said.

"Terrific," Jack said.

The broadcast was well begun, with *CNN Live* on the screen from balmy downtown Miami, Florida.

Greeting Jack on the giant TV was the very handsome smile of Governor Rafael "Rafi" Ros-Rosario, who was not only one of Jack's rivals on the steering committee of the National Governors Conference but was also Jean's hottest old flame—and the man Jack had stolen her from, if that was true.

On TV, coming up quickly behind Rafi was the Florida Democratic machine's superstar on the Hill, Orlando's best good ol' boy, Mickey Mouse's personal congressman, Mr. Speaker of the House Big Luke Rainey.

"Nice to see you, folks," Rainey began to the audience with that sunshine-bright brotherly grin he wore so well—indeed they called him Br'er Luke back home.

Jack had missed nothing, but Jean gave him the glance due a rascal.

Jack glanced at the First Lady seated in the wing chair by the fireplace. Connie's coiffed prettiness and abrupt gestures told Jack that the Jays' melodrama was the same stormy weather.

Jack thought, *Boy, am I tired of the weepy Jays.*

Jack was thankful the strangers in the room were too busy quaffing the good chardonnay and scarfing heartily from Viola's kitchen for him to have to make introductions. They were a

queer-looking group of what Jack could guess were more of
Connie's doctor pals. It was Doctor Constance Jay, after all,
family practitioner specializing in battered women and children,
and she'd once infested the White House with all her drearily
brilliant medical friends: the First Lady of the Healing Arts, the
papers had called her until they'd transformed her into the First
Deserter.

Poor Connie, was what Jack called her. He liked Connie Jay
about the same as he liked any self-satisfied know-it-all with
great legs, but she was Jean's best friend . . .

Lilly, in a pretty print dress, was in the book alcove chatting
with one of the younger doctors. She hopped to her father.
"They're all shrinks," she said of the guests, "every one of
them," and then she smiled beautifully to share the joke with
her father, who had a deep fear of all mind doctors.

Jack looked from the shipwright murals to the handwoven
wool rugs, from the wing chairs to the Colonial settee, and everywhere he looked was the same dour face of a man or woman
with too high a forehead and too crimped a posture. *A coven of
shrinks*, he thought, *and me without a glass of zin.*

The First Lady was at the advance of a trend in weekend
guests. For five months, ever since the president had hospitalized himself, there had been a national seminar on depression
that had blanketed the media with the mysterious vocabulary
of unipolar and bipolar depression, dysthymia, mania and hypomania, schizoaffective disorder, and psychotic depression.
Who could remember all the meanings? And who cared to
learn them?

Jack headed for the lobster stew pot.

On the TV Big Luke Rainey was finishing his joyful introductory remarks to adoring applause from the Miami throng. Everyone liked Rainey. He was more a golfer than a politician—and
his trademark of wearing a golfing visor in the shape of Donald

Duck's bill made him the only member of Congress with a recognition factor in the nation's schoolrooms.

Rainey urged the president forward with a happy "Let's give
him a big hand, folks!" to the audience.

No fanfare, no presidential seal on the podium, just a cordless
mike and a few athletic gestures and here he was again, the
familiar tall, silver thatch–headed and princely Teddy Jay returned to the center of the stage in an excellent blue suit.

"He looks vigorous," the small fellow at Jack's elbow said.
"And stabilized, too. Good color."

Jack took a bowl of stew. "How's that about color?"

"Dysphoria is an illness, you know." The little doctor patted
Jack's ample forearm. "Like breaking several major bones, or
losing a limb. No difference, and when you feel better, you look
better. You know, good color."

What Jack really wanted to say was, "Color him off-the-
hook," but he took another bite of lobster at almost the same
instance the peace of Somes Sound collapsed.

For on the TV, the colorful, undeniably charismatic old
Teddy Jay, the one who could show pity on the spot, who could
croon as good a version of "America, the Beautiful" as he
could of "Camelot," that old Teddy Jay who'd carried forty-five
states and five hundred electoral votes on his visionary platform
of "The New Four Freedoms"—the first ever Michigan-born
chief executive—that supreme politician of the heart of the
heartland came out of his shell.

"Oh, it's good to be with you today, so good to be here. I
don't have much more to say than that. How good it is to see
you. I've missed you . . ."

The president broke off. It was an electric moment. Jack
could see the man thinking on his feet. Jay changed his timbre—
emphatic, driven. Jack thought, *Is he going to resign?*

"What I really have to say is so easy and so hard to say. It's about responsibility. It's about duty. We all know what our duty is. We all know it. We all know what I must do. I've thought about this as hard as I can. I've prayed and prayed for guidance from God and from the spirits of my mother's people. I've waited for a light to lead me. And I didn't know where I would find that light until just this moment . . ."

The president broke off again, casting his gaze from left to right across the field. He was relating both to the camera and to the unseen audience before him. His eyes had the glitter of prophecy.

Jack thought, *No resignation. The face of a crusader. The face of the man who charged along the campaign trail on that white charger of his rhetoric for the New Day in the New Land of our New Dreams. The face of one of the most sympathetic public speakers ever to take the American stage. The face of everybody's favorite daddy.*

"Looking out at you wonderful, brand-new Americans from a hundred lands," the president continued, "I see the light I've been searching for. I see the light in the dreams of Americans everywhere. The light in our homes. The light in our children's faces. The light that America brings to the world. I see it and . . . I see that I can't turn from that light any longer. I've faced my dark nights. My illness. And I've recovered. I've come back. I feel I'm twice the servant I was just a half a year ago. I know what my responsibility is, my duty is. You know what it is. I can't hold back from my duty. I can do no other . . ."

Jack saw Jean flinch.

The First Lady closed her eyes, and there was a tremble across her face. *No, no,* she thought. *This is my fault. He can't get away from them. I never should have left him. He's not strong enough to get away from them by himself. I'm to blame. He needs me. He doesn't have the strength to get away from them. No, no, this is the worst. He's going back to them. The people. The damned people.*

She let her left hand go limp in her lap.

"I ask for your prayers," the president continued. "I ask for all of us to pray for this land we love." His voice was as sonorous as Domingo's. "I ask for you to pray for me. And to see what I must do, because I can do no other. Yes, I must. I must return to my duty. I must. As soon as possible . . ."

The president kept talking, and nodding sincerely, and looking into the nation's eyes with his own black and tender eyes—the look not only of a crusader, but also the look of a troubled man who had faced demons in the wilderness.

The president closed his speech with steely certainty in his posture. "Thank you and God bless you all, my dear, dear friends."

The audience ignited into rhythmic cheers. It was a lustrous crowd of Caribbean and African refugees who had gathered to represent the variety passing through the Four Freedoms National Refugee Act Center. The cameras panned across the brown, black, cocoa, and russet faces like a parent might study a needy brood, and the close-ups were passionate and heroic. The president was a hit all over again to the common of the common.

Jack, watching closely, was impressed. A courageous speech, a high-risk speech, it was probably the performance of Jay's career. Here, at long last, was the kind of man Jack would be pleased to follow. A leader of men and women. A visionary. A risk-taker. A steward. Here was the man who had campaigned for a New World that was as good as our dreams. Here was a president of the United States looking trustworthy, grateful. Here, after two years of sloppy zigzags in office and nine months of bad family troubles, was a bent but unbowed father of his country.

But wait a moment, Jack thought, *what kind of father? A sickly father? An invalid father? A dying father?*

Jack was aware that he had long underestimated Teddy Jay's power with the powers of the weak—the president's pity, his compassion, his bedside manner with the nation—but now, perhaps the president was asking too much.

This isn't a kinder, gentler father, Jack thought, *this is a victim father. Can we deal with a victim in the Oval Office?*

Jack was the only one in the parlor still studying the faces on the TV.

The rest of the luncheon party was focused on the crushed posture of the First Lady. At forty-nine, Connie Jay was a strawberry blond beauty with the raised eyebrows of an intellectual. She was always in control. Except at this moment. Her face was in her palms. Her hair was mussed. Her broad shoulders were collapsed.

Jean came to the rescue by touching Connie's hands. "I'm sorry," Jean said. "Connie, I'm sorry."

Several of the doctors moved slowly in the First Lady's direction; everyone started murmuring.

By this time all four telephone lines were lit, and the throaty low ring was the reigning sound of the house.

Jack got ahold of the remote from behind the fruit bowl and channel-surfed on the video windows. One by one all American networks were cutting into Sunday afternoon sports to headline "Breaking News." Then the CBC came in, and, jumping to the BBC 1 channel off the satellite, Jack started touring European networks breaking in on their evening programming.

The news was spreading like scandal. Jay was back. Garland was out. Anything goes.

If the president had meant to stun the media with his "I can do no other" speech, he couldn't have chosen a punchier method than to make his announcement on a live cable feed from Miami. The national networks, on short notice, had not bothered to adjust their Sunday schedules to handle the live broadcast; only cable news had the airtime to give away. By now, minutes after the bombshell, the Hughes satellites were in a feeding frenzy around the globe.

Jean's attention was for the First Lady. "All right now," she said to Connie. Looking over to Jack, Jean said, "I think we should get ourselves together before— Jack? Jack, can we attend to our guests? Perhaps they would like more wine, and the TV off?"

Jack did nothing about the guests, the TV, or the phones. Lilly tried to cover for her father by moving into the study to take the first wave of calls.

Meanwhile Jack had found the Moscow feed on the cable and went to the main screen to watch a hastily drafted newsreader lean into the camera and read the script. It was the same in all languages, so who needed the translation?

"Just moments ago in Miami, President Teddy Jay unexpectedly announced his recovery from his recent mental illness . . ."

Lilly returned with a report on the phones to Jean, "It's mostly the newspapers and wire services so far. I parked them on call waiting. Senator Bueneventura's on one-two. Senator Cannon's on one-three. And Mrs. Jay's chief of staff, Adam LeMarche, is on one-four."

"Thanks, Lil, you're super," Jean said sincerely. Jean repeated to her husband, "Jack, can we attend to our guests?"

"Oh, Jeannie, I'm all right," Connie Jay said. She cleared away her tremble and got up of a sudden.

Jean slipped her arm in Connie's, and the two best friends stood firm, the frosted blond in jeans and the strawberry blond in a blue pleated skirt—sisters in complexions and posture, the chief difference being that Jean was adamant in the brow and Connie was physically imposing.

Jack, finally paying mind, came over to hand the First Lady a glass of water. "Bottoms up," he said.

"Thanks, Jack." Connie Jay gave Jack the wet-eyed glance of hers that he had long found mesmerizing.

"It was just the jolt of it," Connie Jay said to Jean and Jack.

"I'm all right. We've got calls to take and make." Connie Jay looked to her guests. "We weren't prepared for this, were we? I know I wasn't. But I guess we should have been." The First Lady turned to Jean. "We should have guessed this would happen, Jeannie. Why he called me last Sunday. Why he wanted to come up here. He was thinking like a president again. How it would look to make the trip to me."

Jean said, "I see," at Connie's analysis.

The eldest doctor added, "It is very possible he's as healthy as he says, Doctor Jay. Walter Reed is very able, after all."

The chinless little fellow who had talked to Jack said, "Five months is more than sufficient time to have stabilized, and the recent reports have been sanguine."

"Without pharmacotherapy?" asked another doctor.

"We can assume some," said the old fellow.

Jack detected a professional atmosphere closing in on the room like a fog bank, and he looked for the exit.

Besides, there was a major eruption of international politics out there, and Jack needed his master video system upstairs. Soon there'd be a special treat on the special reports, since it looked like Shy Garland had been caught with his pants down at Wrigley Field. Jack never pushed aside the fact that Jean had once upon a time spent too many nights with her pants off in Garland's bed.

The true motive for Jack's departing was rebellion.

None of the telephone calls was for him. There was likely a task force of cameras headed for the First Lady and the minority leader right now. And there was likely about ten hours of callbacks for Jean as her leadership and members weighed in. Not one of the conversations was going to mention the governor of Maine. All Washington prattle, Beltway palaver, big-deal preening and small-time spinning, with Connie speaking for the First Family and Jean speaking for the Republican Party.

Did Connie need him? Did Jean need him? For what?

Jack cleared the double doors and ran into Special Agent Calcavecchia. "Your 'Peacepipe' is back in the big teepee, Mike," Jack said, using the Secret Service handle for the president, "or did you get that already?"

Calcavecchia tapped his earpiece, through which he was connected with the known universe. "Yes, sir. Just when I thought this job was settin' up nice for a hot summer on the cold water."

Jack laughed and cleared the first three steps up.

Lilly, who'd used the back stairs, caught her father on the second-floor-through landing. "You checking out, Dad?" she asked.

"Just for some TV," Jack tried. "With that mob down there, I can't enjoy the excitement."

Lilly said, "President Jay sure surprised them, didn't he? You too, Dad?"

"You bet. I thought he was washed up. Beached. Now, thanks to what I hear is pharma-something, which I figure is good old Prozac, he's back and the Democrats have got him. And I say, Haw-haw."

"Jean looks worried," Lilly started.

"She got elected to be worried. She'd worry if she wasn't worried. She's the party's Mother Courage of worry. It's her job."

"She and Mrs. Jay must think there's something really wrong with the president, huh?"

"Nothing retirement to his ancestral hunting grounds wouldn't fix."

"Daddy, that's bigoted."

Jack, the one-fourth Algonquin—his grandmother was Abenaki—harrumphed at the upside-downness of language when he couldn't mock Teddy Jay, the one-half Lakotan—his mother was Oglala Sioux.

Yet it wasn't her father's tongue that worried Lilly, it was his wandering heart. She changed the topic to her fundamental suspicion, which was the fact that she knew her father was cheating on her stepmother.

"Are we still flying out in the morning?" was how Lilly's suspicion emerged.

Jack knew she was asking about his rendezvous with Toni tonight. Lilly had been Jack's conscience since Allison's death, and he couldn't hide his passions from her. Not when he was marrying Jean, and not now.

"Departure at 0645 from Bar Harbor. You at the wheel. ETA at Blaine House 0800. You'll make National by 1300 and be making your lasagne for Poppop this time tomorrow. Good?"

Lilly tried, "But what do I do if Jean asks, you know?"

Jack shrugged ruggedly, yanking his blazer and silk tie free and flinging them on his late mother's best thousand-dollar antique cane chair. "She won't," he said. Then he pointed to an upstairs wireless phone flashing red with call waiting.

The nation's business was on those long-distance calls, but as far as he cared, Jean and Connie Jay could have been gossiping about an upcoming "Friends of Big Oil" Ball.

The president might have a date with destiny at the White House. Connie Jay might have a date with a cabal of head doctors. Jean might have a date with any one of her thirty-one charges called the Republican Senate. However, Jack had a date with a magnificent widow lady who could make him glow like a baby when she rubbed those brunette curls against his ruddy cheek.

4 Sunday, Thirty-seven Thousand Feet over the North Atlantic

Red Schofield was napping on his bedroll in officer country in the vast cargo bay of the C-17.

The drone of the turbofans was easy listening for restful sleep, but it didn't come. Schofield was dreaming that he was awake and unable to fall asleep—an old seminightmare of his since his academy days—and when Major Cello reached down to wake him, Schofield felt the weight of his dream fall away.

"Sir, you asked me to get you up, sir. If there was anything about the president or something. On the radio."

Schofield sat up. "What is it?"

"I was up in the Two seat, sir, and I got off the satellite that the president is coming back. The BBC World News Service. It says the president's announced he's gotten better and is going back to work. He said this in Miami. This afternoon, where it's afternoon."

"Jay said this?"

"Yes, sir, President Jay." Cello was a stocky little man with good agility on the balls of his feet. He balanced on the roll of the aircraft. "It said that he's going to take his job back from Acting President Garland. It didn't say when, but I think they mean pretty quick."

"Got it." Schofield couldn't feel his toes. He needed water. He needed to think. He needed someone to talk to. What the hell did Jay's return mean? What the hell was Operation FA-THER'S DAY? What the hell—

Cello asked, "You want me to listen some more, sir?"

"No, get your rest."

Cello, aware that his boss was spooked big-time, but too good a soldier to ask what wasn't meant for him, tried some consolation about the long hop. "ETA puts us on the ground before dark tomorrow, sir. Monday, I mean. We can feed the teams. Two hot meals in twelve hours. It could be worse."

Schofield glanced back at the one hundred and ten soldiers sprawled in the bad light. There were four other Seventeens in the flight carrying identical exhausted displays of his battalion. Twenty hours inbound, three hours on the ground, and now twelve hours outward bound for Occupied Moldova.

Oranges, he thought, *all we've got for them is oranges.*

"You all right, sir?" Cello asked.

"I'm tired," Schofield said.

Schofield jumped up for the head. Peeing made him feel calmer. If he were still a smoker, he'd go up on the flight deck and chat with the air force drivers. Trade war stories. Bitch about the bad air. But he'd let the cigarettes go after his divorce, years back, after the Gulf. Now all he had to stare at in the dark was the ember glow of his worries. And the dials of his watch.

What time was it in Maine?

A coup? he thought. *It's impossible. It can't happen . . .*

Schofield headed for the airstair anyway. Maybe the radio would have something else. Maybe there was a way he could explain to himself why he was so scared—why he'd panicked and made the call at Chaffee.

Toni, he thought. *I had to call you. I'm sorry. There's no one else. I can't call Mac anymore. Toni. Pick up your messages. Make the calls. Tell them. This is no drill.*

5 Sunday Afternoon, Wrigley Field, Chicago, Illinois

At the seventh-inning stretch, the Houston Astros were ahead of the Cubs nine to seven thanks to a ball that stuck in the ivy in left and cleared the bases.

Reluctantly the acting president of the United States agreed to depart the field, even though he knew there's no such thing as a lead at Wrigley when the sun shines in and the wind blows out.

Shy Garland left the stands as triumphantly as he'd entered, shaking hands, bowing to the ladies, grinning to the kids, waving high and low—the glamorous six-footer himself, his dark eyebrows and giant white teeth, his long arms and beautiful clothes, the king of all he surveyed, the most powerful man on earth in his natural element as baseball fan.

How the thirty thousand other fans approved. "Go get 'em, Shy!" they'd shout. "Don't quit while we're ahead, Shy!" they'd yell, and then there was the wonderful hushed chant that now followed him at every outdoor appearance, the choo-choo-like "Shy! Shy! Shy!" as if a great right-hander had just walked off the field.

The truth was that Garland was a great right-hander. Shy Garland was his name, and Christy Mathewson was his hero. The greatest right-hander ever to toe the slab was the acting president's private god. Garland had turned his Oval Office into a Christy Mathewson museum, and he rarely gave a speech without quoting from the Giants' all-time premier pitcher, such as the choice proverb "Get the ball and throw it."

Garland loved baseball more than life. He'd played the game at school, of course; that was part of the legend. An All-Ivy right-hander for Harvard his senior year, he'd come close to turning pro. But then, he'd turned away to the air force. He could hum the high hard one, but he just didn't have the gift to get the breaking pitch over.

Instead he'd made baseball his private metaphor. After the air force, after his tour with NASA, after he'd taken the natural step into Texas politics, he'd decided not to think like a politician—an identity that made him feel like a schoolmaster—but rather to think like a starting pitcher on the mound.

Don't aim, pitch!

Save the strikeouts for the jams; make them hit it to the seven guys behind you.

Never give in to the batter.

It's only a game, play like your life *depends on it.*

Get the ball and throw it!

Baseball was Garland's genius as a politician, first as two-term senator from Texas, then as candidate for the Democratic nomination, and now as acting president.

At the apex of his career, then—the first Texan in the White House since his uncle LBJ—Thomas Edison Garland was going to keep faith with baseball.

Where had Garland been at the tricky hour when the news had come that President Jay was reclaiming his office?

At the old ball game—in his shirtsleeves in a third-base box seat with the mayor's wife along with five recuperating children from the hospital—exactly at game time, with one out in the top of the first, two strikes on the batter, the big Kuwaiti kid with alley power.

Did Garland even flinch when he saw the news flash on the

centerfield scoreboard? Did he rush from his box seat to get to his communications system in the limousine? Did Garland even sweat it?

The answer was he got the ball back and threw it. He was a fireballing slabman. He was ready to go nine.

The answer was also that it was very useful—when the news flashed—to be in the box with the mayor's wife and the five kids, where the press corps couldn't get to him. They could photograph and film him, but they couldn't get close enough to shout a question over the roar of the crowd.

Now that Garland was departing the stadium, the media were gathered at the bottom of the ramp like a gaggle of geese, TV lights on, cameras up, recorders on, phones open, satellites ready.

Shy Garland was ready, too. He turned from the sweaty faces behind him and charged down the ramp in a trot, the Secret Service agents flanking him mightily, and he kept running straight into the midst of the reporters.

"Mr. President, what do you say about the president's statement?" called the three loudest voices.

There were titters at the paradox of the question.

"Give us your take on Jay!" they pleaded.

"What's gonna happen now?" they demanded.

Garland waded farther into the heat of the bodies and took a big breath. He liked the press. He liked to smell the press. Today they smelled like popcorn and beer and fruity perfume.

"I'm real pleased by the news," he announced to the tony brunette from the *Orange County Register*. "Aren't you?" he asked the dainty blond from the *Chicago Sun-Times*. "I think it's the best news we could get besides our distinguished friends in the Senate passing our budget and getting on to do the great work of reconstructing this country," he directed to the meaty boy from the *Houston Post*.

To all of them he declared, "We need President Jay. He's the leader of my party and the father of our country!"

"What's gonna happen?" someone tried again.

"I haven't spoken with the president yet," Garland replied, "but when I do, I look forward to meeting with him as soon as possible and getting on with our job of reconstructing our country! It's been a privilege, for five months, to serve the people of this country alongside President Jay's very helpful and able cabinet and along with my distinguished friends on the Hill. And don't I say it's been fun, too!"

The reporters shouted the more, but Garland was done with them for the moment.

Three girls were blocked back by the special agents clearing a path away from the press corps. Garland, slipping his suit jacket back on now that the still photogs had framed him in shirtsleeves, headed right for the little ones.

"How're you, darlings?" he asked the girls. "Are you having a good time today? Think the Cubs're coming back?"

The biggest girl, perhaps thirteen, looked up from behind her hands and said, "You're so handsome."

"Not as pretty as you!" Garland said, handing the three girls little American flag pins. "And nowhere near as beautiful as Ol' Glory, don't you know?"

Garland was off again in the Secret Service's phalanx of power. The cameras followed him at a jog, since nothing Garland did was inconsequential—everyone had figured that out about the man. The puzzle was correctly interpreting what he was doing, and solving what it meant.

Right now he was exiting the most beautiful baseball stadium in America and crossing over the driveway to the presidential cavalcade of Lincoln limousines and Chrysler minivans and GM squad cars.

Why was he pausing outside the open door of his limousine?

Who were those two men he was talking with? Why was the president delaying his departure? What were they talking about on such a sunny day—the game?

The truth was that they were speaking conspiracy.

"What do we hear from Jay's camp?" Garland asked in his friendly voice. He looked at his watch. "What is it, Q., ninety-six minutes since the announcement?"

"We got the call about fifteen minutes after the president's speech," replied Quinn Roosevelt, Garland's chief of staff sometimes called Q. "It was Joe Friar, front and center."

Joe Friar was Teddy Jay's chief of staff and the major presidential aide to have followed Jay out of the White House in January. Once upon a time Joe Friar had taught Quinn Roosevelt how to make the polls sing and the votes dance in.

"How did he sound?" Garland asked.

"All wound up," answered Roosevelt. "Out of practice."

"He wanted to know our plans for tomorrow," spoke up Hank Lovell, Garland's lawyer and, since the acting presidency, the assistant counsel at the White House. "He wanted to schedule in at the Oval Office. For tomorrow evening."

"Why didn't he just give us a guest list?" Garland mocked.

Lovell added, "Friar did ask that I make sure Abbie Fleischmann's there." Abner Fleischmann was the chief counsel at the White House, left over from the Jay regime, and as far from real information as Lovell could shove him. "I told him Abbie and I are twins on this."

Garland laughed fraternally.

A very attractive young woman, a lean, leggy pale blond who was standing just behind Garland's right shoulder, recorded his laughter on her notepad. Her name was Diana, and her job was to record every word Garland spoke in presidential conversation.

"We told him we'd skip the speech at Cincinnati," Roosevelt said, "and get en route for Andrews now. He said we didn't need to change our plans today, but I told him we'd cover Cincinnati with Mrs. Garland. He asked after your reaction. I said you'd have a statement after the game. Which you just gave them."

Quinn Roosevelt, forty, was a genuine cutthroat. Of course he was related to both TR and FDR; of course he was born to the Oval Office. This time God's joke was that the Roosevelts had come back at the right hand of the right-hander. The devil's joke was that this first-rate Democrat had come back in the stubby teddy bear's body of the original TR, squint and beaver teeth and all.

"I'm having my teams get up the remarks you just gave like a prepared text," Roosevelt said. "It's on the wires momentarily. Global release. And we're rolling tape of you and the little girls and the flags. In time for the evening news summaries in Europe and the morning news in Asia." Roosevelt enjoyed saying, "Drive-time Tokyo and Beijing."

Garland patted his chin in contemplation. "What did you think of the 'leader of my party and father of our country'?" he asked. "It's softer than I wanted."

"It will play just right out of context, sir," Roosevelt said. Roosevelt wasn't a yes-man; he'd had his attack teams write up the line and feed it to Garland that morning, along with five other versions.

Garland reflected, "Let's not use it again. Once for that is enough." Garland changed directions. "Has Iphy gone on?" he asked.

"She's airborne for Cincinnati on a Delta heavy right now," Roosevelt said. "She wants to hear from you when you can."

Garland asked, "Did she understand we had to make it look as if we were surprised by the announcement?"

Roosevelt made a fist. "She said to tell you, 'Lights! Action!' "

Garland licked his lip. How he loved his Iphy.

Garland's third spouse, the Hollywood studio wife Iphigenia

Petropoulos, was a passionate campaigner and a dazzling speaker. Once, her naked affair with Garland, while they were married to other people, had cost him the California primary and the nomination that went to Jay. But now that they were old newlyweds, she'd been the White House's irresistible weapon these last five months for seducing America to the side of What's-Good-for-Garlandism.

Lovell interjected, "We want to talk about the letters, sir. I asked Friar if he'd sent the letters. He said they weren't ready."

"How can they not be ready?" Garland asked.

Lovell shrugged. He was a tall man for a lawyer, and his straw hair and big Adam's apple made him all Canadian River Texas in an Italian suit. "They can get the letters up in minutes, if they want to," Lovell tried.

The letters were what the Twenty-fifth Amendment called for when the no longer-disabled president moved to take back his office. He must send a letter to the president pro tempore of the Senate, in this case Senator Vic Yamamoto (D., Hawaii), and to the Speaker of the House, Luke Rainey (D., Fla.), stating and dating his intentions.

The letters were what started the clock on the cataclysmic section four of the Twenty-fifth.

Roosevelt tried an explanation of Friar's tardiness. "They're shorthanded as it is. At Camp David, I mean. And you know Friar's been holding back to see if it would keep the president back."

Garland complained, "Friar had Jay's speech today ready over a month ago. Is there more to it than just bad staff work? Is Jay crazy to announce without those letters going out immediately?"

Now Roosevelt shrugged, too. "You know, he might be. Crazy, you know."

The fact was that Friar had leaked to Roosevelt on May Day

that Jay was getting restless and wanted a comeback speech prepared. Probably Friar had meant the leak as a friendly heads-up. Perhaps it was also a warning from Friar that Jay was aiming to take back an office he could no longer manage.

Either way, Garland had taken the leak as a shot across the bow.

"Still," Quinn Roosevelt said, turning the discussion to the positive, "the Miami show went as we figured it would. Jay got one look at the audience and let loose that 'I can do no other' line he's been working on. He's back to his old trick of acting inspired. He did plan it this way. Recovered or not, he's still planning and acting like the old Jay."

Garland asked, "Do we still trust what Joe Friar says?"

Hank Lovell constructed a lawyerly equivocation. "He's been good for his word until now. 'Trust' is too strong. He's Jay's till the finish. Too loyal to trust."

"Friar's been holding Jay back," Roosevelt said, "because he loves the man. Not because he wants to do the right thing. Friar's a down-with-the-ship man. You know, he told me as much back during the campaign."

"You'd go down with the ship?" Garland teased.

"Saluting," Roosevelt answered soberly. "But sir, Joe Friar's not the problem over there. You know, the problem's at the top. Friar's trying to hold Jay together. He said to me, 'I didn't expect much more from you just now,' right as we got off. He's beat-up already, and his boss just announced. What's he going to sound like after the press conferences start? That staff work they've put out from Walter Reed—the weekly updates on the president's therapy, the details of his drugs—you know, that's small-time compared to what happens now. Friar knows what's coming at him, and that it doesn't matter if he's prepared or not. It's still too much. I think that's why no letters yet. Why there's no press release—even now, almost two hours after the announcement. Because Friar's shell-shocked already."

"The president just walked up to the camera and popped off and walked away?" Garland asked. It was incredible, Garland judged. With the size of the propaganda machine available to a president—even an invalid president living at Camp David like a rich uncle—not to use it seemed derelict. "You'd think he'd just glance at the Twenty-fifth and spot the part about the letters having to be sent once you announce. Just glance. Who'd believe this?"

Lovell agreed, "It's like the president was dropping back in on us from Olympus."

"Walter Reed's close enough," Garland said. "How do you figure a man you've worked with—a man who whipped you fair and square in the primaries—who's gone touched, as my daddy'd say. Touched."

Roosevelt continued the details. "The president's laying over in Miami tonight, a guest of Ros-Rosario and Rainey and the Florida machine. Here's my thought. Is there any call to think Rafi and Rainey knew this was coming? I couldn't tell from the looks on their faces, on TV, I mean."

Garland made nothing of this suspicion. Roosevelt was paid to be paranoid. But still . . . "A thunderstorm would surprise Rainey," he replied. "And Rafi's too busy running for president of the Antilles."

Garland listened to the quick way he'd dismissed Rafi Ros-Rosario. He didn't like Rafi for good reasons. The best of them was that Rafi was a dark horse in the party. Never a presidential candidate, always a pain. Not the least pain was that back a bit Rafi and he had squired around many of the same women in Washington. They'd done more than that with Jean Motherwell, once upon a time.

"Rafi and Rainey know diddly about Jay's plans," Garland declared.

"Yes, sir." Roosevelt finished the details. "The president's due back at Camp David tomorrow. Friar says they might get into

Georgetown later for a fund-raiser with some Motor City execs. That's why they want to come to us around six. Drive down from Georgetown."

"Do I call the president now?" Garland asked.

"Friar didn't ask for it," Roosevelt said. "I say we let him relax with his breakthrough. So far, they're following along the same course we expected. Why interfere?"

"I'm impatient," Garland answered.

"Tomorrow's the day, sir. Tomorrow at six. At the Oval Office."

"Yeah." Garland heard a roar from the stadium and turned to look above the brick walls.

Maybe the big Arab kid got ahold of one, Garland thought. *Hang a slider in his wheelhouse, it'd go forever.*

Garland turned back to his aides. Behind Roosevelt and Lovell there was a half-circle of moon-faced young men and women standing at the ready. They were Roosevelt's now infamous attack teams, always quick to wire the universe with the praises of Shy Garland and his turnaround administration.

Behind the attack teams were the Secret Service cordon and the state and local police squads. All at attention for the next need of Shy Garland.

Garland needed to get the ball and throw it.

"I don't like waiting for tomorrow," he told Roosevelt.

"I know, sir," Roosevelt assured.

"Where are the frigging letters?" Garland demanded of Lovell.

Lovell stalled with lawyerly trivia. "I don't know, but we do know that Rainey's in Miami with the president. Vic Yamamoto's on the West Coast for the weekend, but he's due back tomorrow afternoon."

Garland relaxed a little. He knew the reason the letters hadn't gone out was that Teddy Jay was a mess, and Joe Friar couldn't manage his job and the president's, and getting the speech delivered today was all they could hope for with their disorganization over there. The broken-down president and his broken-apart staff.

Garland also knew to push things, to make things happen, to move the game along at a steady pace. *Throw strikes.* He looked again at the stadium. What were they not telling him? What hadn't he thought of? You had to hold the whole game in your mind—every pitch, every out—you had to see the win.

Roosevelt tried to distract and console with housekeeping chores. "We've got a barrage of calls coming in, sir," he said, pointing to the rear cabin of the limousine and the White House communications system that was now backing up with every known politician around the world. They all wanted to know the same thing: what now?

"We'll be all night answering back," Lovell tried.

Garland knew they were trying to appease him. He threw the ball again. "I want to do something now, Q."

"Yes, sir. We tell him tomorrow night. We give him twenty-four hours. Then we challenge Tuesday night."

Like a star schoolboy, Roosevelt carefully recited the agreed-upon schedule of their plan, drawn up over the last month by their executive committee, or EXCOM. Jay's announcement. The letters to the Hill. The ninety-six-hour clock. The challenge. The cabinet vote. The House vote. The Senate vote. The presidency.

"And everybody's ready for tomorrow?" Garland asked. "You've talked to everyone on EXCOM since Jay's announcement?"

"Yes, sir. Senators Pickett and Wheat called right away. Mr. Magellan soon after. Secretary Learned . . . and . . . ."

"What about Sensenbrenner?" Garland asked. "What about FATHER'S DAY?"

Lovell shifted his feet. This was the part that scared him, and he made a motion of retreat.

Garland spotted Lovell's mood shift and asked, "What's that, Hank?" Garland kept lawyers around just because he liked to watch them sweat whenever things got rough. "You didn't talk with Sensenbrenner? Is that it?"

Roosevelt paused, and when Lovell didn't answer, he admitted, "No, sir, we didn't get a chance yet, and he didn't call. It's been hectic since the announcement."

"Right." Garland had found the pitch they couldn't hit. The perfect political snob in Quinn Roosevelt had managed everything except for the rough part, the general. Garland knew now he'd been right to test them. Let them surround you with their staff work and you'd never know what they hadn't done. You had to take command of the game yourself.

Give me the ball!

Garland waved at the door of the limousine. "Get me the general immediately. On the screen."

Roosevelt tried to head off Garland's hard-charging. "Are you sure you want to talk with him here?"

"Now." Garland ducked into his limousine cabin to get out of the way of the aides jumping to obey his order to broadcast General Lucius S. Sensenbrenner into the limousine.

Diana climbed in after her boss and folded herself onto a jumper seat.

Garland admired Diana's legs while he took the break to wipe the salt from his face, to wash his hands, to take a long drink of club soda. He should call Iphy. He punched the macro on the panel and within one buzz his wife's personal assistant answered. "My wife free?" Garland asked.

"She's in the restroom, sir," said the aide.

Garland could hear the roar of the wide-body engines. The aide was a Texas beauty named Mayro. Kappa. Runner-up for homecoming. Art deco brain. She made Garland smile.

"Tell her to call me when she's free, Mayro. Ten minutes, no more. And tell her I love her."

Roosevelt's face was at the open limo door. "Sir, the general's airborne en route over the pole to Turkey. The transmission won't be first-rate. Combat quality. You don't want to wait until he lands, do you?"

"No. Do it," Garland said. "And get Sonny Pickett on the next window in."

Roosevelt slipped in beside his boss and touched the screen. A six-by-eight-inch color picture popped out a series of security codes and routings and then there was the hawklike image of Sensenbrenner.

Sensenbrenner snapped off a salute. "Good afternoon, Mr. President," he said.

The picture flickered, the color wobbled, but the voice patterns were solid.

This was a one-way transmission. Garland could see Sensenbrenner, but Sensenbrenner could see only a camera eye somewhere in the cabin of one of the 89th MAC's old Gulfstreams converted to the air force's standards.

"Where in God's name are you, General?"

"We can put up the exact fix for you, sir. I'd say we're seven hours out of Ankara. Over the polar cap."

Garland had no good notion as to why Sensenbrenner was flying to Turkey. What was going on in Ankara? Probably the disasters in Occupied Kurdistan again. Or maybe he was making a stop en route to his pet disaster of Cairo. Garland looked to Roosevelt with a question in his eyes such as *Does the NSA know what's happening in Turkey?* Who really knew what Sensenbrenner was doing next? The man was all action. Garland liked Sensenbrenner just because he never spent more than a day a week in Washington, and this meant the Hill couldn't get at him much. If the chairman of the JCS wasn't testifying, then he wasn't vulnerable to man or politician.

The fact was that Sensenbrenner was Garland's foreign policy. Garland didn't want Sensenbrenner questioned by anyone in Washington but himself. Especially not now . . .

"You got the news of the president's speech?" Garland asked Sensenbrenner. "Of course you did. I'm calling because you didn't call in. I want all of EXCOM calling in."

"Yes, sir," Sensenbrenner said.

Here was what Garland didn't like about the general. He was colorless. Never apologized, never explained—about as far from a politician as he could get and still make policy.

"Hank, will you look in here?" Garland asked Hank Lovell.

The president's counselor squatted down to poke his head and shoulders into the limousine at floor level. Roosevelt shifted to the foldaway seat facing Garland, so Lovell could see the screen.

Pitch, don't aim, Garland thought.

"General, we've got EXCOM up and running. We need the status from your side. Designator FATHER'S DAY. Correct?"

Lovell couldn't stop from muttering, "Shit."

Garland liked the effect. Make the lawyer sweat.

"Sir, FATHER'S DAY is operational," Sensenbrenner returned. "Are you asking for—"

"That's not necessary, General," Roosevelt cut in, making sure his boss didn't hear any more than required.

"Shit," Lovell muttered again.

"You have any questions for him, Hank?"

"No, sir," Lovell replied, "except—yes, sir. General, this is Hank Lovell."

"Yes, Mr. Lovell," said Sensenbrenner.

"What we want to know is: is FATHER'S DAY clear that we don't need it? That we're doing fine with the Constitutional challenge, that your operation is strictly theoretical? Is that clear to everyone there?"

"Sir, we're ready to do our duty," Sensenbrenner said.

Garland grinned. The general might be plain-speaking, but he could cut through lawyer talk.

"My friend Hank, here," Garland told Sensenbrenner, "doesn't know the difference between command and control on this side and operations on your side. He didn't ever get to be a GI like me and Q. and Sonny."

Sensenbrenner returned a flat, "Yes, sir."

Roosevelt spoke up to try to bridge the canyon between the Pentagon and the White House. "Our schedule calls for you to be with us at the White House on Tuesday night, General. For the challenge and the announcement. Wednesday we go to the cabinet. The House and Senate follow. We'll have this wrapped up by Friday at the close of business. No change from our last meeting." Roosevelt emphasized, "And we don't want anything in FATHER'S DAY to interfere in our schedule. Your operation is available to us. But not necessary. Nor desirable. You're the people we don't want to hear from. And when it's over, we don't ever want to hear from. Does this remain clear?"

"Affirmative," Sensenbrenner answered.

Garland liked the tension here between his staff and his soldiers. Who knew what the general had planned? Who cared? The fact of the operation was what was profound. It had been Garland's genius to order up the worst-case scenario of FATHER'S DAY. If EXCOM couldn't get Jay with the Constitution, if something went badly in the week, then there was the JCS option available. The military solution to the Twenty-fifth Amendment.

What Garland especially liked about ordering up FATHER'S DAY was that it had made all the members of EXCOM very much in the game. It raised the stakes. It raised the flag.

It also made certain that no one got out of line. Not even the potent and most popular General Lucius S. Sensenbrenner, who didn't owe his now nearly four-year-old JCS appointment to Garland, was going to look away from Garland's black eyes. Sensenbrenner had taken Garland's deal to join EXCOM. He'd fallen in line to do his duty. Sensenbrenner was completely clear that Acting President Garland was his duty.

"Thank you, General," Garland said suddenly, and he gave the signal to end the call.

Sensenbrenner saluted as his image blanked out.

"Give me Sonny," Garland ordered. "And let's move out for the field."

The word was passed in a wink, and with leaping feet and slamming doors, whistling sirens and blinking lights, the ten-vehicle caravan accelerated out of the parking lot and into traffic patterns that always parted before the president like the Red Sea before the Angel of the Lord.

At sixty miles per hour, the inside of the limousine rocked like a yacht. Garland reached for his club soda and loosened his tie. He was hungry. The Constitution made him peckish. Jumbo shrimp tonight?

The screen popped again, this time with a vivid and deep image of Senate Majority Leader Sonny Pickett of North Carolina.

"Good afternoon, Mr. President," Pickett said. The tall, silver-haired, and statuesque North Carolina tight end (Duke '70) grinned into the camera. He was dressed in a gold polo shirt. He had his feet up by the barbecue pit on his patio outside Raleigh. "We've got sunshine and steaks here for you, come on down!"

Unlike the connection to the general, Pickett could see the president.

"Thanks," Garland returned, "but we'd best get on to the White House and get to acting sober for tomorrow."

"Right you are," Pickett said. He leaned into the camera and lowered his tone to the deep drawl of Garland's best friend and oldest ally and chief conspirator. "You probably haven't seen the tape on Jay yet, but when you do, you're gonna be horsewhipped for what's happened. He's aged somethin' ruinous. And thin as old Abe Lincoln—shit, I think the man's stopped eatin'. We're not up against a whole man. He's a stick. He's an old hickory stick."

"We'll get him when we get him, Sonny," Garland returned.

"Amen to that, Shy," Pickett returned.

Garland threw heat. "I just got off with Sensenbrenner. He's outward bound for Turkey. God knows why. He says he'll be back at the White House for the Tuesday rollout. He says FATHER'S DAY is operational. He says he's clear. What I want to know: tell me this is the man we want. Tell me again."

Pickett replied like a prince. "He's the man we want, Mr. President. He's the man, the general, the hour, the moment of our deliverance. He's the hero we take to the center of the line. He's the win, Shy. I'm more certain than anyone's been down here since Lee rode up the Shenandoah with my gramps. Believe me. He's our shot at all of it in one week."

Garland was half convinced. He decided to be difficult. "One week's all we get. Q. tells me we'll finish by game time at Camden Yards, Friday evening. If not . . . then we have to know we can count on the general for Sunday."

"Yes," Sonny Pickett replied. Pickett knew that Garland was seamlessly serious about using the general's solution. Pickett knew that Garland would not stop until he got what he wanted. "Lew Sensenbrenner is the vote in the Senate. Give me Lew Sensenbrenner for vice president, I will give you the Senate on Friday."

"If not?" Garland asked.

"Then Lew Sensenbrenner is the man for Sunday," Pickett returned with a heavy certainty. "Either way, he's our man."

FATHER'S DAY was named after the last tip from Friar two

weeks before, that Jay planned a reconciliation with his wife and children on Father's Day, June 15. Seven days from now. In Maine. Without the protective net of the Washington air defense. Alone.

"You've told me what I want to know," Garland said. "Iphy's calling now. We'll talk again when I get airborne. And Sonny?"

"Yes, Mr. President."

"Stay in touch. When those letters get to Yamamoto and Rainey, the clock's on. Probably tonight. I'll want to see all of EXCOM tomorrow night after I finish with the president. You and Jesus specially. Late. Pocket billiards?"

Jesus Magellan (D., Calif.) was the House majority leader, and the only other national politician up to Sonny Pickett on the Hill.

"Rack 'em up," Pickett said as his image snapped off.

The caravan accelerated into the expressway. The Secret Service called ahead that ETA for "Big Six"—Garland's code name—was nine minutes to the gate and ten minutes to Air Force One.

Roosevelt let the car rock back and forth on a curve before he spoke his mind. He'd waited silently while his boss and Senator Pickett had dueled over Sensenbrenner. They'd been arguing the same point since they'd first gathered EXCOM on May Day. Sensenbrenner was the key to the challenge and the next week. But would Sensenbrenner hold up?

Sensenbrenner was Pickett's idea. He'd long promoted him in the Senate—a poor-boy brother from Tobacco Road, he said—and it was logical that Pickett would recommend Sensenbrenner as their savior.

Pickett's plan was simple politics. The one-two punch was first to slam Jay as incompetent and second to nominate Sensenbrenner as the new vice president.

What did Sensenbrenner get for his deal? The vice presidency and a way to reinvigorate the armed forces after ten years of cutbacks and rationing.

The whole plan was cynical genius. Roosevelt was most comfortable with the level of cynicism among Garland and Pickett and Wheat and Magellan and Learned and the others of EX-COM. He approved. They were imperial men. He was their henchman's henchman.

The car righted itself and took several bumps over a bridge.

Roosevelt got the president's gaze. "You good and clear about the general now, sir?" he tried out. "He pleases you . . . mostly, anyway."

"The man's a cipher," Garland complained.

"He's straight as the road to hell, sir," Roosevelt quipped.

Garland raised his eyebrows and widened his eyes, a suggestion he wasn't serious.

"How about you, Hank?" Garland asked.

Lovell patted his knees. "Shit, you know what I think. Shit. To execute the man. Even to get ready to execute the man. Shit. It seems more than the Constitution is ready for. Even now. It's a lot to ask of paper. Even that paper. Shit."

Garland enjoyed saying, "We get him easy or we get him hard, Hank. But we do get him."

"Oh, Lord, I do believe you mean it," Lovell replied.

"I always mean it, don't I, Q.?" Garland asked. He looked at Diana and spoke emphatically. "The president always means what he says. That's why I'm the president."

"Yes, sir." Roosevelt had his notebook ready. There were some chores to attend to. "Sir, do you want the leaks started now or when we get back to Washington? And do you want EXCOM called for tomorrow night at nine or later . . . say, eleven?"

Garland answered, "Start the leaks now. Start from our friends in New Orleans. And make sure it gets to the Hill by tomorrow morning. I don't care how. Just make sure they wake up to it. The Republicans must wake up to it. We'll deny later. An EXCOM meeting for the late news. Say the late games from the West Coast. Eleven."

Roosevelt nodded in approval. "The word is given, sir?" he asked.

"The word is given," Garland returned.

Roosevelt touched the monitor beside his seat and waited for the communications system to window up his teams by satellite uplink.

From the moment he'd brought word to Garland on May first that President Jay was planning a comeback until this very moment that his boss had given the word, Roosevelt had not doubted once that they were going all the way. Garland had been watching baseball that day, too—a Wednesday evening Birds-Tigers game from Camden Yards—and there had been no hesitation on the acting president's face.

"He's not taking *me* out," Garland had said, not lifting his eyes from the TV screen and the windup of the stud right-hander. "We're taking *him* out," he'd added.

Roosevelt had believed his boss the instant he'd said it. Take out the president before he takes you out? A big job that required a big son of a bitch. But then that was what made America the greatest empire still in business. In all the world, in all time, there were no sons of bitches bigger or meaner than America's sons of bitches. Shy Garland was the biggest son of a bitch Roosevelt could find in national politics. And Roosevelt knew sons of bitches when he met them. After all, his pedigree included not only the number-one son of a bitch at the turn of the century, but also the number-one son of a bitch of the twentieth century. Now, at the beginning of the twenty-first century, it felt just right to go back to America's roots and show just how a real son of a bitch in the Oval Office got the job done.

Take out the president of the United States? Not how—when?

Roosevelt tapped the macro and popped the sober faces of his team leaders. He spoke two sentences. "This is Roosevelt. The word is given."

Garland smiled and picked up the receiver. He'd talk to Iphy intimately, not on speaker, and he'd talk to her plain.

"Dear, are you there?"

"How're you, darling?" Iphy asked from thirty thousand feet over the Illinois border, outward bound for Cincinnati. "You feeling good?"

"I love you," Garland said. "God, how I love you."

"You love everybody today," Iphy returned.

"Give me a week, I'll love everybody. You, soon as I get my hands on you."

"Oooh," Iphy teased, "promises, promises."

Garland grinned. Roosevelt grinned that his boss was grinning. Lovell wanted to grin at all the grinning, but he was an officer of the court, and he was a very humble officer for a Texan, and there were only seven days to Father's Day, and every one of them was going to mark a new frontier in Constitutional tyranny.

6 Sunday Evening, Hancock Point, Maine

At sunset, a rose-and-violet sky above Southwest Harbor, Jack was as happy as a sailor as he powered up his twenty-foot Boston Whaler and left Somes Sound in his phosphorescent wake.

He called the boat the captain's barge. It had been a Christmas present to Long John's six grandchildren years before from Jack and his three sisters. Since only Jack was at the house year-round—Ellen and Adele were on the West Coast, Bobbie was in New York—it had come to be Jack's boat, the large toy he used to run back and forth to Isle au Haut and his magazine-feature-famous sixty-three-year-old weir for herring. His other large toy, his first wife Allison's B-40 Hinckley, *Louisa*, moored at Northeast Harbor, he used only for overnight trips.

This was an overnight trip, but not the sort Jack could talk about. He was bound for his lover. It was deceitful, it was prideful, it was shameful, but he wanted to go.

He'd been ready to lie his way out of the house after supper—anything to get away from the crisis management spirit that had descended on the house. The constant phone calls, the fax machine whirring away, the First Lady's staff arriving in a rush, the press conference on the front lawn, the bank of TV cameras rushed down from Bangor—all the paraphernalia of presidential melodrama, and all that Jack disliked about politics. What rubbish, was his opinion. Just make a decision and give an order. Just rule.

At the end Jack hadn't needed to lie to anyone. Jean had made a crash decision to go back to Washington at suppertime rather than tomorrow morning. She'd raced off in her red roadster with a peck on his cheek and several pesky reminders, such as, "Remind Viola we are low on staples for next weekend, and make sure she understands that we have at least fifteen coming—and maybe twice that if the president comes over for the barbecue."

And also, "You do remember, it's Father's Day next Sunday? Review, Jack. Your father's coming up. You're a father, Jack. Large family event? Your sister Bobbie is coming for Father's Day. And now the president's probably coming over here for Father's Day. He's a father, too."

And finally, "Be especially nice to Connie if you bump into her at the package store, please? She needs you to be nice to her. She's just the First Lady, Jack—she can't help what the president does or doesn't do."

None of this advice had meant much to Jack at the time, and now that he was out in his captain's barge, his ninety-horsepower Mercury engine at full throttle into a calm sea at ebb tide, nothing about the Jays or their needs meant a whit to him.

What Connie needs, he thought, *is for Teddy to be nice to Connie. What Connie needs is* . . .

Jack let it go. The Otter Cliffs were behind him, Thrumcap and Bald Porcupine Island were ahead. He had his own needs. That's why he was racing around Frenchman Bay in the last light.

The sky was changing quickly, from sunlight to the serene purple of dusk. The island loomed to port. Venus was out like a beacon. There were scattered boat lights, and something big with a mast was scooting across from the Egg Rock light.

Jack throttled down to a low roar and reached for the cell phone in his rain gear. He punched the macro for his baby sister, Bobbie, in New York City.

Sunday night, Bobbie was home early after a matinee. She

was a growth fund manager at Fireman's, and this meant early to bed and early to rise.

"Where are you, Jack?" she asked.

"Out for a run in the barge."

"Where's Jean?" Bobbie asked.

"I called to talk with you," Jack said. "Jean's gone back to Washington on the seven o'clock."

"Jack, you're on Frenchman Bay, aren't you? Don't do this, if you're doing it. Are you?" Bobbie raised her voice: "I don't want you to bring me into this. If you're going to where I think you're going."

Jack didn't like the way this call was going.

Bobbie demanded, "You're going over to Toni Albanese's house again, aren't you?"

Jack knew not to answer. Bobbie had known his soul since they were children. There were thirteen years between them, but most of the time Jack felt she was his twin. After Allison's death, Bobbie had sailed around the world with him and the girls. She was inside his brain. He needed her approval.

"Why are you doing this? Jean won't put up with this. She's going to find out. Why are you trying to wreck your marriage? You've got a good marriage. You're lucky. You've had two good marriages, and I haven't had one yet."

"Bobbie," Jack tried. "You can't know . . . Jean hasn't spent three weekends here since Christmas—since she was elected leader, in fact. What kind of marriage is that?"

"Is that why you called? To complain about Jean? Or to tell me that Toni Albanese's going to save your life? That you should leave Jean the same way Connie Jay left the president? That every marriage in America should crack up because Jay did?"

Jack sighed. This was a terrible idea. How could he get off this line?

"Bobbie."

"Don't cut me off. Jean's busy, okay? You might have noticed
she was on the national news tonight, with the First Lady. Explaining why the country's not going to twist into a pretzel with
Jay coming back. She's a little occupied, Jack . . . she's the
most occupied Republican in the country. She's busy, Jack . . .
she's busy with all of us."

"Sure," Jack said.

Bobbie took a breath, got charge of her tone, and started over
again chastising her big brother for his wandering heart.

Jack knew why Bobbie sounded so peeved about Toni. It was
because Bobbie had introduced him to Toni at a Portland hi-
tech show. Toni was recently widowed and looking to find fi-
nancing for her start-up telecommunications software company,
Enigma, in Ellsworth. Enter Bobbie the fund manager, who'd
been at the Portland show with some of her heavy-hitter corpo-
rate clients. After a brief exchange, Bobbie had offered her
brother the governor, Jack Longfellow, to help find the under-
writers to take Enigma public. A phone call later, Jack had been
talking with Toni. The conversation was immediately intimate
about Toni's widowhood, and within a week Jack had lunched
with Toni in Ellsworth, when he was up for the weekend.

That was Halloween the year before. By Thanksgiving, Jack
was in love with the widow and her two young girls. By New
Year's, they were secret lovers. By Valentine's Day, they'd broken up because it was impossible. By April Fool's, Jack was as
devoted to her as he'd ever been to Allison. He was her hero.
She needed him.

"I want the best for you, honey," Bobbie said to Jack. "Jean
deserves better than this. At least you should tell her."

Jack risked a confession. "I'm going to."

"When?"

"Soon," Jack said. Did he believe this? It sounded okay. "You
know it's not easy to get to talk to her. And she's always with

Dad when she's in Washington. She's never here anymore. The party this, the party that—"

"Jack, you're running for president! Jack, she's holding up your end down there. Don't tell me what she's doing with Dad. Are you crazy? Jack . . . you know what Dad will do if he finds out about this . . . I don't want to know! I don't want to get into this."

"Sure."

Yes, he was running for president. But who was he supposed to talk to? His godawful Democrats at Augusta? His state police escort? His Cessna mechanics?

"Turn around and go home," Bobbie said.

"You're right," Jack said.

"You mean it?" Bobbie asked.

"Let me think about it. Let me go."

"I love you, Jack." Bobbie's voice dropped. She was still peeved. "You might have asked what kind of day I'm facing tomorrow."

"What?" said Jack. He really was too selfish to be her big brother. He tried, "What is it, sweetie?"

"Just that the markets are going to go through the floor tomorrow, that's all. With Jay back, we're going to give most of the rally back. The first-quarter rally. You don't know what I'm saying, so take it from me. We're going down. Maybe not falling off a cliff. Maybe just falling leaves. But that's just my career and all our money. You don't have time for that. You're in love."

It was true. Jack didn't care about the markets. Bobbie was saying that Jay's coming back was going to cause a sell-off in the stock exchanges that had rallied with Garland. So who paid attention? He was in love.

"Bobbie, I'm sorry. I'll call you tomorrow. Good night, dear, thanks. And I love you, too."

As soon as Jack got off, he slowed the motor.

Go home, he thought. *She's right. You're going for a fall.*

Then he powered up, came back around, and churned on toward the three points of land to the north. Lamoine Beach to port. Sorrento Harbor to starboard. Hancock Point dead ahead. Within minutes, he was among the day sailboats at a quay. He tied up at a buoy and, rolling up his trousers, carrying his topsiders, waded to shore.

His heart was pounding, a fact he liked because it made him feel young again. Not the governor, not the minority leader's husband, not the presidential contender, but just Jack Longfellow going over to Allison Hinckley's house—sometime twenty years ago.

The birch and oak tree line swayed in the sea breeze at half past nine. There were cirrus clouds coming from the west. The ryegrass field was awash in blackflies and pollen. Jack felt his lust like an armor. He crossed the road and there was Toni's—a white clapboard Colonial with a kitchen ell. Her bedroom was above the screened porch. The little girls' rooms were dark; however, there was a faint white light in her room. The front door light was out, and this meant she'd locked up tight.

Didn't she get my call? he thought. *Is the light burned out?*

The only way now, without waking the girls, was to use the ladder onto the porch roof. If he'd taken her key he could avoid all this. But it had never seemed right to take a widow's key. He had her heart. He had to leave her something for her own.

Jack banged himself fetching the ladder from the garage and setting it up; he was as noisy as a burglar climbing onto the roof; and he wobbled on the sagging shingles to get to her window.

Toni heard none of this because she'd been deaf since childhood, and tonight she'd taken her hearing aids out to go to bed.

There she was, in her worn woolen robe, with her reading glasses on, with her face greased with lotion. She was making notes on her pocket pc while reviewing her E-mail. Jack thought her beauty itself—with her black curls and olive skin and long Roman nose. She was as dark as his two wives were fair. She was as sensual as his two wives were brainy. She was as much a perfect hourglass of a figure as his two wives were slender and long-legged. In sum Toni was every part of a woman he had never loved before.

Though he knew she couldn't hear him, Jack spoke through the screen, "I love you, Toni."

Something about the shadows alerted her anyway.

"No, no! You're here!" Toni began suddenly. "Look at you. Where're your shoes? Did you come in the boat? Jack, where are your shoes?"

Toni worked at the screen. "You must have called. I didn't pick up. We were away overnight at Mac's parents."

She meant her dead husband Mac's parents down at Belfast.

Jack said, "I did call," but she couldn't hear him.

Toni unhooked the storm screen to let Jack in. Then she reached for her pc's macro key and punched up her weekend incoming messages. They rolled out in a list, and she quickly found Jack's.

She used her company's hearing-impaired package to transform Jack's message to text and windowed it on the screen.

She found Jack's "I miss you," and then pounced over to kiss him on his bald spot as he was crawling in the window on his hands and knees.

"I missed you, too, oh, yes, my yes," she said.

Jack took hold of her by the waist and lifted her high enough to squash her across his chest. He was a broad-beamed six-five to her petite five-six.

Yet he knew to kiss her gently and to keep his forceful nature to his declarations.

"God, I love you," Jack said.

Toni, without her hearing aids, pushed Jack's head back and made him repeat himself so she could read his lips.

"I love you," Jack repeated. "I love you."

Toni beamed. "I should put my ears in."

"Only if we were going to talk."

"I want to talk," she said.

Jack carried her backward. "I don't want to talk."

"But what about President Jay? I saw your house on television. Jean and the First Lady. I want to talk about it. It's very surprising . . . Jack?"

Jack was kissing her cheeks. "I don't want to." Of all the things in all the world, the last thing he wanted to talk about was the Jays. Or Jean. Why was Toni always trying to talk about Jean whenever they got back together? She knew he didn't want to talk about Jean.

Jack kissed her on the mouth, and she kissed back. He laid her across the edge of the bed and slowly lowered himself beside her. She was hot to the touch. He was never more excited than when he first approached Toni's blazing olive skin. He lost himself between the cool down comforter, the starched cotton sheets, and the fleshy aroma of her.

Was the light on? Toni liked some low light on. She was afraid of the dark.

Jack closed his eyes and tasted her mouth again. Everything about her was a taste for Jack. Her apricot mouth, her sugary neck, her salty breasts, her tangy sex, her silky thighs.

Jack's heart was going very fast, and he took a moment to pat his chest down and swallow.

Toni said, "My Jack," and then very little. She rolled over and touched the bedside lamp to dim it to a pale blush color.

The only other light in the room was the glow of Toni's pc with the list of all the weekend's messages.

It was a long list, because Toni had a large number of friends and family who called in regularly—her colleagues in Ellsworth, her mom and dad and two brothers in Orange County, her friends down in Portland, her in-laws at Belfast.

Everybody knew to check in on Toni. Everybody knew she was afraid of the dark. Everybody knew she was afraid most all the time since her husband Mac's terrible and sudden death three years before.

Everybody knew, too, that she wasn't as frightened as she used to be, at night, alone with her two little girls on the Hancock Point West Road, because she had a lover. And everybody knew, roundabout, by rumor and chitchat, that the lover was probably the governor of Maine.

Everybody knew, finally, that Toni couldn't get back to them right away. The phone calls stacked up quickly. She'd get to them in between her children and job and lover and the fact she couldn't always listen; she often had to transfer the messages into text.

The critical message had come in at 7:43 A.M. Maine time while Toni and the girls were down at Belfast.

It showed there on the pc screen, three calls above Jack's. It was from the Arkansas area code, 501. Dialed direct to the Maine area code, 207.

Toni was Ms. Albanese. She was also the widow of MacAndrew "Mac" Schofield.

The call on her message machine was from her Mac's baby brother. From her devoted brother-in-law, Red. From Lt. Colonel Schofield of the 1/14th of the Tenth Division.

Red Schofield had called from Arkansas with an unbelievable message for Toni to pass on to her lover, the governor of Maine.

7 Monday Morning, Georgetown, D.C.

Six hundred miles south of Hancock Point, on the shore of the Georgetown channel of the swollen Potomac, in the Watergate Complex, Jean Motherwell was on her telephone just after 6 A.M.

Jean had jumped from bed to phone in hopes of working through last night's callbacks before today's incoming stacked up. She'd stayed on the phone from the moment she'd left Jack at the house last night until she'd fallen asleep sitting up past midnight. Now she was launched again on her cordless. Her right ear was red; her wrists tingled; her eyes needed drops; she felt sick to her stomach she was so tired; yet she kept at it while trying to make breakfast tea.

Here was the new minority leader at her managerial best. In her floral cotton robe, in her ugly red slippers, her hair mussed, her feet sore, she was working the telephone with a keen sense of the practical game of the capital.

Jean had specifics to offer everyone.

To Senator Goldenburg of Alaska, the Republican conference chair, she said, "Yes, Max, yes, absolutely, Max," as she explained that the Senate budget vote was postponed indefinitely. "We'll talk about it at nine," she added, meaning that she had called her membership to an emergency meeting in the cloakroom to discuss the Jay announcement.

To Elaine Munro, the National Republican Committee chair, she said, "Yes, of course, as soon as we sort it out," when asked to go on a national televideo conference with the party bosses to explain what Jay's return would mean to the party's fund-raising plans.

To the legislative aide for her assistant minority leader, Braun "Brownie" McDonald of Laguna Beach, California, she said, "Tell Brownie, of course we'll miss him this morning, and get well soon," in response to the report that McDonald was going to be laid up another week at Walter Reed recovering from appendicitis brought on by a rough car accident. This was entirely disingenuous, since McDonald was a bitter and jealous rival who felt Jean had stolen the leader's job from him. Jean trusted Brownie McDonald as little as she trusted Sonny Pickett, so she added, "I'll call Brownie myself right after the meeting today, to update him on how we stand."

To the lesser problems of the upcoming week, she spoke bluntly that all committee work was on hold until Jay was back at the White House. No Ocean and Environment subcommittee. No Judiciary committee. No Select Intelligence. No anything—don't bother asking.

Finally she dialed her chief of staff, Ellen Quick.

"I can't talk any more about it until I wash my hair. God, Ell. Everybody wants to know what Connie said when she saw the president announce. I made the mistake last night of telling the story once. Now the versions going around are either pathetic or cruel. It was strange, how the president did it. And if he was my husband, I'd want him in concrete shoes, but who cares now? We've got problems today. That was yesterday's disaster."

To which the practical Ellen Quick replied, "If you could just take one more call, Senator. The networks are bombarding me. All five morning shows want you to appear with Senator Pickett. If you could just give in to one of them—"

"Not Sonny Pickett before we caucus, no way," Jean said. She regarded Halley "Sonny" Pickett (D., N.C.) the trickiest man on the Hill after Jesus Magellan. No way she was going to chat with

Pickett on live television about something as sketchy as Jay's return. "Ellen, you tell them I'm annoyed they think of me as a celebrity head. They want that, tell them to call Iphy Garland."

"Then how about a telephone interview at seven-thirty?" Ellen Quick tried.

"No, nothing until I wash my hair," Jean complained. She walked into the bathroom and turned on the shower. "You hear that. I'm in the water. I'm going to use soap and hot water. I have to do this, Ell."

Jean balanced the cordless between her chin and shoulder and walked over to get rid of her nightgown.

Blocking the bathroom door were this morning's papers, stacked just where she'd dropped them while she'd brushed her teeth.

The headlines were all a variation of the same shocker. Jay was back. Garland was out.

USA Today had boxed Jay's entire speech on the front page, now dubbed the "I Can Do No Other" speech.

Opposite on the page was Garland in his shirtsleeves at Wrigley Field. His grin was as big as the sun.

Jean threw her nightgown into the hamper and stepped into the water. "Ellen, I'm really taking a shower now. I'm getting off the line. I'm going on call forward to you. You tell them all that I'm in the shower."

She flipped the cordless onto the towel pile and put her head in the water. "I'm a mess," she said to the big bathroom. It was the best room in her mother's condo. Mrs. Agassiz Motherwell now lived in Boca Raton with an even bigger bathroom. But this one, in mauve, lemon, and white, with a well-lit wraparound mirror and a Jacuzzi in the bath, was the best bathroom Jean had ever enjoyed, and the bathtub was twice normal size.

I could fall asleep in here, she thought. *Wake up,* she told herself, *you're on duty. Get moving.*

Jean was dealing with a wet towel when the call she'd least expected came in—flashing on the private line for family only.

Jean's pulse jumped. She knew something was wrong. She hit the speaker button.

"Yes? Yes?"

"Jeannie, it's me," began her father-in-law, Long John Longfellow.

Jean relaxed at his paternal tone. "Oh, LJ. You scared me. I scared myself. I'd just gotten out of the shower and . . . it's going to be one of those days, you know . . ."

"Will you stop here for breakfast on your way in?"

"Now?" Jean said. There was something wrong. "What is it, LJ?"

"When you get here," he said.

"Stop this, you're scaring me. Is it the girls? Is it Jack?"

"It's the Twenty-fifth Amendment, Jean, and you're very good to pick up on me."

"Like a book." Jean thought a moment about the clue of the Twenty-fifth Amendment.

No, she intuited. "LJ," she asked, "has Garland gone crazy?"

"When you get here. All four sections. Okay? Thirty minutes?" Then he was gone in the SecDef fate-of-the-nation style that he'd mastered during the Cold War.

Jean started on her hair. Her mind caught up with her intuition. "Oh, shit. No, no, it can't be."

She skipped her last callbacks, dressed in her plain blue silk and best month-old walking-around shoes, and used her cordless PDA to call up the Twenty-fifth from the Americana network and print it out. All systems worked the way she'd paid for them. By the time she cleared her front door she had the hard copy of the Twenty-fifth along with the relevant Twelfth Amendment and the 1947 Succession Act.

By the time she reached the doorman and asked for a cab,

she'd scanned the relevant sections three and four of the Twenty-fifth.

She looked up long enough to get in the taxi door. Her skin stuck to the vinyl upholstery. It was going to get to eighty-five today. There was already a rotten haze off the river.

Jean started to sweat by just drawing out her little white cell phone. She punched her son's macro.

"Hello?" Tim was just getting out of bed in Arlington.

"Tim, it's me. I'm on my way to LJ's. He's got something for me that's got to do with the Twenty-fifth Amendment. All four sections, he said. I need you to scan the columns this morning."

"Okay," Tim said. He wasn't alone. Jean heard a woman's voice.

"Tim, do you want to call me back?" Jean asked.

"No, Mom, it's Anna. She's here."

Jean smiled. Anna Hrbek was a Reuters stringer, same age as Tim, a sensible and bright young woman whom Jean approved of. "Well, then get Anna on it, too. The crank columnists in the *Post,* both *Times*es, the *Journal,* you know. Anything that looks like a leak out of Quinn Roosevelt and his attack teams on the Twenty-fifth."

"Right, Mom. What's up? Garland?"

"Guess for me," Jean said. The cab rocked hard on Pennsylvania Avenue. "One of your big guesses."

"I'm guessing," Tim teased. "There was some wild talk on the cable last night, you know, the flunky channels, about what Garland's options are. The same stuff we heard in January. About challenging the president. You know, Garland has loyalists everywhere, and they like to talk about him as if he really were the president. You upset, Mom?"

Jean said, "It's LJ, he's got me curious, I think."

"He does that to me, too," Tim replied with a laugh. "Garland's a tough guy, but he's not going to challenge the president. It'd wreck their party."

Jean sighed. "Thanks, Tim. I'll call for your results."

Jean's cab plunged into leafy and baronial Georgetown. Jean had grown up here on O Street. Long John's brick townhouse was on P Street, just down from the Georgetown campus. He'd bought this gem in 1956 with two fellow frosh senators (now dead), and after four decades he could afford to camp here and wait for his family to show up, depending upon who was in school in Washington at the time. In residence at the moment were Jack's younger daughter Louisa and one of Jack's sister Adele's daughters, Kelly.

The granddaughters, dressed for their internships, met Jean at the front door with a hushed sophistication that made Jean adore them.

LJ, you old spook, Jean thought, *you've got us all tiptoeing around like it was still Armageddon at the door.*

"Where is he, Lou?" Jean asked.

Louisa answered, "He's in the kitchen making breakfast."

"And watching TV," Jean joked.

Jean owed Long John everything she had in Washington today, and she always came running when he beckoned her to one of his consultations. Jean also adored the man, so it was easy. He'd picked her for the second district seat; he'd picked her for her appointment to his old seat in the Senate. He'd picked her for Jack's second wife. Then he'd helped her pick herself for minority leader.

More recently he'd picked her as the woman who was going to escort Jack into the White House. It was hers and Long John's private deal. Jack and Jean must be picked for the ticket and the election before Long John was picked by God almighty for heaven.

This morning Long John was more interested in a mushroom omelet than eternity. He was at the kitchen counter serving portions, a broad, tall white-haired old man in shirtsleeves and roomy dress trousers who, at eighty-three, had concentrated all his vigor in his deep, ruminating voice. Long John was Jack's size plus thirty pounds and thirty-five tough years in the capital. He looked like an old lobsterman who'd dressed for Sunday supper, which was telling, because this was a son of Swan's Island come to Washington.

"Thanks for coming fast, Jeannie," he began. "I've missed getting you on the phone since this news broke."

Jean kissed him on the cheek. The TV was muted on one of the morning shows. There was a tape of the president's speech rolling at the top of the hour. "I'm hungry now that I'm here," she added. "I've been on the phone about the president all night, it seems. When are they going to get tired of saying the obvious?"

Long John dropped his gallantry a notch and asked after his son, "How's Jack?"

"You know, he wanted to watch television all afternoon after the news. In that way of his. I had Connie and her houseguests over. We all saw the announcement together, and Connie was paralyzed for a moment. Jack just disappeared on me. You know, captain's on the bridge."

It was a private joke between them. It meant that Jack was daydreaming again about going back to sea. It meant that Jack was before the wind on that endless voyage in his mind.

Long John set Jean's plate down, fussed with the silverware and linens, and reached over for his teacup. He held the chair for Jean to sit.

"It looks great," Jean said. She took a big bite and enjoyed the smell of spices. "Aren't you eating?"

Long John settled carefully across from her. He'd had both war-damaged knees replaced, and though this made him as tall as his youth, it meant he must bend his knees with caution.

"Last night at 1776," Long John began about his Sunday evening supper, "I was dining with Father McGinnty. Suddenly Ez Kahn comes in and sits with us. You know Ez? He was at the Pentagon with me. Special Projects. A very steady hand. His son's at State now."

Jean said, "You mean Rocky Kahn? Number two at State?"

Jean disliked Rocky Kahn as a Foggy Bottom bully who liked to mislead the Congress. But since the secretary of state's tumor in April, Rocky Kahn was the boss at State.

"Now you know the source," Long John said. The TV showed a tape of Garland handing little flags to three girls.

"The tale is this," Long John continued. "What we have here is a well-informed source telling me that Garland is going to challenge Jay's return."

Jean said, "Shit, I knew it. When?"

"You knew about this?" Long John asked.

"Not really." Jean slumped at the weight of the bad news. *I knew it,* she thought, *I knew it, I just knew it.* She said, "Tim told me last January that there was loose talk on the cable shows. And when you called me this morning, I made the connection. I have Tim and his girl Anna researching today's columns for the tip from some of Roosevelt's flacks." Jean put her fork down and watched the TV. "Did you know the trash cables have been preaching the challenge since January?"

"If you'd watch TV," he said, "you'd know it, too."

"Come on, LJ, no one ever thought it'd go this far. Not this far. I thought Garland's people were boasting just to keep the president's people in retreat. I mean, Garland's ruthless and all but he's not suicidal. This is just suicide for his party."

"Suicide is ruthless," Long John quipped.

Jean shook off Long John's remark. "I thought the challenge talk was hysteria. Okay, the president's return is a shocker. But Garland's going to wreck the party and the country if he goes through with a challenge."

"Maybe not wreck all of us," Long John said. "That's why I wanted to talk this morning. Before the challenge news hits."

Jean pointed at the TV monitor. "LJ, when it hits the wires, the country's going to start a meltdown. Two presidents! We can't handle it. It's going to paralyze us. Two presidents! The last time we had two presidents, we had Bull Run!"

Long John nodded. *She's got it right,* he thought. *Bull Run. Granddad's dad joined up after Bull Run. Twentieth Maine. Bull Run! Teddy Jay versus Shy Garland! Bull Run! She's got the silver tongue. My Jeannie of the chestnut eyes.*

"There are some useful particulars," Long John offered. "Ez Kahn said that Garland called his Rocky from Air Force One yesterday afternoon. From the cockpit, you know, the way Garland likes to fly the plane. Garland put this question to Rocky Kahn: 'Are you comfortable that the president is fit to resume his job?' "

Jean could see the future. "Oh, LJ, no, this is as ugly as it gets. They're going to challenge by tearing the president apart."

"You watched the president the same as I did yesterday," Long John said. "What did you make of him?"

"I told you, I was with Connie," Jean explained. "And she broke down when the president tried that 'I can do no other' line. It was as if he was a stranger to her. Afterward, she tried to bluff her way through it, but I saw she was worried badly. Then again, who isn't?"

"The First Lady's got a strong stomach," Long John said. "Tell me what you made of Jay."

Jean was thinking very fast. "What do I make of the president?" she said. "I think he's as unpredictable as he's always been, how's that? I think there's an even chance that yesterday was genuine. That means that there's also an even chance that it was cooked up. You remember he did that in the campaign. The brainstorm onstage. The confession, the revelation, the grand conclusion."

"He's great onstage, he's great making eye contact with the cameras," Long John said. "If he was half the politician he is a political actor, he might have accomplished something the last three years—"

"He wasn't the president he might have been—" Jean tried.

"He wasn't any kind of president, with his schoolteacherish 'new man' talk—new this, new that, new freedom from fear, new freedom from want, new anything but new thinking. The same old pie-in-the-sky populist bull!"

"It's powerful bull on the campaign trail," Jean countered. "It's not easy, you remember, to get past the poetry of the president's 'new.' It wins primaries and it wins elections. And it nearly won Maine, as I recall."

"What happened when he actually had to sit in the Oval Office and deal with what we've got? Nothing 'new' about what we've got. Just good old-fashioned American power and glory and pride. What happened?"

"Well—" Jean started.

"He froze up and whined a lot about how set in our ways we are," Long John boomed. "How antigovernment and antitaxes we are. Nothing 'new' there! Jeannie, I've told you. When Teddy Jay says 'new man' he means he doesn't like the man we've already got. No man's good enough for him. He distrusts himself. That's what a utopian is, Jeannie—a doubter, a trickster. We're not what a utopian wants because we're human. He's not what he wants because he's human. The president went into the crapper last January because he doesn't like that we're all full of crap all the time. That's life!"

"LJ, he was sick," Jean protested. "Depression's an illness."

"A very useful explanation for a man who's been preaching that utopian crap his whole life. When we need him to deal with what we've got, what we are, he gets sick."

"It's not as simple as all that," Jean tried.

"And how is it?" Long John said. "Why did his wife leave

him? Why did the press turn on him? Why did he go straight down in the polls? Why did he hospitalize himself, for heaven's sake? Because he caught the blues like a flu? Or because he was the last to figure out that he doesn't like this country the way it is. And since we're not changing, he folded up into the fetal curl."

"Okay," Jean said. She didn't like how hard Long John was pounding the president. But then, it sounded uncomfortably accurate.

Long John demanded, "Why did his wife leave him, then?"

"Okay," Jean repeated. "Connie left him because they weren't communicating anymore, and he resisted her attempts to talk."

"Bull!" Long John said.

"All right, because he was in denial."

"Bull!"

"All right. She left him because there was no love anymore. No trust. What you say—he stopped trusting himself and everyone else, including Connie."

Long John relaxed. "You know, I really don't care about that now. He's not much, but he's what we elected, and that makes him the only president we've got."

Jean relaxed a little, too. The main battle tank in her father-in-law had gone on idle. "You always say it's not supposed to be presidential being the president," she said in passing.

Long John smiled at the wit. *She's the best,* he thought. *She could charm a barnacle.*

He tapped the table. "What I want to know right now is, has the president got the stomach for the fight ahead same as his wife? Do you think he's got it? We saw how he stood up to Garland in the primaries three years ago. Is any of that still left inside him? Can he kick Garland back? Because that's what it will take. The hardest damned kick a jackass ever gave."

Jean admitted, "I don't know, really. I just don't know."

She glanced at her father-in-law and saw he was not going to get off the subject or back off the attack. She pulled the hard copy of the Twenty-fifth Amendment out of her letter case and laid it beside her plate. She put her hand on the four paragraphs. "Tell me I'm panicking."

"You're just ahead of the mob, Jeannie."

"This will explode," Jean said.

"It's been a ticking bomb for thirty-six years. Ratification was February, nineteen sixty-seven. The Twenty-fifth's fourth section is the timer. Tick-tock, tick-tock."

Jean asked, "Did you vote for it?"

"Naw," Long John said with Swan's Island certainty. "They cooked it up in 'sixty-four and 'sixty-five. Everyone had a hand in it. Birch Bayh, Bobby Kennedy, Sam Ervin: they all debated it. They were rattled by JFK's death. What would have happened if he hadn't died on the table. How long would they have waited for him to recover before they made LBJ the acting president. What would the president's state of mind have to be to take the powers away from him."

"So they were worried about mental as well as physical even then?" said Jean.

"They were worried about everything but the obvious. One president at a time. No temporary this or that. This president or not. Plain and straight. I said it then and I'll say it now, for what good it does. Two presidents is a disaster, and that's what the Twenty-fifth creates. Two presidents. The same sort of disaster as two heads or two other ones-of-a-kind. We didn't try out the Bull Run line in 'sixty-five. I like it. Bull Run."

Jean studied section four. "So, the president announces he's returning and sends letters to Yamamoto and Rainey. From the time the president announces his return, Garland has four days to get the cabinet to vote to sustain his challenge. And he needs a majority of the fifteen posts. He has ninety-six hours to get eight cabinet officers to agree with him."

"Correct," Long John said.

"And if Garland does get the cabinet, then he sends it to the Hill?" Jean looked up. "No White House physician. No court. No doctors' panel. Just us on the Hill?"

"Correct," Long John said.

Jean read on. "Since we're in session, we have twenty-one days to respond."

Long John said, "That's what it says there, but figure you more likely have about twenty-one hours. You'll have to move fast to keep the country from panic."

Jean agreed. "There won't be much left if we take twenty-one days."

"Give yourself a day for the House to debate and vote," Long John said. "Another day for the Senate to debate and vote."

Jean continued, "And Garland needs two-thirds from both chambers. Anything less and he loses. He needs two ninety-six in the House. He needs sixty-seven in the Senate."

"Correct." Long John raised a critical note. "About the timing mechanism. Garland has ninety-six hours from when the clock started running to get the cabinet vote. Do you have the exact time Jay gave letters to Rainey and Yamamoto?"

Jean's mind made a logical leap. "Rainey was on the platform in Miami with the president, so . . . Wait! Vic Yamamoto's away! He went to Los Angeles for the weekend!"

Jean drew her little white cell phone like a derringer and called Ellen Quick. "Ell . . . are you moving? I need help. Get this."

Jean gave quick orders to find Vic Yamamoto's press aide and determine if and when Yamamoto had received the letter from the president that he was returning to office. "Rush this. I need it now. I'm at LJ's."

Jean had more calls to make, such as to Tim to find out about the columnists, to her secretary to confirm the nine o'clock with the members. But . . .

Call Connie now!

Jean punched out of her office and hit the macro button for Connie Jay at Somesville. *Does Connie know? Come on, pick up!*

Long John wasn't done with his Socratic briefing yet, but he let Jean spin her webs while he poured himself more tea and tried another hot roll.

Long John had a temperament somewhere between a tyrant's and a Jesuit's. He liked details; he liked Constitutional details; he thought arguments were good for showing the mettle of the mob. Long John was in all things a learned Puritan and an honorable man; he was also a brawler, a son and grandson and great-grandson of fishermen who wouldn't back down from the sea or the Devil. Long John's father had been hit by a stroke at eighty-one while getting in his traps; something had clicked off in old Jock's brain and he'd gone into the sea with his hands on the line.

Long John aimed to die like that, on the deck, ready for hauling. Jean was his idea of a strong back to haul with. Long John had seen every major battle in Washington since the Korean crisis of '50, when he'd come to town as a thirty-year-old freshman congressman from Maine's second district. He knew a battle coming by the way the drums sounded. This one was going to be Bull Run and more.

Jean couldn't get through. The First Lady was doing her morning rounds at the clinic. Jean left a message with the First Lady's chief of staff, Adam LeMarche. *Call me as soon as you're free.*

Jean was about to start another round of calls when Long John interrupted.

"Let's visit my rhododendrons," he suggested. He picked up

his walking stick and got himself erect on his two prosthetic knees. "It's not too hot for it yet," he added.

Jean understood she could use some of Long John's ministrations.

"Okay, but I've got to be in the cloakroom at nine," she still complained. "I've got to talk them down from the budget vote we've just canceled indefinitely. And I've got to figure out what to tell them about this . . . And Brownie McDonald's in Walter Reed with appendicitis, you know, so I've got to run the whole show—not that he's much help."

Long John didn't answer. He called upstairs to his granddaughters that they should come say good-bye to the senator before they went to the museum.

Long John knew he was too old now to be anything but obvious about his affections. He did love his granddaughters. He'd waited so long to marry after the war, that when he'd started having children—Jack was his eldest—he'd been thirty-five. Three healthy girls had followed. He'd been in love with children ever since. They were God's triumph.

And other sentimental claptrap, Long John thought to himself. *Concentrate, John,* he thought, *this is going to take all you have left. Don't overthink it. Let's lay the traps and let the shedders walk to us.*

Jean and Long John took a silent turn down the flagstone path. He walked fine on his new knees; the walking stick was the pose of veteran power.

There was an oak tree as old as Bull Run in the next yard that fanned out its arms to keep a third of Long John's hedges in shadow while leaving the platoon of rhododendrons free to the flaming southern sun. Long John liked the heat and humidity. He'd grown up in a lobsterman's drizzly damp cottage on Swan's Island. Maine's cloudy summers made him grumpy. He was fresh and cheery now.

"What's your plan about the challenge, Jeannie?"

Jean shrugged in surprise. "I don't know. You know, I hadn't thought about it yet, it's so new. Do I back the president or not, you mean?"

"What's best for you and Jack?" Long John tried.

"For next year? Why, I suppose it's best if we don't back the stronger of the two, because we'll have to . . . We back the president, LJ. It doesn't matter about next year. We back the president."

"And what will that get you?" LJ asked.

"You mean if we back the president, then we'll get whipped, right? So why should I back a loser? Because he's my friend, how's that for a reason?"

"The best."

"It won't mean much against Garland," Jean said. "If Garland is going to do this, he'll probably hit us with everything he can think of, won't he? And he wouldn't try it if he didn't already believe he had the win. Won't he win, with or without me?"

"It's a high probability," Long John said.

"He can get the votes, LJ, I can feel it. On the cabinet. On the Hill. I don't know how he's going to do it, but I can feel it."

"I admire your feeling," Long John said. "We do count hands anyway. Give Garland the cabinet majority by just scaring them with the obligation. Give him the House by opening his check-book. The Senate, that strikes me as altogether another problem. Too many members who still look Garland in the eye. Too many princes like him."

"Sonny Pickett'll break heads for his buddy Shy," Jean said of the majority leader.

"It will take something emphatic," Long John remarked. "What about your side of the aisle?"

"You remember that sixty-seven for them and thirty-three for us means Garland wins. We can't stop him, even if I hold all of them."

"Correct."

"But I can make noise, can't I?" Jean said.

"Correct."

"And noise is what passes for a campaign speech eight months to New Hampshire?"

Jean's tone was still suspicious, but she was feeling keener. Long John was onto something as Machiavellian as she'd ever heard from him: Foe of my foe is my friend. *But Teddy is my friend,* she thought. *But Teddy is going down,* she thought. *Nothing to lose but lots to win.*

Jean said, "LJ, you're being real hard here. We're talking about a Constitutional crisis, and you want me to think about New Hampshire."

"Last time I checked, every time we go to the polls there's a Constitutional crisis," Long John said. "Are we going to pass power peacefully, or are we going to tear each other's throats out?"

Jean propped her hands on her waist and drew back her shoulders. "I guess I agree. I guess Jack and I are either running for New Hampshire or we're running away. I guess I've raised about half a million bucks to pay the campaign committee. I guess it means we're serious. I guess we have to fight Garland now or next February. I guess we fight him now. Is that what we're doing? Are we fighting him now because we're going to be fighting him later?"

"Garland's the king," Long John said.

"And when we fight him in February, it's for all of it—it's for a fight we can get the votes to win. The electoral votes."

Long John said, "A king is a king until you take it away from him. And the best way we know how is at the polls. Short of that, there's disaster."

"You mean the shortsighted Twenty-fifth?"

"I mean the ruinous Twenty-fifth. A king is a king until some-one takes the crown. A king never gives up the crown. If he does, he's no king and might never have been. President Jay gave it up, so he's no king. Acting President Garland's the king, and he won't give it up."

"Does it matter that we're a republic?" Jean tried.

Long John spoke softly in his hardest rhetoric. "Jeannie, only the accident of history that made us a republic is the reason we might ever get that crown away from the likes of a king like Shy Garland."

Jean felt her chest contract. She was cold at the fingertips but damp at the brow. "Wow, LJ, I feel like such a fraud! Is this me? Am I really doing this? I wake up in the night sometimes and I ask myself if I have lost my mind. What happened to the little Holton Arms girl in a ponytail on O Street? Where did my daddy go? Where did nineteen sixty-eight go? Am I this big-deal sena-tor? Am I married to Jack? Are we really running for the White House? Doesn't Nixon live there? Is this world true or am I out of my mind? Do you know what I'm talking about?"

Long John grumbled in that distinctive manner of his, like a great old pine giving way in the wind. "My dear Jean," he said, "you're the best I've ever seen. Sometimes you just take my breath away. You make a speech like that on the floor and they will follow you to the Gates of Hades."

"Not through?" Jean teased.

"They'll want amendments on it," Long John teased, too.

Jean felt stronger. He was helping her. She hugged his meaty arm. "All right, I get it. We fight because we fight. Thanks for reminding me. Sometimes I begin to think we're all here in Washington to do something beside fight, you know, to govern or something like that."

"Only sunshine soldiers talk about governing," Long John

said, swinging his cane in the direction of the Capitol Building to the east. "The rest of us are too busy punching back as hard as we can."

"Is that your Tom Paine who said that?"

Long John grinned. "Our Tom Paine."

"They had all the moxie back then," she said.

Jean looked at the rhododendrons in bloom. Perfect white petals like bridal veils for the bees. A perfect day for love and pollination. A perfect day for a picnic. And she was going to the stale Senate cloakroom to tell thirty or so spoiled brats that they were going to fight Garland for the good of the Grand Old Party—and for New Hampshire.

Jean said, "I guess I better call Jack, too, and tell him we're not just supporting the president. We're running against the White House. 'Garland's the king.' And, wow, are we in for it now."

8 Monday Afternoon, Augusta, Maine

At Augusta, on the shady lawn at Blaine House, Jack's day was half done, and he was trying to find some peace at a small picnic he was hosting for the James G. Blaine Historical Society—two dozen wealthy hobbyists who looked after the historical accuracy of the furnishings of the governor's mansion.

The potato salad at the picnic table was the most peaceful thing about the day.

Like many small-state governors with a limited staff, no lieutenant governor, and a part-time legislature, Jack spent his days being badgered by the favor seekers from the towns and counties, ignored by the deal makers on the House and Senate committees, and just generally harried by a schedule that delivered up needy delegations every twenty minutes.

There was no escape from the grind when Jack was camped at Augusta. The governor's rambling clapboard mansion, Blaine House, was just across a narrow street from the gold dome of the Statehouse and the parking lot–ringed executive offices. The governor's office was only ninety-five of Jack's giant strides from his bedroom. And wherever he went the cell phone in his hip pocket made him instantly available to anyone who talked past his three assistants.

The part of his job that Jack was very good at was giving orders. When his daily appointments called for decisions, he found the work engaging and exciting. Two decades as a deep-water sailor had left Jack as God almighty on the ship of state—a governor who took most seriously anything that threatened his command's well-being.

Then again Jack's reputation was a dilemma for him as governor. It was Captain Jack the people loved at election time—the boss who always brought the ship home safe—the amazing hero who had actually brought out the tanker fleet at Walvis Bay back in '99.

Yet it was Chaplain Jack the people wanted at budget time every other year—the all-ears pastor who could somehow make the ship work despite the leaks.

At this moment, Jack was trying to maintain himself as Chaplain Jack while he listened to Ralph Beale explain how he was about to publish a monograph on the visit of President Ulysses S. Grant to the home of Speaker of the House James G. Blaine on that serene August Tuesday in 1873.

"I have unpublished photographs, Governor," Ralph Beale

said. He was about seventy, with long white hair and longer
fingers, a dandy from Portland, where he'd cochaired Jack's
fund-raising for Cumberland County. "Group shots of Grant and
Blaine, with both senators Lot Morrill and Hannibal Hamlin and
the governor, too, Sidney Perham. Grant spent the night in the
master bedroom. Your bedroom. There was a band concert, I
have photographs taken before dark. Grant didn't come down
for the music. The whole presidential party filled the house.
What a day, and here, right where we're sitting. The history
of it!"

Jack bit into his American cheese sandwich. His mind was not
with Grant sleeping through a band concert.

Rather he was thinking of how little he'd accomplished for his
nine o'clock meeting with the Speaker's numbers woman and
the chairperson of the House Appropriations Committee, the
fearsome Bonnie Nash.

"The next day," Beale continued, "the governor received the
presidential party formally at the Statehouse . . ."

Jack added up his morning fifty ways and still got a budget
agreement that, according to his legislative aide Dick Schecter,
was well short of a two-thirds majority in both chambers. Exactly
where he had been last week. Stuck in the mud.

Beale proclaimed, "On Thursday night, Mr. Speaker of the
House Blaine hosted a reception here for President Grant . . ."

The bald truth of it was that Jack cared only about the wetlands anyway. He didn't care about the lard in the state retirement plan, he didn't care about the fat in the education
commission, he certainly didn't give a hoot about the perks for
the party hacks who still riddled the state payroll no matter how
many times Jack ordered them severed. What Jack cared about
was how the bloated state budget drained not only his treasury
but also the wetlands. Here he was in a resourceful capital city
of thirty thousand, in a creative state of one million, all of it

growing to burst its seams from the Kittery Bridge to Presque Isle, and yet he was the only person in the state who took time to worry about what made Maine green and great—the wetlands.

"The seventeen-year-old Nellie Grant wore a white silk . . ."

What did a balanced budget matter if those wetlands were the price? Maine had the last pristine bogs in New England. When they were gone, it was all gone. Not just Keep Maine Green. Keep America Wetland. For the cattail and red-winged blackbird, for the spotted sea trout and blue crab, for the canvas-back duck and sago pondweed, for the cypress remnant everywhere! Fight!

"The next morning, I can tell you, Governor," Beale said, "there wasn't a room in the house that hadn't been turned upside down by the crush of Republicans!"

Jack slumped his huge GOP shoulders. He wanted to do right for his magnificent wetlands, and yet he was beaten down every day by all these bizarre arguments over reamortization of debt and the minimum retirement age of freeloading jackasses. It was stupid. He was purging the pork so he could cut the sloppy budget so he could reduce the brutal tax burden so the sensible folk who didn't work for the state could grow their businesses and hire more workers so the state coffers would fill up for the capital projects that would expand the infrastructure that would then threaten the wetlands. Who was he, the friend or the foe?

"And that wasn't the last time Blaine House shone like a gem when it hosted a presidential party," said Beale.

Chaplain Jack finally paid attention. "I hope you'll put me down for your monograph, Mr. Beale."

The three coiffed historical society ancients at the picnic table beamed at Jack's thoughtfulness.

"My dad's a big fan of Grant's," said Jack.

"Well, sir," said Beale, "it's no secret we're all fans of yours, Governor. And some day soon, I feel, Blaine House will finally add a president of her own to American history."

The ladies tittered. Beale primped. Jack chewed his sandwich.

Then the cell phone in Jack's coat buzzed the alert for Jack's family-only line.

Jack, thinking of peril whenever his daughters were flying commercial jets, said, "Excuse me, I should take this," and picked up.

"Jack dear, it's me, can you talk with me?"

"Sure," Jack said as he gulped. It was Toni, and she sounded fragile and scared. "What is it?"

"I don't know really."

Jack excused himself from Beale and company. He stepped around the buffet and headed toward the tulip beds. "Toni, tell me. I'm here."

"When you left this morning . . . I was looking at my messages. The ones I'd missed like yours?"

Jack glanced back at the picnic and Blaine House. "I miss you already. I missed you soon as we swung over Hancock Point."

"This isn't about us," Toni interrupted.

Jack controlled himself. The flying trip down this morning had been a hasty muddle—rendezvousing with Lilly at Bar Harbor airport, liftoff at dawn in Jack's Cessna, then Lilly's questions about where Jack had spent the night, with him smelling of Toni and desire.

Toni said, "I held off calling you because I'm so unsure of myself. I tried to call him, but you can't get anywhere if you call the Pentagon. I have no one to tell but you, because it's about you—"

"Call who? What about me?"

"Mac's baby brother, Red. I told you."

"Tenth Mountain. The battalion commander, in Moldova. Is he okay?"

"Just listen. He called yesterday from Arkansas. From some-place called Fort Chaffee. He said he didn't want to leave the message on my machine, but it was all he could do because the Seventeens were coming and he was going into lockdown. He said you would know what all of this means."

"He knows about me?" Jack asked.

"You remember, on Valentine's Day, when we broke up? I wrote Red about it. I know I shouldn't have told him. But you know what? He wrote back that he likes you. He says you're his idea of a good politician. Because you're a sailor. And because of Walvis Bay, you know. That's why he wants me to tell you."

"What!"

"All right." There was a low whistle. Her hearing aids occa-sionally caused feedback. "Red says there's a task force ready to kill the president if he doesn't resign. He says the task force is assigned to something called EXCOM at the Pentagon. He says the plot is called Operation FATHER'S DAY."

Jack asked flatly, "How does he know this?"

"He says it's his task force. Task Force Schofield. He says he thought he was going into a training exercise, some sort of readi-ness test about security. But he doesn't anymore. He says that they don't give out go codes after exercises are over with. He says his go code is 'Happy Father's Day.' Is this making sense? He says he's working for Generals Sensenbrenner and Brecken-ridge."

Jack said, "Holy shit."

"Do you believe it?"

"What else did he say?" Jack was walking in circles now, the captain on his quarterdeck demanding damage control reports.

"I don't understand all of it. Let me transmit it to you."

"No, Toni," Jack said. "Keep it the way it is. Let's slow this down. Did he say where we could reach him?"

"I couldn't get past the Pentagon number, where all you can do is leave a message on E-mail. I don't know what to do next. Red said to tell you because you'll know what to do. Because of your dad. He mentioned your dad. He called him 'my first boss.' "

Jack asked, "He mentioned Dad by name?"

"Red's been a soldier since he was seventeen at West Point. He graduated in 'eighty-two. Wasn't that when your father was secretary of defense?"

Jack said, "Yes." Jack thought, *Storm warning.*

The Blaine House side yard was no place for thinking. Jack said, "Hold on, I'm going to get upstairs."

Jack tucked the cell phone in his hip pocket and headed back to collect his coat and reading glasses.

It took Jack more than a few moments of broken sentences to get away from the Blaine Society ancients. And then he was finally into the center hall and up to the only privacy he had in this vast house—his bare-bones bedroom and book-lined chart room.

Yet Jack wasn't quick enough to avoid the alarming coincidence that, while he was mounting the steps, his cell phone buzzed again on his family-only line.

Now he had two family calls waiting.

Jack sat down in his straight-backed chair, stared ahead at the open window on Capitol Street, and punched the macro.

It was Jean from the Senate cloakroom.

"I've got to run," Jean said, "but I've been needing to talk to you all morning. Can you give me a second?"

Jack slumped. "Yes."

"Don't bite me," Jean said. "It's this. LJ picked up on a rumor last night that Garland's going to challenge the president. Do you know about the Twenty-fifth Amendment? I've had Tim and his girl Anna and my Ellen chasing the rumor since I left LJ this morning, and we can't pin it down. It may be true. It's still a rumor. I didn't bring it up at the caucus with my members this morning. We just talked over the president's return, and the budget. I might have to move fast down here. If the challenge is coming, LJ recommends we back the president and fight Garland. Fight him now because we'll be fighting him in New Hampshire. You okay on this?"

"Yes."

"Jack, are you all right?"

Jack lied badly. "No, it's okay."

"You sound really out of it. This is me, Jack. We've got a campaign committee in New Hampshire. You follow? If this is true, the news is going to swamp the country, and Shy Garland's going to batter the Hill like a storm surge. I'm going to fight him. I'm going to take my members against. We don't have much of a chance. But I'm finally applying for Senator Stonewall's job. Do you approve?"

"Sure, Jeannie. I'm sorry, I understand."

"Uh-huh." Jean muffled the receiver to talk to someone else. When she came back, she said, "I'll call later. I love you, Captain."

Jack said, "Yes," as Jean clicked off.

He didn't do anything momentous. He was reacting to a crisis in the old familiar ways. First, you feed the crew. Second, you feed the engine. Third, you feed Poseidon, whom landlovers know as fate.

Jack punched on Toni.

"Here I am. Let's start with what we know from the beginning." Jack put on his reading glasses and opened his notepad.

Toni, too, had gathered her thoughts, and when she spoke

again she sounded not the tentative lover but rather the chief
executive officer of a sound growth company, a proficient
woman of means and sense.

What Jack learned was that Lt. Colonel Schofield had called
Toni's machine yesterday morning when she had been at her in-
laws' at Belfast. Just about eight o'clock Maine time. Schofield
told her he was calling from Fort Chaffee. Schofield told her
that he wanted her to tell Jack and his father what he had to say.
Schofield said he was in command of a task force that was assigned to a unit called EXCOM under the command of Lt. Gen.
"Brick" Breckenridge, vice chairman of the Joint Chiefs. Schofield said he had his orders directly from General Sensenbrenner, chairman of the Joint Chiefs. Schofield said he and his
battalion had flown into Chaffee to conduct an exercise to inter-
cept and capture and execute a mock president of the United
States. Schofield said his assignment was now called Operation
FATHER'S DAY. Schofield said that he was headed back to
Occupied Moldova into lockdown for at least four days, no more
than seven days.

Toni added, "He ends the call by telling me he loves me and
the kids. He says it three times. Like he was saying good-bye."

Her voice thickened with grief. "He said I wasn't to get into
it. Just pass on the message and, you know . . ."

"Toni, you all right?"

"Yes . . . he said to tell you to help me if he can't anymore,
but, you know . . ."

"Yes, I do," Jack said.

Toni spoke quickly now. "Jack, Red's just not anything like
this. At Mac's funeral, he was heartbroken, but he was a rock.
He told me he'd promised Mac that, you know . . . that he was
going to take care of us, you know . . . He worshipped Mac,
and yet he buried him without . . . And Red, he's the nicest
man. He doesn't have a wife or children. He's the kid brother

who always liked visiting us when he could. And for Red to ask for help . . . it's just not like him, not a man like him."

Jack wrote while she talked. He circled the principal points. *Sensenbrenner. Breckenridge. EXCOM.* Jack wrote down, *Garland?*

"Jack, talk to me," Toni insisted. "What's going on here?"

"Whatever it is, he wants you to stay clear."

"This is me, Governor," Toni said. She was peeved by the paternalism. As tender as she could be, what held Toni Albanese together was a brave soul that didn't back off from trouble. "This is my family. This is my husband's brother. I love Red. If he's in it, I'm in it. Now, tell me, what do we do? You apparently believe enough of this not to cut me off. Think out loud for me."

"I'm not good at that. I get carried away."

"Help me, please. I think something horrible's happening to Red." Toni's panic showed: "Please, dear, help me!"

Jack didn't want to give in—too many years on the bridge as God almighty—but he couldn't turn away from her need. It was part of what he loved about her, that she was courageous enough to be needy. "All right, what do you want to know?"

Toni asked, "Is it true?"

"It sounds like something rough."

"Why kill the president? What's he done that the army—"

"There's a problem, Toni," Jack interrupted. "About Shy Garland . . . and about President Jay's fitness. You can't figure how bad a problem."

"Okay, so there's . . ." She changed directions. "But why . . . why did he call me about it? You know, why me? To tell you? What can I do? What can you?"

"If it's true, Toni," Jack said, "he's desperate, and he called the only person he could think to ask for help."

"But if it's true, if there's a plan to kill the president, why not call . . . the FBI or something? Or . . . the White House?"

Jack thought, *And say what? And who would believe him? Who would even talk to him?*

Jack bypassed Toni's question. "From what he said he was on his way out again. He had one call in him. He called you."

"But why me?"

It made brutal sense to Jack, but he tried to explain mildly, "Toni, I don't know the guy, but I can try to look at it from his side. It might be that you're the only person he knows who would believe him. And even you're struggling . . you see, he's cornered. He's got a battalion, and he's cornered."

Jack said what he was thinking aloud. "They've tasked him to kill the president. They've made him an executioner. He doesn't want to do it. But he will do it."

"Jack, tell me something I can hold on to."

Jack decided it was most fair to be blunt. "If it's true, he knows what will happen to him and his men. They don't let shooters come back, Toni, you understand. You don't come back from this stuff. That's the record of this sort of thing—this sort of coup, anyway."

"He was calling to say good-bye?" she asked.

"Yes," Jack said.

"It can't be true, then," she tested.

Jack aimed to sound hopeful. "Maybe not."

Toni looked for a way out. "Can you stop it? Can your dad?"

"He took the risk that something we have could," Jack said. "Maybe he got one phone call. Maybe he got more than one. I wonder who I would've called—if I could've called. To get one call out of the trap he's in."

"Isn't there anyone for him?"

"He's a soldier, Toni," Jack tried once more. "He does what he's told. Now he must be in a place where no one's telling him anything that helps him. He might not have anyone to ask. He's alone with the loneliness of command. He's alone in Occupied

Moldova with no one to trust but his men. Whom he can't talk to about this, who are as helpless as he is."

"He must be terrified," Toni said.

"If he's the tough guy you say," Jack noted, "he's smart to be very scared."

"I hadn't thought of it that way."

"And now he's made that call to you, he's broken his oath. So his toughness is gone, too. Hell, he recorded the call. He stood there and spoke out what he knew. Guts is what that took. Like he was daring his bosses to come and squash him. There's nothing left for him now. Oath, toughness, you, all gone. He's alone like . . ."

"Like us," said Toni. "Like me."

"Yes," Jack said.

Toni sounded dead: "He called me because he loves me and wanted to say good-bye."

Jack assured her, "I'm not ready to give in to that kind of thinking. I don't like this, but we need a lot more information. Maybe he's scared. Maybe he's just confused. Maybe he's sorry he made the call and wants to take it back. We've got to try to find out more. It's what he wants us to do, at the least."

"You know what to do?"

"Yes," Jack conceded. "I know I've got a call I can make."

"Your dad?"

Jack sighed. "Yes . . . Christ!"

Toni was quiet for a few moments, and she punched up her pc at home and ordered it to store all her Sunday messages into her most secure locked box. This was what Enigma did, after all, for in a world of cells and satellites, there was a premium on software that could hide secrets as deep as Moby Dick.

"I've stored the message here," Toni said.

She sounded stronger than before, and continued to display her backbone.

"I'm here until six-thirty, when I've got a meeting at the parish hall. Sunday school retreat, you know. After that I'm at home. And Jack, I understand, the logic of this is obvious. Red wants you to tell your dad. But I know you're probably going to have to tell your wife. Red didn't mention Jean, but he knows who she is."

"Thanks, Toni. I've got to think."

"I love you. No matter what has to happen between us, you've helped me and I'm grateful. I'm not going to faint on you, Jack. You'll really upset me if you treat me like a fainter." She ended with the fear back in her throat. "Please, help Red, Jack. Please help me."

Jack got off after a consoling good-bye. He stuck the notepad and the cell phone in his coat pocket and went downstairs.

At the front door, he told his state trooper escort Pearlman that he was going for a walk and wanted some quiet.

One moment he was in the cool front hall at Blaine House, the next he was across Capitol Street and striding in the sunshine into the park and down the slope toward the river. He was hatless, wearing his reading glasses, and, for all the lunch-hour joggers to see, he was headed for the river.

He knew what he had to do. He had to call his dad. To do that, he had to get help. He flipped the cell phone and called his baby sister, Bobbie, at the World Trade Center.

"Governor, I'm trying," Bobbie's loyal assistant Milvian said. "She's been on the line constantly . . . she's got them backed up." Milvian was very politely suggesting that Jack call back. "Why don't I have her call you?"

"I'll wait, Milvian. Thanks."

From the tension in Milvian's voice, he could tell it was not a good day on Wall Street.

After a minute of Mozart on hold, Bobbie's scratchy voice snapped, "Jack, is it you, honey, what is it?"

"I need your help again," Jack said.

"Now? It's really not a good time. What is it?"

"It's about me and Dad," Jack said. "I've got to tell him some bad news, and I need to figure how to do it."

"What are you going to do? About you and Jean and Toni Albanese? Jack, no, no."

"It's not just that. It's more than I can say."

Jack heard a door slam. Bobbie had retreated from the chaotic trading floor to her see-through office in her opaque building in her impenetrable city.

"Let me get my breath. It's two o'clock," Bobbie tallied, "and the bonds are tanking, the Dow's off three percent, the NASDAQ is off two percent, the dollar's heading south and taking my sixth biggest holding with it, and gold, for kickers, is trying to find its wings"—she took another breath at the gloom on her monitors—"and you want me to tell you how to tell Dad that you're leaving Jean for another woman."

"Not that."

"Jack!"

"I have to tell him about Toni in order to tell him what I have to tell him. I don't think he'll listen. He and Mom never had this happen to them."

"Don't count on it. Dad's as male as you are, and you're all occupational hazards." Bobbie sighed. "What else can go wrong today? Criminey. Will you grow up! You and Jean are going to the White House. You don't take girlfriends with you. It's not allowed. Jack! Tell Daddy for me he should bop you!"

Jack said, "This wasn't a good idea to bother you."

"Why not! You just wanted me to tell you that you're in trouble."

"I shouldn't have called," Jack said.

"Don't sound like that. I hate it when you sound lonely— Shit, will you look at that?"

"What?"

" 'Phone' just gapped down a buck."

"It's bad there, huh?"

"Bad?" Bobbie giggled. She was six feet tall, could finish the marathon in three hours, and her tennis forehand was brutal, so giggling made her appear a happy Amazon. About infidelity she could fire up; about the markets she was a sport. "Oh, Jack, haven't I taught you anything about this business? You future chief executives have to learn that when AT&T gaps down a buck, it's very bad."

Jack had heard a headline news report at noon that the market was down sharply. "I'll get off. You've helped."

"I could use a little help once in a while, too. You and Jean have your rules, but you might have mentioned to me before the rest of the planet that Teddy Bear was getting well enough to come back."

("Teddy Bear" was Wall Street's mocking name for Jay.)

"We didn't know any more than you or the First Lady," Jack explained. "And Connie was knocked down by the news."

"Her and me and the bond futures. The big boys hate her husband, and they didn't know how much until he says he's coming back."

Jack realized that Bobbie might be telling him something critical. Perhaps the shakiness of the markets wasn't a sidebar to the challenge but was part of Garland's planning. If Garland was about to demand a vote by the cabinet and the Hill, wouldn't he calculate that he could count on the markets to side with him by selling off? Wouldn't he use financial panic as a weapon?

Jack asked, "Say that plain, Bobbie, about the bonds."

"You should see the short stuff tanking. Why?" Bobbie sensed trouble. "You know something?"

Jack couldn't tell Bobbie the whole story. He could try to probe.

"I guess Garland's been good for business, huh?"

"Good for business! We love the guy! Up eighteen percent since January! Of course, that was before today." Bobbie smelled a clue. "Do you know something about Garland?"

Jack evaded, "I've got to call Dad."

"Don't leave me like this. You never care about the Street. Why do you ask about Garland and business . . . Oh, Jack, is it that bad? Can it be that bad? What's worse than exchanging Shy Garland and his diamond mine of a budget—for Teddy Bear and the Handwringers?"

"I have to leave it."

"Jack!" Bobbie dropped into her chair. "I'm your baby sister. I've got your grandchildren's security in my hands. I've got to know something."

"Bobbie, I can't. Let me call Dad. I'll ask him what I can tell you."

Bobbie got very calm. "Just tell me this. Is it getting better?"

"No," Jack confessed.

"Is that 'no,' " she tried to joke, "as in go to cash, buy a gun, and margin the Hudson on gold futures?"

"Thanks, Bobbie, I love you."

"You're really making me nervous."

"I'm sorry. I've got to call Dad."

Jack punched off and leaned against a V-shaped oak trunk.

Call Dad, he thought, *and tell him straight out. If it's all nuts, then I deserve what happens. If it's not all nuts . . . ? Garland, you bastard. This is your doing. Garland, how nuts are you?*

Jack reached for his cell phone at the same time Bobbie on the twelfth floor of Number Four of the World Trade Center reached for a macro key on her speakerphone.

"Bernie, it's Bobbie," she began to her technician, who was in a sunless room beneath Two Galleria Tower in Dallas. "What's the Dow floor if we spike down seven to ten percent from here? Say we do it on the open tomorrow."

The technician didn't speak. He played his keyboard and transmitted the chart to a window in Bobbie's monitor.

Bobbie's eagle-wing eyebrows flapped toward heaven as she stared into the two-dimensional image of a meltdown.

In Georgetown, those same eyebrows in the original flapped even higher when Long John heard the first sentence in Jack's call.

"Dad, I've got to tell you about a woman I know and something real bad about the president . . ."

"Sure, Jack," Long John said. "Tell me."

9 Monday, Occupied Moldova

Red Schofield arrived back on the Left Bank of the Dniester River fourteen hours after leaving Sensenbrenner and Breckenridge at Fort Chaffee.

The battalion came in the same way it went out, the four C-17s hitting the emergency field like bottle tops come to earth in lumbering rolls and then, the troops leaping off, spinning off again in gigantic roars.

After a nap to restore his brain, Schofield was out of his field tent and looking around the bivouac.

The same black fields, the same meadows and beech trees and river rats. The same bad weather clouds. He was back in Occupied Moldova. It wasn't a nightmare. Or was it?

He ducked inside and found his weapons locker under his cot. He pulled out the .22 pistol. Here was the fact. He'd shot the president with this. Two rounds, one in the heart, one in the head.

Then what did I do? I panicked. I made the call. Toni. I cried for help. I went nuts. But that was nuts, wasn't it? Kill the president? Nuts!

And now what?

Get dressed, take care of the men. You're locked down. You've got nowhere to go. Until they call. Until Sensenbrenner . . .

A quarter hour later, Schofield had a mug of coffee in one hand, the written status reports from his captains in the other hand, and he was telling his orderly, Sinai, to call his driver.

"You gonna do rounds now, sir?" Sinai asked.

"Yes. And then a shopping expedition. Fetch Ky, will you? And get me the motor pool." Schofield took the field phone from Sinai after he'd made the connection. "Sergeant, get me up a shopping convoy. Yeah, yeah, now. We're going into Bendery. Yeah, we'll be back by dark. Make it ready to roll at . . ."

Schofield gave the orders for a shopping expedition into the big manufacturing town of Bendery on the Right Bank of the river. He could order Cello to go, but no—he wanted to go.

Meanwhile, he was going to make his rounds and try to cheer everyone up by announcing he'd have thick lamb and good wine for mess tonight, and pastry galore. And maybe some new videos, and maybe . . .

The problem Schofield faced, now that he was back in Moldova, was that his men were flat. He didn't have to see it, he could feel it. Four days in the air on bad food and their reward was back where they started. Flat. And flat was vulnerable.

He had to go into Bendery. But what about lockdown? He had to go, or he was going to have six hundred and twenty-two trapped animals.

Schofield's battalion was deployed on two catercorner collective farms that had been abandoned in the first years of the fighting. It was a defensible position, with springwater, fine vegetables and fruit trees, and a whole village of peasants to take care of housekeeping. Over the last five months Schofield had come to think of himself as a farmer with a six-hundred-man family. No matter the weather, no matter the day of the week, Schofield knew he was going to get into his Hummer with Corporal Ky and drive around the fields calling upon his company commanders. And his captains—Brauchli, Engelmann, Incavaglia, Wesson—were going to come up from driving around their platoons and report to him that all was well.

It was called peacekeeping. Schofield liked it best when it was as peaceful as a linden tree. He could direct the squadrons to pick wild pears and wild cherries; he could send his scouts out to hunt deer and hare; he could worry about the foxes in the hen coops; he could just generally trouble himself that the men were making baby dolls of the teenaged girls along the river.

In all he could keep his men secure as long as he kept them inside his perimeter. There hadn't been any mortaring from the Right Bank since February.

Hunkering down inside his own wire wasn't what NATO had had in mind when it gave in to the Moldovan Ministry of Defense and dispatched troops into the middle of a civil war between guerrillas, partisans, goons, renegades.

But Schofield knew from years of training that the only peace he could keep was his own peace of mind—and maybe keep the peace between his outfit and the Argentine battalion dug in five kilometers to the south and the new Indonesian battalion dug in three kilometers north.

In Occupied Moldova, there was no peace to be found on either side of the river. Out there were three and a half million partisans from the Prest River to the Dniester and then from the

Dniester to a meandering border with Ukraine thirty kilometers to the northwest. And the only thing those millions of ethnic Russians, Ukrainians, Romanians, and Gagauz had in common was the black soil of the steppe and the hatred of foreign invaders called peacekeepers.

Who knew what the politics of the Trans Dniester Moldovan Republic and the Moldovan Republic and the Gagauz Republic were? Who cared about the twelve-year-long slaughter by brothers and sisters? This was spectacular farmland. Close your eyes and you could smell Indiana. And yet they had been killing one another over it since the Soviet Union had crapped out and the black steppe between Romania and the Ukraine was torn apart like Christ's robe.

For Schofield, what all this chaos meant was that he was going to keep his battalion on the farm until they were ordered off again for another exercise.

He wasn't acting irregularly. This was the Joint Chiefs' version of peacekeeping; this was Sensenbrenner's famous "button-up" policy. Keep your head down and let all the bad guys hate you. As long as the bad guys hated you, they weren't going to cut one another's throats much. And as long as you weren't taking incoming, you were keeping the peace.

That Monday afternoon, Schofield's rounds confirmed that, though all might be peaceful on the farm—stags and roes and white-tailed eagles so unthreatened by all this disciplined firepower that they were poking around the meadows—all certainly wasn't well with the men.

Morale was cracked like a pot, and the silence in the bivouacs was a misery. The cocks crowed; the larks and song thrushes and wild geese were noisy with hunger; and his soldiers were not ready to fight.

Back at his field tent, Schofield looked out upon the pigs behind his headquarters company position. Then he drank good coffee, ate fresh corn and hot black bread and blood sausage, pulled on his armor, and went outside to climb into his Hummer with his RTO, Corporal Ky.

"How's our luck?" Schofield asked.

"Okay, sir," Ky said wearily.

"Okay to be back, isn't it?"

"More okay than still airborne," Ky allowed.

"The men are down," Schofield told Ky. "And there's not much we've got to do about it."

Corporal Ky kept shut. He knew his colonel was thinking out loud. He knew Schofield wanted to do right.

What Ky didn't know, what no one in the battalion knew, was that they were locked down. The 1/14th was as isolated as if it were on the moon. Operation CAR ALARM was done. Only Schofield knew about Operation FATHER'S DAY.

"You think Bendery will make a difference?" Schofield asked.

"Maybe," Ky said.

Schofield blew out his lungs. He didn't get paid to feel good. Okay, he'd try to buy them off with sirloin and wine.

An hour later, Schofield was in the second vehicle as they crossed the last good bridge over the deep Dniester at Bendery.

The lead Hummer pulled ahead and then gave a hand signal back. No mines on the bridge—not yet anyway.

The bridge had never been mined, but there was no reason to assume anything. This big river town was the best black market within reach, and that made it the most dangerous zone for the peacekeepers.

The bad guys were a partisan gang called the Black Sea Cossacks.

An Indonesian patrol in two vehicles had been hit by a partisan RPG last month.

Schofield had placed Bendery off limits in mid-May, after he'd lost two men to ax-wielding muggers.

Also, this was June, anniversary of the outbreak of the civil war between the two banks of the river, and some freelancing patriot might decide to celebrate with an antitank mine.

Prudence was to stay out of Bendery. They weren't going to run into the Black Sea Cossacks today, nor any of that heavy equipment the Cossacks rented out to the gangs, but then it only took a sixteen-year-old with an AK-47 to start a firefight. The peasants cheered when the target was an American. Schofield had lost three men to snipers on the opposite shore in the spring rains. They didn't give bodies back; you had to go in and shoot them out.

Nevertheless, Schofield had made his decision. Bendery was critical.

They moved into the stone-paved market square down by the long quay. Eight vehicles, twenty-five men, including all his cooks and supply noncoms, and three fire teams, along with a half-dozen peasant women from the collective farm, who would translate for them. Here was the American army at the farmer's market. Watch your back.

Tom Owen, the battalion Top, was in charge of security, and he deployed his sharpshooters to the church tower right away and sent the Hummer with the light machine gun up the rise to command the square.

Schofield waved to the local potentate. His name was Ostapenko, and his title was Chairman of the Executive Committee of Occupied Bendery. Schofield had sent word ahead that he was coming in and wanted to deal.

Ostapenko walked across the square and saluted. "My colonel!" he shouted in German. Ostapenko was an ex-major from the old Soviet 14th Army. Back then he had been fat and smart; now he was old and fat and dangerous.

Schofield liked Ostapenko because he was dependable. Give him money, and he delivered.

"We want good stuff," Schofield told Ostapenko in German. "Good meat, good candy, and if there's champagne, I'll take it all on consignment. We'll pay you for the good stuff only. And lamb for the battalion. How much?"

Ostapenko grinned and wrote down his figure on a notepad.

Schofield glanced over and nodded, then signed his name to the page, so Ostapenko could get the paymaster to honor it in American dollars.

"My colonel, you were gone!" Ostapenko shouted, pointing to the sky across the river.

Of course Ostapenko had known about the battalion's four days away. Whatever the battalion did was watched closely by the Black Sea Cossacks—the local goons—and reported back to Bendery, where the resistance was headquartered.

Ostapenko was a collaborator with the resistance as well as the black marketeer.

Schofield didn't care this afternoon. He strolled across the square. The river traffic was heavy here; anything that would float was carrying the harvest down to the Black Sea and to the rich black markets in Asia Minor and the smoldering Caucasus.

The square was filling up with cigarette smokers come to beg from the American kids who didn't smoke.

Ky joked, "Here come the paparazzi, sir."

The local press corps was gathering on their motorbikes—correspondents from Moscow and Kiev, stringers from the European services. There were probably two or more minicams on the way to record the return of the rich Americans.

Every now and again, if the weather was good, there were American correspondents passing through as they sailed up and down the Dniester covering the Moldovan civil war.

Schofield turned away from the gathering commerce.

He looked first to his Top, Tom Owen, who was seated like a

cocky Saint Gabriel on the roof of a Hummer, watching his charges, weapon at the ready, expecting the worst.

Schofield looked up the seventy-three stone steps to Printing House Square, and to the red-roofed printing shop to the left.

It was midmorning. She was probably busy. But maybe she'd have time for a pastry. Ky could watch her little girl, Tanya, and they could talk.

He thought, *Good idea. I need to talk with somebody I'm not in charge of.*

Schofield signaled Owen he was going off scene; then he waved to Ky, and they started up the stone steps to Red Schofield's new friend, the porcelain-skinned war widow Christina Perzhu.

The market women parted in Schofield's path. The huge American in battle armor and his squat Sancho Panza wearing a manpack transceiver were climbing up to Christina's. Everyone knew the story. Christina was too serious for a pretty young woman. It was good for her to have a man. This man was rich. He couldn't have his own wife. He was too lonely for a young man.

Minutes later, Christina let him into the print shop and kissed him on the cheek.

Schofield hesitated and said, "I missed you," and then he reached into his vest. He'd brought her a present from the Able Company's mail drop—a white cashmere sweater a specialist had bought by mail order for his girl, who'd subsequently ditched him.

Christina said, "Thank you, thank you, my sweet man, thank you!" in smart English. She smiled brilliantly, complementing her porcelain white skin and startling yellow hair. Twenty-eight years old, and widowed by the war—her dead husband had been a Black Sea Cossack killed by Left Bank snipers—she wasn't shy about good luck. Having Schofield call upon her was a fantasy, and she was ready to enjoy it.

Christina spoke slowly in Russian, "They said you'd gone. Last week. Flown away."

Schofield translated to himself, held up his hand. "We're back now," he said in bad Russian.

"You're not leaving again?" she asked.

Schofield fibbed, "No, no," and sighed until she kissed him on the mouth very softly. Schofield blushed at her hot touch. He was the shy one, in the same way hundreds of thousands of American GIs the last hundred years had blushed at their amazement to have a girl of their own.

Christina had two girls; the six-year-old was at school, while the three-year-old Tanya was in the little yard out behind the shop, playing with the neighbor's children.

Schofield gave Ky the toy makeup kits that he'd gotten from the mail drop for the babies, and sent him to deliver. "We'll be upstairs if you need me," he said.

Ky eased off the manpack, told Tom Owen's RTO in the square where he was, and obeyed his colonel.

Soon, seated upstairs in the apartment Christina had over the shop, Schofield was chatting away just as if he'd come home from the office. His easy remarks quickly ran to his hard complaints. Not too long after that, Christina was in his arms. She felt like cotton candy, and she smelled like the morning meadow.

Schofield looked at his helmet, at his holster, at the clock.

He wanted to go back to her bedroom. He also wanted to talk. She was only twenty-eight, the same age as his sergeants, but she understood a lot more than they did about men who don't want to be tough all the time.

Or did she? She put her cheek against his cheek and spoke in Russian now. "When can you stay with me like a boyfriend?"

Schofield concentrated on the translation. A boyfriend? He suddenly felt very old. What did she understand? That he was a warlord. That he was holding the battalion together all by himself. That . . .

"Please, Red, please," she said, pulling at his buttons, putting her knee against his belt.

Twenty minutes later, out of the release and the guilt and the pleasure of her softness and wetness and muscular neediness, Schofield's mind fell back to his worst fears, and soon, falling slightly away from Christina's wet body, he was drifting off into his nightmare thoughts.

What if back in the world is a dream?

What if Bendery is the end of the world?

What if I never heard Sensenbrenner give those orders?

What if I never made that call to Toni?

What if this scared little family is all I have to worry about?

What if FATHER'S DAY is a nightmare?

No, no, he thought—*what about Toni's scared little family? How is grabbing Christina helping Toni?*

Why did I make that call? I heard Sensenbrenner's order. I could have refused the order.

No, no: the textbook says to acknowledge the order is to obey the order.

So why did I make the call? I talked. Why? Why?

Because I panicked?

Because I don't want to be alone?

Because I'm in love with Toni? Am I? Is that why I'm here with . . . with my blond Toni in Bendery? Because I should have asked Toni to stay with me after Mac . . . Because I'm jealous of . . .

No, because I'm going to die. Because I'm dead. Sensenbrenner ordered me to my death. With a .22, I'm going to die.

What's going on back home? Why do they need an operation to kill the president? Why . . . ?

But what if . . . ?

Why did I call Toni?

What can she do? What can the Longfellows do? What can anyone do?

The go code comes, we go.

But . . .

So much sex and death and defeat was twisting Schofield's mind to confusion. He was ready to admit to anything. That he coveted Toni. That he hated anyone who had his Toni. That he hated his duty. That it was all useless.

The two rifle reports outside the window were not a dream.

Schofield came alert instantly. He got his Beretta in his hand and was at the window without dressing.

The siren started up. Tom Owen was recalling. Big trouble.

Ky called upstairs, "Colonel, recall! Sergeant Owen's buttoning them up." There was a squawk of the manpack. Ky cried louder, "Three-minute recall! Somebody's down, sir!"

"Right there!" Schofield called back, reaching for his pants. "Shit! Shit! Shit!"

He had no dreams. He had no nightmares. All he had was orders.

And now he had a soldier down.

10 Monday, Occupied Kurdistan

General Sensenbrenner drew his Beretta as he was charging up the street.

He had to dodge the hysterical Kurds running away from the blast crater. There were only a few minutes gone since the car bomb had torn open the bazaar, yet already, in this sticky evening heat, the sour, sick smell of death was like a warning to run for your lives.

Sensenbrenner wasn't backing off. It wasn't in him. He was one of those soldiers who marched to the sound of guns.

He was also a first-rate officer. The very best officers have the very best hearts. And that explosion had torn a hole in the heart of the world.

The bomb had gone off right outside the courtyard entrance of a popular tea garden. There was a ten-meter-wide crater across the street that had chewed away the edge of the courtyard's thick wall. Worse, the detonation had turned the archway into the muzzle of a cannon that had spewed shrapnel into the patrons.

The shredded sign above the archway read in Turkish, "House of Honor."

What was wrong was that there was screaming from the courtyard. Everyone on the nearby street had been blown dead by the concussion. But in the courtyard they had only been raked. You could hear the screams fifty meters away.

And those high-pitched shrieks were from children.

Sensenbrenner had to go to them. It was part of what held him together. Poor boys cared about poor boys and girls.

Sensenbrenner's four bodyguards gave him cover while they advanced in a zigzag trot toward the tea garden. The mob was gone now. All that remained was the screams. Sensenbrenner skirted left around the crater. He could feel the heat of the hole and smell the nitrates. He could guess plastics, probably from the Turkish army arsenal. The crater was like an open grave of body parts.

"Point!" Sensenbrenner called, and one of his bodyguards, the little corporal Filizzola, took the lead to the courtyard.

No one hesitated. This called for rapid coordination. Sensenbrenner's men knew that the worst mistake in any ambush is to hesitate.

Filizzola squatted to the right of the shattered archway. There was only one way to go in, and that was to go in. Sensenbrenner came around the left side of the crater and stopped against the wall, squatting in the rear-facing position. The general glanced along the edge of the tin-topped roofs on the other side of the bazaar.

A stupid place for an ambush—no high ground, no exits—but then Kurdistan wasn't a place for wise men.

Team leader Sergeant Sandoval squatted down and handed the general a Kevlar helmet. "Pot on, sir."

Sensenbrenner shed his beret and pulled on the helmet. He had been in his good field uniform in respect for the military governor. Now he was caked with black dust.

Sensenbrenner signaled Filizzola. "On my count," he commanded. "Three. Two. One."

The point man jumped into the archway and vanished into the dust. A second bodyguard replaced him at the wall.

"Clear!" the point man called back.

The shrieks from inside rose up again in a mad rhythm of pain.

The second bodyguard plunged inside as backup, and another bodyguard took his place.

There were sirens from down the street—a mobile patrol coming up in two Hummers. A Comanche gunship darted past the fallout cloud from the blast and then down toward the crater for a look-see.

Swiftly the brigade's security response teams were closing in on what was left of the bazaar.

Sensenbrenner understood that the bomb was a warning shot. He had been about a half kilometer away in a convoy with the military governor. The Kurd resistance—the PKK—couldn't mount the resources to strike directly at the visiting general. But they could kill their own women and children in a show of savagery. At the explosion the convoy had deployed in a defensive perimeter. The military governor, a fat burgher who'd gone to school in Munich, had told Sensenbrenner in German, "Pay no mind is my advice."

Sensenbrenner had said nothing; he'd just sprinted toward the screaming.

Presently an NCO brought up a fire team on a dead run. The NCO knew the general was here, and not until he was certain the general was secure did he grab the horn from his RTO and call up to the gunship.

All this happened in rapid sequence: Sensenbrenner alerted the RTO, "Friendlies inside, soldier!" The long wasp of a Comanche flitted directly over the courtyard and hung there with its twin cannons like a double stinger. The sky turned pink and indigo to the west. The American peacekeepers kept at their job.

After a pause, Sergeant Sandoval spoke to his general. "Welcome to Diyarbakir, sir."

What was left of Diyarbakir. Once the capital of Kurdistan

here in the upper Tigris River valley, it had been reduced by siege and terrorism to a rubble of refugees attached to an airbase. The Georgians and Armenians pressed from the north. The Iraqis pressed from the south. The Iranians pressed from the east. The Turks in faraway Ankara had begged NATO for protection before they lost everything beyond the Taurus Mountains.

The American forces had been airlifted to the rescue one more time. It was called peacekeeping, it was also called mercenary; but whatever you called it, the GIs showed up and buttoned up and that was the end of the big trouble—and the beginning of all the little troubles.

Sensenbrenner gave a thumbs-up, and then without a glance back he plunged into the archway with two fretful sergeants on his tail.

Filizzola had used his rifle to lever up a table. The child with the throat wound couldn't move. The screaming was from underneath the fallen cooking table. Sensenbrenner, Filizzola, and Sandoval pitched in together to lift it, burning their hands on the searing metal. But what were their burns to the misery underneath, where they found two infants buried by hot coals.

The babies, trying to crawl free, had only gone into the worst of it.

Filizzola grabbed one child in his arms, doused him with water from his canteen, and ran for the archway and the Hummers.

Sandoval grabbed the other, a girl. "Sir?"

"Go," Sensenbrenner said, releasing Sandoval from his side.

Sensenbrenner stepped back. What was it he saw? Two old men were dead in their seats at the back wall, frozen in place as if they were a mural. There were wounded bodies in every direction. And the babies under the coals.

He thought, *Where have I seen this before? What courtyard? When?*

Many hours later, after supper with the regimental noncoms and a twenty-minute nap, Sensenbrenner was in the communications room at NATO headquarters.

There was a scheduled video call from the acting president, and Sensenbrenner was waiting for the satellites to make the connection.

His hands were bandaged, silvadene and gauze, and he couldn't stuff them in his fatigue pockets to hide the irregularity. The regimental chief of staff was behind him, chatting with Sensenbrenner's aide about the next events. The schedule called for a nighttime flyover of the river. Then liftoff for Cairo at 0100 hours.

There was new trouble at Cairo. Sensenbrenner didn't want to think about it yet.

He wanted to remember something about the devastated tea garden. What? He was only half listening to the briefers. He was mostly staring down on this blacked-out quarter of the city.

The tea garden. The slaughter. Where had he seen it before? Then he solved it.

Mexico, he thought. *The archaeological dig. The ancient acropolis at Cacaxtla. Eight hundred* A.D. *The warrior merchants. The mural on the north plaza. The blood-soaked scene of ritual sacrifice. The jaguar men and the bird men. The bird captain's mouth open in a scream. Yes.*

He'd stopped at the dig three years back, during a visit to Mexico City. It had been one hundred and twenty degrees under a great shed. The grim fact was that the archaeologists had found the remains of children buried beneath the plaza—the bodies cut up and burned in sacrifice. The horror of prosperous priests burning children. About the time of Charlemagne, eight centuries after Christ, eight centuries before Cortez. Enterprise and savagery and genius. Burning children to death in thanksgiving.

"Sir, the call's coming in." Sensenbrenner's junior aide spoke calmly. His name was Yudron, West Point '99, and his parents were Bhutanese immigrants living in Colorado. "Do you want a chair, sir?"

Sensenbrenner asked for his beret. He had to arrange his thoughts now. The president was calling.

He'll want a report. No . . . he'll want to know when . . . no, he'll want me. He wants me to come home. The vice presidency.

Sensenbrenner shook his head. The carnage today had rocked him more than he'd figured.

He thought, *What will the president want?*

EXCOM. Yes, EXCOM. He'll want a report to EXCOM.

Will he want to know more about FATHER'S DAY? No. No, he knows not to worry about operations.

Is FATHER'S DAY ready? I took the order. What kind of order was it? It was the president's order. A direct order.

What's wrong with me? Is it EXCOM? Because they're politicians and not soldiers . . . ?

I took the president's order. I'll keep my place. I'll do the job.

What else will he ask? Yes, my hands, he'll want to know what happened.

And?

The vice presidency. He wants me home to make me vice president.

In exchange for what? In exchange for the force structure. He's going to give me the force structure back. At least, he'll stop the bleeding. At least, that was the deal.

Sensenbrenner stepped in front of the field version of the televideo camera, a dull green contraption that resembled a toaster. Combat quality, one-way projection to the White House.

His head felt very heavy. Burning children on purpose. A

millennium later, still burning children on purpose. His head was heavier and heavier.

On May 1 Sensenbrenner's head had felt just as heavy as he'd stepped in front of the president in the Oval Office. That was the day that Acting President Garland had offered the deal. "We need your help over a bad patch in the road, General," Garland had said. And then he'd made the offer. Quid pro quo. All the power of the White House in exchange for the capability of the Pentagon. What was required was a single operation that would probably never be used.

Operation FATHER'S DAY.

I took the deal, Sensenbrenner thought. *I wanted to take the deal. To protect my command. To maintain our readiness. To save what I can. Because I wanted to.*

I sold the force to save the force.

Poor boys care about poor boys and girls.

The satellite made the connection. The signal lit up. The camera light blinked on.

The chairman of the Joint Chiefs of Staff saluted the acting president of the United States.

11 Monday Evening, the White House

"General, what's happened to your hands?" Garland asked.

A few minutes later Garland finished the call when he was satisfied that Sensenbrenner understood he was to be there tomorrow night, that Sensenbrenner understood that the challenge was going forward, that Sensenbrenner understood that EXCOM was pleased with him—and so was Shy Garland.

Quinn Roosevelt, seated out of sight of the video unit, suggested otherwise. "What's wrong with our general?"

"He did sound distracted and dismal," Garland admitted. He crossed the small room to his desk and made a note on his pc. They were in his private office, here on the second floor of the White House. Garland didn't like to work in the Oval Office; it made him feel he was on a sound stage, and he found the other second-floor rooms overfurnished and overdecorated.

Only here in a room he had made his own—sparse Western trappings, simple woven rug, a plain wooden table for a desk, a giant framed NASA photograph above the mantel of Major Garland hanging in zero g's over the Gulf of Mexico—did Garland find the peace of mind he needed to think well. Inside Garland the chief executive was the boyishness of the ranch hand, the ballplayer, the astronaut, where form followed function and less was more and every detail was nailed down.

"You saw his hands?" Garland asked. "I wish he wasn't such a bloody-minded champion or whatever you want to call it. Why is he in Diyarbakir? Kurdistan's been stable for months. He didn't have to go there, and he certainly didn't need to get wounded. What's he trying to prove?"

Roosevelt remarked, "Perhaps that he's too busy for what we need of him?"

Senator Pickett, the third man in the room, spoke up. "Goddamned, don't even joke about that one, Yankee boy. We need old Lucius S. more than we need friggin' C-SPAN."

The long-bodied, silver-maned majority leader was draped over a hard-backed bench in front of the TV monitor. Dressed in tan dress slacks like Roosevelt's, with a black polo shirt like Garland's, the skillful and reedy-voiced Halley "Sonny" Pickett of Raleigh, North Carolina, was entertaining himself by channel-surfing through the government cable shows.

"Course I realize it's a tonic for you," Pickett continued to Roosevelt, "to hold our most sacred institutions up before your magnifying glass and look for the holes, but don't do it in my earshot this time. Amuse me and keep your tongue."

Garland spoke up. "Now, Sonny, Q.'s wasn't that poor a comment. You do have to wonder why he's in Turkey when he knows we need him here."

Pickett cursed the TV, "Crap," and blanked the screen.

Sonny Pickett and Shy Garland were longtime pals. Everybody knew they'd been partners in a previous life—"Maybe the same little satrap," was the joke.

The other joke was that the only reason Shy Garland had left his power base in the Senate for the Guy In Backseat on Jay's ticket was that he'd left Sonny Pickett holding his coat. If Garland was "Big Six" Mathewson, the all-time ace right-hander, then Pickett was his raunchy major league manager, Muggsy McGraw, a man who once did anything—lie, cheat, break an arm, attend the Ziegfeld Follies—to win the pennant.

Garland continued to think aloud. "And if something did happen to our general, then what do we do? Do we have a fallback position? Do I do the press conference anyway and hold up a cardboard cutout and say, 'He's with us, brothers and sisters, really'?"

"You misunderstood me, sir." Roosevelt spoke to Pickett. "Or perhaps I should say, I misrepresented my position. What I meant to say is that we can't do without the general. It's way too late to start over on this one. We don't have the staff work to do the polling and prep work for another candidate."

"Oh, sweet Savior, it ain't funny if you're bein' funny, and I can't tell," Pickett mocked Roosevelt.

Like many Washington politicians these days, Pickett distrusted Quinn Roosevelt—the president's most loyal cutthroat.

To underline his protest, Pickett leaned back around and directed his remark at Diana the scribe, who was seated primly in the corner writing verbatim notes. "Make sure you get that this Johnny Reb wasn't laughing at Billy Yankee's misspoken remark." He emphasized, "Without the general, we're just pissin' the wind here."

Pickett addressed Roosevelt with a cruel tone. "Bang your pair together, Q., and try to imagine that sound if you had just one. That's what we'll sound like without the general on our side this time."

"Sometimes, Senator, I don't know when you're serious," Roosevelt complained.

"I do," said Pickett.

The snit passed. The three men, Garland, Pickett, and Roosevelt, were comfortable with one another's ambitions. At heart they were practical men, not ideologues, and they'd long worked well together.

Garland even knew when to make light of their disputes. "I am allowed to think the unthinkable thirty seconds a day, you know. It's weary-making to be right as much as Q.'s teams make me right. Besides, we'd scare the Hill to the Baptists if we pitched Sensenbrenner overboard. They're going to squeal as it is—"

"Hah!" Pickett offered. "I tell you the squealing's going to come from the goddamned pen across the aisle. Jeannie Mother-friggin'-well's going to wet her pants when she sees old Lucius S. marching to the microphone Tuesday."

Garland was taken with Pickett's wit. "Have you heard from Jean?" he asked.

"She don't want me," Pickett said. There was no reason to mention Garland's old romance with Jean Motherwell, so Pickett did anyway. "Don't want a piece of me, neither."

Roosevelt contributed, "She should have the tip by now. We gave it to Long John Longfellow, and he's her guru."

"She'll call a press conference eventually," Garland said, "and then we'll hear all about her moral claims." He was thinking about claiming the morals of another Jean Motherwell—the trim little blond widow congressperson who'd propped herself comfortably in his bed, once upon a time. Actually they'd been mostly in a bunk down at the boat basin on Sonny Pickett's thirty-four-foot runabout. Garland thought, *The scent of her long legs. The grip of her long legs. The view of her long haunches.*

"Anyway," Garland added, "we've got the head count without her. Maybe she doesn't go the press conference route."

"I'd rather she stay at home," Pickett said. "I know we've got the votes, and I know we can buy that Orange County troll McDonald for a song, but my back still tells me this is going to be a pisser. Even our friends are going to get hot and bothered on us when they figure out we need them. And that crackpot Keebler's going to get on TV and preach his 'Shall We Gather at the River?' recipes just to see who he can shake free from us. Shit, he's the one we should be stomping on. Not poor little mixed-up Teddy Bear."

Garland noted Keebler on his pc. He hadn't considered in depth what Keebler was going to do with the news. Then again, who could? Keebler was only as deep as a flash flood, but just as scary and all mud.

" 'One war at a time' is the quote, I think," Garland said. "Isn't that right, Q.? One war at a time. Stanton or—"

"It was Seward," said Roosevelt, "just down the hall in the old cabinet room."

"Oh, f——, not more Yankee hosannas," Pickett teased.

"I've always liked that remark," Garland said. "It makes sense. It's how you win it all. One game at a time. It's going to work, Sonny. And the polls are with us, right, Q.?"

Roosevelt made a note about Jean Motherwell. Then he made another about Gus Keebler, the billionaire sheriff of Yuma

County, Arizona, who came within closing distance when matched head to head with Garland.

"All our polling focus groups say it works," Roosevelt answered. "Even when we ask the question straight-up hostile—'Is this a coup?'—we get back a six-out-of-ten approval."

Garland thought, *The last pitch, not until the last pitch of the last out of the last inning of the last season.*

Garland was also thinking how much simpler the whole game would be if the president would cooperate with the inevitable and resign.

Garland would have his chance to win it all in about an hour because President Jay was due downstairs in the Oval Office, at 6 P.M., for a sit-down meeting about the supposed transition.

Meanwhile, Garland made notes on his pc about the linchpin of Sensenbrenner. He liked the general, but not as a friend. The class difference explained their distance—Garland of River Oaks, Sensenbrenner of Tobacco Road—yet there was also their temperament. Garland was intuitive and romantic. Sensenbrenner was predictable and classical. Garland gave orders. Sensenbrenner obeyed orders.

In contrast, Garland and Pickett were twins in the Senate—too alike to choose from—and their alliance was more cunning than profound.

But then again Garland's teaming up with Sensenbrenner was like the magic of sun-kissed opposites—a marriage made in Congress. They had been allies since Garland's heady days as chair of the Senate Armed Services Committee. Together, Garland, then a senator, and Sensenbrenner—then in charge of both the plans and the force structure directorates on the Joint Staff—had drafted the Garland-Magellan Military Reorganization Act of 1 January 1999, which had scheduled the long-term revamping of the armed forces—cutting up to seventy-five percent of the force, reducing the officer cadre by ninety percent, and concentrating command of the armed forces in the hands of the streamlined Joint Staff.

For the first two years of the Jay administration Garland, together with Sensenbrenner as sitting chairman of the Joint Chiefs, had accelerated the phase-in of the Reorganization Act and worked to transform the battered and demoralized Pentagon into a slim and most proficient military organization.

Together, Garland and Sensenbrenner had projected American power on every continent by playing the strategic roles of the good cop and the bad cop. For example: Senator Garland the peacemaker had negotiated the cease-fire at Walvis Bay in '99 while General Sensenbrenner the peacekeeper had held Brick Breckenridge's amphibious Operation FLAMINGO over the heads of the hostiles like a dagger.

Together, Garland and Sensenbrenner had contributed the only foreign policy success of the Jay administration—the Walvis Bay Peace Accord, which they had fashioned in imitation of the Cairo Pact they'd helped shape under the previous administration, after the failure of Operation MEMPHIS FRIENDS to secure earthquake-torn Cairo.

Now together Garland and Sensenbrenner were going to save the country from the headless President Jay.

Or so goes the fairy tale, Garland was thinking.

Garland brooded aloud some more to Pickett and Roosevelt. "Maybe the general's bandages will help us tomorrow. The press loves him already, and if we could play it up as a combat wound . . . Another Purple Heart?" Garland frowned. "Forget it. The general won't go along. Sometimes I forget that he's a very colorless fellow. It's his job that gives him the pizzazz. Diyarbakir!"

"He's no politician," Roosevelt said.

"He's a goddamned two-thirds majority is what he is," said Pickett, flipping on the TV monitor again. "Look at this shit they've got on . . ."

Garland made more notes to himself about Sensenbrenner.

Why is S. blue? Garland wrote.

Did S. do that to himself deliberately? Garland wrote.

Also: *Is this stress showing on S.?*

Garland abandoned psychology. He was tired of figuring out motives.

Garland told the operator to get his father on the line. He wanted to check with him once more about tomorrow.

Moments later, Garland used the receiver to speak respectfully to his stately octogenarian of a horse-thief father, the famous Lynch Garland of Houston. "Daddy, you sure you don't need me to send one of my Gulfstreams down there for you?" Garland's accent always dusted up when he talked with his father. "Iphy thinks you shouldn't have to fuss yourself. She's ready to fly down and fetch you and the boys herself."

Garland had two sons by his first marriage, his NASA marriage, and one son by his second marriage—his senatorial marriage—and the boys lived with their mothers in Texas.

"Let her come on down," Garland proposed to his father. "It's not a problem for Iphy—she said to tell you. And you could get in early and have a siesta. We're going on air about seven our time, and it'll be close if you fly commercial. The boys'd like it, too. Please, Daddy, nobody's to think you're losin' it if you need help with your grandsons . . ."

Sixty minutes later Garland was dressed beautifully in a new blue pin-striped suit and brilliant white shirt, and he was standing on the porch outside the Oval Office waiting for his wife.

It was a lush, soft evening, the roses in the garden spraying scent like a fumerie. Garland had rarely felt more charged up and confident.

Iphy's entrance raised his game to another level. She came striding out the Oval Office doors like the lead taking command of the set, which was true, for no woman is more of a leading lady than a studio wife. She was a redhead this month, with her eyebrows as black as her eyes. She'd chosen a white-and-blue suit with huge shoulders to match Garland's formality, and she was wearing her real diamond studs, not the paste. Her heels were as sharp as her fingernails.

The effect was that of a burning eagle flapping to earth.

Garland breathed in her perfume. *Did I marry her? Look at that profile! Look at those legs!*

"You're gorgeous," Garland told her.

"Never mind turning my head now, this is business," she replied with her spectacular smile. She ordered, "You take my arm, darling, and when the president gets close to us, you pass me over to him. I want to feel what he's got inside him, and the best way to do that is on his arm."

"Is that true? Where'd you learn that?" Garland asked.

"You know, I usually can't recall which project," she said, "but it was one of those mysteries, and I had to do everything to hold up the production end. The concept was a moll who goes straight."

"Straight to me," Garland teased.

"I love it when you talk dirty," she said with that grin again. It was a famous grin, so provocative that when she'd used it during the California primary everyone had known that she and Garland were lovers.

Iphy nodded down toward the Rose Garden, where the countless White House aides were signaling that the presidential party was approaching from the parking area at the west gate.

It was like a meeting of two tides, with two sets of Secret Service presidential protection teams about to crash together on the emerald lawn.

"Here we go," Iphy said. "And try to hit our marks, will you, they're set up just right."

Iphy wasn't teasing. The studio wife in her could feel the television cameras deployed along the edges of the garden as an Eagle driver could feel illumination.

The acting first couple stepped down to greet the forty-third president of the United States.

The president was not hiding his feelings or his fatigue as he crossed the lawn toward the Garlands. He had been in town all afternoon. He'd flown back from Miami to Andrews at noontime, and then, after a nap, he'd attended a garden party in Georgetown put together hastily by some of his oldest fundraisers from Detroit. They were excited that the president was back in good health again. Their pleasure had raised the president's spirits, but then, afterward, coming down in the car, he'd felt his mood drift.

How do I feel? he thought. *A little lonely for Connie.*

The TV cameras on either side of the lawn picked up each step of Jay's walk back into history. The live cable feeds featured close-ups on his strong cheekbones, compassionate gaze, and generous mouth from the moment he cleared the shrubbery blinds.

The president had long since stopped worrying about how he looked from day to day. No reason for a display from him at all today, he figured, and he was dressed plainly in a good double-vented suit, like a rising Chrysler executive. Despite his weariness, he glided with his distinctive relaxed gait, a man who understood how to carry power like Atlas. He was trailed by his chief of staff and a few White House hands who'd come out to greet him in the parking lot beforehand.

The man was come home. This was his house, Jay knew; the American people had put him in it with five hundred electoral votes, and he had come today without need of proof or pomp.

He intended to make a bigger show of his return when he took the White House back on Friday.

That was it, wasn't it? he thought. *Today is Monday, and our plan is that we're back on Friday?*

Still, now that he was in the Rose Garden again, he felt the same thrill as his first day in office here. Five months at Walter Reed or Camp David, with all the privileges of his office, weren't to compare with the sensation of being president at the president's house. The winged mansion looked good to him—bright white like a clean sheet of paper and neat as a flagship. The whole park looked grand to him in this June light. Thomas Jefferson's mounds, Andrew Jackson's magnolias, Eisenhower's pin oaks. He was ready to go to work, if not today, then next week— as soon as he got things put back together.

As soon as Connie comes back to help me, he thought. *Connie. I should have Connie with me. I should call Connie later. She'll be watching this on TV. No. She told me she doesn't have cable at her house. Maybe she'll see it anyway. I should smile for Connie and the children.*

The two presidents met at the dead center of the marks. The cameras couldn't choose between them. The close-ups failed. Iphy's grin overwhelmed the focus.

"Mr. President," Garland began, "we're so pleased you were able to come today. We thought we could start in the office, you know, some photos, and then have a light supper, a working supper."

"Thanks, Shy." The president corrected himself. "Thanks, Mr. President. It feels good to be back here today. I wondered, on the way down in the car, what it would be like to walk up to the house. I told myself it might feel like an old pensioner dropping by his office. But no, it doesn't feel as if it's a place I've left behind me. It feels as if I'm coming back from a long trip. When I left, it was snowing a little that day—yes, there were flakes—and the roses were all balled up like shivering cats."

"I like that idea," Iphy said, "and now look at them, like great lions!"

The president smiled at Iphy's remark. "You've kept things so well for me, Iphy, thank you both. You never know what you might need in this life, and it's a lucky man who has friends who keep his house so well. All these brave lions."

"You look so happy," Iphy said, crossing from Garland's side to Jay's and taking the president by the left elbow. President Jay was a left-hander, and so Iphy had him by his strength.

The president was also a tall man, and his silver thatch was like a permanent wreath that made him seem even larger. In fact he was an inch over Garland and a head taller than Iphy. Yet he had lost a deal of weight and some of his excellent posture during his illness, so he seemed enclosed by the Garlands. It was easy for Iphy to do more tugging than boosting on his arm. The president and Mrs. Garland proceeded across the lawn at Iphy's pace. It looked like a caregiver and her charge. President Jay's legs were wrong. You could see it on the TV. His knees were pointed inward. He was stepping crookedly. He was slumping down to Iphy's side.

Behind the two presidents, Quinn Roosevelt fell in with Joe Friar. The two were far enough back that Friar could make a safe remark to Roosevelt.

Joe Friar started, "He's tired out by the day already, Q."

"We all can see it," Roosevelt said.

Friar got to his point. "I've heard a nasty rumor you're going to try and sandbag us today. That you want something for your work. A payoff. There's nothing to it, is there?" he asked.

"What's the man say?" Roosevelt asked of the president.

"I didn't bother him with it," Friar said.

"Are you really out of shape? You couldn't ask him?"

"He didn't want to be asked," Friar said.

Roosevelt said, "You *are* out of shape. In the old days, you would have had overnight polls for talking papers. You would have had the teams spinning the big foot press all four points of the compass."

Friar agreed with his protégé. "It's been five months. My reaction time's off, I guess. So's my paranoia. This isn't a job you can practice for. You're in shape, though. I saw that clip from Chicago. Slick. 'Leader of my party and father of the country.' "

Roosevelt said, "The boss worried it was too soft."

"But a good bite out of context, eh, Q.?" said Friar.

"You taught me," said Roosevelt.

The two chiefs of staff were like butlers discussing their lords. Both of them ate too much and drank too little water; and they both hadn't had a vacation since the turn of the century; and they both sneaked cigarettes when they could; and neither one had a marriage to brag about or more than a half day a week for his kids. Once they had shared a campaign victory. They had liked each other since, in the way two rival catchers like each other—the old pro Friar and the hot rookie Roosevelt.

But not today, not this way. Friar sensed the trap. Roosevelt baited him.

"Seriously, how rough is it going to be?" Friar asked.

"All the way, Joe," Roosevelt said.

"I'm not going to ask what that means," Friar responded. "And the man I trained wouldn't tell me anyway."

Roosevelt twisted his mouth—not quite a smile.

They were on top because they had the people, he thought about Teddy Jay and his Joe Friar. *In the primaries, they beat us because they had the people. We had the machine, but they had the people, and whenever things got tight, whenever we closed, Teddy Jay could always go over our heads to the people with that "new world" speech of his. In the election, we cleaned up be-*

cause with their people and our machine, the GOP was nothing but bystanders.

But now, Roosevelt thought, *we've got the party, we've got the machine, and we've got the people—and Teddy Jay's got memories.*

Up the steps to the portico, Roosevelt spoke once more to his mentor. "The man you trained would tell you to look at the polls. Look at the polls, Joe. You taught me. Always look at the polls."

Friar turned sideways to ask, "And what do your polls say?"

"They say, 'All the way,'" Roosevelt spoke again, this time with bite.

Inside the Oval Office, the staff let the photographers in for a few minutes. Garland distrusted these dog and pony shows, though he'd been good at them since NASA. He had Iphy to shield him. Certainly one of the reasons he cherished Iphy as the political animal she was—a studio wife was a politician who earned real money—was that her presence relieved him of the spotlight before the game.

Iphy loved the camera, and the camera loved Iphy. She twirled back and forth to steal every shot. No lens could get past Iphy's face, that queer combination of narrow-set, aroused eyes and sheer marble cheeks and her eagle's beak over that famous naughty grin. Each time Iphy pushed her cameo against Garland's cheek, or about one centimeter from Jay's, the cameras whirred. No one wanted a shot without her. No one could miss that she made Garland look sexy and Jay look bushed.

Iphy was also good at fielding the shouted questions of the White House press corps.

"When do the movers come, Mr. President?" they asked Garland.

"We just brought our overnight bags, don't you know," Iphy responded, and then, waving at the Christy Mathewson museum exhibits around the room, she added, "and a few of my husband's old baseballs."

"What about the budget, Mr. President—Mr. President?" they asked both men. "Are you together on it? Are there significant differences? Wall Street seems to think so. Any comment on the negative reactions of the markets today, Mr. President—Mr. President?"

"We're all long on America, aren't you?" Iphy responded.

And then the jabs directed at Jay. "What about your recovery, Mr. President? Don't the American people deserve the facts of your recovery now that you're back here in the Oval Office?"

This was an unfair question, as there had been a full-dress medical press conference at Walter Reed that morning in which the president's physicians and consultants outlined the dimensions of his illness for the twenty-fourth time in twenty-two weeks, lectured generally about the wisdom of facing up to an affliction that all estimates said weighed down ten million Americans, and commented vigorously at length on their opinion that the president was fit and trim—more so than he'd been in many years.

Still, Iphy, waiting a long count for Jay to say nothing, responded with a cunning soliloquy.

"What the American people deserve is our thanks for the one million four hundred and thirty thousand 'Get Well' cards and letters the president has received that have done the trick. The American people gave the president their prayers, and I don't care what the doctors say, I know that prayer is what makes people better. Don't you all know that by now? Not doctors. Prayers and love."

The press was swept from the room like a buffet table cleared of snacks. Garland liked the press the more he held the top job. They were like a good dog. Feed 'em right, and they'd hunt. And what headlines they'd write you if you just kept winning.

President Jay liked the press, too, though he'd had weak relations with them the last months before his collapse. He'd wanted to persuade them. They'd wanted to be persuaded. He'd just not connected. Then his carping and whining had worsened—conduct that was now clearly recalled as the tip-off of his decline. After the First Lady had moved out of the White House, the dialogue between the press and the chief executive collapsed. He'd have to rebuild, he knew. The sympathy vote was a head start, he knew.

I wish Connie were here, he thought. *Connie could do this. Connie's got more class than this mob. Connie. I should call her as soon as I get out of here. Or wait till Sunday? What would she like? Connie.*

Garland took Iphy to the door and kissed her on the mouth in parting.

She said, "Break a leg."

He answered, "It won't take that long."

She said, "I'll be waiting for you," and there was the grin once more, this time with punch, for she liked romance after photo ops.

The president was in the catbird seat before the dark fireplace. He arranged himself with his long right leg crossed over his knee and his elbows resting neatly on the arms.

Garland changed vantages, to the straight-backed chair at President Jay's left hand. Friar and Roosevelt pulled their low-backed seats in line with the president's sight. The arrangement was one of deference to a president—or to an invalid.

Other senior staffers, such as Garland's lawyer, Hank Lovell (sweating in the air-conditioning), and Jay's longtime friend and White House chief counsel, Abbie Fleischmann, sat along the sweep of the wall. Garland's omnipresent scribe, Diana, was within earshot by the side exit, while Jay's scribe, Duncan, was seated by the New York Giants baseball uniform.

The sharp snap of the doors shutting was the start. Nine men, five women, walnut and oak floor, blue rug, off-white drapes, Chippendale armchairs, gold sofas, Revere silver tray of crystal water glasses and an etched water pitcher, Charles Marion Russell's *Fording the Horse Herd* over the bureau and George Henry Story's *Abraham Lincoln* over the fireplace, and the clock struck six-thirty.

Roosevelt addressed President Jay. "Sir, we have a letter this morning from Mr. Speaker Rainey informing us that you look to resume your duties on Friday morning."

Joe Friar interrupted his protégé. "Is there a problem?"

"We don't have a comparable letter from Senator Yamamoto," Roosevelt commented.

"It's all in order, Q.," said Friar. He was writing on his notepad. "We got the letter to Yamamoto last night. He just hasn't written you yet. Do you want me to call? We can have it here immediately."

Friar spun his head to look at the twin counsels, Abbie Fleischmann and Hank Lovell. "Is Yamamoto's letter to them a problem, Abbie?"

The sagelike Fleischmann, a corpulent grandfather who'd been left far outside Garland's private circle for five months, shook his head no. Hank Lovell shuffled his big wingtips.

"There is a problem, Joe," Roosevelt responded to Friar.

Friar and Roosevelt didn't look at each other as they argued. They spoke to the carpet or to the flags behind the desk.

"The problem is the Twenty-fifth Amendment," Roosevelt qualified. "We have our responsibilities to the Twenty-fifth."

Roosevelt addressed President Jay. "We have very heavy responsibilities, sir."

President Jay was not ceremonious and never had been. This was his staff; he had hired all these people once upon a time; he was the boss. He cut off the fencing by asking Garland, "What is it?"

Garland held his hands palm out and wide apart in a gesture of candor. "We don't think we're ready on this, sir," he said to Jay.

"What's that mean?" asked Jay.

"Don't do this," Friar whispered to Roosevelt.

"It's not the time, sir," Garland said. He liked the way this sounded, and he amplified, "It's not *your* time."

The president, wan and willowy, sat forward and declared, "You don't want to do this, Shy."

"Mr. President," Garland continued, "it's out of my hands. The Twenty-fifth Amendment is the clearest guide we have from here on. We're here today to help the country through what'll probably be a bad patch in the road. We have it in our power to help everyone get along together, not just to help ourselves here."

"This is double-talk," said Jay.

"What's in the Twenty-fifth about this?" Friar complained to Garland. He was treating Garland like an equal. Roosevelt didn't like it, but he let it go.

Garland carried on. "Mr. President, the plain talk is that I am asking you to resign your post. Today. Now . . ."

Garland let the word "Now" hang in the air. He didn't think Jay would go for this argument immediately. He was showing him his good stuff right off. He figured he'd have to work for the out.

Strike one.

No one in the room was breathing evenly. Friar found he couldn't close his mouth. Roosevelt liked the southern light on Garland's sober face. It made him look gifted.

Then President Jay surprised the room with a show of force and command: "What you're asking is impossible, you know.

Even if I wanted to, I couldn't. You see, Shy, you're not fit. It's not *your* time. I didn't want to say this. But you want to hear it, I guess. I made a mistake three years ago by making you my running mate. It was my mistake. You're not ready for this job."

Garland blew out his cheeks. *Boy, this guy can still hit. Don't make that mistake again. Nothing over the plate. Paint the corners.*

"We disagree," Garland said. "I expected we would, didn't you? We see it our way. And we'd hope that, given time, you would join us. Yesterday you forced this on us. We want to do the best by you we can. You deserve the best."

President Jay relaxed in his chair. He smiled dully, and then there was the change in his face that meant he was thinking. With an electric glimmer in his smart eyes, his inspiration came out. "You want to hear what I make of you, I can tell. You want to hear why you aren't fit. Let's pretend you just asked me. I can tell you . . . reluctantly."

"Mr. President, you don't owe me an explanation," said Garland.

Garland realized the president was going to swing away. What else could he do?

"It's because you're immature," Jay told Garland. "That's why I'm in this job and you're not. The party in the end recognized that I was the man they wanted to be their leader. Not you, Shy. They couldn't go that far, not yet. And then the American people confirmed that they think the party made the right choice. For now."

President Jay cleared his throat. He needed a drink of water. No one was helping him. He was alone.

"You see, this job isn't a reward for being popular," Jay continued. "It's not a vindication either. Or what you've made of it, a victory lap."

President Jay was looking at the president's desk—at his own desk that he'd brought from Lansing.

"You've got some growing to do, Shy," Jay continued. "You might get there. But for now, you're not ripe enough for the job. You're like a great athlete, aren't you? On the field, you shine, but off the field, when you have to live like a normal human being, you embarrass yourself, you bore yourself. There's also the paradox that by the time you're mature enough to handle the fame, you might have lost your skills."

The president fell silent and eased into the comfort of his seat.

Garland didn't talk back right away. He let the eerie pause that followed serve as proof that Jay had lost control. Garland did half believe this now. The man was barren; the man was depressed.

Eventually Garland replied as if he were offering consolation. "Mr. President, I can see you'll need some time to think about this. Unfortunately we haven't got much time. I'll need your answer by tomorrow. Twenty-four hours. Or I will have to proceed with my responsibilities."

"An ultimatum?" asked Jay. "Just say it. It's an ultimatum, isn't it? You're threatening me in this room with an ultimatum?"

Garland liked the moment, two men in fair combat, the pitcher and the hitter, anything goes. Garland went into his windup and fired, "Sure."

Garland thought, *Strike two.*

"You see what I mean, Shy, you're embarrassed to be flummoxed." Jay was as philosophical as he'd ever been, here in his office, in his house, with his staff. "You don't know what to do if you're not out there with the fans roaring for you. How do you spend money? How do you make friends? How can you be sure who likes you and who likes that you're the superstar? What about your new wife?"

"I'm sorry for you," Garland said, "that you'd lose yourself and make a remark about Iphy."

"I'm sorry for all of us," President Jay said.

"You do understand my responsibilities?" Garland pressed. "Tomorrow we must have your resignation, or we must proceed with the Twenty-fifth's provisions for challenge."

Strike three.

"What I understand is that I came down here for a visit today looking to resume my office on Friday morning," the president stated. "And what I found was a welcome mat that was laid over a lion pit." He glanced at Garland. "A red-headed lion pit."

Garland nodded; the president's rhetorical gifts were welling up, and he knew to step aside.

Roosevelt knew that it was a good thing there wasn't an audience present, because Jay could win anyone to his side when he wanted to.

"You know, Shy, you've put me right off my day," the president said. "I recall now how you used to do that all the time, except that I always tried to overlook it as just more of your showboating. But now I see that you just couldn't walk away from that prima donna nature of yours, that—"

The president broke off. Halfway along on what was gathering itself as a withering criticism of Garland's style, Jay lost his way.

The president glanced down at his lap.

Why do I have to lecture them? he thought. *Can't they think for themselves? Don't they see that this is a terrible turn? A stupid turn? Why do I have to be the one to say the right thing? Do the right thing? Can't they solve this?*

The president threw his hands out like a man who was quits with his subordinates.

Get away from them, he thought. *This isn't worth debating.*

Get to a place where I can sort this out. Maybe Connie will call. Maybe I should call her?

The president stood abruptly. It was time to go back to Camp David. He didn't want Marine One.

I could use some air, he thought. *An evening drive. Roll down the windows. Admire the roses. Connie thinks roses are the petals God drops to soften our path in this hard life. Connie.*

"I suppose we'll have to argue about this later," the president told them all. "At least, I'm sure I don't want to go to dinner and argue. So I think I'll pass on your invitation to have a working supper here and go elsewhere. If that doesn't inconvenience you and Iphy."

Garland was standing now. He said, "I understand, Mr. President. You need time to think about all this—"

The president cut Garland off. "You know, Shy, you really shouldn't invite a man to eat if you're not going to feed him. I've been off my feed, but I'd really worked up an appetite tonight. Now . . . maybe we'll get a burger on the road."

With this peculiar remark about food, from a man who rarely ate red meat, the president started for the Rose Garden.

Since all doors opened for him as if by wizardry, he kept on across the porch, down the steps, and through the invisible rose clouds.

12 Monday Night, Georgetown

"All I can do is tell you the truth, Dad," Jack said.

"You can do a hell of a lot more than that!" Long John boomed back. "You can tell me why you've done such a thing to yourself! A woman! God almighty, Jack, for a woman!"

Jack felt his exhaustion yet he remained standing at alert in his father's kitchen in Georgetown. It was nearly eleven o'clock. Without supper or much water, Jack had flown his Cessna 172 from Augusta to National against tricky headwinds and with a pain in his stomach. Jack was genuinely frightened of his father's temper. Yet he couldn't back away from this trial. His father had ordered him to an audience. His father had commanded him to explain his sins.

The truth was there was no explanation Jack could think of. He'd done it because he wanted to. Now, what could he say?

"I'm sorry," Jack tried. "I didn't want to hurt anyone. Dad, I'm sorry."

"Do you love her?" Long John demanded.

"Yes, sir," Jack said.

"When are you telling your wife?"

"It's not like that, Dad."

"How is it, then? Tell me about how it feels to lie to all of us! All the effort we've put into your campaigns! All the time Jean spends raising money for you! And you do this to that wonderful woman! You—"

"Dad," Jack said, "I'm not here to defend myself. I've done

rotten things, okay. But that's not why I called you today, or told you about Toni. I didn't want to. You're the one who started guessing."

"Plain as your face!" Long John bellowed.

"But Dad, why I called you was because of Schofield. Because of EXCOM and FATHER'S DAY. Because of the Garland challenge to Jay. Are we going to pretend I didn't tell you all that and spend ourselves arguing about what an idiot I might be? I am? Dad . . . what Toni says . . . she might be talking about the real thing. You know it."

"It's a lie! A coup out of the Tenth Mountain! A damned lie by a damned liar's woman!"

"Everything's a lie that you don't want to hear," Jack replied.

"You try to ruin our family with a damned affair, and you make remarks about what I do?"

"Ruin our family? Come on, Dad."

Jack knew this was a stupid remark the instant he'd spoken it. He lowered his head in shame.

It was just then that Jack saw in the corner of the room that his daughters and niece were watching from upstairs.

Also just then Long John poleaxed his son with his walking stick.

The first blow staggered Jack toward the sofa.

"You're a liar!" Long John cursed.

The second blow caught Jack's left elbow.

"Why did you do this?" Long John demanded.

The third blow missed, and Jack caught the stick in his left hand.

The girls were screaming at them to stop. Lilly took the lead to shout at her grandfather, "Please, Poppop, please!"

The two males drew apart. Now there was enough shame for the whole house.

Long John held his arms open and let Lilly embrace him.

Louisa and Kelly stood by until Jack took charge of himself and embraced them.

"I'm sorry, dear ones," Jack said to the children. "I'm very sorry."

Louisa was crying. "Please don't fight with Poppop, Daddy."

"No, no, no more," Jack said. "We've stopped now."

It took more than a half hour to calm the girls down, and even then they went back to bed not trusting the grown-ups.

Jack and his father were contrite by the time they returned to the kitchen table to share orange juice and some toasted cheese buns. They both knew they'd been caught at child abuse. To have lost their tempers, to have let things get that crazed between them with the girls helpless in the house, to have failed their promises to their deceased wives that they would be good fathers—all this weighed upon the two men like pain.

In relief, the only thing they could think to talk about was EXCOM and FATHER'S DAY.

"All right," Long John said, "let's pretend it's not a damned lie. Tell me again, who is this Schofield, and why do you believe what you've heard?"

"But, Dad, it doesn't matter what I believe," Jack argued. "How about you? Do you believe it?"

Rather than lose himself again in denial, Long John snapped up the cordless receiver. "Let me make some calls . . . and we'll see."

"See what? We haven't got that much time, you know, if—"

Long John cut in, "We'll see who Schofield is and why he's talking like this, and why he wanted us to know."

"How?"

Long John punched the numbers. "There's only one place I know that has answers to everything about the One-fourteenth of the Tenth Mountain."

"You mean, at the Pentagon?" Jack asked.

13 Monday Night, the White House

Much later Monday evening, after the battle in the Oval Office, Shy Garland was upstairs on the second floor of the White House, in the traditional First Lady's dressing room.

He was standing behind Iphy. She was mostly in his arms, with her right hip and back to him, so she could rub against him as he stroked her rib cage and breasts.

"I love you," he told her.

"I know you do." Iphy was unclothed except for a white teddy that touched her hips. "But you know I love to hear you say it over and over."

Garland whispered, "Over and over and over."

They'd kept the lamps off; the room was lit by the reflection of the lights on the grounds through the single window. It was a tiny room in a peach-and-white floral pattern—as dainty and precious a chamber as Garland's office was rugged and unbreakable.

Garland liked making love to Iphy here. It made him feel ardent, like the top hand sneaking in on the cattle baron's daughter. Iphy played any role Garland could think up. She preferred the demimondaine gone noble, but if he wanted she'd play the lady gone bawdy, she could handle any guise.

Iphy asked, "Are we going to get over to the post, pardner?" reaching back for his buckle and zipper. "I need something to hold on to."

"I love you," said Garland.

Iphy fixed her stance and arched up, and Garland got a little lost for a few minutes—the fleshy part of him that was with Iphy just rocked in a soaking pleasure, while the brainy part of him that could violate space and time just roamed around his memory, swigging the power of the moment.

Garland had assumed he was ready for the power of the White House. But this evening there was more rush than ever before. His heart was going too fast. He felt very hot—and then came this plunging cold, as if his loins were thrown in an ice bath. The old driver in him felt redout coming. He saw the dots of negative g's. He lost color vision. His legs were going. He crumpled at Iphy's ankles.

Iphy laughed at first, not realizing what was happening. Then she threw herself down beside her husband. "What! Are you all right, honey? Shy, what is it?"

Garland's face was blotchy red. He'd felt this part before. Liftoff: the riptide of gravity followed by the nothingness of zero g's. He lay flat out on the feathery carpet. "Phew," he whispered.

"You scared me," Iphy said.

"It was great," he said.

"What happened? Are you okay? You sure?"

Garland shook off his confusion. He had no strength and let Iphy raise his head up and lay it across her thigh. His trousers were at his feet about a thousand miles to the south. He recovered quickly. First his sense of smell found sweet and salty Iphy, glowing above him like the roundness of a red full moon. Then his sense of humor found his wit. "I think I just screwed the Constitution."

"Hey, it was me."

"I know, darling," Garland said. "You think you're what Jefferson and Madison had in mind?"

"Hey!" she said, and then she kissed his lips and asked

hoarsely, "Want to scoot over to the divan and go for the Bill of Rights?"

Garland did and he didn't, and he slipped into the paradox of passion—when too much is less than none.

Iphy understood, and soon she had her husband up and washed and dressed—as sharp as ever for the meeting called for 11 P.M., in the third-floor Billiards Room.

Six men fit very snugly around an excellent green billiard table and under a cloud of blue cigar smoke.

Garland in his bright white shirt and cream linen pants and Pickett in his all-black sports clothes circled the table like mimes, lining up their shots and banging away. Neither was a good pool player, but both were enthusiastic and their excellent mood suited the framed photos of grinning presidents that filled every inch of the walls.

Quinn Roosevelt sat by the archway with a tall beer in his hand. He was watching the big monitor that hung from braces in the corner of the room. Several of the late local news channels were displayed in all the windows on the monitor. The sound was off, so the fun was guessing what the top stories would be on each of the channels.

Roosevelt spoke to Magellan in the next chair. "We're the lead story—but I say the second is the zoo. The new bat caves."

Jesus Magellan, House majority leader, veteran Los Angeles politician, and news junkie—his baby boy was married to the boss of CBS News—clicked his fingers and said, "Wrong choice, Q.: bat caves'll be number one. Hundred bucks."

Across the room, Billy Wheat, Senate majority whip and Harvard boy, was on the phone with his new wife, Kentucky Savoy, the film star, who was home with their ten-month-old daughter. "I'll be late, I don't know, sweet. But it's just a fever . . . how much is it? Kentucky, if you want to call the doctor, call her. It's what we pay for . . ."

Hank Lovell sat in the next chair, beneath the large black-and-white portraits of FDR at the racetrack and Eisenhower on the links at Burning Tree.

Lovell looked neat but exhausted; he'd been in meetings since six that morning, and he expected to start again tomorrow with the same schedule. A president was a dream client, because the meter stopped only for sleep; but then, the demand was crushing. Lovell was losing weight; he was skipping doctor's appointments; he'd not been home to Texas in a month.

And tonight, after an ugly yelling session with senior White House counsel Abbie Fleischmann over the challenge, Lovell had to make his brain work well enough to conduct himself as recording secretary of this meeting.

This meeting was EXCOM, the acting president's executive committee in charge of the challenge of succession under the Twenty-fifth Amendment.

Lovell flipped up his mini-pc and called up a file from his server downstairs. He punched the key for his secretary, who was still on duty with his whole staff in the Old Executive Office building, and he scratched in another note to call a full legal staff meeting at 6 A.M.

If he ever got to sleep tonight. If this meeting ever started.

Garland was in no hurry. He sank the two ball in the side pocket—*click, clunk.* He moved to the corner and lined up a table-long shot on the green six ball.

"Ha!" Jesus Magellan called and reached out for Roosevelt's hundred-dollar bill.

"Amazing," Roosevelt said, paying off. The new bat caves at the Washington Zoo were the lead story. President Jay's return to the White House was second—and even then they used a long-range shot of Jay, Garland, and Iphy walking together in the Rose Garden.

Magellan joked, "Got to get used to it, Q., we're way down

on the shopping list. Just background noise to them. They pay for the bat caves, they pay for us, and who're they more proud of?"

"But bat caves?" Roosevelt returned. "We're behind bat caves?"

Magellan turned his cigar over and looked at the blue smoke.

"Isn't hard news fascinating?" he asked. Jesus Magellan, fifty-six, had been one of Garland's inner circle ever since they teamed up on the sponsorship of the Garland-Magellan Military Reorganization Act. What Garland saw in Magellan was California's forty-eight electoral votes and one tough party operator. What Magellan saw in Garland was a cowboy spaceman who was also plenty talented enough to hold the party together after victory. Three years before, Magellan had devoted his Southland machine to Garland in the California primary, only to lose to Teddy Jay because of the Iphy Petropoulos affair. Then Magellan had helped convince Garland he should take the VP post when it was offered by Jay in a show of party unity, and he'd even made the VP nominating speech for Garland at the last convention. Magellan, more than Jay's people, had delivered California to the party in the election; and Magellan, more than anyone else on the Hill, could deliver the House for Garland in the challenge.

Quinn Roosevelt thought Jesus Magellan the best political brain on the Hill, way ahead of Sonny Pickett, because Magellan was the only man in the party leadership who wasn't running for president in his daydreams.

Garland sank the six ball. Things were good. The corner pocket was forgiving. He'd left the cue ball on the far rail—not much to work with.

"You're hot tonight, boy," Sonny Pickett said. He waved his big cigar over the table and smiled.

Garland leaned around to glance at the monitor. He frowned

at all the newsreaders. "Could I get one of those windows with the Giants game, please? Just one?"

"Giants are up two–zip," Magellan reported, checking his sports-line watch.

"Excuse me, Mr. President," Hank Lovell began in his thinnest voice. "Are we waiting on the secretaries to begin the meeting?"

Lovell meant State Deputy Rocky Kahn and Defense Secretary Archie Learned and Defense Deputy Ben Mica.

Roosevelt didn't look away from the TV while he stated the details. "We told 'em eleven-thirty; it's early yet. I asked Rocky and Ben to pick Archie up on their way in from Andrews, since they're coming in from London. We figured it'd be more discreet with one car than all three going past the gates this late. They're probably coming up now."

"Go ahead, Hank, they'll catch up," Garland said, banging away at the four ball, "and skip the old business, let's move on."

Lovell began weakly. "What I have is very brief. Since the meeting at six-thirty, we've not heard back from President Jay's staff. I mean from Joe Friar. Not that we expected it. Now . . . tomorrow, presuming we don't hear any more, we're looking toward a full press conference at seven P.M. Is that right, Q.?"

Roosevelt drank his beer, foam on his lip, and nodded. "Right. 0700. I expect we can grab the lead story tomorrow night, right, Mr. Majority Leader?"

Magellan laughed. "So long as no kid falls down a well, God forbid. You giving odds on another hundred bucks?"

Pickett leaned on his cue stick and chewed lightly on his cigar. "I want to hear the facts again," he told Lovell. "Give us the chronology. Specially when my general gets here."

Pickett blew smoke at the middle of the room.

Magellan pushed his legs straight out and stretched, blowing smoke at the center pocket.

If anyone was ever unaware there was a head-to-head competition between the two majority leaders on the Hill, all that was necessary was to watch the two of them blowing smoke in each other's direction—Magellan's Cuban tobacco smoke, Pickett's Carolinian tobacco smoke.

Hank Lovell, crisscrossed by jealous winds, tried to maintain order: "Seven tonight, we gave President Jay the word. Seven tomorrow night, we go live on TV and announce the challenge to the nation. By seven Wednesday evening, we push for a cabinet vote on the challenge. On Thursday, we send the challenge to the House. You first, Mr. Magellan. And our hope is that you can push the vote through by seven P.M. Thursday. Then, by Friday, we expect to be sending it for a vote in the Senate. Senator Pickett, Friday is what you agreed to. Correct?"

"Excuse me," Billy Wheat asked with the receiver still at his ear, "what's seven P.M. for? Every day at seven P.M.?"

Roosevelt quipped, "Drive-time coast to coast for starters, and it makes the Tokyo stock market opening."

"Oh," said Billy Wheat.

What was clear was that Quinn Roosevelt didn't mean the challenge as a Constitutional exercise; he meant the events of the next few days to rock the world.

"We're as regular as the Danville train," joked Pickett, looking to Magellan. "Jesus, you do figure you can deliver me the House by Thursday, say seven P.M.? It'd be real good. I could use the momentum to break arms all night."

"You know I can," said Magellan. "I got three hundred votes now, name by name . . . you want the names now?"

"I believe it," said Pickett.

Magellan exaggerated, "I can make 'em vote for the pope. God forbid."

Garland liked the sound of his two heavy lifters cooperating with each other.

Roosevelt liked the sound that Magellan and Pickett weren't taunting each other.

Garland missed the five ball. "Shoot," he exclaimed.

"Go back a bit," Pickett asked Lovell. "Where's my general in all those seven P.M.s?"

Lovell checked his list. "General Sensenbrenner is due in from Cairo tomorrow afternoon. He's scheduled at the White House tomorrow by five P.M. for a briefing before the press conference. Our thinking here—Q.'s thinking—is we should bring him in the west gate well before we call the press in, so we won't have problems with the nosy bodywatchers."

"Good, good," Pickett said. "Long as Sensenbrenner's here, we're fine. Praise the Lord and pass the brass hats. Brass and circuses, I'm telling you, brass and circuses. We're just fine. You like it, Mr. President?"

"I like it," Garland admitted as he, too, missed the five ball. "It's your shot, Sonny."

Pickett grinned on his cigar, perhaps a little too self-congratulatory, for it got Magellan's back up.

Then again, their little spat was typical of the way the party ran the Hill—with friends like these, who needed an opposition?

"I have a question about General Sensenbrenner," Magellan started. He stood up to the table, a lordly brown man, expertly dressed in a blue silk suit and a flower-painted tie, with two gem rings on each hand. He waved his cigar like a baton. "We don't know where the general stands on all this. We know he's in with us, you say he is. But what does he think? You know, what's he got in here?"

Magellan patted his barrel chest over his heart. This was the oratorical Magellan on low volume.

"We're making him number two on our team," Magellan continued, "and yet what do we know about him? You see him sitting around with us next week, do you?"

Pickett was peeved right away, and he defended his choice bluntly. "Lucius S. is the same sort of stone this country's built on. You got that, Jesus? He's State and Defense and NATO all together. He's worth a division anywhere we send him, and you might notice that, thanks to Teddy Jay, we ain't got too many divisions left to send."

"Okay"—Magellan cut Pickett's energy off—"he's a patriot and a hero, that's not what I'm asking." Magellan reached out an orator's hand to Garland. "Mr. President, you hear what I'm saying? This man's a uniform. He's not a politician like us. We don't know much about him. I'm not here to go along. I'm asking questions now we're going to need answers on later."

Pickett shot back, "You're a little late in the day to ask questions. This ship's launched, and you're either on board or you ain't."

The backdrop of this disagreement was that Mr. Majority Leader Magellan, who did not daydream about being president, had fancied himself as the proper choice to be Garland's vice president—by temperament, by region, by tribe, by talent. Sonny Pickett's advocacy of Sensenbrenner had pushed Magellan's ambition aside. Magellan still resented it. Pickett was still stubborn about it.

Before he'd chosen Sensenbrenner, Garland had been half leaning Magellan's way. The man did have zing, and he did bring a lot more to the ticket than brass buttons. After all, how many electoral votes, went the argument, did a uniform have?

But then, Garland knew he wasn't running for the electoral college, he was running for two-thirds majority on the autocratic Hill; and he'd gone with Pickett's "brass and circuses" recommendation.

Magellan let Pickett's crack settle on the table, then he kept at his game. "What I want to know is, what's he going to do for us next week? Not tomorrow night. Next week. What's he going to deliver?"

Hank Lovell tried to make peace. "General Sensenbrenner has signed on to every finding of this committee, Mr. Magellan. He's been on board since our first meeting. He's cooperated fully with all our requests. He's provided his staff services, and he's—"

Magellan hammered, "He's a uniform, Hank, what else d'ya expect, except he'd cooperate? We gave him an order, and he's carrying it out. That's not news. But what do we do with him when he's out of uniform? When he's—"

Pickett barked, "Hold on!"

Roosevelt got to his feet and caught Garland's gaze. The message was that this wasn't going well, and it was time to douse the flash fire.

Garland waited.

"You're asking," Pickett continued to Magellan, "if we can trust him. Is that it? Can we trust Lucius S. Sensenbrenner? Can we trust a man who's put himself out there for thirty years? Can we trust a man who got his hands burned up bad today in combat in goddamned dusthole Kurdistan? In combat!"

Magellan wasn't backing off. "Yeah, can we trust him, Sonny? We're giving him the keys to the kingdom. Can we trust him when he takes the guns off?"

A welcome interruption was that the three missing cabinet secretaries trotted into the room with the rush of a transatlantic flight in their posture. The vigorous Rocky Kahn said, "Sorry," and Defense Secretary Archie Learned threw down his raincoat and folio case and said, "Mr. President, I was ready to get out and swim. There's got to be a better way than circling across the ocean."

"You might want to circle back," Pickett mocked, "since Jesus here is asking if we can trust Lucius S. with our nuts."

Little Ben Mica, the best bean counter in the cabinet, responded, "Whoa."

Roosevelt addressed Pickett. "Perhaps we should take down the volume, Senator."

"I didn't start it, he did," Pickett said.

Magellan replied, "I'm not asking anything you wouldn't if Sensenbrenner was my boy and not yours."

Garland knew he had waited long enough. "What do you want us to say, Jesus?"

"Make me feel good about it," Magellan said. "We're right up on top of the rampart, we're going over tomorrow. We're going to put this country through a rough week. I want to feel good about the mystery man. I know it's late. I'm going on my instinct."

Garland looked to Roosevelt to handle the matter.

"He took our order," Roosevelt said, "didn't he, Mr. Magellan?" Roosevelt asked Learned, "Isn't that correct, Mr. Secretary?"

Archie Learned nodded. "He's provided all the teamwork we've asked—always."

Roosevelt spoke to Magellan again. "You understand, he took our order on every detail. On FATHER'S DAY, for example. What else could we ask him to do? He saluted us and he put the operation together in less than a week."

"That's what you say," Magellan shot back.

Hank Lovell perked up. "Now you see, that's what I was saying, how do we know what General Sensenbrenner's done? We don't actually know anything about FATHER'S DAY."

Garland came to his full height. He'd heard sufficient. It was time to take command.

"We all have our assignments," Garland said. "You do your job, the other guy'll do his. Rocky, Archie, Ben: you deliver me the cabinet. Jesus, you deliver me the House. Sonny, you and

Billy hand over the Senate. And the general, he'll do what he's told. Does anyone doubt it? You're right, Jesus, he's a uniform. And he's wearing it still. He'll do what he's told. We told him FATHER'S DAY, he put together FATHER'S DAY. We told him he's going to be vice president designate, he said, 'Yes, sir.' "

Garland's temper was showing, along with that vacant look of his that scared his subordinates. He might be about to treat them as space debris.

"What's going to satisfy you?" Garland asked. "You want me to order FATHER'S DAY tonight, Jesus? Is that what you want?"

"No, no," Magellan relented.

"And you, Sonny, you're the one who pushed for FATHER'S DAY. You're so worried about our nuts, you want me to use the go code to show how big our nuts are?"

"Now, Shy," Pickett muttered, lowering his head and his tone, "you think it's a shit-kicking idea."

"I do!" Garland roared. "I do! Wax the turkey. Shit-kicking. Get this, Di"—Garland turned toward a make-believe Diana, since she'd been sent home long since—"I think it's a shit-kicking idea to show we've got the biggest nuts anytime we want. Biggest shit-kicking nuts in the universe."

Garland hinted at where his anger was about to take him when he switched to black humor: "But it would be wrong."

Nobody laughed.

Roosevelt came to the rescue of EXCOM. "We're all challenged, Mr. President. All of us. Just feeling our way through."

Garland ceased fire. To charge his team up again, he said, "Now let's review the good things in our bag of tricks, Hank. Tell us about Treasury and our Old Boney, and how we're going to sack that little money changer and drop him in the river."

"Well . . ." Lovell started about the imminent firing of Treasury Secretary Dean Bonaparte.

"And how we're going to declare war on the stuck-up Frogs," Garland said.

Garland suddenly saw the eight-ball shot he'd left on the table. An easy line into the corner pocket. Sonny Pickett saw it, too. Garland grimaced as Pickett took the shot. It sank like a stone. It sank like the world's markets were going to sink when they learned what kind of game Shy Garland was playing with the Twenty-fifth Amendment.

14 Tuesday Dawn, the Pentagon

Past 5:30 A.M., Jack directed the limousine to the River Entrance of the Pentagon.

The driver was Creole from the Indian Ocean island of Mauritius, and he apologized for driving fast and not knowing the right exit from the Arlington bridge. "Sorry, boss," he said.

"It's tricky for first timers," Jack said. Jack knew the big town much better than he liked to pretend. He'd escaped the capital's culture for boarding school when he was twelve, and yet he'd found, no matter how far he'd run off to sea, that his memory was loaded up with the T-squared grid of Monsieur L'Enfant's river bottom of a District.

Jack climbed out of the front seat and opened the back door for his angry father and his anxious daughter Lilly.

"Okey-dokey, Lil?" he asked Lilly apart from his father. "It's a fishing expedition, that's all. Like they used to do on Poppop.

You remember, when he was indicted? We're looking for facts like that. I'll explain soon, and I promise we're not going to fight."

"All right, Daddy," she said without punch.

Long John overheard and grumbled.

"Dad," Jack complained. "We're showing Lilly we can work this out."

"All right," Long John agreed.

Jack took his daughter's arm.

The reason Jack had brought Lilly along was to prove to the girls that their elders were not male monsters in a multigenerational chain of Longfellow abuse. This morning, the girls had come down to the kitchen with puffy and mournful faces. They were too well schooled in the modern family to be argued out of their assumptions about last night. Jack had glanced at his father, and Long John had glanced at his son, and then—pausing in their debate—they'd firmly surrendered.

Jack had immediately proposed that Lilly, because she didn't have school later like Louisa and Kelly, accompany him and Poppop to see that all was well.

For Jack, this wasn't entirely a gesture of peace. He was aware that the teenagers were forcing him to deal with his anger toward his father.

His father had gone too far, was Jack's opinion. Nothing, not infidelity, not even the White House, could justify caning.

For Long John, at the same time, Jack had gone too far for caning to matter. Not just keeping a mistress. Not just betraying Jean. Not just throwing away the nomination. But to accuse Sensenbrenner—to go along with a story so bald and stupid—

Or so went most of Long John's thinking now that he'd had a night's phone calls and sleep to consider Jack's behavior.

Then again there was the one credible part in one hundred about the tale of EXCOM that had brought Long John to the Pentagon at dawn.

Jack directed the limousine driver to wait, then turned to his father. "Okay, Dad, we're set," Jack said. He looked into the massive fake columns of the River Entrance. It was already busy inside with the arrival of the day watch. "Will everybody be on time?"

Long John answered, "My people do what I say."

Jack thought, *He's gone into his Stalinist mode. The Last Dictator.*

Long John was dressed for autocracy in one of his senatorial gray suits of armor, complete with gold tiepin and gold watch. Long John studied his timepiece, and precisely on time two merry matrons dressed in generous summer dresses came rushing past the guards and metal detectors and out the swinging doors to hail Long John.

"Mr. Secretary, ooohie," said Betty Valentine.

"And Jack—Governor!" cried Mrs. Patricia Sergeant Major Tucker Fredericks, or simply Patty.

Jack leaned to let Betty and Patty hug him.

Once upon a time the women had been Long John's executive secretaries, when they were under fifty-five and Long John was under sixty-five—back in the Cold War days when Long John held the high ground as SecDef of the Reagan administration.

Betty demanded of Jack, "This can't be Lilly?"

Betty was the wisecracker, Patty was the grind, yet neither was a woman to be taken lightly. Back when Long John had been indicted by the special prosecutor for tyrannizing Congress, Betty and Patty stonewalled the investigation so deep that Justice had abandoned hope.

Betty and Patty hugged Lilly in turn. "Why, you're your

mother all over again," Betty allowed. "Except taller," Patty noted.

Lilly, who hadn't seen the two women since she was in the fourth grade, returned, "I'm still the same inside."

"Aren't we all, sugar?" Betty joked.

Betty and Patty did not try any familiarity with Long John. It was the rules of the Pentagon. Once an almighty secretary of defense, you were always one, like being King Lear on the Potomac.

"Are we going in, Dad?" Jack asked.

"Soon," Long John said.

Jack knew not to protest the delay. His father had been up late telephoning Betty and Patty about today's expedition. And this morning he had been up early to telephone someone else.

When Long John's old crony Ezra Kahn arrived in a cab, Jack gave up trying to figure what his father had in mind next.

"Mr. Secretary," Ez Kahn said in a hasty greeting, tipping his straw hat to the women.

"Let's move it," Long John announced as he pushed through the swinging doors with his old vigor of attacking the morning.

Betty and Patty hung visitor's badges on Jack and Lilly. Long John and Ez Kahn had their IDs from all their OSD advisory groups.

Following Long John was like processing with a pope over the ruins of Rome.

And what ruins, Jack could see, for the building was in sorry shape from its heyday as master of the universe—closed-off bays, torn-up floors, plastic tarps, carpenter's toolboxes. Down Corridor 8 for the D Ring, Betty remarked to Jack, "Not much of a Pentagon anymore. The joke is Triangle."

It was a crack, but she was talking about the new DoD—how, under the phase-in of the Military Reorganization Act, the five sides of the Pentagon were being whittled away so that the military had only three-fifths left, and all of the remnant piled atop itself—the army, air force, navy, and marines so tight together they joked about a Pentagon assignment as bunking in rather than staffing up.

Jack managed the polite reply, "It's not the bad old days, is it," but then didn't finish his remark.

Maybe it was the bad old days. Maybe a decade of cutbacks had pushed the uniforms to desperate measures. But a coup? It was unthinkable. It wasn't in the American mind. It wasn't even in the American gut.

The truth was that even Jack couldn't think what he was thinking.

I don't want to be right, Jack thought, *except I am right. Garland, you crazy bastard.*

Betty and Patty led the charge to the elevator banks with almost no acknowledgment of their own age or of Long John's knees. The elephants had been trying to retire them for years. Direct from high school for the federal jobs that opened for Negroes in the panicky summer of 1950 (including combat), they had raised families and grandfamilies on their salaries, and were, like the building, monuments of labor. Also, they were most retrainable and stubbornly unpayoffable and, after all, they could move the package and feed the bears.

For their latest putative last outpost they'd been parceled out to the logistics office for the Office of the Secretary of Defense's Under Secretary for the Mapping Agency.

Betty and Patty were now travel agents here in the C Ring in outer SecDef country.

Their office was a cubbyhole inside a squirrel cage that smelled of photocopies and coffee.

There wasn't space for Jack's and Lilly's long legs, so father and daughter sat on book boxes and poked their feet toward the open doorway.

Long John sat on the cluttered credenza; Ez Kahn leaned to his side like the apprentice.

Despite the squeeze, Betty and Patty were ample hosts, serving their own brewed coffee and fresh-baked buttered rolls before shimmying into their desk chairs and firing up their monitors to wait on Long John.

Mr. Secretary Longfellow began, "What we're after is a damned lie." Long John swung his long legs like a pendulum beneath the credenza. "The worst damned lie I've heard since they said Andropov was pro-West."

No one reacted.

It was 0554 hours.

The day watch was far below on the second floor in Joint Staff country.

Betty and Patty focused on their old boss. These were the men and women who'd cracked the Commies like pecans.

Betty remarked, "Sounds like a green door."

"No one's asked us to find a green door since you left, Mr. Secretary," said Patty.

"His name is Schofield," Long John said. "G. M. Schofield."

Betty's and Patty's hands slapped the keys and the trackballs; the monitors flashed like wildfire.

Jack felt cold of a sudden. It truly wasn't a game anymore. His father despised him, okay, he could recover. But this search for Schofield wasn't something he wanted to deal with.

"Army guy?" Betty asked.

Jack responded, "That's Lieutenant Colonel G. M. Schofield. No serial number."

Patty found Schofield first. "Battalion commander. The One-fourteenth of the Tenth. Stationed south of Bendery. Occupied Moldova, Mr. Secretary."

Long John said, "Read it for me, Ez."

Ez Kahn, a little man in a seersucker suit, put on his reading glasses and leaned into Betty's monitor.

"Here," Betty said as she highlighted the data.

The Pentagon's hi-tech was about ten years out of date—mainframes and minis alongside networked pcs off of file servers, coaxial cables alongside fiber optics, very little cordless stuff, handsome but hodgepodge software—and it lacked the unified communications systems that were now standard for the S&P 500 and even available to Jack at Augusta; yet the Pentagon still worked reliably, and its database was godlike with every grain of sand in the Pearl Harbor file of military history.

"Fast-tracker," Ez Kahn interpreted the facts. "Out of the box from West Point, 'eighty-two. Top ten percent of his class. From Boston. Appointed by Tip O'Neill."

"Did I know him?" Long John asked.

Patty answered, "You attended the Point's 'eighty-two graduation. You would have given him his degree."

Long John nodded. This meant he'd shaken Cadet Schofield's hand.

Ez interpreted onward. "He's zigzagged his way up. Germany and everywhere in Artillery, then into Intelligence at Chuachuqua. He got out of Intelligence in 'ninety for a combat command and made it to the Gulf as a replacement. Company commander at Carson. He was here in 'ninety-four and 'ninety-five. Staff College at Norfolk. Industrial College here. Then Operations of the Twenty-fourth at Benning. Then CENTCOM staff. Then Tenth Mountain Operations before Jericho fell. He got his silver oak leaf and his battalion in 'oh-one. Like I said, a fast-tracker . . ."

"Jericho fell" was Pentagon slang for the reorganization, as in when the Garland-Magellan Act had sounded the trumpet and Jericho's walls had come tumbling down along with the force structure.

Jack had heard all about it for a decade. Long John and Ez Kahn had fought it from their advisory groups, and both had testified before Congress numerous times on what they called a disaster. Twelve active divisions to thirty-five brigades. Twelve carrier battle groups to four. Twenty-four active air wings to eight.

What "Jericho fell" really meant was that the guys at the sharp end of the stick believed they'd been handed the short end.

Ez Kahn finished the acronyms that characterized Schofield's career.

Patty asked, "You want hard copy on anything?"

Long John shook his head no. "What's he care about, Ez?"

"He's one of the righteous," said Ez Kahn. "Except . . . he married and divorced early. Married an army lieutenant who separated from the service in 'ninety-two. No children. No remarriage. The mark against him for higher command is he's a lone wolf. His benefits are signed over to his parents and to . . . his brother's family. Is this what you wanted?"

"Name of the beneficiary?" Long John asked.

"Mrs. Antonia Albanese-Schofield. You want more on her, don't you?" Ez Kahn tapped the trackball.

What Ez Kahn knew about was payroll and benefits. That had been his job for Long John: Under Secretary for Special Projects. Once upon a time, Ez knew where the bodies were, warm and cold.

"We can have access to her numbers," Ez Kahn qualified. "She's running a public company with an air force contract. Two air force contracts. Enigma. You want IRS?"

"Hey, Dad," Jack tried, "Toni's not the problem."

Long John frowned at Jack. "What else?" he asked Ez Kahn.

"She's disabled," answered Ez Kahn. "Hearing loss. Ninety percent in one ear. Seventy percent in the other. Looks like major debt on her company. Her husband died three years ago. Lymphoma. She's got family . . . you want her family? No military personnel."

Lilly was trying to be polite, tucked up against her father, but as Ez Kahn kept on about Toni Albanese's life, Lilly pulled at her father's hand.

"I'm sorry, Lil," Jack said. "You see, Schofield is Toni's brother-in-law and . . . I'm sorry."

"It's okay, Daddy," she said.

"It's not okay, not slightly," Long John declared.

Jack saw the cane move.

Lilly clutched her father's hand.

Jack squinted and braced.

When the blow didn't come, Jack stared back at the window in the monitor that showed Schofield's mug shot. That was Toni's Mac's face—without much hair and with a chin like a ledge. Maximum soldier. Hard guy.

Jack said, "Just leave Toni out of it."

Long John ordered, "What we need is Schofield's latest assignment. Something new. Very now."

Betty and Patty locked and loaded. Ez Kahn took the trackball. There weren't any secrets from them; they had played in every sandbox in the building; many of those sandboxes had been built for them; and what Betty and Patty didn't remember their way into, Ez Kahn did.

The truth of it was that these semiretired public servants were a few of the perhaps four thousand people still alive who had invented the myth of the omnipotent Pentagon.

"We have his outfit near Bendery since January. On the Left Bank. You know where that is?" Betty windowed up a map of Moldova and used the mouse to point and shoot in on a winding Dniester River until she got a dot called Bendery to flash.

"He's had casualties," Patty contributed from her side. "Lots of paper. A new trail. Tasked by the UN as of April. Indonesians, it says here, and Argentines as of the first of the month. Under UNPROFOR command, consulting the Moldovan Ministry of Defense."

"Newer than that," said Long John.

"You mean EXCOM, don't you?" asked Betty. "It's a green door, all right. Is that it?"

Ez Kahn touched Betty's keyboard. "Bypass it. Walk him backward."

Patty called over to Ez Kahn, "Here's something that kind of jumps out. Is that Fort Chaffee's signature, Betty? Yes? Your fast-tracker spent last Sunday at Fort Chaffee. For about three hours. Task Force Schofield, with two attached fixed-wing squadrons. Look at Schofield's routing in. See that, Betty? I show major assets in and out of Bendery. What is that symbol for, Betty?"

"Got it. It's a rapid response lift," Betty answered. "Mr. Secretary," Betty said, using the mouse to highlight a lengthy paragraph of acronyms and numbers on her screen, "we have an airlift here. Schofield's battalion, the One-fourteenth. Out of Bendery Friday night. Is that what you're after? Some boys and girls were lining up their ducks on this one. It's beautiful. C-17s out of Dover's 436th MAW. That task force got treated like a golden goose."

Patty asked, "You want more detail on the fixed-wing asset? They had Ospreys."

"No, not for now." Long John tapped his cane on his foot.

He's beginning to believe it, Jack thought. *He's halfway to buying this. Holy shit.*

"Ez," Long John started, "tell me where General Breckenridge was last weekend."

Betty remarked, "The purple suiter's purple suiter," and delivered the vice chairman's itinerary to Ez Kahn.

Ez Kahn toggled. "He started at Pendleton Saturday morning . . . Marine breakfast with a thousand noncoms. Andrews that afternoon. Fort Hood on Saturday evening. Fort Chaffee on Sunday morning. Back in the building Sunday evening."

Jack knew Breckenridge from Walvis Bay. Brick Breckenridge had decorated Jack after the tanker exfiltration. It was so
hard to imagine him part of this. The super marine. The black
gyrine. The peacekeeper.

Patty was ahead of everyone. "Breckenridge has the key to
EXCOM. Breckenridge owns EXCOM. The action officer is
Colonel Johnny Jones—Breckenridge's boy, director of the Joint
Staff. You got that, Betty?"

Betty worked her trackball. "What I've got is that there's no
way in that green door, Mr. Secretary."

Long John said, "Tell me where General Sensenbrenner was
Sunday morning."

Jack licked his lips and drank coffee. His father sounded
no less angry; however he also sounded tougher, more controlled.

Betty and Patty answered together, "Fort Chaffee. He came
in from Cairo for those two hours, then he was gone again. To
Turkey. Diyarbakir. Look at that."

"What?" Patty asked as she toggled. "Oh, my. He was
wounded yesterday. General Sensenbrenner was hurt. Last
night. Look, Ez, isn't that it?"

Ez Kahn hummed. "Burn case. No hospitalization."

Long John stood from his perch and asked, "Last questions
for now. Where was Archie Learned on Sunday? And where was
Ben Mica? Chaffee, too?"

Betty said, "I do wonder," and then punched fast enough to
shoot back, "Not Chaffee, Mr. Secretary."

Patty joined in. "Mr. Secretary, Learned was in London . . .
and he still is, according to this. The NATO conference of minis-
ters. And Mr. Mica was in town. It says here personal business. I
happen to know it means his daughter was getting married. It *is*
June."

Long John settled on the credenza like a bear.

Jack guessed at what Long John had found. "You think it has a limit? Not Learned and Mica? They cut the OSD out? Just the uniforms? Some sort of vest-pocket operation out of the White House? Call it EXCOM for executive committee—isn't that what JFK called the Cuban missile crisis group back in 'sixty-two?"

Long John didn't intend to answer.

Jack tried harder. "Maybe EXCOM's just Garland's little gang? You know, Sonny Pickett and Jesus Magellan and like that? Bypassing the National Security Council? Like you did with Teheran and Baghdad? You think Schofield's a cowboy backup shooter?"

Long John had heard enough. "I don't think anything of the sort," he said.

Jack was impatient. "Then ask about FATHER'S DAY. Why're you being so roundabout? If this is NSC stuff, if they used the chain of command, then there's an NSC finding in there, I understand the rules."

"You don't understand anything," Long John said.

Jack replied, "I got enough to know something's rotten. Ask about the operation and this go code. Ask."

Long John wouldn't respond.

Ez Kahn tried. "It's behind the green door, Jack, do you understand?"

"No," Jack declared.

Betty, trying to keep peace, said, "They mean that there's probably nothing there. The action officer keeps the music in his pocket. General Breckenridge owns the door, the key, the action officer, the music, everything."

"So who can get in?" Jack complained.

"Not us," Betty answered. Patty added, "We've gone as far in as we can, Jack."

Betty said, "Believe us, we're sure. Your father had them

build the green doors twenty years ago. And you know the kind
of things we put in them."

Jack thought, *It's Garland. Garland's behind the door. He just
won't say it. But he thinks it's Garland like I do.*

"Dad?" Jack started, then let it go.

"Jack . . ." Long John started, and then changed his mind
and addressed Betty and Patty: "Thanks."

"Thank you, sir," Betty said; and Patty would have saluted if
she'd moved at all.

To Ez Kahn, Long John said, "Let's get to it."

Ez Kahn said, "Am I looking for Rocky?"

"Your choice," Long John said.

Jack finally understood why his father had asked Ez Kahn
along this morning. Not just for his experience. But also because Rocky Kahn was number two at State, and now the de
facto boss.

If State was in EXCOM, Jack knew, then so was the DoD.

Ez Kahn tapped and toggled. He found his son's file, since
the Pentagon tracked its rival lords.

"He wasn't at Chaffee," said Ez Kahn. "He was in London all
weekend with Archie Learned. He arrived back last night at
Andrews."

"Conclusion?" Long John asked.

"When he called me Sunday afternoon, to tell me about Garland's call, to tell me that I should tell you . . . he said he was
at the office."

Long John nodded gravely.

"Does that mean they're all in EXCOM?" Jack asked.
"Learned and Mica and Rocky?"

Ez Kahn looked brokenhearted; he answered, "It means my
son lied to me about the Twenty-fifth Amendment."

"Sons lie," Long John said, standing up.

Jack stood, too, and knew not to reply. He held out his hand

for his daughter. He had to show her that her family could work
this out without anger and fear.

"It's time to call Jean, Dad," Jack said.

"Yes, it is," his father replied. "And that's the first correct
thing you've said this morning."

15 Tuesday, Occupied Cairo

Sensenbrenner was exhausted by the three-hour briefing at the
embassy, and he knew he should go straight back to the Shera-
ton for a nap.

But everything from the NATO team had sounded so gloomy,
so futile—another food riot at the Camel Market, another car-
bomb assassination on Tahrir Square, another monthly shortfall
of vaccines for the refugee camps, another five thousand arrests
in three weeks—that he needed to get away from his own
thoughts.

*I'm losing the city—we're losing the city—it's slipping back.
Every advance since the quakes, going.*

*And why? Defeatism. Fanaticism. The blind rage of the blind
ignorant. The terror of the terrified.*

January 6, 2001, a day so black it made doom look accurate.
Four hundred thousand dead in the earthquake and aftershocks,
most of the big mosques broken or destroyed, six million beg-
gared, a seam opened like a wound from Memphis to Heliopolis,
fifty years' labor crushed or burned, massive civic breakdown, a
vision of the end of the world at the birth of the century.

And now, thirty months later, nothing was working, nothing. Sooner bail out the Nile than fit the broken pieces of Cairo back together.

Sensenbrenner ordered his driver, "Take me down to Old Cairo, all right, Corporal? You know the best way?"

Sergeant Sandoval, the team leader of the bodyguards, leaned over from the front seat. "We got wheels-up coming at sixteen hundred hours, sir."

He meant that departure for Washington was at 4 P.M., in just four hours.

"I just want a drive," Sensenbrenner admitted. "No walk-about. It's too hot. Tell the boys."

Sandoval radioed the following security team van. They were going south on Suleiman Pasha Street into the oldest part of the city, where nothing wider than a cart could get through. The vehicles would be useless if they missed a turn, and they had to watch for the worst-case scenario. Car bombs were the weapon of choice in Cairo. And Sensenbrenner, with two brigades of American troops bivouacked at the airport, was the target of choice for every primitive in the Mediterranean.

Sensenbrenner didn't care about security procedures. He'd long ago accepted that he could wear armor but he couldn't dodge fate's bullet.

What Sensenbrenner did care about was Cairo. He liked the vast whirl of the city, regardless of the depravity of the heaped stone and dust. He especially liked the Old Cairo neighborhood where men and women had lived and died for a thousand years. Looming stone-built houses on narrow streets, dung-covered walkways, the pure sensation of feeling the dreams and deaths of centuries.

He started feeling better as the sedan slowed near the Roman fortress. He lowered the window and smelled what he thought of as the stink of conquest. How many generals like himself had floated through this precinct. How many conquerors had come to Cairo in just this way—tired, curious, despairing, fascinated.

Maybe there's time to do some drawing, he thought.

Maybe we could go over to the City of the Dead. I could finish those pieces . . .

Up ahead, there was a glimpse of a minaret that had reeled sideways and been left untouched for three years. It leaned at an incredible angle but had neither fallen nor broken. In the cruel sunshine, there was a daggerlike shadow across the thin street. A perfect image of Cairo. Timeless. Ironic.

"Stop the car here, please," Sensenbrenner asked.

He rolled down the window, pulled out a sketch pad from his portfolio, and chose a good piece of charcoal.

But no sooner had he made an estimate of the perspective than the SATCOM phone lit up.

Sensenbrenner's aide, Yudron, reached down to take the call. "Sir, yes, sir, he's right here, sir."

Yudron looked over and said, "It's General Breckenridge."

Sensenbrenner made a few more strokes and sighed. They wouldn't let him be. They pursued him with their worry. He couldn't ever . . .

He took the hand receiver. "Yes, Brick," Sensenbrenner began. "I'm here."

Breckenridge was at Camp Pendleton—at his office away from his office with his devoted corps.

"Sir, I'm sorry to call so soon again—"

"It's all right. We've just finished at the embassy. A nightmare of a briefing. You'll get the report by fax . . ." Sensenbrenner came back to the point. "What is it? Did Mr. Roosevelt call again?"

There was the usual delay for the scrambler and for the pulse to bounce from Old Cairo to the satellite and then back down to Virginia.

"Yes, sir," Breckenridge answered. "He's called twice this morning already. About your ETA at Andrews. I told him all was nominal, but—you know—he says he's just confirming . . ."

"What else did he want?"

"He said to tell you that he'd thought it over and wanted Emily—Mrs. Sensenbrenner—present at the press conference today, sir."

"All right." Sensenbrenner knew all this. Breckenridge was off balance.

What was bothering Breckenridge, Sensenbrenner knew, was that his number two didn't know what was going on, and yet he was now the errand boy for the White House and that priggish pest Quinn Roosevelt.

"Sir?" Breckenridge started, about to ask what was not his need-to-know.

"Forget it, Brick," Sensenbrenner advised. "Mr. Roosevelt is carrying out orders. You'll have the picture by this evening, your time."

"Yes, sir," Breckenridge allowed.

Sensenbrenner had given Breckenridge charge of the EX-COM package without ever telling him what was going on, or who he was working for, or what was going to happen.

Still, Sensenbrenner wasn't going to explain. No one else was going to have to take the responsibility for following the president's order. It was his own duty. The end.

Sensenbrenner changed the topic back to Africa. "I need a briefing on the Nairobi congress. Can you get a team on my aircraft at our stop at London? With the updates on the intercepts. Full dress."

"Yes, sir," Breckenridge said.

"I'll lay over at home tonight. I'll sit in on the warlords' briefing tomorrow, so tell Jones to make it as broad as possible. That means I want a decision on the Vandenberg mess. I want to get out of town again tomorrow morning. Catch the tail of the London conference. Then back here on Thursday to prepare for the Nairobi meeting. Understood?"

Breckenridge wanted to sound firm but he was clearly lost and without his bearings. "Understood, sir."

When Sensenbrenner got off the call, there was a strange scraping sound from underneath the car.

Sensenbrenner ignored the sounds at first. They started again, like metal, like wood, like fingers.

He glanced at the toppled minaret.

What's holding it up? What's holding Cairo up? What's holding it all up?

The scraping sound deepened. Annoyed, Sensenbrenner opened the door with a shove, and as it swung open, it hit something.

Lieutenant Yudron said, "Oh, Jesus—"

"What is it?" Sergeant Sandoval asked, leaning over to look.

It was a legless boy on a wheeled board. Covered with a rag, face pocked with sores, toothless, the child was a living horror but undeniably alive. He'd rolled right under the carriage. He didn't know what he wanted. He just wanted, and he pushed his hand up into the car. He touched Sensenbrenner's boot.

"My dear God," Sensenbrenner said. "My dear God, forgive me."

16 Tuesday Morning, Capitol Hill

Jean was having a bad day by 7:30 A.M. when Jack first called her private line at her Watergate digs and got the machine.

She was already at her office. The immediate task at hand was a televideo conference call with four strong-minded members of her leadership—Assistant Minority Leader Brownie McDonald of California from his hospital room at Walter Reed; and from their Senate offices Conference Chairman Rip Abbott of Arizona, Conference Secretary Merry Mars-Grassley of Kansas, and National Senatorial Committee Chair Cindy "Cat" Belleau of Louisiana. For fifty minutes they were discussing the story of the day, the week, the decade—yesterday's Oval Office powwow between Garland and Jay.

The Twenty-fifth Amendment was mentioned so often it made the senators sound like scholars.

The word "challenge" was used like a thunderbolt.

Yesterday morning, only Jean and a handful of her peers had heard the leak that the challenge was coming. Ellen Quick and Tim Seward had worked the phones all day to get nowhere past the early version that Garland was calling the cabinet about the challenge.

Last night only Jean, among her leadership, had been prepared to resist Garland; and Jean had made a very difficult phone call to Connie Jay to tell her that the capital was preparing a stake and tinder for her husband.

By this morning, with word of the impending challenge

spreading over the Hill like gossip, Jean's position was taking on wide Republican support.

Jean's agenda throughout all her calls, and again on the televideo, was as simple as muscle. If Garland was challenging Jay, then the Republicans in the Senate were going to fight Garland to the last ditch. Win or lose. Fight.

At 8 A.M., Jack gave up calling her machine at home and punched up her office. He got Ellen Quick and emphasized his message for Jean was urgent.

It wasn't until about eight-fifteen, as Jean got off the conference call, that she could have learned that her husband was in town.

"At his father's," was how Ellen Quick reported Jack's whereabouts.

The distracted Jean, assuming Jack was at Augusta, misheard this as "About his father."

"Did he say what?" Jean asked.

The muddle was the result of obvious confusion—since they were standing by the passageway in Jean's frantic office suite at the Hart Building.

Jean's staff was hopping and skipping, because their boss had a confab with the twenty-eight available of her thirty-one Republican senators at nine sharp. There was no old business. There was only the new business of fighting Garland.

Ellen Quick explained about Jack, "I asked him if I could help." Ellen was a lean young woman who could move her whole face into punctuation marks. "I told him it was a lousy morning and could he ring later."

Jean didn't get to reply, because she was startled by checking her digital desk clock. She was due at the Senate Conference Room in thirty minutes for her first showdown of the day with Brownie McDonald's surrogates.

She stuffed her little white cell phone in her best bag and

offered, "Okay, I'll call him on the run—it's probably something about this weekend, you know, Father's Day," and that was all she made of Jack for some time.

"Come on, Ell, I'm not making these callbacks." Jean looked at the list of sixteen Republican senators who wanted her attention. "I'm seeing them in thirty minutes, and they want me to hold their hands now. What am I? The caterer?"

Jean shed her comfy old walking shoes for her new dazzling heels.

Where's my necklace, she thought, *still on my neck? Did I get all my buttons?*

Jean wiggled her toes. "We've got to get in front of this thing, Ell," she said of the Jay-Garland rumors. "I had them under control last night. But now this Oval Office story. How did they think Garland would do it, issue the president a strong warning? This is a Constitutional crisis coming."

"It's not quite a real enough story yet to get control of," Ellen Quick said.

"It's real enough for our dear laid-up crafty care bear Brownie to sniff out the possibility of double-crossing me and backing Garland. You know what he tried out on me? 'If this be treason, well, gosh, let's make the most of it.' What a ham he is. Even for an ex–TV actor, he's a ham. Isn't that somebody like Nathan Hale?"

"Patrick Henry," corrected Ellen Quick of the double doctorates. "And he was talking about fighting King George, not anointing Shy Garland."

Quarter to nine, Jean was up and running stiffly for the door and the elevator, with the long-legged Ellen Quick in trail.

Jean knew if she took the Senate subway over, she'd have to talk to her distinguished friend in the majority—so she headed for the atrium and the outside.

Get a cab, Jean, get your head straight, check your buttons. Call Jack.

Jack did not get called, for Jean's job stole her mind again and again.

In the atrium, Jean ran into Nan Cannon and Sue Bueneventura—actually Nan and Sue were twenty yards away on the other side of the giant Calder piece—who had their own hot new versions of the leaks.

"I hear the cabinet's already voted, ten to two with one absentee," said Sue. "Did you hear that?"

Jean said, "I wouldn't bet on any count that didn't add up to fifteen."

"I wondered about that," Sue said.

"I've heard that our Secretary Pigeon," Nan Cannon said of the terminally ill Secretary of State Cal Mooney, whom she despised as so dovish he was a pigeon, "is getting out of chemotherapy to vote for the president. The man can't stop vomiting, and he's going for a man who can't stop crying."

"Tough talk, Nan," Jean said.

"It's a tough business, counting on the near dead to hold up the near nuts."

Jean said without conviction, "Why don't we wait till we get better information?"

To which Nan remarked, "You still afraid of Shy? I'm with you, Jeannie. I'm going with you on this one." Nan cracked, "Stand up to your man!"

"Lighten up, Nan," Sue remarked. "We're all with Jeannie."

"Thanks," Jean said.

"I told you we'd have to fight him eventually," said Nan, who was even tougher than she talked—a Republican rock down to her claws. "You didn't want to dig in. Well, Senator Not-a-Stonewall, you've just found your place to dig in. He's not going to get away with this one without paying top dollar. Fight him, Jeannie."

"Yes," Jean agreed.

What's wrong with me? she thought. *Last night I was ready to fight. Why do I think something's wrong here? Is it the president? Is he worth fighting for? Connie's not sure, is she? Am I sure? Can he stand up? I should call LJ. I should call Jack. Call Jack.*

Jack didn't get called, for no sooner had Jean slipped the scolding Cannon and consoling Bueneventura for the heat of another roasting day on the Hill than she ran into three more senators who were also searching for cabs—two Democrats and her own Nickie Skaggs of Wyoming.

They gave her the latest twists of the tale.

"I hear Jay broke down and cried like a babe in arms," said Wiley Frost of Vermont. He made a cradle out of his elbows. In his tan suit and ponytail, he looked like a chubby bride planning a family.

"We hear Treasury's getting the sack," said the darling of the natural gas boys, tiny little Senator K. O. Kaganovitch of Oklahoma City. "Not just Old Boney, the whole staff. Garland's cleaning house tonight!"

Nickie Skaggs, who was taller than a drink of Big Sky moonshine (he'd played the NBA), rocked Jean when he ducked over to her just out of the cab at the plaza entrance of the Capitol and said, "Miz Jean, I got the White House going on the record and denying everything."

"When?" Jean asked.

"High noon," Nickie said, "and you heard it here first. Shy is ridin' the high lonesome on us. Look out, Jeannie. I don't like the feel of a boy like Shy on the high lonesome, ya get me?"

"By 'high lonesome,' you mean you think he's going to win the challenge easily?"

"If he's the boy I know he is," Nickie confirmed, "bridle in his teeth, guns blazing. He's going to win or we're all going to lose."

"Thanks, Nickie," said Jean, who took the warning seriously. Garland was acting despotic. What did that mean beyond the challenge?

Jean had to sprint after that, using Ellen's long arms to screen her way through the press at the door.

It was still so early that none of the media stars had climbed down here to wait in the Crypt. The stringers were avoidable, since they tended to be idealistic young women who were way too hands-off of the ideological old women in the Senate.

Jean did wave hello to Tim's sweetheart, the dark-eyed Reuters stringer, Anna Hrbek.

Anna called over, "Please, Senator, can you help me?"

Jean responded with a silent smile.

The national media were behind on this one. Without a confirmation from the White House, the press had to sit on its pcs and wait for a miracle—or a denial from Quinn Roosevelt's attack teams.

Once Jean was into the cool air of the Capitol Building, it was hopeless for her to have a moment to think about Jack.

Jean's next two hours were devoted to hard bargaining in the Senate Conference Room—a chilly marble chamber with the glamour of a catacomb. Twenty-eight Republican senators from thirty states, joined by their whispering staffers like so many Iagos, devoted their energy to badgering their leader Jean to tell them what they should do next. Jean not only chaired the tussle, she also served as the chief talking point.

There were more than a few remarks loaded up with double entendre about Jean's past affair with the looming Shy Garland, such as "Boy's got a head on him, don't he, Jean?" and "Let's get down to the skinny, Jean, eh?" Jean endured the medieval blather because it was her job to guide these mostly shiny vanilla knights (Sue Bueneventura was café au lait) of the Grand Old Party to genuine consensus.

In the end, Jean knew that if she pressed her agenda to fight the challenge stubbornly—win or lose—to the point that the Democrats had to vote in lockstep for the two-thirds majority, then she would get her way with her membership.

First rule and last rule for a leader on the Hill was to play like an actor and act like a dictator.

In the end, too, Jean's twenty-eight gathered members didn't want to go their own way. They wanted homogeneity. They wanted to lose together. After twenty solid years in the ever-sinking minority, the party knew best how to say no to the White House.

Besides, Brownie McDonald, the jealous ham of an assistant minority leader who wanted to say maybe to Garland, was still at Walter Reed with his appendix scars healing.

About eleven, the conference ended with excited grumbling when word arrived from staffers that the White House was going on cable within the hour to make a statement.

Also, the eleven-up news flash on the Americana news service out of the PDAs and pcs propped on staffers' knees used the word "denial" in a teaser about the Twenty-fifth Amendment.

More darkly, there was also mention of a sell-off on Wall Street.

Members scattered in cliques to find monitors and clear reception for their electronics.

At the door Nickie Skaggs gave Jean a confidential smile.

Jean smiled back. *Good tip,* she thought. *Anything goes if they're denying,* she thought. *What next, Shy?*

Jean let herself be strolled down to the Small Rotunda by her pals Nan and Sue and Merry Mars-Grassley, who were happy to criticize her performance. Jean's temper might have flared if Nan had made one more crack about how Jean had to bark back louder at what she called the Dirty Old Man Syndrome. Sue and Merry interrupted enough to let Jean drift in her thoughts. She felt wrung like a swimsuit, and her shoulders ached from throwing them back, and it wasn't even noon.

"Anybody want a ride?" Nan asked. "I'm going to lunch early and enjoy today with a gin fizz."

"Sounds nutritious," Sue said.

"Can't. I'm presiding on special orders today," Merry said. She was a bountiful honey blond whom the old men liked to have around to tell stories to. "Call me later," she said to Jean, and skipped back toward the Senate chamber. " 'Bye."

Sue complained, "They pick on her too much," as Merry vanished.

"She likes it," said Nan, "and she also likes a certain reckless war hero from the Plains, is what I hear."

"No!" Sue teased, and Jean laughed at the long-playing romance called the Hill—an *As You Like It* she'd enjoyed in her day.

The three reached the private door that opened onto the corridor of the leadership offices at the back of the building.

Nan groaned, "The penguins are feeding."

She meant the media. What they'd run head-on into was the ruckus in the Rotunda, where the news folk were waiting on the gossip of congresspersons who were emerging from the opposite House and Senate corridors. The TV lights were flashing on the big portraits of Jefferson and King. The dome above crackled with echoes of the feedback at the setup. Behind the ropes and the guards the ever-polite tourists, who were paying for all this entertainment, stared from face to face trying to recognize the famous nose or eyebrow.

All this was rule-of-law as usual.

What caused an unusual upset was that at just that moment a small line of scrubbed high schoolers were frightened by the cable boys lighting up for live feeds; and the kids veered from the Rotunda toward the Small Rotunda, overrunning Jean and company.

Jean slumped back against the marble to let the kids by. In her loose blue New York suit, her tight shoes, her slippery makeup and damp hair, with her bladder full of coffee and her stomach empty of calories, she was not ready for what happened next.

First, Anna Hrbek slipped through the dazed teenagers and reached Jean to deliver her surprising information with one rush of air: "Senator, you've got to help me. We've got it from Abbie Fleischmann at the White House. He's saying that Acting President Garland threatened President Jay last night to resign in twenty-four hours or else. An ultimatum, is what he said."

Nan, Sue, and Jean opened their mouths with a silent "What?"

Second, Ellen Quick came out of the passageway door behind Jean and, spotting her boss, signaled Jean with a high wave above the skinny kids and bantam senators that something was alarming.

Third, before Jean could react, that very tall man in a navy windbreaker coming in behind Ellen turned out to be Jack.

Jean shot upright and turned full-face to her husband. She felt numb; she choked out, "What are you doing here?"

Jack reached her in a step and spoke over the senators and confusion, "I've been trying to call you all morning."

Jean's peripheral vision registered the wonder in Nan's and Sue's eyes at this unexplained entry of the governor of Maine.

Jean's primary vision saw all trouble, and she demanded, "Is it Long John? Has something happened—Jack!"

"No, not Dad, it's us, we've got to go. I've got to tell you something."

"What? Tell me."

Jack swallowed and said, "Dad's outside in a car. We've got to go. We need you. We've got to go see the president."

"What? Jay? Now? What?"

Jack wasn't paying attention to who was eavesdropping when

he said, "We've got to go see Jay," and he wasn't even sure where he was when he took ahold of his wife's arms and pulled her close.

He thought, *Get it done, Jack.*

He bent down and whispered into her right ear with a swelling hysteria: "You won't believe me, but a woman named Toni Albanese at Hancock Point, her brother-in-law's a battalion commander in the Tenth Mountain, and he called her on Sunday and said he's part of a plot against the president. I found out about it yesterday and came down last night. Dad and Ez Kahn checked it out at the Pentagon this morning, and Dad called the president for an appointment. Now. At Mount Vernon. The president's at Mount Vernon right now, I don't know why. And we need you. Dad needs you. The president will listen to you. We got an appointment because Joe Friar gave us one, but we've got to make them listen. Jeannie, I've done a rotten thing, and I know it, but this isn't about me. I don't know how else to say what I think. Jeannie, I think there's a plot out of Garland's people to eliminate the president if they can't get him with the Twenty-fifth like you told me, with the challenge. Cowboy backup shooters out of Europe, Jeannie, I swear to God they've gone nuts, they're all nuts. Garland and Sensenbrenner and Breckenridge, Jeannie. And we've only got Dad and Ez and Dad's old secretaries Betty and Patty. We need your help now. We've gone as far as we can without you."

Jack didn't really embrace her while he said all this, he just stood with his arms containing her, a six-five hulk surrounding a five-seven beauty.

Jean's mind took it all in quickly. However, her body betrayed her. She went as cold as stone. Jack was telling an unbelievable tale. Somewhere inside it was falsehood.

Toni Albanese? Who?

Jean said, "Jack. Okay, Jack. We can go. Where's LJ? Outside where?"

The role reversal was instant. Jack the aggressor became the dependent party with the halting step, and Jean, the defender, became the momentum and voice.

What else can I do? Jack thought. *I have to tell her the truth. I have to.*

"Ell," Jean said, and then as Ellen Quick opened the security door, Jean left the public behind and led Jack down to her little Capitol office.

Nan and Sue followed and came into the office right behind Jean to stand like sentries at the open door.

Jack crashed to the chair and hung his head. *No other way,* he thought.

"Ell, get me Timmy on the phone," Jean ordered, and then to Jack, "I know you didn't mean to, but you said all that with a Reuters reporter within earshot. Fortunately, she's Tim's girl."

Jack said, "Christ, I'm sorry, I didn't . . ," and then realized he was being stared at by Nan and Sue, and said "Christ," again.

Jean took the cordless with her son on the line. "Tim, I need you to call Anna and make her see you right away. She's outside in the Rotunda, I just left her. Jack's with me. Promise anything. She's heard something she wasn't meant to. I don't know how much she has, and don't let her quiz you. Get her and keep her with you until you hear from me. Tell her I need her help on this. Thanks."

Then to Ellen Quick, Jean said, "Did you hear what Jack said?"

"Enough," Ellen said.

"Then get Connie Jay for me, please, and tell her or her Adam that I'm going to be calling in the next hour or so and she has to have a telephone with her and be where she can talk freely. Say it's about the president."

Jean punched off and turned to Nan and Sue. "What do you want to do about what you heard?"

Nan said, "Heard what?"

Sue added, "Exactly."

"I'm sorry, Jeannie," Jack tried to Jean; then, turning to Nan and Sue, he said, "I didn't mean to mess you up on this, if I have. I didn't realize you could hear me."

Nan said, "A man has a right to see his wife when he wants. Come on, Sue. How about that gin fizz?"

Sue nodded. "Sure."

"Thanks," Jean said. "I'll be calling."

"Whenever you need us," said Nan. "If I believed everything I heard around here, I'd be an old woman."

Sue moved over to kiss Jean on the cheek.

Then they were gone. Jean told Jack to sit still and went into the wc to pee and organize herself.

Time to decide, Jean thought. *Time to go to Long John. Trust LJ. Shit! You total bastard, Jack Longfellow.*

With that, Jean came out of the wc, grabbed her white cell phone bag, and told Jack to follow her. She led down the back stairs to the Crypt and out the plaza door into the heat.

Long John and Ez Kahn were in a white town car across the park in front of the Library of Congress.

Halfway along the walkway, Jack started, "I'm sorry, Jeannie. I didn't mean it to happen like this—"

Jean interrupted, "Who's Toni Albanese?"

Jack thought, *Tell the truth, it's the only chance.*

"A woman I met last fall," Jack said. "She lives with her children on Hancock Point. She runs Enigma in Ellsworth, you know it? She's a widow."

"Since last fall?" Jean answered her own question: "You mean, since I became leader?"

"It was around then," Jack said.

"Do you love her?"

"I don't know. I'm so sorry."

Jean declared, "You're a fool."

"Jean, I'm really ashamed I did this to you. I never thought."

"We agree on that," the prosecutor in Jean said.

"Please forgive me."

Jack felt himself begging. *I am a fool,* he thought. *Shit, shit, shit.*

Jean stopped the giant by turning on him twenty yards short of the cab.

"I'll say this now, and we can get on to Dad. We're badly hurt, Jack Longfellow. You and me, as a married couple, we're hurt. You didn't do this to *me,* you did it to *us.* Don't make more of how I feel just now. And don't you think to ask me to forgive you again! That's not fair, and if we're finished, we must try to be fair to each other. For now, we're going to put what you've done to us away in a private place, and we're going to go on without dragging it out again and again. Later, when we're alone again, we have to deal with it, and I don't know what will happen. Usually, nothing good happens. Those are the odds against us. Do you understand me?"

"Yes," Jack said.

Jean pulled away from him and turned to catch her father-in-law's wave from the cab.

She thought, *Mount Vernon? Why's the president at Mount Vernon?*

17 Tuesday, Occupied Moldova

Schofield knew he was losing control of himself. He knew it, and he was trying to talk to Cello about it, Tuesday afternoon, at the battalion laager.

Yet it was coming out all confused. He sounded angry, when he actually felt scared.

"We've got the information we paid for, Mario," Schofield told Cello. "We've got to move on it. I think we do."

"Sir, it's late in the day, it's going to rain," said Major Cello. "Going into Bendery now, sir, it's too late."

"The information's good," Schofield said, flapping at the note that had been delivered from Bendery. "And it's good for now, not tomorrow."

"But, sir . . . we're locked down . . . we're—"

"I say what's locked down and what's not locked down!" Schofield barked. "And no one suspended perimeter defense. This is perimeter defense—if I say it is!"

They were standing at the edge of the operations field tent. All the scrupulous S-3 staff was watching the boss and his deputy argue. The battle staff was waiting to plan this way or that. Schofield was tough to plan for anyway, because he was intuitive about his decisions, and most of the battalion's orders were written about ten minutes before they were delivered.

"We lost Augenthaler," Schofield insisted. "They did it on purpose. We can't let it go."

"It's gone, sir," countered Cello.

They were talking about the sniper kill the day before, while Schofield was in bed with Christina. A sniper had made a throat shot on a specialist named Augenthaler. He had died in gasps for air. He drowned in his blood. Schofield had gotten there in time to hold a nineteen-year-old boy while he begged for air.

A throat shot at several hundred meters was evidence of a professional. With his pot and body armor, Augenthaler was a tough target. Only a throat shot could have done it. Only a professional could have made it. Augenthaler had been murdered by a monster. Schofield wanted to strike back.

"It's not anything we can control," Schofield continued. "We paid Ostapenko for this. What're they going to make of us if we don't move? This was the damned Black Sea Cossacks. They did it to see what we'd do!"

"Sir," Cello said, "they've done it before, they'll do it again. It was a test, because they don't know why we went away. They're taunting us."

"They did it for nothing!" Schofield shouted. "For nothing!"

Cello, a thoughtful man who liked his boss, didn't want to make it worse. He said, "What do you want us to do, sir?"

Schofield relaxed his grip on the box of the SATCOM—the satellite uplink he wasn't allowed to touch in lockdown.

Then again, the strange fact was that, in lockdown, Schofield was the absolute authority in this sector of the Left Bank.

The Argentine and Indonesian battalions were peashooters in comparison to the 1/14th. Eighty kilometers upstream, there was a NATO headquarters and a Canadian battalion at the capital, Chisinau, but they weren't coming running even if they were called.

And Schofield wasn't calling—not in lockdown.

No NATO, no United Nations, no EURCOM, nothing was

going to interfere with Schofield now. He was exempt from all orders but one, from EXCOM.

Schofield wasn't thinking about EXCOM just now. He was thinking about revenge.

"What I want," Schofield said, "is a strike team in thirty minutes. And Bradleys, I want a Bradley on point and a Bradley rear guard."

"Sir, we talked about this," Cello tried. "You take a Bradley into Bendery, you can't control the firefight. They'll see it as provocation."

"Thirty minutes," Schofield said. "And I'm taking the column. Strike team from Charlie Company. Lots of bullets, Mario, lots of bullets, damn it. They murdered that boy. He was eating ice cream. He was nineteen. Damn it! Lots of bullets."

Cello tried one last time to slow down the episode by suggesting Schofield ask for gunship backup from NATO. "You want me to call Chisinau for air? Get an Apache flight down here."

"No air," Schofield said. "We're making an arrest, not an assault, got it?"

Even Schofield knew that sounded hollow, and he ignored the exhales and raised eyebrows of the operations staff.

Schofield strolled up and down the muddy ruts on the battalion's Broadway while he waited for the scramble and his column to assemble. He was right, damn it. He was going to take the strike team into Bendery and make an arrest. And then he was going to cart the murderer to this side of the river—where he was the law—and shoot him like a poacher. Not like an enemy soldier, like a poacher.

Schofield watched the black clouds billowing up from the river. He could smell the weather changing.

Good. Dart into town in a soaking rain. It'll keep them indoors. Make an arrest. Shoot him like a mad dog.

Like a president!

Schofield turned away from his own thought that he was cracking up.

Toni. Where are you? What's happening? Tell the damned Longfellows! Help me.

18 Tuesday Afternoon, Mount Vernon

On the ride to Mount Vernon, Jean found that her mind and body were at war.

Her mind told her to listen to what was being said. Her body told her to rage in revenge.

Sitting in the backseat with Long John and Ez Kahn, her head cocked and her gaze on the back of Jack's shoulders, she found that her knees started shaking under her hem; and when she locked them together, she found that her hands were shaking; and when she buried them at her waist, she felt her heart pounding.

She wanted to scream at Jack: You did this to me. You son of a bitch. I'm supposed to forgive you? What have I been doing while you've been off screwing another widow? What am I to you? Don't I matter to you? Why did you make me marry you? I didn't want to! I didn't want any of you bastards. I knew I shouldn't have! It was better with Will being gone than with you being here!

Instead, Jean sat and listened to more treachery and rationalizing.

What jackasses men are! Every one of them! Who cares what happens to them! In the end they screw you anyway!

Long John's remarks didn't help her warring moods. "Jack's lied to all of us," he confided, "but not on this one . . ."

Or, "Jack's my son, and I'm ashamed of what he's done, but we have to help each other . . ."

Or, "The president's not much, but he's all we have. Like Jack, he's all we have, Jeannie, and . . ."

Jack, in the front seat with the Mauritian Creole driver, Parsifal, listened to his father run him down and said nothing in reply.

Jack's thoughts were broken defenses, such as, *Okay, so she's never going to believe me again.* Or, *Where does it say that I have to be married?* Or, *What a mess.*

Every now and then, Jack also thought, *Do I believe this is happening? A cowboy backup shooter?*

The journey to Mount Vernon was a quick half hour of talk. Long John told Jean the tale flat. He emphasized nothing; he doubted nothing. It was his opinion that you didn't tell the minority leader of the Senate how to think unless she asked for help.

Jean was his dear daughter-in-law, but she was also the most potent weapon they had right now. He needed Jean's help. The country needed Jean.

Long John thought, *It comes down to this—we're all in this together, but we make it or not because of old Ag Motherwell's darling little girl Jeannie of the chestnut eyes.*

Into the swelling Virginia splendor along the muddy Potomac, they came to the elegant and understated entrance of Mount Vernon.

Long John asked Jack to have the car stopped over by a roadside concession. Then he told Jack and the driver to get them all hot dogs, milk and soda, and chips.

Jack said he wasn't hungry, and Jean shook her head no as well.

Long John said, "Do what I say, Jack. We're all going to eat something before we go in. I know about this sort of meeting. Eat beforehand. You might not get to eat later."

Jack and Parsifal trotted off.

Ez Kahn got out of the car to take what would have been his pipe stroll if he still smoked his pipe.

The groves were swaying in a hot breeze, and the only unattractive noise to be heard was the occasional vehicle rounding the bend on the country road.

Long John tucked his double chins and spoke to Jean. "Jack's gone. You want to ask any questions?"

Jean said, "We're sure about what Jack says?"

"Because of the source?" Long John said. "Yes, I thought about that. She's had a security check because of contract work with the air force. We're as sure of her as we can be at this point."

"It's a hard case to make," Jean said. "On the word of someone we haven't questioned."

"We've made the case," Long John said.

Ez Kahn, who'd overheard, ducked back in from the open door and added, "We haven't tried my son. We think he's a member of EXCOM. We can ask him."

Jean asked, "Will your son be voting instead of Cal Mooney?"

Ez Kahn shrugged. "It's an assumption."

Long John said, "It shouldn't get to the cabinet vote. We don't want it to get to that vote."

Jean gathered her doubts all together. "LJ, it's going to go to the cabinet, you know that. It's after twelve o'clock, isn't it? If we turned on the radio, we could hear a report that the White House has denied the rumors of a challenge. You know what that means. Before Jack found me, a reporter I trust—Tim's girl, Anna Hrbek—told me that Abbie Fleischmann has gone on record this morning to say that Garland gave Jay an ultimatum last night in the Oval Office. Twenty-four hours."

Long John sighed. "Garland gave the president an ultimatum? In the White House?"

Ez Kahn made a sound of disbelief.

Jean answered, "That's what I'm told, and Garland's going all the way. Probably tonight, is my guess. And now we're going to go to Jay and say what? That there's a plot against your life? On the word of a woman we don't know and a Pentagon database search that was jury-rigged by . . . ?"

Long John grumbled and urged, "Go on."

"I have to say it," Jean said. "I have to remind you that I'm going in there with the word of two indicted if unconvicted Pentagon officials from a Republican administration, with the word of the loose cannon Republican governor of Maine who is already running for New Hampshire, and with the word of a strange woman we . . ."

Jean didn't finish. It was hers to decide. That was why Long John had brought her to the gates and halted. He'd stopped arguing back. This was her choice.

She asked, "What do I say when Jay asks why there should be such a plot? If they can get him with the Twenty-fifth, what's this for—this 'cowboy backup shooter,' as Jack calls it?"

Long John answered the question: "I think it's a gut check."

"What's that mean?"

"They came up with it to prove to themselves they have what it takes to steal the presidency."

"That's it?" Jean asked. "A little-boy-dare thing? Who can jump from the highest tree? Who can kill the president of the United States?"

"I know what it sounds like, Jean." Long John explained, "It's also what we did up against the Soviets. Only then we called it Launch on Warning. To prove that we were going all the way, that we believed in MAD, that we had what it took to shoot first. That's what Launch on Warning was—a first strike in sheep's clothing—and it was national policy for decades. If we couldn't get what we wanted, we were going to blow them out of existence."

"And yourselves, too."

Long John rolled his bushy eyebrows and poked his walking cane at his shoe top. "We won."

Jean sat silently when Jack returned with the box of food. She was thinking many paradoxes now. Men were rotten double-crossers. Men were what you had to stop the rot and the double-cross. Long John was telling her the truth as he saw it. Long John was part of the problem for more than fifty years. First Strike! Mutual Assured Destruction!

Why listen to them? Jean thought. *They came up with MAD. What woman would point a gun at her baby's head and say "I'll shoot if I don't win"?*

And what about FATHER'S DAY? Men like them come up with things like this. It's named for them!

Liars, cheats, fools, bullies, sons of bitches. Shy Garland is a lying son of a bitch. And Sonny Pickett, and Jesus Magellan, and Rocky Kahn, and Archie Learned—all lying sons of bitches!

Just like Jack, she thought. *My very own son of a bitch, Jack.*

Jean finished half her hot dog and drank some milk. She did feel better. She felt sharper at least.

Walk this to the edge, she thought. *Look into the pit.*

Jean told them, "I'm going in with you. You can tell the president what you know. I'll give you that much—you'll have your hearing."

Parsifal dropped them at the entrance and was told to wait in the parking lot.

At the gate, the rangers accepted Jean's credentials and said that she and her party were expected.

The rangers also said that President Jay had arrived by car this morning and asked to spend some time in the house. Tourists were being let in to stroll the grounds and take photographs. Only the house was closed off.

A few quick-witted sorts in the national media had found out where the president had gone and were congregating in the parking lot, because the rangers had made a decision to keep them off the grounds. Frustrated, none of the press personnel was keen enough to recognize Jean—the foxy frosted blond on the arm of the big fair man with the jawline—until it was too late and she was through the gate.

Mount Vernon is primarily a lush, breezy farm with a simple farmhouse and useful outbuildings built on a rise over a deer park down to the river's edge.

Jack took Jean's arm and led her up the gravel carriageway to the house. Now that he was here, Jack was feeling stronger. The food helped. The clean Virginia air and bright June sun helped. The confession he'd made helped the more. He'd done his part; he'd let his father and Jean make the president understand.

The truth was that the more Jack thought about Operation FATHER'S DAY, the more he was impressed by it. It was shocking, it was incredible, but it wasn't unimaginable—not for Shy Garland. Maybe not for the president, either. Jack had watched Jay and Garland campaign three years back. They'd won five hundred electoral votes, they'd carried forty-five states—and almost taken Maine. They were formidable competitors and overwhelming demagogues, both of them. Jack didn't like Teddy Jay—he thought of him as a whining Big Brother—and he despised Garland, who was Prince Charlatan, but to choose between them, he preferred Garland's deviousness to Jay's poor, poor pitiful me.

Shy Garland would be much more fun to beat next year.

Also, Shy Garland had made a bad mistake. He had put together a coup with a problem in it. He had probably made sure he had the votes for the challenge. But he had not made sure he had the shooters. Not all of them.

Jack thought, *Know your weapons, Shy. Leave the guns alone unless you aim to use them. Shoot to kill about one click after you aim.*

You lose, Shy, Jack thought.

The door of the house was open. Chief of Staff Joe Friar met them just inside the central hall. Friar looked first to Long John and Ez Kahn. "This isn't the best day so far," he said quietly.

Then Friar bowed to Jean. "I told them I'd try, Senator. I asked him if you could come in—and he said he doesn't want to talk to anyone."

"Where is he, Joe?" Jean asked.

Friar rolled his body back and let his eyes indicate that the president was somewhere at the back—off the piazza at the river side of the house. He added, "I did try. And I didn't promise."

Friar was talking in a half-whisper, as if this was a funeral parlor and not the middle of the plain house that birthed a nation.

"We only need a few minutes," Jean said.

"He's just not feeling sociable," Friar said. "You can understand that. It's been a bad night and the day's getting worse. You heard about Abbie—what Mr. Fleischmann's saying about last night's meeting?"

Jean replied about the White House counsel, "I was told there was an ultimatum."

"There was, but Fleischmann's also saying that the president folded up and walked away."

Jean asked, "Is that what happened?"

Friar said, "It was criminal. They were like criminals. Cutting up the spoils. If you understand me. We made those people. And Garland, we made Garland. We could've left him chasing starlets forever. I talked the president into offering him the two slot. Me. Party unity. What a joke that is! I walked over to his hotel and delivered the invitation. I did it. And to listen to Garland say, 'It's not your time'—I swear, it makes me sick. I know it says

in the Twenty-fifth that they can do that, but there wasn't anything legal about what I saw. Criminals."

Jean liked Joe Friar. At forty-five, he was a chunky, balding
workhorse who took his wife and kids to church—he was a faith-
ful Catholic like his boss the president—yet also took his family
for granted. He wasn't smart or careful about the usual precious
Hill feelings, true, but he was also a steadfast manager, like
Ellen Quick, and he had those qualities rare in public service,
nerve and loyalty.

Jean suggested, "I can get Connie on the line. If that's what it
takes. We need to talk with the president. And talk with you, too.
It's important enough that I'm going to say that it has to happen.
What will it take?"

"He's turned away every call," replied Friar, glancing from
Jean to Jack, from Long John to Ez Kahn, in order to emphasize
his point. "You wouldn't believe who he won't talk to . . . Everybody's heard something of what's happening, and . . . It's
why we got in the car this morning and drove around. We came
here to get away from the calls."

"Did Connie call?" Jean asked.

"No, she didn't," Friar answered quickly. He looked back to
the open door to the piazza again. "You'd get Connie?"

"She's waiting to hear from me," Jean said.

"I've been hoping he'd call her. She can calm him down the
way I can't. But . . ." Friar said, "She's the one call he might
take."

Jack watched his wife's face as she pulled her little white
cell phone out of the bag and punched the macro key for the
First Lady.

She's very good, he thought. *She's as bullheaded as any of us.
More. Elephant bull.*

"Connie, it's Jean." She swiveled away from Friar to stop on
the doorstep. Out there the gusts were crossing the tulip

poplars. In here the small house smelled of the hot river wind up from the orchards. Jean didn't talk very long, and she didn't explain much. When she turned back, she handed the cell phone to Friar. "She wants her husband."

Joe Friar vanished out the back door.

Jack beckoned the special agent with the metal detector and told him to sweep them now, they were going on to see the president.

Jean appreciated Jack's confidence in her bargaining. *Whatever else,* she thought, *Jack's a pro. Like me. Like all of us.*

Friar reappeared without the phone and bowed again to Jean. "Okay. He wants to talk now. Okay with you if he sees you on the lawn? There's like a little park. If he starts to walk, you go with him?"

"Joe . . . ?" Jean started, then swallowed her question.

"Just help him if you can," Friar said.

"It's why we came," Jean argued.

Long John addressed the central hall as much as the others as he said, " 'I walk on untrodden ground. There is scarcely any part of my conduct which may not hereafter be drawn into precedent.' "

Jean took Long John's arm. "Is that our Tom Paine?"

"The former owner here," Long John said, glancing into Washington's study on the way out.

The Longfellow party followed Joe Friar across the piazza and down the slope to the deer park. The view was stirring down through languorous tree boughs and coloring shrubs to the broad, deep flow of the Potomac.

Forty yards across the tailored lawn stood the rail-thin president, hands in his suit coat pockets, smiling shyly toward Jean.

The president had been sitting on a white wooden chair, with a wooden table beside him. He'd been writing in his diary. Jean recognized the plain black cloth binder. Connie had given it to him the night of the election. Jean had helped her order it special for him in New York.

The pen, Jean thought. *That's the one I gave him. With an inscription on the base: "For my best friend's best friend, Love, Jean."*

Jean felt her heart. The president looked desolate. There was a child's loneliness in his eyes. To go from the triumph of the election to this in twenty-five months? Who could accept that this was the same man who'd stolen Washington's heart with his inauguration pledge to "make the world safe for every child"? As a candidate, Teddy Jay had been so sensitive, so sweet, so lyrical—and as a president he had been so kind, so polite, so keen on children—and now, what was left?

Long John's right, Jean thought, *he's all doubt. He doesn't trust himself. He's not tough enough for this—and maybe he never was.*

First Connie left him, she thought, *and then he left the country, and now the country's left him . . .*

But, wait, she thought, *I can help him. We can help him.*

"Thank you for seeing us, Mr. President," Jean began.

"I'm sorry, I shouldn't have made it so difficult," the president replied.

His glorious baritone was well rested. Yet he was obviously off center. He was looking at Jean's excellent new shoes, at her first-class legs. He couldn't look her in the face. "Connie . . . she said you wouldn't be here unless you couldn't be anywhere else." Jay waved the cell phone in his left hand as if it were a person. "Connie said you were here to help me."

"She's right," Jean said.

"How is she?" he asked about his wife. He put the phone on the table. "She sounded . . . nice."

"We're all concerned for you," Jean said.

"I know. I'm sorry. I was looking forward to seeing Connie and you this weekend and . . ."

The president was not crying. He didn't want to cry anymore. He bobbed his head in pain.

"Everyone's looking forward," Jean said. "The kids, too. Little Ted especially. We thought we'd have a barbecue in our garden if the weather holds. The lupines are out."

The president almost cracked at the sound of his youngest son's name. "I know," he managed.

Joe Friar stood behind the president like a one-man backdrop.

Jack, Long John, and Ez Kahn stood in a line behind Jean, waiting to be called upon by their chief executive. After all the doubt, these were public servants, and Jay was the living office atop the republic they honored.

"I've brought Secretary Longfellow and Mr. Kahn to help me," Jean continued. "And my husband," she declared.

The president glanced up.

Jack had the feeling that Jay hadn't realized he was here. The white mansion, the well-appointed barns and stables, the abundant deer park, the vast lawn, the weeping willows and towering poplars, the brown river, the pregnant breeze—and the president was missing all human contact.

"Hi, Jack—Governor," the president said softly. "Mr. Secretary. Mr. Kahn."

"Mr. President," they each said with bows, no one going forward to shake hands.

He's gone, Jack thought. *This is iffy.*

"It's mine to begin," Long John said of a sudden. "What I have to tell you makes me wish I had a chair. No. It's better I don't. I sat down once at one of these—and couldn't get up."

Long John planted his walking cane like a battle flag and balanced on it, head up, weight well distributed, a fisherman on the job.

"Mr. President, within the last twenty-four hours, we have uncovered what we believe is a military plot to kill or capture you with a battalion of American infantry. Its designator is Operation FATHER'S DAY, and it's being run out of the Joint Staff. There's an outfit called EXCOM. My opinion is that EXCOM stands for Executive Committee. It very well goes across the river to the White House. EXCOM. And unless you know differently, I'm going to tell you what we know in full . . ."

Long John kept talking in an unwavering flow of clarity. Dates, times, dispositions, quotes. No one interrupted him. He was half a century of government and eighty-three years of oratory. He made his points as fixed as stone cuttings. Schofield. The 1/14th of the Tenth Mountain. Sensenbrenner. Breckenridge. Fort Chaffee. EXCOM. Mrs. Albanese-Schofield. Jack, Rocky Kahn and Ez Kahn, Betty and Patty. Jean.

He stressed again and again EXCOM, EXCOM, EXCOM.

Significantly Long John did not mention the acting president. He spoke to the facts only as he had investigated and marshaled them. EXCOM was the closest he could get to Garland, so he emphasized it as the driving force without defining it.

Long John couldn't have painted a darker picture if he'd used blood. And then, with the savvy of a boss who'd listened to hundreds of similar briefings in his day, he brought it to a blunt close.

"We asked Jean to help us see you today. We—Jack, Ez, and me. Jean brought us here. But what I've told you, we three believe it, and as far as I know, we three are the only ones who do."

Long John waited to see if Joe Friar's face was going to reveal anger or fear. Nothing. The president was all sunken-eyed pity, but Joe was blank.

Long John underlined, "Unless you believe us, we'll be the only three who do."

Jack liked his father for taking the fall so that Jean didn't. Jack spoke up. "I believe it, Mr. President."

Jack didn't like the absent gaze on Jay. Nor did he like Joe
Friar's reticence.

Jack told himself, *Get it done.*

"I believe," Jack said, "that EXCOM's being run out of the
White House." Jack proposed, "EXCOM is a White House
working group. This is my version. I believe that Garland's chair-
ing EXCOM. And who's on it? I'm guessing Garland's old cro-
nies Sonny Pickett and Jesus Magellan. And Garland's factotums
Rocky Kahn and Archie Learned, and maybe even Ben Mica.
And Sensenbrenner—he's certainly a member. Garland's made
him his private soldier, Lucius S. Sensenbrenner."

Friar winced at the names as if they were blows in the face,
and at Sensenbrenner's name he bit his tongue.

Jack continued, "If you look at EXCOM closely, you'll see it's
what's behind Garland's campaign to get rid of you. They've
cooked this up. I know I'm speaking out of turn, but there it is.
Plain talk, Mr. President. Dad didn't say it, Jean won't, so I will.
This is Garland's work. The challenge is Garland. EXCOM is
Garland. FATHER'S DAY is Garland."

Ez Kahn said, "That's what I think, too, Mr. President. I don't
like saying this, but I think my son's a member of EXCOM. I'd
also like to think he wouldn't have participated if Garland hadn't
ordered him."

Jean held her say and waited to be called on.

The president still hadn't reacted.

Joe Friar, a much shorter man, stepped closer and looked up
to Jay's profile. Friar's face was beginning to change now. The
jaw was slacker, the neck was pinker.

Long John saw fright in Friar's eyes.

"Mr. President?" Friar prodded.

"Thank you," the president said. "Thank you all. I know this
couldn't have been easy . . ."

The pause was followed by a provocative silence. Jean heard

the breeze as if it were a threshing machine that was going to level them. Jack watched the president's eyes and realized they weren't focused on anything in the foreground.

The thousand-yard stare, Jack thought.

Long John felt too old to go along with such poignancy. He figured that either the president was strong enough to fight for what was right or he wasn't going to be president.

Long John said, "If you're waiting for my recommendations, Mr. President, I'm ready, and if you're not, then stop me."

No one commented. The president did rock from one foot to the other.

Long John continued, "My recommendation is that you call General Breckenridge and ask him straight out if it's true. Then fire him and the director of the Joint Staff, Jones. Then you call General Sensenbrenner—who's overseas at last look—and order him to Camp David. That will give you about twelve hours to rest and wait for all the members of EXCOM to call you. I suggest you put them on hold and make them wait on hold. When Sensenbrenner gets in—about midnight tonight—sit him down, you and him, and order him to write out a confession and sign it. Then fire him. By then, there won't be any challenge coming your way. And by then Garland will have offered his resignation, too. So your job is to pick another vice president. You could do that for breakfast. My recommendation is Luke Rainey. He's Speaker, so he's already in line, and there's the precedent of Nixon and Ford."

Long John was almost enjoying himself—he *was* enjoying himself—and he halted a long count to see who was listening.

Jack and Jean were stunned. Ez Kahn had heard it all before, the Last Dictator running the world. Joe Friar watched very somberly. It was the president who was wrong. His body was turned aside. He was watching the river.

Long John thought, *He is or he isn't fit. It's the damn Twenty-*

fifth. You're either president or you're not. Dead or not. Damn Twenty-fifth.

"Any questions for me, Mr. President?"

Joe Friar showed his strength when he stepped in front to cover for his boss, to ask what his boss should have been asking.

"Why do we believe this?" Friar asked.

"Because I do," Long John said. "And one phone call to Breckenridge will seal it."

"Okay," Friar said, "and what authority do we have to make these calls? To order or fire anyone?"

"By God, Friar, there's only one man in the country who took the oath of the president, January 2001. And he's standing here."

"But—" Friar tried.

"Damn the buts!" Long John preached. "Damn the Constitution to save the Constitution! You are the boss. No other boss here. Don't 'but' me. Buts didn't get us here. Buts don't live here! You make the call, they pick up. You give the order, they salute and obey. You tell them to take out their hearts and hand them to you, they're doing it. I know these boys. They were mine. I trained them. Best damn bunch—the best—and Sensenbrenner is . . . To make Sensenbrenner into a thug. That they would do this to him. That he's got to go down for them. A man who's worked so hard to hold it together. A man you could've backed up when they were taking his force from him as if he were a shoe clerk . . ."

Long John reined in his zeal. "Sensenbrenner and Breckenridge will do what you tell them beyond your understanding of duty. They will march into fire. You have to tell them. Someone has told them to go one way. Now it's yours to tell them to go the other. They will obey you."

"All right," Friar said, still uncertain how far he should risk his charade. Friar's glimpse was going from the president to Jean to Long John to the president, the good butler studying his place.

Jean tried once more. "Mr. President, are you satisfied you've heard what you need to hear?"

The president came alert. "Yes. Thank you, Mr. Secretary. Governor. Mr. Kahn. Walk with me, Jean."

Jean looked to Jack for reassurance. Jack nodded to her.

Stupid—funny I still do that, Jean thought, as she stepped away with Jay.

They didn't go far, across the lawn in the direction of the stables and the tomb. The sky was like blue cereal with creamy cumulus clouds floating by. It was two o'clock and hot.

Jean took his arm. "I don't know if we've helped you."

"What does Connie say about me?" the president asked.

"She loves you," Jean answered honestly.

"What does she think of what I've done?"

"I don't know. I do know she's looking forward to you coming up."

"Yes." Jay swallowed. "I'm better, you know. I am. It's a difficult thing to explain. It's not the flu, but then again, it feels like it sometimes. As if you can't lift a hand. Or do anything for yourself. And your thoughts get all jumbled up. There's this distance you feel. I was fooling people about it a long time. Myself included. Not Connie, though. She saw it. Finally, I did, too. And that's when I did the right thing, Jean. I put myself into the hospital. It was the right thing to do."

"Yes it was," Jean said.

"I am better, Jean," the president insisted.

"I can see that you are."

"Yesterday, when I walked into the White House, I felt almost all the way back from whatever had ahold of me. I did feel better. Yesterday."

"Not today?" Jean asked.

"Perhaps not. In truth, maybe I've been hurrying this."

"You don't need to do it all by yourself," Jean said. "If you say so, I'll have about ten million voters here in an hour. That's the cable audience. And another one hundred million by tonight. We can show them you're ready to face whatever's coming."

Jean knew she had to risk more. "I believe what Secretary Longfellow said. I believe he's figured it out, and I believe he's got the way out. They're weak-willed, Mr. President . . . Shy Garland and his people are weak-willed. They wouldn't have put together such a scheme if they were strong. It's why we can stop it, because they don't believe in themselves. They're trying to prove themselves. That's what FATHER'S DAY is, some sort of self-infatuation. I see that now. I figured it out when I listened to my father-in-law. And I think they're weak to have obeyed such orders from Garland. I don't excuse them. Weakness will out. EXCOM is weakness. If they were strong like they pretend, they wouldn't have come up with this whole thing. If they were strong like they want to be, they never would have given such an order to General Sensenbrenner, and he never would have taken the order."

Jean tightened her grip on Jay's arm. "You've already proved the important things." She could feel the president's slim arm. Jack's was Poseidon's in comparison. "What you did, facing your illness by yourself in front of the world, that was more coura-geous than Shy Garland ever will be. I know Garland. He's a think-he-is. You're what he thinks he is. Seeing you like this, seeing you trying to do the right thing, I admire you more than ever before. I believe in you. We all do. And we're not going to let them have their way. We're going to fight. Right with you."

"Thanks." The president stood still and dropped his arms so that Jean parted from him.

"I want you to know why I'm not feeling better today, Jean," he continued.

Jean felt he was deliberately skipping all her remarks about EXCOM. As if he didn't want to think about it. As if betrayal were impossible for him.

"It's because it feels as if I'm doing all the work," the president explained. "And I'm not as strong as I was. I need time to get back my strength. And they're not giving me that time. You see, you can come back from an illness. But perhaps you can't come back from letting people down. And I did do that. I let them all down in January, and they won't forgive me for it."

"You don't think the whole country's like Shy Garland and his gang, do you?" Jean asked.

"No. But then again, aren't they? Don't they all want a strong leader? Don't you? Isn't it a crime not to be strong?"

Jean protested, "You don't believe that."

"Don't I?" he asked.

Jean waited, certain that he was coming out of the trap he'd let himself be put in by EXCOM. To be right about his illness? Or just to be strong regardless? It was a ruinous dilemma for a man as rational and patient as Teddy Jay. On the campaign, in office, in his whole life, he'd usually made decisions on the basis of what he called the right thing to do.

And now? Jean thought. *What's he think is right? To fight? Or to wait? To be right? Or to get tough and kick back like LJ wants?*

He's never ever going to be a son of a bitch, she thought. *Like Shy. Like Jack. Like LJ.*

Jean started to coax the president toward LJ's fighting side. "Mr. President, I think that—"

The president wouldn't hear her out.

"I think I should have some time to decide. Thanks, Jean. Senator. Thanks for all you've done. I just need some time to think now. This is one of those decisions I have to make alone.

And tell Connie I do love her. It's not because I need her. I love her. You do understand."

Jean wanted so much to understand that she could have blown up in frustration, but then she wasn't here to be satisfied, she was here to obey, too.

Jean departed Mount Vernon with her party and only a few clues as to Jay's mind.

None of the clues was encouraging.

Later, back in the limousine and heading back to the city, Jean had a chance to recount her conversation with the president. She came to a hard conclusion.

"He's alone up there, and he doesn't know what to do," she said.

"I'm reminding you that command is lonely," Long John said.

"Are we going to keep fighting on this?" Jean asked. "Or, you know, do we just give it up right now and say we make the best of a lousy situation?"

Long John's instant response was, "We're going to do what you say, Jean."

Jack turned back to look at his wife.

Jean thought, *They want to fight.*

She said, "Then I don't see any need to change our position. Do you, Jack? If the president won't resist the challenge, that's his decision. We gave him the weapon to fight with, this EX-COM, and he wouldn't use it. Maybe we can. Anyway, use it or not, we're still fighting. We were fighting yesterday when I heard the leak. We were fighting this morning when the White House got tough. And we're fighting now. Nothing's changed. For the party and for ourselves."

She touched Long John's sleeve. "For New Hampshire, I suppose, if we get there."

"Thank you," Long John said. He leaned back and thought about beaming. It didn't come. To fight the White

House. To fight for the White House. There was a battle up to his training.

Jack said, "I'm sorry, Jean, for making this even rougher than it should be."

"Tell me later," Jean countered, and then, because she wasn't the minority leader all the time, she looked out the window to Virginia. She kept her strong, wet chestnut eyes fixed outside the car to keep from having to consider her husband's strong, brown, and faithless eyes.

19 Tuesday, Occupied
Moldova

Schofield let Tom Owen and the little acrobatic lieutenant from Charlie Company, Bob Olsmith, handle the strike in Bendery.

It was textbook. You go in with maximum force. You put foxtrots on all the exits. You probe. You snatch.

The problem with the textbook was that they were up against urban guerrillas in a city that was split among several murderous gangs—half of whom wanted to link a Right Bank city to the Left Bank forces—and the worst of the gangs was the cutthroat Black Sea Cossacks, made up of the old Soviet Fourteenth Army.

The target tonight was a small stone house on a sloped brick-paved street. This was the crowded part of the town, but the target stood along the railroad tracks, where the tract houses were lined up like toy soldiers. The address was 13 Feodor

Close—two stories, about nineteen feet wide, with rubble on one side where a larger house had been torn down.

According to the informant, via Ostapenko, the shooter's name was Mircea. That's all they had except for the fact that Mircea was a member of a Right Bank gang called the Burundiki, or field rats.

So went the tip. Schofield didn't trust it, not really, but whom did he trust in Bendery? Christina? Maybe.

Schofield sat in his command vehicle about a half kilometer back from the target street. Beside him was his S-2, a lieutenant named Flynn, who was in charge of developing all the intelligence for the battalion. Though he was a sharp soldier, with good languages, he was usually overtaxed by his task to keep all the tribes, gangs, and partisan forces comprehensible.

Flynn asked, "You want to give the go, sir, or do you want me?" Flynn waved the horn. There was squawking from the strike team. "They're asking."

Schofield said, "Tell Olsmith it's his call."

That should do it, Schofield thought—*because Olsmith will ask Tom Owen, and Tom Owen knows everything about bash-and-snatch.*

Schofield stepped out of the vehicle into the rainfall. It felt frigid and cleansing. A hideously black sky, wind like a body blow, rain in sheets, as if the Dniester were curling up and dumping everything including the fish on the town. A man couldn't see twenty meters across the street. The whole population was battened down. Only bad boys and the U.S. Army would go out on such a night.

Only bad boys and good boys and boys like me, Schofield thought. *What kind of boy am I?*

Ky came up beside his colonel. "Sir, down at the bridge, Green Leader reports two sets of lights on the road from the Left Bank."

Schofield heard trouble. Why should there be anything moving across the river? He didn't want to overreact. He told Ky, "Nothing across the bridge until we bug out, tell Green Leader. It's our bridge until it isn't."

Schofield leaned into the vehicle and told Flynn, "Whistle up Olsmith and tell him to get it done. Go."

Within a minute, there was a flash and then a sharp popping sound from the target house. Another two minutes, and there was a call that they had several suspects in custody and needed a better translator.

Schofield was tempted to say, Drop them in a bag and we'll take the whole house back with us.

"Ky," Schofield started, "get me Green Leader."

Ky handed over the horn. Green Leader was Sergeant Childers, who would hold the bridgehead until the river dried up, and he had two Bradleys as assistants. "We've got the package, Childers," Schofield said. "Give me your picture about those headlights."

"No sweat, sir," Childers said. "Lights gone. I don't know what that was. We can't see zip down here, and then there was these two vehicles over there. Freaky."

Schofield hopped into the Hummer and told the driver to get him to the target house. He didn't like this. He had a bad feeling about lights on the road that disappeared. Without that bridgehead, he was cut off.

The house was dripping rainwater and filled with smoke. They'd detonated several stun grenades going in, and one had set fire to the upholstery in the parlor. Only now did they have a fire detail on it, pouring foam an inch thick on the broad plank floors.

There was the low wailing and cackling sobs of the women in the house.

Tom Owen had the suspects in the kitchen area out back.

Two males, heads down and hands bound behind their backs, the young one about twenty-five, the older one about forty, dark haired, shaven, good clothes, good shoes, no rings. Probably father and son. Both of them tattooed on the backs of their left hands. The death's-head tattoo of the Right Bank gangs.

There were also three females, left unbound: an old woman; a matronly sort with very short hair; and a young woman, fair, good looking, bad complexion.

Four small children under ten were penned up in the pantry, crying for their mamma, the short-haired woman—and their papa, probably the young man.

"What a choice, huh, sir?" Owen called out to Schofield. "We found 'em eating dinner. The old guy there, he went for the telephone. No way."

Flynn knelt down and spoke to the old woman. It was good F-2 style to go after the senior female for a hostile interrogation. He asked her politely for Mircea—who was Mircea? This one? That one?

Lieutenant Olsmith came banging down the staircase from the house search. He had an AK-47 in one hand and the carrying case of a telescopic sight in the other. He took out the scope and handed it to Schofield. "Look at that, sir, German made. How do you figure they got ahold of it?"

Owen looked at the scope. "Jeez, that's worth more than—"

Two specialists brought down a crate and dropped it on the foam. Popping it up, inside they found two Beretta 9mm, with U.S. Army serial numbers, and a stainless steel Ruger Mini-14 and boxes of rounds. Also a ball of what looked like C-4. Also a .22 pistol with a silencer—an assassin's weapon.

Then the hardest detail—the posters.

"What do you bet we can match these"—Olsmith poked at the Berettas—"with the numbers from Miner's and Brown's."

Lieutenants Miner and Brown had been robbed in Bendery

in April. At the time Schofield had figured it was a mugging. The men had been at a cathouse. Now—it looked like terrorism.

"Here you go, sir," Olsmith said, handing up one of the posters.

These were the Wanted posters printed up by one of the local gangs. They'd been finding them on trees and walls since April. The artwork was conscientiously crude—a line drawing of a GI in body armor with a swastika on his helmet. The GI's boot was crushing a gravestone with the Moldovan symbol—the white eagle. Written in Russian and Romanian was the promise of a hundred-dollar reward—written $100—for a GI, dead or alive.

It was signed "Justice Committee."

At the bottom of the poster pile was the infamous Wanted poster with Schofield's name on it. They'd spelled it "S-K-O-F-E-L-D." They'd drawn him with Dracula's teeth and a skull and crossbones on his helmet.

Olsmith said, "This Mircea guy is one of their hit men, sir. If he's Burundiki."

"He's Burundiki," said Flynn. "Look at this." Flynn picked out a rat skin from beneath the C-4. "That's their totem."

Schofield grunted at the fancy word "totem." He didn't disagree, though, and picked up the .22 automatic. Well oiled, good balance even with the silencer. He took up a Wanted poster, wrapped it around the pistol, and went back with Flynn into the kitchen.

"Which one is Mircea?" he asked Flynn.

Flynn said, "They're pretending they speak Ukrainian. They—"

"Tell her I want Mircea," Schofield ordered. "Tell her I don't want to hurt anyone else, but I want Mircea. Tell her now!"

Flynn started translating simultaneously in Russian.

"Tell them that rifle there belongs to Mircea. Tell them he killed one of my people with it . . ."

The short-haired matron was wailing deeper.

"Tell her he shot twice. The first shot made my boy raise his head up and expose his throat. The second shot tore out his larynx. Tell her . . ."

The children were screaming at the unmistakable threat in the booming alien voice.

"Tell her if she doesn't give him up, I'm taking both—"

Ky walked in beside his colonel, and he had the phone horn held high.

"Sir, it's Green Leader," said Ky. "He says those lights are back on the river road—"

Schofield didn't have time to react to this bad news, because the next moment there was a squawk on Olsmith's RTO's manpack, and Olsmith took a call from his lookouts.

"Unfriendlies, sir," Olsmith reported, two fingers in the air, "two police cars. Black Sea Cossacks patrol, at the tractor factory back there. You know?"

Schofield told everyone, "Radio silence, they might have scanners."

Olsmith flicked out the kitchen light.

Tom Owen looked at Schofield and spoke everyone's thought aloud: "They got a tip, maybe. This is a setup, maybe."

"Maybe," said Schofield.

Owen reversed his worry. "They're just cowboys, maybe. Don't know we're here, maybe."

With the radios down and lights out, there was nothing to do but wait. Schofield marched through the house and stood on the stoop, with the rain pouring down in a cascade. There was no use hiding. The street was dark as a river bottom.

Damn this town, damn this country, he thought.

The police cars turned the corner and slid by. One left turn, and they were dead men. The cars were diesels. They made knocking sounds as the rain popped on their hoods. They were within fifty meters of Schofield's position.

Damn this street, damn this whole f——

The Cossacks patrol kept going by.

Schofield should have relaxed his guard. At least he should have eased up on his dark thoughts. His reaction was in the opposite direction and murderous.

He charged back into the kitchen. "You tell me," he shouted at the woman. "Tell me!"

He pulled the .22 from his belt. He slipped in a clip. He flipped off the safety. He squeezed the trigger.

T-phut!

The man on the left fell forward, a bullet in his throat.

T-phut!

The second man collapsed sideways, a bullet in his throat.

The two men didn't die, they jerked for air, just like Augenthaler.

"Shit!" said Flynn, trying to give first aid.

The women were berserk, jumping on Flynn's back, screaming and crying out.

Schofield raised the .22 again, at the face of the old woman.

"Damn you to hell, tell me who's Mircea!"

"Sir!" screamed Tom Owen. "Sir!"

"Tell me!" Schofield insisted.

2 0 Tuesday Evening, the White House

Shy Garland leaned forward and pushed the damask ottoman closer to his father's boots.

"It's friendly to use the furniture, Daddy, we're stayin' awhile."

"Don't like other people's hand-me-downs and leavings," Lynch Garland complained. "Recall me to hard times."

Garland laughed at his father's joke. The national antiquities as leavings. How the father pleased the son. How the son liked to appreciate his father's dry wit, such as his lifelong recommendation: "Politics and business don't mix, but pure politics is big business."

At eighty, the elder Garland was no politician and glad for it—a desert-burned, long-nosed rancher in a cowboy's Sunday suit of clothes complete with shiny brown boots, a string tie, a ten-gallon sombrero, and a hatband of rattlesnake skin. Of course he was not what he appeared. Texans favored misdirection about their true source of wealth. Lynch Garland was a bond vigilante—also known as a banker—and the nearest he'd ever come to hard times were the bankrupts he played cards with at Houston's River Oaks Club.

Iphy glided over in a cloud of perfume. She gently knelt before her father-in-law and eased his iron-hard legs up on the doily of the ottoman. "We'll get new-made furniture for the family quarters here, I promise, honey," she said. "Just as soon as we move in permanently."

The Garlands were in the overdecorated Yellow Oval Room upstairs at the White House.

It was about a quarter to seven on a hot, fragrant evening on the Potomac.

The acting president was due downstairs in the East Room for his press conference presently.

Rather than sit around in his TV makeup and discuss the obvious with Quinn Roosevelt, Garland had taken the time to visit with his father, who'd flown up from Houston that afternoon. Lynch Garland was all the family Shy Garland needed to please. If the patriarch approved, then the rest of the numerous Garlands—Garland had two younger brothers, eight uncles and aunts, and sixteen first cousins—would follow like longhorn steers trailing on to water at the cottonwoods.

Garland's three sons had already gone downstairs to get good seats. However, Lynch Garland wasn't to be moved. He wanted to watch the excitement on television from up here—with yellow damask sofas, Chinese porcelain, a ballroom chandelier, and three windows on the Washington Monument.

Shy Garland spoke to the steward who'd just come in with the tea service. "Is that cream heated up?" The steward nodded yes. Garland inspected his father's comforts once more. "You all set, Daddy? TV's on, tea's on, scones and tarts and whatnot are coming up hot buttered, and Iphy and the boys will be right along after, for supper."

"When're you comin' after?" Lynch Garland asked.

Garland tried his own dry wit. "I expect there'll be a considerable few phone calls I'll have to take, don't you?"

Lynch Garland laughed in appreciation. "Yes, sir, considerable few. Well, tell 'em to buy bonds on the way down. With you in, the government's gonna be good for its debts again."

"Thank you, Daddy," Garland said. The supreme compliment in the Garland family was that a man was good for his debts. Garland leaned down to touch the rattlesnake hatband for luck. It was a family heirloom from the wildcatting days and would be the eldest son's in time. "I love you, Daddy," Garland added.

Lynch Garland gave a speculative grunt. He'd never felt relaxed with his son's ability to be direct.

Iphy kissed Lynch Garland on the edge of his lips and said, "Turn the sound on sometime, Daddy."

"Faithie didn't like the sound neither," he said, meaning his wife and Garland's mother, Faith Folsom Garland, who had passed away while watching TV five years before. "Sound's for the changeable sort."

Garland laughed again. He could hear the lesson from his childhood: "If you don't want to change, don't listen."

Husband and wife departed the Yellow Oval Room for the long corridor. Garland felt as uplifted as a live oak in a hurricane. Iphy took her man close by the arm as they sashayed down past the Oriental screens.

"Mr. President?" a young aide called instantly.

Iphy pulled Garland behind the big blue screen. "Want to go for the well-screwed look tonight?" she whispered. They were both crisply dressed in black and white, for the solemnity of the occasion, and the only festive color on them was her bright lipstick, which complemented her even brighter red hair. "How about just the randy-for-it look?" she tried and yanked him tight by the belt.

"To choose so dear," Garland teased back. "Shoot for the satellites or shoot for you?"

"Hoooh," she growled. She kissed him at the edges of his mouth and left a speck of lipstick on his chin, like a marker to warn off the very ambitious groupies out there tonight.

"Mr. President? I'm sorry to disturb, sir, but Mr. Roosevelt—"

Garland replied, "Yes?" while leaning out from behind the screen with Iphy holding him by the privates.

"Mr. Roosevelt says he needs you in your office, sir. On the phone, sir, it's the president telephoning."

Garland thought, *Jackpot.*

He led Iphy quickly by the hand down the corridor to his cowpoke-bare office.

Quinn Roosevelt was standing in front of the window with the receiver in one hand. "Yes, yes—all right, Joe," Roosevelt said into the phone, "he's coming now, just a moment."

Roosevelt punched Hold. "They're still at Mount Vernon. Incredible. All day they've been there."

Garland liked the delight on Roosevelt's usually unanimated face.

"It's the history of it for him," Garland explained. "He campaigns the same way, remember? Always the set-piece historical landmark to help him think."

"I don't know what he's thinking now," Roosevelt said. "Friar is tight-lipped. And real dreary."

Garland took hold of Iphy's hand and punched the speakerphone. "Yes, Joe, I'm here now."

"Mr. Acting President," Friar said. "The president has just now asked me to answer your request from last evening . . ."

Garland didn't like Friar's tone.

"The president's opinion . . ."

Garland thought, *Lose the attitude.*

". . . is that we should look to the Constitution."

"Hey," Garland snapped, "I've got seven minutes. You folding or what?"

Joe Friar replied, "No, definitely not. Nothing like that. The president asked me to urge you to follow the Constitution."

"Explain that," Garland ordered.

"I'm not sure I can," Friar said. "I guess he means we're going to see what happens with the Twenty-fifth Amendment followed to the letter."

Garland thought, *Throw a strike.*

"Put him on or I go with what I've got," Garland said. "And what I've got right now is that the president is about as straight as a snake crawls."

Garland had intended to walk up to the camera and announce his challenge and his choice of General Sensenbrenner as his vice president. Any deal from Jay was a bonus. But what kind of offer was this?

Friar was off the line for a moment, probably to consult with the president.

Garland waited while watching the digital display clock on the TV monitor. The cable networks, still waiting for the beginning of the press conference, were replaying the noon White House announcement that had denied there was a challenge in the offing. Roosevelt had sent Jay's press secretary out to tell the Big Lie. The young woman had an impenetrable facade—Delilah Little Crow was her name, one of Jay's native American troupe from his Lansing regime—and she did what she was told.

Iphy puckered her lips to Garland.

Quinn Roosevelt held up five digits. Five minutes to get downstairs to the East Room. Roosevelt pretended to be pulling something down with his hand—as in, Flush this guy.

Garland thought, *This is fun.*

There was a click, and Joe Friar was back on the line: "The president is unavailable."

"Are you bluffing?" Garland asked. "I can't tell. I can't say I care, either. I've got responsibilities here. Are we on the same page of the Constitution? Read the part about 'ensure domestic tranquillity.' You want to see my phone log? You want to glance at what the markets did today? And that was after I had to deny it all at noon. Is anybody there with you paying attention? What the blazes do you mean he's unavailable?"

Friar responded slowly. "I mean he's asleep, I think, sir.

Asleep in the chair. I was talking with him, and I came over here to make the call, and when I went back . . . Do you think I should wake him?"

Garland asked, "He's really asleep in a chair? That's about right. In fact, it's perfect. I like it." Garland spoke out for Diana the scribe, who was standing behind Iphy. "At the last moment of his presidency, the president was asleep and couldn't come to his own call to the White House."

Roosevelt waved three fingers, but Garland was enjoying himself. "Tell me what he wanted to say, Joe."

"I have, sir," Friar responded. "When I left him to come call you, he was reading. I swear, I didn't know he'd gone to sleep. He's out of my sight from here. It's not a cordless phone."

Garland thought, *Friar's stunned. Fan the guy.*

"All right," Garland said. "We've got to get on with it. You've done your job."

Garland started to punch off, then pulled back to ask, "Joe?"

"Yes, sir?"

"You really still at Mount Vernon?"

"Yes. In Washington's study. We've been here all day. Maybe we should have eaten supper. I've got to do something about him falling asleep. I don't like it. He looks all right."

Roosevelt showed two fingers. Iphy tugged.

Garland's last question: "What was he reading?"

"You know, his Bible, sir," answered Friar.

Momentarily, Garland and Iphy were down the grand staircase and then parading on their marks down the center of the red-and-gold carpet to the waiting lectern in the East Room.

From the distance, the TV cameras picked up the grace of their walk. The audience spotted their self-assurance. In a world of foxes who know many little things and hedgehogs who know one great thing, here came Mr. and Mrs. One-Absolute-Certainty: we're the stars.

There was a clattering hush as the press corps and the guests rose to their feet.

Then a voice called out, "Ladies and gentlemen, the acting president of the United States."

Forty still cameras salvoed with mechanical click-clacks. The TV lights twinkled like the firmament. No one talked.

And then Shy and Iphy were there together, square shoulder to square shoulder, at stage center to the satellite uplink.

"Thank you for coming out on short notice . . ." Garland began.

The TelePrompTer displayed the script. Garland shook it off and decided to try a breaking pitch. The big right-hander went into his windup.

"Within the last hour I've communicated with the president . . ."

No smile, no hurry, he thought. *Let them return to their seats. Avoid the camera's eye. Paint the corner with a fade-away.*

". . . It was a frank and helpful exchange. We talked about our responsibilities. We talked about the jobs the American people want from us. I want to speak to the American people tonight about our responsibilities. About our jobs. The president and I, our work is a privilege to us. Our work is to obey the Constitution with all the power God gives us . . ."

Garland glanced to the row of seats to the left, where he'd ordered the cabinet assembled like a Greek chorus. Two of the fifteen were not present. Secretary of State Cal Mooney was permanently invalid. Secretary of the Treasury Dean Bonaparte was missing, because Garland had ordered him to stay away, because Garland was going to fire him tonight after an appropriate amount of time twisting in the wind.

"Our work, too," Garland continued, "is to follow your instructions with good, sound, dependable government. Not wait for tomorrow. Not return to yesterday. Not hope for the best. Good, sound, dependable government . . ."

Garland glanced to stage right, where General Sensenbrenner was supposed to be seated with his wife.

Sensenbrenner was exactly in place, ramrod, awesome, attentive.

Throw the heater.

Garland started, "Unfortunately . . ."

It was 7:02 P.M. in Washington, D.C.

The North and South American markets were closed after a brutish day of sell-off in the morning on the rumor of the challenge, then buyback at midday on the fact of the White House denial, then sell-off again at the close. The markets were opening in Asia within the hour. Every set of eyes on the floors of the markets in Tokyo, Hong Kong, Beijing, Seoul, Bangkok, Djakarta, and Sydney was trained on Garland's brow.

The acting president was cool. The traders knew what it meant when an American cowboy was cool. Sundown.

When Garland said, "Unfortunately . . ." the first wave of sell orders hit the futures like a tsunami, and the bond boys went fishing for bids at the bottom of the sea. At the currency desks the dollar was in flames and ballistic. In the commodity pits gold was a big yellow bird lifting off.

On the Harkness stage in the East Room of the White House, General Sensenbrenner watched the acting president speak into the camera's eye.

Pray God, Sensenbrenner thought, *pray God all the little tyrants out there don't look into the president's eyes and ask their witch doctors if this is the night for their little shot at paradise. Two commanders in chief. We've got two. The tyrants and warlords and potentates out there can smell uncertainty like blood. Two C in Cs. You can't get a Go/No Go with two C in Cs . . .*

Sensenbrenner wanted to scratch the loose bandage on his left hand.

The medic on the flight back had said it would take another week. He was going to lose some skin on both hands, but the worst of it was on his left hand. The red skin on his right palm stung to touch. He wanted to scratch between his fingers. He clenched his teeth.

Garland kept talking, and the still cameras kept clicking, but Sensenbrenner wasn't paying close attention. His mind was still out there where the orders had gone out within the hour. The acting president had signed on with the JCS recommendation to advance the readiness—up a notch. At sea, the two carrier battle groups were at general quarters. In southern Europe and southern Asia, the fighter wings were prepped. The two dozen ready brigades were fully staffed. Military bases and distant laagers were as restless as a billy goat.

Sensenbrenner knew trouble was coming. He didn't know when, but he did know how and where.

Like a nightmare.

At the weakest point.

Sensenbrenner also knew training was the way to stop trouble. Training was the way to stop a nightmare at your weakest point. Train, train, train. Train like you think. Train like you fight. Train, train, train, that was Sensenbrenner's faith, that was his standing order.

Sensenbrenner's story was fifty-six years of training. Dyslexic, he'd trained himself to read and write fastidiously, and even to write verse. Out of a broken home on Danville's Tobacco Road, he'd trained his mind to win an R. J. Reynolds contest for an appointment to West Point, where he'd taught himself to read German, Latin, Greek, and Hebrew—the warrior tongues. Commissioned in 1969, he'd trained himself to serve and to obey regardless of the trouble. The catastrophe in Vietnam, the phony peace of détente, the burden of hodgepodge postings all over the globe—artillery, armor, airmobile; battalion, division, corps, army—Korea, Germany, Texas, Colorado. Through all this trouble he'd obeyed and served and trained—even trained himself to do line sketches of the ruins of vanished empires he'd visited, from Babylon to the Yucatán, from Luxor to Angkor Wat.

The training was religion for him. Even now, even after the last decade of haphazard drawdowns in force structure, Sensenbrenner continued to train himself and his command to stand up to whatever was coming their way. No questions. No complaints. No retreat. Fight the ship with your bare hands, fight to the finish. He'd given a large part of his last decade to drafting the blueprint for the Garland-Magellan Act. He'd distinguished himself from his three-star peers by cooperating with the congressional hacking and slashing in order to save what he could. In reward they'd given him the top job he'd trained for throughout his career. His response was to keep training.

He didn't have half enough out there. He knew that. Four carriers was a shadow. The fighter wings and bomber squadrons were a trace. Thirty-five active and reserve combat brigades was a last ditch. But what remnant he had was the best-trained armed force in Western history. Without elite troops anymore, without adequate air- or sea lift, without even two full marine brigades, what was out there was six hundred thousand fundamental soldiers—all interchangeable parts of a smart, tenacious, tireless war machine that could and would pound any enemy to jelly on instantaneous command.

Crucially, Sensenbrenner had trained most of the officer corps for the last ten years—the last four at JCS. Everyone with brass owed his or her career to Sensenbrenner's faith in training.

The proof of his faith was what his fleet and wings and brigades had done at Cairo and Walvis Bay—textbook chapters of what training could do right.

He'd trained them all, he'd led them all, and now, after four years as chairman, it was part of the training to pass them on to someone new. Perhaps Brick Breckenridge. Perhaps not. That was up to the commander in chief . . .

As soon as we have our C in C sorted out, Sensenbrenner thought. *Two C in Cs. Trouble coming. My hands sting. Listen to the president. Where's Emmie?*

Sensenbrenner found his wife Emily's eyes. She wasn't on the stage with him, for they'd set her off to the side, with the White House staff. He wished he could've provided her a more formal escort and entrance to the White House—he'd been able to telephone her only on the ride in from Andrews—but then, this was supposed to be a discreet affair. She did look very well turned out tonight for an army wife who shopped at Fort Myer. None of the glamour of the press women, none of the aura of the staff women, but a clear sense of command about her, the CO's wife, a slender blond girl from Atlanta who, after four children and two hundred thousand miles of household moves, had matured into a resolute, kind, pretty brown-haired grandmother, the old man's wife, the general's lady.

Emmie didn't know whether or not to smile back at her husband, so she at first blinked quickly and nodded.

She thought, *He looks so tired. When will they let him rest? Maybe this will change things. Maybe he can stay home more than one night in ten.*

Emily Sensenbrenner gathered her best smile. She looked at her husband with the best love in her soul. Was it enough? What else could she do for a man who was about to be nominated for the vice presidency?

Sensenbrenner saw Emmie's look and let his eyes thank her. *She's the best,* he thought.

The truth was that neither of them thought much of the plan tonight. But then the two of them were so army after thirty-four years of marriage to each other and to the army that an order was an order, a posting was a posting. The president gave the order, they obeyed. The vice president's house at the Naval Observatory was the posting. They prepared to move again. To serve and to obey.

Then what? It was a fair question that Emmie had asked Sensenbrenner on the telephone two weeks before, when he'd first told her of the president's decision.

Emmie had asked, "What happens to us afterward? Are we going to become politicians?"

All he'd thought to answer was that he was just going to fade away like all the other vice presidents. Eighteen months more, and they could go to Italy again, and he could sketch the fall of the Roman Empire at leisure.

Or so went EXCOM's plan.

Garland got Sensenbrenner's attention back by changing the cadence in his voice. He changed from the gravity of the announcement of the challenge to an upbeat, confident drumroll in preparation for announcing Sensenbrenner's name.

"I want to have your questions," Garland was saying to the press corps. "We're moving into trackless territory here and learning together, and it's right that we talk about it like a family. But before I open this up to your questions, I want to show off my first decision as we move toward resolving our difficulties together. There's no fuss to this. My decision is about a man who's better known than I am . . ."

Garland allowed himself a small look of fulfillment. The camera caught his eyes gleaming.

"General Lucius S. Sensenbrenner, who's been asked to join our team here as my vice president, and who's agreed . . ."

The facts of the Twenty-fifth had already stunned the audience.

But now, by announcing Sensenbrenner as his nomination for the vice presidency once the challenge was resolved, Garland was wrecking the room.

Three hundred members of the press corps shifted their

rumps to keep from falling on the floor. The pens scratched the monitors, the fingers rattled the keyboards, the national networks opened up and fed the satellites to five continents regardless of the local times.

Everyone was tearing apart their leads and rewriting.

Not "Acting President Garland announced today that he is challenging the ability to govern of President Teddy Jay by invoking the mechanisms of the Twenty-fifth Amendment . . ."

Rather, "Acting President Garland, challenging the ability of President Teddy Jay under the mechanisms of the Twenty-fifth Amendment, has named General Lucius S. Sensenbrenner, Chairman of the Joint Chiefs, as his vice president designate pending the outcome of the most serious constitutional crisis since the Watergate scandals . . ."

Garland gestured, and Sensenbrenner came to his feet.

"Come on up here a moment, General," Garland ordered.

As Sensenbrenner stepped forward he felt the heat of the lights, especially on his hands. He also felt stiffness in his limbs, and it surprised him. This was stage fright, he knew; after all these years of showdowns and ceremonies, he felt the fear of stepping up to the national stage of history.

Breaking the breathless silence, there was sudden applause from the back of the East Room.

Sensenbrenner heard the approval as he heard the gasps and whisperings of the press.

What he couldn't hear was that six hundred thousand men and women in uniform were coming to their feet and cheering as the word was passed around the earth as fast as light could speed. The old man's in. We're going to get some now. We're coming back. Look out, bogeyman. You spell number one: "U.S.A."

Sensenbrenner halted a stride from Garland and, out of habit, gave a quick salute.

"Yes, yes," Garland teased in his polished ad lib manner,

sticking out his right hand, "you'll have to get used to shaking hands, now, General, won't you?"

Sensenbrenner, ignoring his burns, gave Garland his right hand. No one made note of the bandages, though the joke tomorrow would be that the general looked like he was playing with fire.

Garland pulled Sensenbrenner close for the still photographers to pop away from all angles. The two men were physically unequal. Garland was tanned, trim, square shouldered, a salt-and-pepper-haired beauty. Sensenbrenner, six inches taller, looked as slim, stern, and immovable as a fence post in army green, and all those ribbons only made his face seem plainer.

"We'll have to help him get used to all of it, won't we?" Garland asked the audience. "I'm counting on you to help him. He knows how to scare the daylights out of the outlaws. Now we're going to have to show him how to kiss babies and"— Garland yanked his hand from Sensenbrenner's adamant grip— "not crush my fingers."

The ham humor was appreciated. At all times Garland knew that if he made them cry, they'd love him—but if he made them laugh, they'd worship him.

"Say a few words," Garland asked Sensenbrenner.

Sensenbrenner stepped to the center of the podium and froze a moment.

"I want to thank the president . . ." he began. Garland hadn't told him he would have to speak. He realized he sounded scared. He told himself to relax and say what he meant.

He started again. "This is an honor. Not for me. For the uniform I wear. For the millions who've worn this uniform before me. And who wear it now. Thank you. And thanks to all of you who know what it means to follow the flag . . ."

Sensenbrenner broke off. He didn't know how to read an

audience. Not a civilian audience. What did it mean that they were staring at him? He couldn't see much into the lights. But they were silent out there. The cameras clicked, but the people were not reacting as if they were pleased.

He thought, *Did I say it wrong? Remember the little demons watching. Say it again for them.*

"I want to say one more thing," Sensenbrenner added. "You know about what's ahead better than me. I'm a soldier. Soldiers don't know what will happen in the next half minute. I do know this much. Anybody thinking the armed forces of the United States of America are less ready tonight than this morning: you're wrong."

Sensenbrenner backed away from the podium and saluted Garland, then came to attention a stride away, eyes straight ahead, not flinching as those at the back of the room got to their feet applauding, and even the press corps bobbed their heads in recognition of a genuine flag-waver.

They were applauding very loudly now. There were cheers. There were wet eyes.

Garland widened his amazed eyes and thought, *This man is colorless? Who said that? Did I say that? Well—brass and circuses, Sonny says—brass and circuses. We could have found a reincarnation here. American Caesar II?*

It was 7:25 P.M. in Washington.

Across the Pacific the markets were in free fall.

At home the republic was waking up from a dream to find that it wasn't a dream.

On TV the bulletins were unanimous in all American time zones.

Shy Garland was playing a Constitutional game called the Twenty-fifth Amendment, and the clock was running. Ninety-six hours for the cabinet to vote to sustain the challenge. After that, twenty-one days for the Congress to vote to sustain the challenge. No time-outs. No interference by the courts. No recount. Winner takes all.

Garland took back stage center.

"Now I want your questions," he said, "and I'll handle them fast as I can."

Garland gestured back toward Sensenbrenner. "For my friend the general up here," he said, "I suppose we'll save him for those of you who ask your questions *wrong*."

Part Three

THE NEW
PRESIDENT

21 Wednesday Morning, Georgetown

Downriver at Mount Vernon, President Jay slept and stirred and slept until he wasn't able to sort between his dreams and his fears. Sitting upright in a two-century-old chair made for a man half his size, the president deteriorated into silent sobs sometime near midnight Wednesday morning.

Upriver at Georgetown, Jack sat upright in his father's kitchen and channel-surfed on the TV, chasing the cable shows that were talking compulsively about the fire-in-the-hole called the Twenty-fifth Amendment and the pyromaniac called Shy Garland. The instant reaction to the challenge was decidedly mixed—the celebrity commentators mucking up all distinctions among the relevant strictures of the Twelfth and Twenty-second and Twenty-fifth amendments and the 1947 Succession Act. The simple conclusion offered by the competing and confusing voices was that the presidency probably belonged to the one who said he was the president, as long as someone else didn't say he was president, too.

Jack stared into the monitor as if it were a friend he could tell his troubles to without threat, and he kept at his blurry-eyed pursuit until his long night of feeling sorry for himself was cut off by word of the president's latest collapse.

At the precise quarter-hour the word came, Jack was eating a hot turkey and tomato with mustard on rye sandwich and telling Lilly that she should get on to bed; he was shipshape.

Jack said, "I'll get going at sunup. I'll be back at Blaine House by noon."

"That's too much flying on too little rest, Daddy," Lilly objected. She was in a turquoise silk dressing robe that Jack knew would have been her mother Allison's choice as well, and she looked to Jack as perfect as the Allagash River. "I should fly you back," Lilly said as she reached for some ice water. "I can; there's not much for me here until my internship starts."

Jack didn't want to argue anymore, not with a woman anyway, and he let his eyes drift back to the mute screen.

He knew he should have departed at suppertime—get in the Cessna and put ten states between himself and this wicked town. He'd called Cory Saltman and Dick Schecter and, after debriefing them on the day he'd missed (all Democrat shenanigans on the budget), he'd promised them he would make his nine o'clock. Then he hadn't moved from his seat. He hadn't wanted to do anything so clear-cut as leaving since Long John, Ez Kahn, and Jean had dropped him here like a truant after 3 P.M. From what he could see of his knuckleheaded attitude, he probably wasn't going to move from this excellent Shaker chair until either he saw the sun light up the rhododendron in the garden or his father walked through the door and told him what Jean was saying about him now.

It was upside down, Jack knew, that the son was waiting up late for the father to come home to tell him what the girl said about the son's misbehavior. But then Jack also knew that his father was more in love with Jean than he'd ever been, and that his marrying Jean was ninety percent his father's idea and the other half was Jean's. He'd been a miserably happy widower after the first five years, and was hardly threatened by going to Blaine House an old unmarried salt. The courtship of Jean Motherwell finished that fantasy—truth, it'd been fun to track down such a cosmopolitan duchess in her world-class pearls and towering shoes—but now where was he?

Lilly put the water glass in the sink and tried to comfort her father once more. "Daddy, you be sure to get me up for your breakfast. I'm in Gramma's room tonight, so you won't have to worry about waking Lou and Kel. Okay?"

"I love you," Jack said.

"And I love you, Daddy," Lilly said. "And Jean loves you, too."

Jack said, "Thanks, Lil."

He watched his daughter climb the stairs with her slide walk that was so exactly the same as Allison's that he felt haunted. Jack didn't think of Allison every day anymore; however, he missed her tonight. He'd been young then, a man at sea and home, and all things had seemed possible. Now he felt awkward and lead-footed and put-upon—a provisional member of the political class, a loser.

What am I going to do about it?

The answer was, It was up to him. For this was not a foolish man, this was a first-class sea captain tossed up on the beach by fate who, despite his worldly success, hadn't yet given up on the dream of going back to sea.

Half of Jack Longfellow aimed to be captain of the ship of state; the other half aimed for open water and a fair breeze.

It was shortly after Jack's exchange with Lilly, with the house as quiet as the sirens of the District would permit, that the car pulling up out front had the same six-cylinder knock as Parsifal's town car. Jack launched himself on his long legs to clear the davenport and to go by way of the backyard, charging around the house to leap the side fence and come up hard-winded on his father on the front walk.

"Where's Jean?" Jack started.

"Andrews," Long John said.

"Air Force Base?" Jack asked.

Long John kept going past his son, *tap, tap, tap* up the steps to his house. "Here," Long John said as he fished for his key. He handed Jack Jean's smooth white cell phone. "She wants to talk to you. And try to get the facts straight. I've got to get the girls up."

"Why? What?" he tried.

Long John was enjoying himself—mastering the universe, concocting the moment, and punishing Jack. He said, "My advice is don't forget you're not on the bridge; you're crew. Get your orders and carry them out."

Jack slumped and scowled.

"You want to know why? The president's fainted or some such thing. After Garland's announcement he just started sobbing or some such thing. I don't know all of it because I haven't seen him—Jean and I were at her office when Friar called—but I know that Connie Jay's taking over now. The First Lady's ordered us to bring him to her. She's taking over. Look at the facts, and get them straight. Jean and Connie Jay are going to be commanding us for a while. Can you deal with it . . . ?"

"Can *I*? But Dad, you're the one who—"

"I'm learning," Long John claimed, and then he was gone into his hallway, calling, "Lilly, get up, Lilly, it's Poppop! . . ."

Jack punched the macro button and sat on the front stoop. "Jean?"

"Jack?" Jean said. "I'm on my way to Andrews with Tim and Anna. Has LJ told you? I'm expecting the president's caravan to meet me there in the next half hour. We're taking one of the president's little planes. For Bar Harbor. The Secret Service is stinking about it, but we had Calcavecchia burn some ears. We'll be into Somesville by dawn. How soon can you get everyone here? I need you to stop at my place and get my pc, it has my notes in it, and I forgot to set it up so I could call it. Ellen will meet you there, she's coming along, and she'll have Sue with her."

"You mean Sue Bueneventura?"

"Right. Nan Cannon's flying up in the morning."

Jack hesitated. He didn't know why the senators from Florida and Indiana were being brought in, but then he did a conscientious thing and demoted himself to the fo'c'sle. "Okay," Jack said, "How's the president?"

"Connie's not certain, since she's diagnosing by phone, but she thinks he didn't eat and skipped his medication and is just worn out. You saw him same as me, he's let himself waste down to a stick."

"But is he quitting?" Jack asked.

"No one's quitting," Jean said. "I don't think LJ'd allow it, and I also don't think we're in a position to quit, know what I mean?"

"Garland was outrageous. I'm glad we're not quitting. He was just outrageous. He and Sensenbrenner up there like Romulus and Remus. Christ. Knowing what we know, Garland was totally outrageous."

"All right, Jack, you don't like the guy."

"That's it."

Jean allowed herself a snort about the double-think of her husband—that he should be jealous about her past entanglement with Garland while overlooking his own ongoing infidelity with Toni.

"Connie's on the phone to Ted right now," Jean continued. "She's talking him down. Joe Friar's got one of the Walter Reed doctors meeting us. We're all right as long as we get out of town before they know what to do about it. You know Quinn Roosevelt's a rat. Your dad says the White House is too cocky to care what we're doing, but I don't know. I guess your dad's right as usual."

"He said you were in charge," Jack said.

"Come on, Jack," Jean said.

They shared a smile despite their troubles and mistrust.

Jean kept talking, and Jack started moving to prepare for an airlift home. He thought, *Get your orders and carry them out— and mind your manners.*

In not more time than it took to marshal three sleepy teenagers, one sleepy senator's chief of staff, one sleepy senator from Florida, and one wide-awake octogenarian despot, Jack and Parsifal and Parsifal's cousin, Athos, who drove the second car, had delivered the party to the other side of the Beltway at Andrews Air Force Base. Jean was waiting for them along with the president's party. They cleared security faster than usual, thanks to some savvy phone-ahead work by the First Lady's special agent in charge, Mike Calcavecchia, who was running this airlift by remote command from Somesville in the middle of a hot night.

Departure wasn't immediate. The delay was caused by a mistake from the part-time press officer attached to Jay's outfit at Camp David, Harriet Boxwood, who'd indiscreetly telephoned the pool reporters assigned to watching President Jay. The press demanded to be included on the evacuation and wanted at least three seats on the flight north.

Long John disliked the media more than old age, and he'd held his nose at Jean's decision to trust her son's sweetheart, Anna Hrbek. He listened in on Harriet Boxwood's complaints to Friar and then ended the dilemma by reminding Friar that they

weren't going to Mars, they were going to Vacationland: the
reporters could follow from National Airport in the morning,
and buy their own tickets.

By 2 A.M. the presidential party was strapped in on one of the
89th MAC's tidier executive aircraft, a Gulfstream V dubbed Air
Force One-Half, and liftoff for the Hancock County–Bar Harbor
Airport followed as smooth as sea moss.

22 Wednesday Morning, the Pentagon

On the second floor of the Pentagon at the River Entrance, the
Joint Staff of planners, action officers, and dexterous briefers
were standing around looking competent.

Colonel Johnny Jones, the straight-backed, perfect sable director of the Joint Staff, was standing at the gateway from the
anteroom and clicking off the briefers as they passed him.
"Some meat," he'd say. "Get some meat on the bones," he'd say
to each new J-staffer as he or she entered the sanctum
sanctorum of the building.

This was the Tank, and in the airless, windowless, limitless
Tank competence was the highest acclaim, and Johnny Jones was
the ringmaster.

Outside the chamber, in the anteroom where the J-staffs and
ready briefers waited in suitable batting order, it was first light
on another steamy Potomac day, and this briefing session had so
far lasted fifty-nine minutes, exactly according to schedule and
orders.

But inside the Tank, tied by wireless pcs, PDAs, PCSs,

multiwindowed monitors, and videoscreens to the JCS situation room down the hall, there was a timeless feel. It was all days, all hours of all days, all minutes of all hours of all days in the Tank.

Sensenbrenner favored formal briefings—full dress, mechanical, *click-click-click*—the old "slide and glide shows" that now used multiple media and even live video feeds from anywhere. Sensenbrenner called for these big shows whenever he was in the building. It was standard operational procedure to break at least half of the briefers. You didn't go into the Tank to succeed, you went in to survive with a rating of competence.

This morning's fifty-nine minutes had ranged over a long list of incompetence, from a measles pandemic in the Philippines to machine parts shortages at Walvis Bay to the proselytizing among the suicide squads in the Kurdistan refugee camps to the priest kidnappings in Colombia to the smoke damage at Vandenberg Air Force Base. The appropriate J-director (defense, manpower, operations, logistics, plans, command and control, force structure) stood behind each briefer like a mother ready to accept the blame for an errant child.

Around the table the Joint Staff conducted themselves like judges interrogating suspects. As usual Chief of Naval Operations Admiral Meriwether did most of the heavy lifting. Kip Meriwether, fifty-four, was the bright-eyed, bald-headed, tightly wound star prosecutor in the Tank. He routinely crushed briefers and hacked down operations and wasted action officers. And this morning he had destroyed everyone from J-3 Operations directorate. They were puddles. Full colonels were soaked through their blouses. The J-director was struggling to keep from making a fist.

Johnny Jones kept clicking, "More meat."

Meriwether did such a good job breaking wills that the wraith-thin air force chief, the famous pug-faced Filipino American Clark Catedral, and the army chief, the famous pug-faced Romanian American paratrooper Izsak, had only to sit back and check off the plans that were dead on arrival.

Brick Breckenridge, at the chairman's right hand, was serving double duty as both deputy director and marine commandant, so he didn't get as involved in the questions as the others.

Johnny Jones was Breckenridge's contribution to the session, running the Joint Staff like clockwork. "More meat . . ."

Fifty-nine minutes of this hammering was routine, and so was the following one minute of silence.

Sensenbrenner, sitting ramrod straight at the head of the table, closed his briefing book and looked to Clark Catedral.

The minute was done. The drab walls, the throbbing cursors, the color bar charts and careful wire diagrams on the monitors— everything shut down.

Sensenbrenner said, "I want Space Command on the carpet. What happened at Vandenberg is unacceptable. Do we clean house, or do we not clean house?"

The big boss had cut through all the talk. Vandenberg. The smoke damage in the VAT. Clean house. Heads were going to roll. The air force was either going to give them up or it was going to have them taken.

Clark Catedral kicked the leg of his chair. "We clean house," he said.

Next package: Sensenbrenner looked to Meriwether. "*Teddy Roosevelt*'s up anchor?"

"At sea," Meriwether said, nodding at the digital clock showing Greenwich time in the big pc, "one hundred and forty minutes ago."

"What about the president?" Sensenbrenner asked.

"We got word from the White House an hour ago," Meriwether said. "They asked for permission to board. We replied affirmative."

Breckenridge contributed, "The president's flying out on Marine One, sir, to mess with the petty officers. Marine One's lifting wheels in ten minutes."

Next package: Sensenbrenner spoke to Izsak. "Cairo, Mickey—Cairo's a nightmare. It's not our people. It's not the food riots. Not the cholera . . . it's . . . Yesterday, there was this little beggar boy, on one of those boards, like a skateboard. Legless. His face . . . the sores, the mouth . . . You see, he'd rolled up underneath the car. He . . ."

Izsak didn't know what to say. Was this an Operations question? A Form 9 for Central Command? Call NATO's J-3? Was the boss talking about beggars? What did beggars have?

"Yes, sir?" Izsak said.

Sensenbrenner fell silent. The Joint Chiefs watched for the chairman to tell them what he wanted done. You didn't debate with Sensenbrenner. You tried to get ahead of his direction and follow from the front. Better, you ran the action from way out front. Sensenbrenner demanded competence by firing any flag officer, any three star, any C in C who didn't anticipate the next street fight and get there with maximum firepower.

But this morning the Joint Staff was thinking, *What's wrong with the boss?*

The question was in all the faces around the table, in the eyes of the weary planners and busted briefers, and even Johnny Jones had a hesitation in his clicking as he watched for Sensenbrenner's gaze to focus.

And wasn't Breckenridge trying to cover up the boss's upset? Wasn't Breckenridge hovering over Sensenbrenner like a nursemaid?

Eventually, what every member of the staff told him- or herself was that it was because of politics.

It was the vice presidency.

Last night's announcement had stunned the building and left the chiefs and the Joint Staff speechless. No one had known about the vice presidency, not even Brick Breckenridge or Johnny Jones. To keep a secret that big so well was the kind of detail that made Sensenbrenner a legend and made the fact of his elevation a puzzlement.

Vice President Sensenbrenner? Out of uniform? A politician? Campaigning? Presiding over those oddball characters in the Senate? Hobnobbing with twenty-four-year-old lawyer staffers on the Hill? Hanging out with the Democrats? Raising money?

Not our boss.

Breckenridge stood up and waved to Johnny Jones. Jones clicked, and the anteroom door swung full open; in swept a line of stewards carrying trays of orange juice and a lush breakfast bun, doused with butter icing.

"Sir, you know," Breckenridge said to Sensenbrenner, his full, fleshy face exploding with a generous grin, "it's what we could do on short notice."

The chiefs took glasses of orange juice. There was a decoration on the big breakfast bun. It was the seal of the vice president of the United States done in red, white, and blue frosting. There was a single candle.

Breckenridge gave the toast. "Godspeed, sir."

Meriwether, Catedral, and Izsak added, "Amen."

Sensenbrenner was standing with a blank smile on his face. He felt so tired. They were such good people. These fifty here, the six hundred thousand out there . . .

I did it for them, he thought. *I took the president's deal for them, didn't I? To hold them together. To do what I can to give them what they need to do the job. For them. Didn't I?*

He felt too tired. He needed to return the toast.

What is it? That beggar boy? Where had he seen him before? No legs. That ruined face. Why, God? What can I do for all the poor boys? All the poor boys I left in the field. All the poor boys that nobody's ever bringing in. All us poor, poor boys.

Sensenbrenner let his sense of doom take hold of him. "Absent friends," he said to Catedral and Izsak. And to Kip Meriwether and Brick Breckenridge, he gave the salute to the navy dead. "And all those boys still at sea . . ." and then he blew out the candle.

23 Wednesday Dawn, Mount Desert Island

Jack didn't get to talk much on the flight to the Bar Harbor field.

The Gulfstream cabin was like a single parlor, and the doctor from Walter Reed, a fair-haired man named Bruce Futter, wanted quiet for the president to sleep.

Jack had hoped to get some moments with Jean or Long John to find out what their plans were. But Jean was deep in a huddle with Sue Bueneventura and Ellen Quick; and Long John was sitting forward and passing notes with Joe Friar. This left Jack back with the Secret Service, the girls, and the sleeping President Jay, who was tucked up by his seatmate and longtime secretary, the blue-haired Marthe—who was Teddy's second cousin on the Lakota side, a grandaunt of great trustworthiness and taciturn strength.

The only other person who interested Jack was Jean's tall, nimble son Tim Seward. But he was most taken with the attention of a very pretty European woman named Anna Hrbek, who Jack was surprised to learn was the Reuters reporter who'd overheard him at the Capitol. Anna Hrbek's inclusion struck Jack as paradoxical, given that they'd ditched the networks and the bigfoot press at Andrews. Jack puzzled what his father was up to.

Before Jack could figure out his father's machinations, he was asleep; and before he could dream—or have a nightmare about the vulnerability of a lone aircraft coming down in a swirling low-pressure center on an uncontrolled rural field—they were on the ground at Bar Harbor and taxied to shutdown.

There was an eerie wet first light outside, too gray for night-time, too dark for daytime.

As soon as the steward lowered the stairs, Connie Jay was up and in the door. She looked good to Jack, sleek wet from the storm and glowing with energy as if just off horseback, wearing a cheery heather country-living sweater and black suede car coat, with that handsome, sober doctor's face of hers, concern mixed with confidence.

The president was clearly passionate to see her, and they didn't wait for privacy to embrace and kiss.

The First Lady leaned around her husband to address Long John and Jean. "Thanks for bringing him home to me. You, too, Sue and Ellen. He feels so good to me, just so good . . ." and then she took her husband by the arm. "Let's get everyone settled at home before we talk. Is that good for you, dear?"

"Fine, yes," pronounced the president. He looked toward the hatchway and asked after his youngest children. "Where's Ginny and Little Ted?"

"Asleep, where we all should be," said Connie, nuzzling her man. "I didn't tell the children you were coming—we can surprise them. Wait'll you see the house. It's one of the old cottages the Rockefellers built for their servants. Built with granite from the quarry right next door and shingle-finished. Right on the water, across from Jack's. Right, Jack?"

"Yes," Jack managed.

At the same time Connie was being gracious, she was reaching over the president's shoulder and indicating to the Walter Reed doctor, Futter, that he should go on ahead with the fat briefcase containing reports about the president's last five months.

It was clear to Jack that the First Lady was taking over the president's care—no more quarrelsome White House physicians (President Jay had replaced three in three years); no more Walter Reed think tanks; no more dysphoria consultants on cable network shows. Doctor Jay was now the president's specialist.

Connie turned her attention to logistics. "What time have you got, Jack?" she asked.

"It's 0520," Jack said in the naval manner. He pointed to the open hatch and the mist. "About ten minutes to dawn," he added, "in all this muck."

"Thanks, Jack," the First Lady said. "All right with you, Joe?" she asked. "We'll sit down about ten?"

Joe Friar answered, "We'll be ready."

"Good," said the First Lady.

Long John said, "Ten o'clock."

President Jay didn't offer much of substance. He did speak to Marthe, but Jack couldn't overhear him. At the door he called back to Jean, "Thank you. I wasn't sure, but now I am. It's good to be here. I should have left Washington months ago. Maine looks very good."

Jack wished that the president looked as good as Maine. The man was ashen, and his usually mighty voice, which had been sonorous yesterday, sounded frail.

Jack hoped for an explanation about the meeting at ten o'clock, and when it didn't come, he decided to constrain his curiosity and try patience.

After all, this is Maine. I'm the governor. Eventually they'll tell me what's going to happen.

The 89th MAC had landed the president's limousine a half hour before, and it pulled forward to the staircase at the Secret Service's signal.

The president's party filed down the stairs slowly. The rest of the caravan pulled in line as soon as the president was at his limousine—three minivans and two station wagons for the other passengers and the baggage. Bar Harbor was a clean, small civilian field, bordered by ryegrass fields and the rich wetlands of the Narrows. Ordinarily, at this hour, the airport would be as quiet as mud. The Secret Service had roused the local staff and authorities' staff from their beds, however, and there was a crowd of attendants at the ready and, in the upper parking lot, five state police cruisers with their lights bright as Polaris, waiting to form up with the president's caravan for the short drive across the causeway onto Mount Desert Island.

Before departing, the First Lady's special agent in charge, Calcavecchia, conferred with the president's special agent in charge, the hefty former Notre Dame ballplayer Kleczka; and then the two of them approached Jack. "Governor, good sloppy morning, yes, sir," Calcavecchia said. "All right with you if we order up more state police cruisers?"

Kleczka added, "We'd like to have trooper teams on rotation, sir, eight hours max."

"Yes, definitely," Jack declared. "I'll sign the order when it comes."

Jack didn't want to alarm the agents, but he did think about Red Schofield when he started giving orders again: "If I can make some other recommendations?"

Calacavecchia and Kleczka waited attentively.

"You can draft all of Barracks J," Jack said. "Set up a command center for the town at the Repertory Theater—it's empty till the season starts. Call on all the shopkeepers and tell them to lay in stores for the extra demand when the press corps arrives. And we'll need a National Guard helicopter in here with maintenance teams, in case the president wants a ride about. Park them here with this aircraft, and use my troopers to guard the field.

And call the Bureau of Fisheries and get a launch round the clock in the Sound. I'll leave the Coast Guard at Southwest Harbor to you, but the commander there's a friend of mine, and he's got some new cutters that'd be good to patrol off the Cranberry Isles."

"Yes, sir!" they both acknowledged.

Jack reminded them, "We know there's an invasion of camera crews coming at us by midmorning, but the island doesn't, so have my troopers wake up the motel owners from here to Bar Harbor and get the rooms aired out. Make sure you alert the park rangers, will you? We could open a campsite early for the TV semis. That way we'll know where they are."

Calcavecchia was grinning. "Yes, sir."

"Last details," Jack told Kleczka. "Acadia Mountain, on the west side of the Sound, that's the high point over the old Rockefeller place where the president's staying. How about a ranger patrol on the walking trails up there during daylight? And Sargent Drive on the east side of the Sound commands a view down on the house—so I recommend you put one of my cruisers up there and rotate the team every eight hours."

Kleczka saluted with his eyes. "Done." Everyone guarding the president disliked the media and knew that, given any chance, the TV crews would climb a hill for an eagle's-eye view.

"My last recommendation," Jack reviewed, "is that you establish a security working group with the troopers, park rangers, National Guard, island police, Fisheries, and the Coast Guard at Southwest. The Sound is a five-mile-long bathtub—deep and cold and protected by the hills. Lock it up."

Calcavecchia and Kleczka jumped to duty.

Jack felt excellent after his generalissimo talk with the Secret Service. This was the first respectful attention he'd received in days, and it made him think he should take care of himself before he saw his father and wife again.

If he'd abandoned his Cessna in Washington, he didn't have to abandon his old Jeep Cherokee, so he told the girls to go on with their grandfather, and he let the president's caravan go on without him.

This gave Jack the freedom to veer into Somesville and drive down the west side of the Sound, shooting past the turnoff to the president's new roost at the old Rockefeller place, and accelerating down the nine miles to the working anchorage of Bass Harbor.

He aimed to breakfast at Tom's Blue Plate Cafe with some genuine fishermen—sailors who'd grown up with his father on Swan's Island. Jack knew that, unlike his family, the old salts would treat him right.

24 Wednesday Morning, Arlington National Cemetery

Generals Sensenbrenner and Breckenridge descended into the rolling rows of headstones. The early morning breeze was up from the river and over the grassy grave plots like waves lapping at a stony coast. The gusts flapped the tiny American flags at each site, making a strange *clop-clop* sound across the lawns.

The generals' mirror-bright shoes left shallow footprints as they walked from the car on Roosevelt Drive down the few yards to the grave of George C. Marshall, General of the Army, Secretary of State, hero of heroes.

Breckenridge waited while Sensenbrenner bent down to touch the headstone.

"I like it here," Sensenbrenner offered, "do you?"

Breckenridge rocked on his heels, unsure what to say.

"All these men from the history books," Sensenbrenner said. "Here they are. In the end, here's what's left for us to honor."

"Yes," Breckenridge agreed cautiously.

Sensenbrenner said, "We're going to spend a long time here—or, our earthly remains are. How do you feel about that, Brick?"

Breckenridge was a devoted Roman Catholic. He hadn't thought much about eternity; he'd concerned himself with conscience. But then, he'd been lucky: his wife and children and grandchildren were all healthy, and when he'd buried his parents, they'd been at the end of full lives.

He had buried a lot of marines at Walvis Bay, but he didn't have a way of connecting that madness to this park.

Breckenridge thought, *What does he mean, how do I feel about Arlington?*

"It's a beautiful place," Breckenridge tried.

"Beautiful enough for eternity?" Sensenbrenner asked.

Breckenridge was puzzled. He'd attended so many ceremonies here over the years, during his three previous postings to Washington, that he'd come to think of Arlington as part of his job. Tomb of the Unknown Civil War Dead. Joe Louis. The Argonne Cross. Walter Reed. And of course his choice, the Tomb of the Unknowns.

But what about eternity?

"I guess so." Breckenridge checked his watch. 0635. Sensenbrenner had a flight for London in fifty minutes. And he had a briefer waiting for him at Andrews to load him up with the papers he needed for the NATO confab.

Sensenbrenner stood up. "Brick, you're a good friend."

"Thank you, sir."

They turned together to look down on the Potomac and across to the swelling haze over the low city.

Sensenbrenner started in a quiet tone, "I want to tell you what happened to me this morning—in Cairo. I started talking about it in the Tank, but . . . It's about a beggar boy. We were coming out of the embassy. And I asked to drive down to Old Cairo. You know, where the river narrows. You remember, I took you there last year. Where the old Roman fortress was, the ruins?"

"Yes," Breckenridge answered. Cairo was a fascination to Sensenbrenner. Cairo and Rome and Jerusalem and Athens. The old Roman Empire. The boss liked to draw the ruins. Breckenridge couldn't draw much. He liked to sing, but that wasn't very military.

After a long hesitation Sensenbrenner continued. "There was this little beggar boy. Maybe ten years old. He was born without legs below the hips. He was on this cart. He begs for coins. He works for these big handlers, who turn the kids into Fagins. You know, Fagin in *Oliver Twist*? There's not much Dickens about Cairo. What I saw is so wrong, and it made me feel so wrong. A failure."

Breckenridge straightened his forage cap. He was perfectly dressed in the robust marine olive drab. The ribbons on his chest glistened in the sunlight.

"Do you understand why I'm telling you this?" Sensenbrenner asked. "I feel a failure. That I've gone the wrong way. I haven't helped. That child, what chance did he ever have? What have I ever done for him? Why did God put him here? To live like that, no parents, nothing to love, his sores, and they beat him, and when he touched me . . . I felt . . ."

Sensenbrenner let his chest heave.

"I've felt that way, sir," Breckenridge admitted. "It's when I'm most tired."

"What I felt when the child touched me," Sensenbrenner

said, "was what I imagine death will feel like. A rotting body. But a wonderful soul. I'm sure that child has a wonderful soul . . ."

Breckenridge was listening closely.

"Brick, if anything happens to me," Sensenbrenner started again, "I want you to take care of me. Help Emily. She and the boys will need your help. Bring me back here. No matter where my soul is, I want my body here. It makes me sleepy just to look at it."

Breckenridge respected soldiers who felt they were going to die. He'd had the feeling. It came and went. You didn't deny it. You marched.

"Yes, sir."

Sensenbrenner turned and they strode evenly back up to the car. He knew he had to get on to Andrews. He knew he was due in London for tomorrow morning's briefing.

He also knew he was going to become the vice president of the United States.

What would George Marshall make of this? To take off my uniform and go across the river? Marshall did it. And how did the politicians treat him? Like an interloper. Like a fifth wheel.

"I didn't like keeping last night's show secret from you," Sensenbrenner said to Breckenridge. "The White House—the president's chief of staff, Quinn Roosevelt—he asked me to keep it under my hat. Actually, I was ordered by the president's executive committee."

"I understand," Breckenridge said, then using the critical acronym. "It was EXCOM."

"That's right, EXCOM," Sensenbrenner said. "The outfit we've both been working for."

Breckenridge said, "I understood it must be something like that. Last Sunday, at Chaffe, I figured it was something like that. EXCOM'd asked you to run an exercise like that. So you had me pull a line unit out—one that wasn't in a high-profile laager— and get them to you for the exercise."

"You did it fine," Sensenbrenner said. "The battalion did fine. The One-fourteenth. Fine. And the CO, Schofield, a good officer. Fine job."

"He did the job, all right," Breckenridge responded, adding unnecessary details. "A good officer, yes. Class of 'eighty-two, from the academy. I pulled his file. Schofield. He was on my central staff. Johnny Jones knew him at the academy. And by the way, I had him wrong—he finished above Jones, in the top ten percent. They call him Red."

Breckenridge knew he was stalling. Yet he wouldn't go any further. He wanted to ask about FATHER'S DAY. It had been the unsaid detail between them for three days now—in person or by satellite—and Breckenridge knew that they had to get past it. That operation at Chaffee had been one of the strangest he'd ever organized and witnessed. Not the worst—Walvis Bay was the nightmare in his life, the night landings that'd turned to massacre. But still, even for the Puzzle Palace, FATHER'S DAY was strange soup. And the White House had ordered it up?

Brick Breckenridge was the good soldier, too. He obeyed. He waited on his boss.

Sensenbrenner looked to his right to the massive shoulders of the Pentagon. He held his tongue. He, too, wanted to go one step further. The logic was compelling. EXCOM was the president's outfit. EXCOM had made him the vice presidential nominee. EXCOM was FATHER'S DAY. So President Garland must be directing not only the challenge to President Jay but also the preparation for FATHER'S DAY.

But did Breckenridge understand that FATHER'S DAY was not Sensenbrenner's idea? That it was a direct order from EXCOM? That Sensenbrenner had obeyed the order but did not intend to carry it out? Never expected to carry it out?

Does he know I had to do it? That it was the only thing that will stop them from taking us down to the level where we can't do the job? Where what we'll wake up to is massacre after massacre? Where there will be only Kurdistans and Cairos out there?

I had to do it! We've got noncoms feeding their families with food stamps! We've got no spare parts for half the forward-based commands. We've got ten days' ammo in the Pacific! Space Command can't afford to rebuild Vandenberg! We've got battalions out there without backup! Our hospitals aren't much better than Grant's! The carriers don't have enough drivers to go around!

"I want you to know . . ." Sensenbrenner started, but then he changed his mind about candor. It would be over soon. Maybe by Friday. That's what Quinn Roosevelt had said last night. The challenge would be sustained by Congress by Friday. All done by Friday night. And then he could bury EXCOM's plan with all the other horrors in the Plans directorate.

I'll be in Cairo. Maybe I can find that beggar boy. And help him.

". . . about FATHER'S DAY, Brick," Sensenbrenner said. "Only I give the go code."

Breckenridge looked directly at his boss's grim profile. Breckenridge didn't speak. He lowered his formidable chin and nodded.

25 Wednesday Morning, Somes Sound

Bass Harbor's gray shingles and white clapboards were heavenly in the fog. The clouds were pressing down on this peninsula of the island like a soft cheese, and the morning sea breeze was clean and dense with the tide meeting the spring pollen head-on.

Jack felt stronger the moment he turned the Cherokee up the bumpy gravel to the water's edge. He climbed down to the noisy hum of the tide and opened Tom's heavy old door with a clomp. He sat on his usual stool and said, "Usual, Tom, thanks."

The dozen or so old men in the long, chilly room acknowledged Jack with their dark eyes and infinitesimal head movements. Being Mainers as well as Downeast salts, no one spoke unless spoken to, and then not much. The governor wanted to be alone with his raft of flapjacks and bucket of orange juice, then the governor was going to be left alone. Think it'll lift later?

Jack looked out on the creaking ebb tide, stacked lobster traps, and bobbing trawlers and came to some of his better senses. He wanted to call Toni. She was probably still asleep. He was a chicken not to have called her last night. He must call her.

But first he called his baby sister—Bobbie, the only person he knew besides salts who'd be at the office at quarter past six.

"It didn't go so well with Dad," Jack began. "It's me, Jack."

"Criminey, you sound underwater. What's that sound?"

"That's an old ventilator. I'm at the Blue Plate. Just flew up from Washington with Dad and Jean and a whole crew, including our dear wounded Mr. Jay. Dad really ripped into me about my friend Toni, and so did Jean, and now I think they're disowning me."

"Add me to the list," Bobbie said; she sounded peeved—and not only about the family, also about her portfolio. "You might have been less baffling Monday, about Garland and Jay and all, and I might have got out of the way of what's coming to my poor long positions."

"I couldn't say any more," Jack said, "and I'm sorry I couldn't, but what I knew was from Jean and . . . It's all a mess. I was hoping I'd still have a place with you if they throw me out."

"You serious?" Bobbie asked.

"I don't know. Dad's gone Lord High Sheriff of Acadia on me. And just for the thrill, I think he's about to counterattack on the White House."

"I wish I knew what you were talking about—what's Jean doing? Did you tell her, too, about this woman?"

"Jean says we're finished."

Bobbie got to her feet with a slap. "No!"

"She gave me the odds."

"What are you going to do?"

"*Louisa*'s paid for. How about the Southern Ocean? Elephant Island? You game?"

"Jack, you've got to be serious. I love you, Jack. Please, don't get that lost-boy voice. It kills me. We need you, Jack. You've got to hang in there with Dad and Jean. You must promise me."

"I want to, but they drive me crazy. Why do they treat me like this?"

"It's just Dad's way . . . you know, he pushes everyone hard, and he's always pushed you hardest—especially from the moment he got the idea to launch you to the White House, you know—and Jean, she loves you. I've seen it, Jack, she's in love with you. I know."

"Sure."

"That lost-boy voice, again. Please! Stop it! It's bad enough here."

Jack eased up. He was as sick of his own self-pity as anything else. *Try caring about someone else,* he thought. "How bad is it there, Bobbie?" he asked.

"You want to know?" she asked.

"It's Garland, Bobbie, I can tell you that much. He's engineering this. He's cooked up the challenge and the scary stuff."

"No kidding. His name's on the radio so often this morning it sounds like he's a cereal. And 'scary'? How about 'horror show'? Firing Old Boney and his whole staff is a horror show."

Jack said, "What are you talking about?"

"You missed it? It was on the wire this morning at three A.M., just in time for London futures opening. Old Boney's out, and so's everyone at Treasury down to the doorman. Massacre. Garland's fired everyone down to the doorkeeper and put the Treasury in Quinn Roosevelt's hands. Here comes New Reconstruction with Lynch Garland's Houston pals in charge of the revenue stream. Tight money and tighter nooses."

Jack was amazed. Garland had fired Treasury? Just like that? "I didn't know," he said.

"That's just for starters this morning," Bobbie said. She punched her keyboard, and the clicks were like the ticking clock. "Tokyo closed down three percent last night, Hong Kong down three, and Sydney only one percent because of the gold shares. And that was before we heard about Old Boney getting the boot. Now, with two hours left at Frankfurt, the DAX is off five percent; so's the CAC-Forty in Paris; and in London, the Footsie's off seven! Percent! You want to know where Teddy Bear's Motor City is trading in London? GM's down two and a half, Ford's down two, and Chrysler's down one and one-half. Bucks!"

"How bad does it get?" Jack asked.

"Picture a black train rushing across the Atlantic for the Street. Picture all the traders getting onboard. Picture the wreck when it slams into the opening. When they can open. When!"

"It's Garland who's doing it all," Jack said. "He's cooked this whole thing up to panic people. Nothing's wrong except Garland's personality. This is all a phony crisis to get his challenge passed by the cabinet and the Hill."

"Jack, there is something very wrong, and what's wrong is doubt. Don't you remember what I taught you? Doubt breaks markets. Trust makes markets. It isn't Garland, Jack, it's our good old friend fear of the unknown. We're going to give it all back, everything since January—every penny, and then they'll start on our halfpennies!"

Jack talked consolingly with Bobbie as best he could, given his general amateurism about the markets, and he stayed on the phone longer than necessary to try to make up to her. He was a selfish fool, he knew. Hitting on his baby sister for sympathy. Splitting the family against Dad. Fretting about himself instead of things that really mattered, such as . . .

Jack called his press aide, Cory Saltman, and asked for her help to postpone the weekly governor's supper with the State-house leadership; then he called his legislative aide, Dick Schecter, and asked for his help to make a deal with the Aging Committee about reamortization if rates were going to back up; then he called Ralph Beale at Portland to thank him for the luncheon; then he called State Treasurer Robby Thredgold to chat about what the markets were doing to the state bonds (okay, so far). In fact Jack called everyone he could think of to be nice to, solicitous of, or candid with—he wanted to tell everyone everything about Jay, but he held his tongue—right up until it was after eight and he could call Toni at home after the kids were off to school.

Instead he got her housekeeper, a Chinese national with a weak vocabulary: "Miz Toni gone, yeah! Gone way! Who're you!"

"This is Jack Longfellow."

"Yeah, Lun-feywa!"

"What?" Jack said, and then he had a chill up his back and guessed Long John's shenanigans: "Did she go to the Longfellow house? Did someone come and get her? Men with badges?"

"Yeah! Lun-feywa! Gone!"

Jack was hastily into the Cherokee and racing up Route 102, through Manset and Southwest Harbor. He slowed for the

troopers who'd set up a temporary outpost at the turnoff to the
old Rockefeller place and the president. He rounded through
Somesville, where he had to crawl along because of the network
semis and TV RVs that were arriving in convoys like the Winnebago and Harley fleets of the summer tourists. The drivers were
out of their cabs and scratching their chins over small maps.
Welcome to Vacationland.

Jack accelerated up Route 198 into the fog bank spilling out
of the Sound. Quickly he was down onto Sargent Drive and
down the slope to his own turnoff. He left the Cherokee at the
gravel's edge and took the front steps in a trot. The front door
was open.

Jean was sitting with Sue Bueneventura in the central hall.
They were both washed up from the journey and changed into
denims and loafers; they were both seated with cordlesses to
their chins, talking to Washington while they made notes on
their handheld pcs. Jean covered the mouthpiece and said,
"Your father's looking for you."

Jack demanded, "Is Toni Albanese here?"

Jean didn't flinch. "She's in with LJ," she said, nodding at the
parlor doors. "It was his idea," she added. "He needed to be
sure of the facts."

"Why? Who cares! What's he up to?"

Jean looked her husband over. He was a salt-air mess. And he
had that guilt-soaked look of his, the one that made him dangerous with his anger.

She didn't feel angry. She'd been surprised by her reaction to
meeting and talking with the woman, with Toni Albanese, whom
the Secret Service had delivered before eight. She'd felt jealous
and devalued and tricked and threatened, yes; but not angry.
She'd felt no fire when she shook the woman's hand. More
disappointment, to be truthful, and also embarrassment, that the
two of them should have to meet like this. Jean had looked at

Toni Albanese and thought, *How young she is. Is she forty even? And how dark-eyed and sweet and bouncy. Yes, clearly a perky little brunette with a mop of curls.* She also had thought, *She's all wrong for Jack. Jack likes blonds. He always has. And Jack likes a temper. This one doesn't have a temper. It doesn't make sense . . .*

And then Jean had noticed the tiny hearing devices Toni Albanese wore. Both ears. And Jean had thought, *A pretty little disabled widow with two small children and a start-up business. Of course. Jack needs her neediness. Admiral Jack to the rescue.*

Jean answered Jack slowly, "I'm busy here, Jack. Brownie McDonald's threatening to check out of the hospital. Why don't you ask your dad?"

"Okay, but it stinks," Jack said. "She didn't do it, I did, and we shouldn't drag her into this, whatever it is."

Sue came off her call and asked, "Do you two want some privacy?"

Lilly, who'd run to the entryway from the summer kitchen the moment she'd heard her father come in, called, "Daddy, do you need breakfast? I've got a Western omelet ready to pour here for you."

Ellen Quick opened the parlor doors and came out with a notepad in her hand. "Governor," she said formally to Jack, "your father's been asking for you. And also, you have a call from Dick Schecter about—"

Jack pushed past Ellen Quick and, trying not to trip on the Persian throw rugs, came upon what he had half expected and doubly feared.

Toni, in a charcoal business suit, was firmly seated in his mother's favorite blue silk wing chair. And Long John in his suspenders and mud boots was in his own wicker rocker. Both were laughing at one of Long John's charming little witticisms.

"Good, Jack," Long John said, "we need you now."

Jack ignored his father for Toni. "Are you okay? I'm sorry, I really am . . . you see . . ."

"I'm fine, Jack," she said, putting down her coffee mug. "And I feel much better about Red. Your father wanted to talk with me about Red—he says that there's a way to help him. Red doesn't have to just march off the cliff. Isn't that what you mean, Mr. Longfellow?"

"Fluid, yes," Long John said.

"Yeah, yeah, fluid," Jack interrupted rudely. "Life is fluid, Dad. The ocean is fluid, Dad."

Jack sat on the brocaded ottoman with a thud and hung his sandy head. This was the worst. They wouldn't even give him room enough to feel ashamed of himself. They wouldn't give him anything! Crushed by Dad. Humbled by the heart. Docked by Garland.

Fight the one you can get at. Fight Shy Garland.

"Damn it, Dad!" Jack looked up. He was mad. He was going up on the bridge. He was taking over from the old man and the eternal sisterhood that yoked him. He was in command.

"Let's get on with it!" Jack declared. "Enough of this maneuvering. Are we going to go at Garland or are we going to talk about it?"

Long John, his pink cheeks brightened, asked, "Yes, Jack?"

Before Jack could start, Jean and Sue Bueneventura walked into the room with the phones still at their ears as they chatted with their Hart Building staffs. There was a firestorm breaking out along the Beltway. It was arson. Quinn Roosevelt was pouring the gas. Garland was playing with matches.

Tim Seward came up from the kitchen area, flapping a handheld pc that was broadcasting this morning's highlights of Garland's firestorm.

"Headlines coming in," Tim said to everyone without realizing there was a story breaking in the parlor, too.

"You know Old Boney's out of Treasury, but did you know they gave his whole staff thirty minutes to clean out their desks? In the middle of the night. Hauled them in there for it. And there was a guard detail to take them to the front steps for a photo op at three A.M."

Sue Bueneventura muttered, "No stuff."

"But you want to hear the best so far?" Tim asked. "Garland's transferred out the whole Trade staff. And put in his mouthpiece Hank Lovell as our Trade rep. And Lovell's first move this morning was to say that we're pulling out of GATT if the French don't drop their tariffs on our foodstuffs. Not discount. Drop. Lovell's giving Paris an ultimatum. Farm pricing his way or trade war!"

Jean said, "Garland likes ultimatums, doesn't he?"

"As a president, he's a great monarch," Sue said.

Tim added, "And did you hear—"

"Hold on now, Tim," Long John insisted. He turned their attention back to his son. "Jack's got something in mind, I think. Is that right, Jack? What do you mean, go at him?"

Jack was ready.

"I'm finished with hearing what Garland's going to do. He can reposition himself from evergreens to redwoods, and he'll still have his neck hanging out. What I want to hear about is what we're going to do about it. *Our* news."

The others stopped dancing around the room.

Jean signed off on Washington and opened up her eyes to a most unusual Longfellow event: father and son were dealing with each other in person—two identical sets of eyes, two identical jaws, two temperaments on collision course, or was it parallel?

"You tell us, Jack," Long John encouraged.

Jack asked, "Is President Jay onboard with us?"

"We'll see at ten," Long John said. "In a half hour—for our appointment over there."

Jack asked, "How about Connie—is she ready to hear our case?"

Long John answered, "The First Lady is hearing the story now in full from Friar. My guess—and Jean's—is that the First Lady will want to fight when she hears the details of the Oval Office ambush. She's stubborn enough. We don't know about the president. We'll have to go by what Joe Friar says about his boss, and what he told me on the flight up was that the president wants to abide by the Constitution. Go with the Twenty-fifth. See it to the end. Friar's got good sea legs, you know, and he says that the Twenty-fifth is driving the president's mind for now. Such as it is. The Twenty-fifth, I mean."

Jack spoke of the Jays. "We do this *our* way. They come with us and do what they want with the room we get for them. We're looking at Concord in February, not Washington in June. Friar knows it, or he's not the man I think. Jay'll know it, too, if he's the guy he has to be to stick it out."

Long John stretched out his legs. "I'm listening."

"All right, let's make it quick," Jack said, "and we'll make the meeting on time. Across the Sound. Timmy, tell Lil to get the barge uncovered and the canopy up."

Jack began his customary walk on his make-believe bridge. His posture, his tone, his gestures—everything was transformed from the petulant son of the last few days into a poised professional leader at his job.

"Five recommendations," Jack started, holding out his right hand with fingers spread.

Toni lowered her gaze. Jean watched Jack's performance carefully. She knew what he was doing. He was taking over. Was she pleased? She wasn't certain.

"First. We need proof of Red Schofield. We go to him to get it."

"Yes," Long John said.

Jean breathed heavily. This was the same as Long John's plan—the one he'd cooked up last night.

"But Jack—" she said.

Long John raised his right hand to stop her.

Okay, she thought, *it's good for them to make up and think alike.* But she had to ask the hard question anyway, the one Long John hadn't filled in. "How do we get it?" she asked.

Jack replied, "Occupied Moldova. And I'll need a native with me. Timmy, your Russian's serviceable?"

Tim answered, "It can fry eggs, sir." Tim pointed to Anna Hrbek standing behind him. "Anna can do some Romanian. And she's been to Budapest."

"You volunteering?" Jack asked.

"I'd like that, sir," she said with a smart smile.

Jean held her tongue. Tim and Anna with Jack in a war zone. No! No! No!

Jean's restraint didn't get a chance to break down, because then another woman's willpower spoke up.

"I'm going, too," Toni Albanese said. "In fact, I've already volunteered. Your father already asked me, and I agreed."

Jack glanced at his father.

"My reaction is negative," Jack said. "We're pros. You aren't, Toni. I think you should stay clear. And anyway, it's what Red Schofield wants. He said he wants you out of it."

"The question is whether you're going with me," Toni said. "Since I think I'm the one Red will want to see. And will listen to."

"But, Toni, it's not—" Jack said.

"It's my family, Jack," Toni said. She was not a reticent negotiator. "This is about my family. Red called me. It started with his phone call to me. Remember, I called you? And you told me you could help. You have helped, and now you can help me some more and take me to Moldova and Red. Red and I are how it started, we're how it's going to finish."

Jack saw that Toni was dug in, and he sidestepped the contro-
versy. Did Dad go along with this? Did Jean? Jack couldn't
figure them, so he kept on with his mind.

"Second recommendation," Jack said. "We need to slow
down the Twenty-fifth process. The three votes coming. Can we
get Rocky Kahn to listen to us, or has he gone over to Garland?"

Long John sighed. "Ez called his son last night. Roosevelt
made Rocky an offer he couldn't refuse—and unless we can give
him a reason to side with us, Rocky's in Roosevelt's pocket."

"And with Treasury canned," Jack argued, "and Cal Mooney
too sick to vote—so Rocky Kahn votes for him—and Archie
Learned probably in Garland's hire, and the vacancies at Commerce and EPA . . . well, I give Garland the cabinet vote. I
don't see any certain way we can stop the cabinet vote. Garland's
going to want to rush the cabinet. Use that ninety-six-hour re-
quirement to scare them into action. Today, probably this afternoon, for a press release tonight. It's how I'd do it."

"My expectation," said Long John, "is that they'll want to
announce the cabinet vote by this evening to gain momentum
for the Hill."

Long John watched his son carefully, thinking how satisfying
it was to have Jack take charge with exactly the same plan he'd
already designed.

"We'd do best to fall back and get ready to slow the Twenty-
fifth down on the Hill. Garland's going to want to rush there,
too. He'll claim that the Twenty-fifth's call for a twenty-one-day
period to debate is dangerous for the country."

Long John said, "When they wrote the Twenty-fifth, they just
picked twenty-one days out of the air. It was a fantasy."

"We don't have any strong hands in the House," Jack continued, "so I'd leave it to whatever Joe Friar can do. Probably not
much. He's got the Michigan delegation of sixteen, but not
much more than that to go up against Jesus Magellan's majority
machinery."

Jack nodded at Jean. "We'll make our stand in the Senate, Jean."

"We haven't got the numbers, Jack," she answered.

"I know—how many can you count on?"

Jean answered, "Maybe half—sixteen of my thirty-two. Brownie McDonald's going to get out of the hospital eventually, and he'll probably go over to Garland and take Cindy Belleau and the southerners with him."

Jack nodded in agreement. "Okay, so we have sixteen. Perhaps we can get another sixteen from Friar. I know it's not enough to stop it, but it's enough to debate it, and maybe slow it down for more than a day."

Jean answered honestly about the prospects of the challenge vote on the Senate floor. "It'll take a miracle to stop Pickett if he wants to bull us aside. We can try. We can talk. But a filibuster is out of the question, you know it."

"You can find a miracle for us," Jack said.

Jean sighed. "Thanks."

Long John looked to Jean. "You can use what the Twenty-fifth gives, Jean. I see that today more clearly. I've disliked the Twenty-fifth so thoroughly, I wasn't looking at what we can use it for. If Garland can use the twenty-one days' time line to argue that the Hill should rush, you can use the twenty-one days to argue for deliberation."

Jean shook her head. "Okay, but—"

"We need to buy time to get to the weekend," Jack said. "The weekend is when we can dig in. By then we can count on Jay's forces rallying. We can mostly count on television time—the Sunday shows, or *Sixty Minutes*. You know, make the president the underdog. But what will most rally the country to the president is my third recommendation."

"The vice presidency," Jean said.

"Right," Jack said. "We need to prep a vice presidential successor. Someone to answer Sensenbrenner with. Someone to rally Jay's forces to. I like your choice of Luke Rainey, Dad. As Speaker, he's third in line anyway. And he's plenty lovable, and he's got the Disney money and the Florida machine—Rafi's machine."

"Yes, yes," Long John said.

Jack asked, "That's why Sue's here, isn't it?" He looked into Sue Bueneventura's brilliant brown eyes. "You and Jean are going to Florida, Sue? You've got a meeting scheduled with Rafi?"

Sue answered, "We've got the appointment. But I've been thinking that Rafi's going to want something in trade for helping us. You know Rafi."

Jack did know the governor of Florida fairly well. He'd gone marlin fishing with him at the governors conference in the Keys two years before, when they'd discussed politics and women— mostly Jean, Jack's newly wed bride and Rafi's old flame. Jack knew Rafi's charm was endless and his powers of persuasion were potent; and Jack also knew to be firm with the governor of Florida, El Presidente Cubano.

"What Rafi gets," Jack told Sue and Jean, "is his Luke Rainey groomed and ready for the vice presidency. No promises. No other deals."

Jean nodded at Jack's bargain. This was Long John's plan to a jot. Offer Rafi nothing, just ask how much Rainey would be worth to him and Florida.

"We're outbound for Miami this afternoon," Jean noted, "if the president and Connie agree to the deal."

Ellen Quick came into the room. "Excuse me, but it's a quarter to ten . . . if you're going to make the appointment with the president and—"

"Let's move it," Jack said, "we'll finish on the way over." Jack jumped toward the double doors, giving orders as he walked.

Ellen Quick and Tim Seward were to stay here with the phones. Lou and Kelly were to monitor TV for more Garland news. Anna Hrbek was on her honor to keep the story in her pc and not on the fax lines. Everyone else was to get to the mudroom for wet-weather gear. Jack helped his father with his coat and then took his arm to help him get down the wet back steps and through the soaked formal garden.

"You know Jean's right," Long John told his son. "She can't stop Pickett if he forces a vote on the floor."

"If I were Sonny Pickett, I wouldn't try to get past Jean," Jack said.

"See that you don't," Long John warned.

Jack lowered his head in acknowledgment that his father had scolded him again—and at least this time it wasn't by threatening him with his walking cane.

On the wharf, Jack helped his father into the Boston Whaler and then helped Jean and Sue and Toni down into the well. He told Lilly to take the wheel. "Make it an easy trip over, Lil, we need to talk a little more."

It was a flawless rainy morning on the Sound, with choppy white water and skimming white gulls, the ebb tide turning at the express-train rate of four knots, the wind changeable and meteoric off Acadia Mountain, and Jack in the well on his knees, talking politics.

"My fourth recommendation," Jack called over the slapping water and low rush of the drizzle on the canopy, "is that we need to counter the pro-Garland propaganda on TV!"

"Of course we do!" said Long John.

"We can't use the president," Jack said, "and we can't do it ourselves! Not even you"—he turned to his wife—"can go on the talk shows and go directly against Garland. So we need a big mouth who'll do what we say and pop off at Garland. I say we need Gus Keebler!"

"I don't like this part," Jean said.

"What's that?" Long John asked, since he couldn't hear
clearly in both directions. He was having fun now—this was raw
politics—and he didn't want to miss whatever Jack or Jean said.

"You know what I mean!" Jean called back. "I told you last
night I didn't like using Keebler!"

"Keebler, yes!" returned Long John, who liked Keebler as the
most unambiguous demagogue in America today.

Jack didn't mind they'd already had this argument; he continued, "We send you to him, Dad, correct? You and Nan Cannon?
Is that why Nan Cannon's coming up this morning? Because she
hauled Keebler over at the FTC hearings three years ago?
You're taking her along? You've got a sit-down tonight at Yuma?
Face-to-face on the Colorado River? You, Nan, Keebler, and his
cooking show?"

Long John nodded. Perfectly devious.

They were talking about Arizona billionaire builder and de-
veloper Gus Keebler and his very popular cable TV show, *Southwest Cooking with Sheriff Gus Keebler*.

Jack asked his father, "He's on tonight, right? He tapes a half
hour before broadcast? You go to him and tell him what we
know about FATHER'S DAY and see what comes out of him on
TV, right? Eleven P.M. our time?"

"Yes!" Long John called. "We'll be back tomorrow! Watch the
television! Tonight!"

"Daddy, shall I land us?" Lilly called.

Jack looked out on the landing at the old Rockefeller place.
The cliff rose straight up out of the water on one side, and on
the other the house's grounds rolled into the old Hall Quarry.
Lilly had taken as long as she could to cross over and still make
headway. Jack waved to the Secret Service agent on the floating
raft. "Longfellows for the president!"

The agent spoke into his headset to communicate to the command center in the two-car garage. He waved back to Jack to
proceed.

With the soft thump of the port bow, Jack leaped out and tied off the Whaler. "Okay, everyone?" he said, leaning down for his father first. "Let me help you."

When Jack turned back to offer his hand to Toni, she leaped nimbly past him and up onto the raft. Jack puzzled momentarily about her motive. Was she spurning his help? She hadn't said a word since their disagreement over Moldova.

Okay, he thought, *okay. She doesn't have to like me anymore. Okay.*

It was a brief, dark moment for Jack, in the bobbing craft, and then he turned back for Sue and Jean.

The old Rockefeller place was a gloomy presence with a clapboard addition. It sat up across a sloping lawn that was dotted with children's toys left out in the rain.

The most distinctive feature of the house was the second-story deck that jutted out from the master bedroom. Special Agent Kleczka, the president's man, was watching the Longfellow party from the deck.

At the back door of the mudroom Special Agent Calcavecchia, the First Lady's man, was waiting for Jack. "You all set, sir? They're waiting for you in the front room."

"Boost my dad, will you, he's tough on steps."

Jack helped Sue Bueneventura out of her raincoat. Her shoes were soaked from the boat, her hairstyle was ruined by the damp, and her fingers were red from the cold. "And this is June?" she said, blowing on her hands.

Upstairs, in the wide dining area that overlooked the lawn, the president was seated in an overstuffed chair at the picture window. The First Lady was beside him on a high stool. The long, narrow room was luxuriously done up in bright floral upholstery patterns, excellent watercolors, and new Orientals, and Connie Jay had obviously worked hard to give it a homey feel by bringing her little children's chairs and

tables into the dining area alongside the cherry wood en-
semble.

Joe Friar and the First Lady's chief of staff, Adam LeMarche,
were at the dining table with their pcs lit up, and there were
junior staffers hanging back at the entryways.

The president, dressed now in cords and a red flannel shirt,
came to his feet to greet the women, and he bowed a little to
Toni as he took her hand.

"Thank you for coming this morning, Mrs. Schofield," the
president said. "It's very kind of you. And all you've done, I've
been told, very kind of you, and much appreciated."

Toni appreciated the attention and stepped back beside Long
John like a girl with her father.

The First Lady also went forward to shake Toni's hand. The
two women were a contrast in size and manner—the delicate
brunette and the authoritative and towering Connie Jay.

Jack, waiting for the welcoming to pass, aimed to steer the
conversation to his way of thinking. His family was about to go at
risk, and he wanted the president to be outright about his support. It wasn't that Jack doubted the Jays' loyalty. It was that he
wanted certainty that he was working to help a man who could
be helped.

Joe Friar began the meeting by getting to the point.

"There's been an opportunity now to present your thoughts
to the president in full, Mr. Secretary," he said to Long John.
"And we want you to know we're in agreement."

"You mean we go to Schofield?" Jack asked, ticking off his
points with the precision of accusations. "I go to Schofield in
Moldova—" Jack corrected himself, "I, along with Mrs. Schofield, go to Colonel Schofield, and we get his statement to use
against Garland and General Sensenbrenner?"

Joe Friar nodded.

"And," Jack moved to his second recommendation, "we assume Garland is going to get the cabinet and the House vote, so we look to holding him up in the Senate. Jean holds him in the Senate with what she can rally from her side of the aisle and what you can offer from your side."

Joe Friar said, "It's what we can do just now, until we get more information."

"And," Jack continued to point three, "we offer the vice presidency to Luke Rainey. Jean and Sue—today—go to Rafi Ros-Rosario and offer the vice presidency to Luke Rainey. You're agreed on that?" Jack asked. "The Florida machine is being invited in?"

The First Lady took a big breath and touched her husband's arm.

The president jerked alert. "Yes, Governor," the president said. "The Speaker . . ."

The president let his sentence fall off.

Connie Jay finished for him, "We're fine with Luke Rainey." Then she explained why in self-justifying detail. "He's always been a favorite at the White House. He stood with us on all the big fights on the Hill. He's raised as much money as anyone for the funds. And he was so good to help the president last Sunday in Miami."

Jack didn't care about Rainey's credentials for the Democratic Left, and neither, truth be told, did the Jays. Instead Jack couldn't resist spelling out the jeopardy here. "You're offering a lot of clout to the Florida machine," he said.

"Yes, Jack," Connie Jay said impatiently. Her eyes flashed on Jack and then on Jean.

Jean responded to her best friend, "We think we can handle the governor of Florida, don't we, Connie?"

"*You* can," Connie Jay teased back, with the dig at Jack.

Jack pushed the First Lady harder. "And you're agreed that we go to Gus Keebler. Tonight. In Yuma, and tell him the story.

Knowing he's going to put it out on television?"

Connie Jay made a face at Keebler's name. Jean exhaled a guttural sound of disgust. The First Lady and Jean reviled Keebler as a misogynistic bully, and they weren't going to hide it even for the president.

Joe Friar said, "We understand. What is it you want us to say?"

"That you're backing us all the way," Jack answered quickly. "That we're not going to go out there and get left out. That when it gets nasty—because it is going to get nasty—then you're going to get nasty, too. We're hitting back at the White House, at Quinn Roosevelt's apparatus and Sonny Pickett's apparatus and Jesus Magellan's, too, and all the rest of that rough bunch in your party—and Garland's not going to roll over if he figures it out. Or his boy Roosevelt does."

"We get it, Governor," Joe Friar said to Jack. "You don't have to like us to help us."

"And I don't like your rough bunch," Jack said, "and you don't like the rough bunch in my party, if we've got any still standing. That's not what I'm asking. We're volunteering. Are you asking for volunteers?"

Connie Jay tried, "My husband's taking the responsibility, if that's what you mean." She was not pleased to be shoved around by Jack's rhetoric. She reached for her husband's hand, then drew back and said, "What else do you need to know?"

Jack liked that Connie Jay was irked. She wasn't going to promise more than she could deliver. He decided to ask for more.

"We lose the cabinet vote today, right? And we lose the House tomorrow, right?" Jack asked.

"They're gone," Friar said.

"That's what we figured," Jack replied. "It comes to the Senate. How many of your side can you deliver to Jean in the Senate? To get us to the weekend. To stall the vote at least until the weekend. How many?"

Friar turned his palms up. "I've been on the phone . . ."

"How many?" Jack insisted.

"Eight for certain," Joe Friar said, glancing at the pc on the table and up at Adam LeMarche.

Jean didn't hide her disappointment. "Just eight, Joe? I can get sixteen or more of my people, perhaps more if Brownie McDonald stays in the hospital."

"Or we keep him there," Sue quipped.

"Eight," Joe Friar repeated.

The president's face revealed no reaction to the fact that of the sixty-eight senators of his own party—most of whom he'd campaigned for—only the two from Michigan and six others were reliable in the crisis.

"All right, eight is what I'll take for now," Jean said. "I've got work to do before we get to the Senate floor anyway."

"I know we're not offering you much," Friar said. "I can hope for more if I get more time on the phones. And . . . I wish it was more, Senator."

Jean addressed Connie Jay. "It's more than you started with on the National Refugee Act and all the rest of it you got past me."

Connie Jay didn't smile.

The president came out of his peculiar silence to ask Toni, "Please, Mrs. Schofield, you haven't asked any questions. You're going so far for us. Isn't there anything we can do for you?"

It was a most considerate remark, and Jack honored the president for thinking of Toni's feelings in the middle of all this horse trading. Jack liked the president for his manners, and decided he wanted to help the man regardless of how shaky he was.

To get Garland, Jack thought. *I want to get Garland.*

"No, thank you," Toni told the president, "except, you can

help my brother-in-law, can't you? From what we've learned, he's only obeyed orders so far. I'm sure he wouldn't go farther. He's a loyal American—and he lives for the army, and for the defense of his county. He . . ."

Toni was struggling to keep her statement explicit. Her face was all pain.

The president came to her rescue. "I can do a deal for him, Mrs. Schofield. And you tell him that for me, will you?"

Jack didn't want to break off the meeting without one last try at clarity.

"Mr. President, we're going out today. I'll be back here Friday morning. With Schofield's statement. Is that right with you?"

"You mean, Jack," the president replied with sudden candor, "will I use Schofield's statement to stop the challenge? And the answer is that I will do whatever it takes to carry out the duties of my office. That is what we're arguing over, isn't it? If I'm able to do my duty? And I am able."

Jack couldn't hope for more. The man's voice was fragile, and he looked as if he were wasting away in the cheeks, but he'd said the right thing about duty.

"Thank you, Mr. President," Jack said. "Friday morning it is. All of us back here."

26 Wednesday Afternoon, the White House

The White House air-conditioning was acting up, just a little, and Quinn Roosevelt ordered it shut off for repairs sometime around noon. He also ordered every one of the six dozen sealed windows in the West Wing pried wide open.

Garland liked the prankishness of the idea and teased Roosevelt, "It's a Galveston day in here already. Shame we can't dig a pit in the garden and rack up some real meat. Wouldn't a whiff of barbecue finish off what's left of their gentle little Yankee stomachs?"

Roosevelt shrugged.

"No, no, it's sufficient," Garland judged.

These climate arrangements were for the cabinet meeting that was called for three-thirty. By then the West Wing would have heated up like a bog, the Cabinet Room would resemble a sauna, and there was going to be a new national standard for sweating out a vote.

Garland had been sweating out his vote getting since dawn on a most blazing hot and humid day along the mid-Atlantic coast—with thunderstorms expected around dusk on the Potomac.

Garland was having fun, yes, but he was working hard, too—aiming to squeeze an entire presidential campaign into about nine hours of photo ops jumping out of Marine One before he came back for the cabinet vote.

At dawn, he'd lifted off in his sleek Osprey from the South

Lawn and raced into the red rays over the black ocean to land on the supercarrier *Theodore Roosevelt*, just sailed from Norfolk, to the roaring cheers of the crew, the orange juice toasts of the officer cadre, and the live camera feeds of the cable news. Then he was off again to the Sojourner Truth Community Preventive Health Clinic in Baltimore, where on live TV for the network morning shows he pulled on an apron and dished out scrambled eggs and buttered pieces of home-baked bread to a line of preschoolers and their siblings, who sang for him, "The Eyes of Texas Are Upon You." Then he flew to Washington's Crossing State Park in Pennsylvania, along the rye fields and rushing current of the Delaware River, where he jogged over to a Victorian gingerbread house and called upon Mrs. Joycelyn Montana, who'd just come home from the hospital with quadruplets. Garland explained to the local TV morning show hosts that Mrs. Montana had sent the White House a birth announcement the week before in which she'd promised to name two of her babies for Shy and Iphy. Garland said, "It isn't enough to cross rivers or kiss babies anymore, I need to store up the treasures we receive from heaven."

By eleven-thirty, Garland was showing what a Texas politician can do on the campaign trail if he has an aircraft that can fly five hundred kph and land anywhere. He'd stopped at a truckers' café outside Orange, New Jersey, where he'd answered questions about this morning's trade war with France—"I don't like to pay all that much extra for French champagne, do you?"— and then stopped again at a nineteen-foot-wide appliance store beside a parking lot in Fort Lee, New Jersey, where he'd answered questions about his budget. The store just happened to be so close to the national business cable studio that Garland was able to dash onto the set and give a two-minute live interview that was meant both to speak to his father's worldview ("My daddy's always said to buy bonds in all weathers and especially when there's a sale") and to hedge the hard questions about last evening's massacre at Treasury ("For now, I'm handling Treasury personally"). And then, lifting over the George Washington Bridge and racing down the Hudson to land at the heliport off the World Trade Financial Center, Garland had picked up New York's mayor and immediately directed Marine One to hop over to Queens, to the stables at Belmont Park.

"I first aimed to eat at the Waldorf like a proper chief executive," Garland had told the wall of cameras and bevy of Queens politicians that awaited him, and then he'd mounted a sorrel mare and remarked, "but every time we come into town, there's a traffic jam. The next best thing I could think is to have a hot dog out here with champions and take me a little saddle time." Garland pointed at Manhattan's spires in the hazy sunshine. "And maybe get some of those folk to set aside their worries for an afternoon and come out and enjoy a pretty pony."

By 3 P.M., Garland's campaign had returned to the White House via a half-hour stop at Potomac County's Burning Tree country club (where he'd had a lime soda with Sonny Pickett at the clubhouse). In the day's work so far, Garland had left behind him a score through the media markets of seven states and the District.

By three-thirty he'd cleaned up and changed his clothes, and, in a Sea Isle cotton white shirt and one hundred percent cotton navy slacks and a hand-painted silk tie, with handmade half boots, he was ready to go to work on the cabinet votes.

The Twenty-fifth Amendment was most serious business to Garland—this was his World Series—and therefore, following his good instincts, he was treating it as a great game.

The cabinet officers were waiting for Garland as punctual as NASA.

"We'll need some large pitchers of iced tea," Garland told the steward as soon as he walked into the long, steamy, low-lit Cabinet Room, "and a tray of iced-up glasses with lemon and lime twists and some mint leaves." He cooled his face with one of the little Oriental fans he'd fetched out of the White House vault. "And get a fan going, one of the big ones that rotates," he added.

Garland looked over the melting faces—seven men and seven women in the cabinet, nineteen aides of many stripes—as they all tried a smile at him.

"Mr. President, good to see you," began the tanned, athletic Rocky Kahn, Harvard '76, as he rose from the leather-upholstered chair beside Garland's. With Secretary of State Cal Mooney too sick to serve—State was the senior department, and Mooney, until he resigned, was fifth in line to the presidency—Rocky Kahn, as deputy secretary of state, was taking it upon himself to head up the headless cabinet.

Garland beamed at Rocky, whom he liked a great deal as a manager of all those chatty embassies out there. "Yeah," Garland returned.

Then again Garland was most cordial all around, shaking hands and exchanging pleasantries with President Jay's potentates as he made his way to his seat—and handing them each one of the delicate Oriental fans.

Garland was especially gracious to the seven female executives, who were usually led by the outspoken EPA boss, botanist and longtime Jay confidante Doctor Jennifer Choco. However, Jen Choco had resigned in April to take charge of the World Bank, and since Garland had not yet sent a replacement nomination to the Hill, the deputy administrator, Sacramento farmer Lisa Alwyn, sat in EPA's place.

This vacancy meant the United Nations representative, famously tough-minded Doctor Goldie Klingelhofer, former NIH director, former New York governor, was the instinctive leader of the females, if they'd follow her.

"I had a chance to send my congratulations to General Sensenbrenner last night," Doctor Klingelhofer told Garland as he shook her hand. "I like that man," she added.

"I'd hoped you would," Garland said.

Quinn Roosevelt caught his boss's glance and tapped his throat. *No choke,* Garland thought. *All's well so far,* he thought.

As Garland reached the presidential chair, he was bothered by déjà vu. He was thinking, *What is this? Some room I've seen in some movie? Iphy'll know,* he thought.

"Excuse me," Garland said to his officers, who were murmuring among themselves. He strolled to the north wall, to the fireplace and the portrait of Woodrow Wilson, and looked back down the longboat shape of the table, the drapes wafting in the hot breeze, the limp flags, and the ladies and gentlemen in light print dresses and bright white shirtsleeves. Then he told his aide to give him his wife on the cell phone.

Immediately the call was placed and within moments Garland had the connection in his hand; he huddled with the bust of Benjamin Franklin in the niche.

"I've got this puzzle bothering me," Garland started to his wife, and then he explained to her that he'd seen this room somewhere before. Had he dreamed it? Or was it a movie?

"What's that?" Iphy asked back. She was signing her book on Chicago's Fifth Avenue as part of her day-long campaign trail up the Mississippi River valley—Vicksburg, East St. Louis, Chicago, then deep into Jay country at a PTA meeting among the Detroit palaces in Auburn Hills, Michigan—and she sounded distracted. "You sound a little irritable, dear. You all right?"

"I just wanted to know the name of the movie I'm thinking of, if it is a movie. It bugs me. You see"—he glanced over his shoulder at the cabinet—"their faces are flushed. Sleeves rolled up. No one smoking—but they're fidgety."

"*Twelve Angry Men,* with Henry Fonda," Iphy answered, "is that it?"

"Yes, yes. I love you," Garland told her.

Garland walked back to his chair. Quinn Roosevelt was signaling from the doorway that he wanted to let the media in for photographs. Garland held up his hand to have them wait.

"Have you all seen the movie *Twelve Angry Men*?" Garland asked.

The surprise topic worked. Fourteen important heads snapped to alert.

"I was just thinking—I called Iphy to make sure—you know, how the jury goes into a hot room, a lot less comfortable than this one, even today, and they figure they can get this over with. Let's vote the man guilty and get on home. But there's this one fellow, played by Henry Fonda, who says, 'Well, now, I don't know . . .'"

Garland checked the eyes across the table. Five of the cabinet women were sitting opposite him, with Goldie Klingelhofer directly across. Doctor Klingelhofer was smiling like a sunny Siamese cat.

"You do remember that ninety minutes later or so," Garland continued, "this one doubter has changed everyone's mind, and they vote the accused not guilty. Now I was thinking, is that what I want to do? Should I be the Henry Fonda character and start, 'Well, now, I don't know . . .'"

His long and folksy way around his introduction paid off, for everyone in the room ducked their faces and chuckled some.

Garland understood partisan politics so perfectly—make 'em laugh and your nastiest enemy will have to maintain he or she respects you—that he rushed to take advantage of the opening.

"What I've asked you here for today is to help me and the country over a bad patch in the road. I asked the president for his help on Monday night. Mr. Jay was unable or unwilling to come over to my way of thinking. I'm no lawyer, but I think I can make a good witness, and I expect you to ask about my motives. As Iphy would say: my motivation."

Garland broke off before he stayed too long on his point. *Change speeds.*

"Now let's get the working press in and show the country we're doing our duty—and, yes, what I'm going to tell them is that we're here in this room as long as it takes. Until we get a verdict—from fourteen *good* Americans."

The camera crews surged into the room. The iced tea pitchers were passed hand to hand down the table. The TV lights poured ten degrees onto the carpet. The boom mikes hung over the table like panting vultures. The White House press started shouting out their questions.

Garland sat back in his comfortable chair and enjoyed it all. He had his good stuff today. He could feel his slider break. Maybe ten Ks. Maybe thirteen.

"Mr. President, have you heard from President Jay? We understand he's gone to his wife's in Maine. Did you—"

"Mr. President, can you tell us about calls from overseas? We understand the president of Russia called to congratulate you for a 'palace coup.' What did you—"

"Mr. President, what d'ya say at the stock market's plunge? We hear you're handling Treasury yourself. What can you tell the public about—"

"Mr. President, what's going to happen if—"

Shy Garland answered with jaunty wit, all earnest smiles and measured blinks. There was nothing new to say, yet he knew there was always a new way to say the obvious so that they'd love the sound of your voice being evocatively predictable. Garland kept pitching and the press kept eating it up—a president was perpetual copy—and then it was time for serious business, and the media were invited to await the next word on their comfy chairs in the pressroom.

Room smelling of excited humanity, Rose Garden birds chirping and swooping outside the east windows, portraits of Thomas Jefferson (Garland's favorite president) and Sojourner Truth looking on, the acting president began again most soberly, "The Twenty-fifth Amendment charges us with a very explicit responsibility. I have mine. You have yours. Section four states that the president 'shall resume the powers and duties of his office unless the Vice President and a majority of either the principal officers of the executive department or of such other body as Congress may by law provide, transmit within four days to the President pro tempore of the Senate and the Speaker of the House of Representatives their written declaration that the President is unable to discharge the powers and duties of his office.' "

Garland looked across to Goldie Klingelhofer and spoke formally. "As acting president, I challenge President Jay's ability to discharge the powers and duties of his office."

Doctor Klingelhofer nodded. In her crisp rose dress and fine gold jewelry, with her trim white hair and sturdy profile, she could not have been more sobersided if she'd worn angel wings. At seventy-four, a lifelong liberal Democrat, Doctor Klingelhofer had a portfolio stuffed with the achievements of a public career of rectitude and truth. No one doubted her moral courage. She'd faced down more real bullies out of New York's tribal battles than all the others in the room together. And her support in the New York primary had helped Jay defeat Garland by a plurality three years before.

Also crucially, for today's meeting, Goldie Klingelhofer was a medical doctor, trained as a pediatrician, Hunter College and New York Medical School.

Garland knew that if he won over Doctor Klingelhofer, he'd won, for none of the other women officers or deputies—Interior, Commerce, Labor, EPA, Health, Transportation, and Edu-

cation—was potent enough to override her; and the men—
State, Defense, Justice, Housing, HHS, Agriculture, and Energy—without Old Boney's dissonance at Treasury, would follow
Kahn and Learned. It was an open secret that Jay had tried to
name Doctor Klingelhofer for chief justice as the first nonlawyer
on the court in one hundred years, but that she'd deferred to the
Mexican American jurist Maximilian.

Garland was ready to try a new sort of pitch with Doctor
Klingelhofer. He'd throw her a big fat easy open and hope she
didn't bother to clear the fence.

"Doctor Klingelhofer," Garland said, "I need your help especially, because I'm feeling the risk here, and I know we've talked
so helpfully about the sort of mistakes that get made when you
feel at risk. I feel the weight I've put on this table. I feel your
worry as well as my own. I wish there was another way. I wish
you could help me find another way. We've got to find a way out
of this room together."

Goldie Klingelhofer was not so readily disarmed. "Thank you,
Mr. President," she said. She leaned forward and leveled her
gaze into Garland's. "I do want to help—"

Quinn Roosevelt, seated behind his boss, held up one finger
to an aide to ready the forearm-thick portfolios of Jay's medical
records. There was no physician confidentiality now. The
Twenty-fifth didn't ask for it; the Twenty-fifth didn't recognize it.
Had the drafters of the amendment, Bayh and Powell and Brow-
nell, thought that it would be otherwise when the crisis came?
Had the senators such as Bobby Kennedy thought that ethics
could stop so momentous a step as a challenge of a president's
ability to serve? Quinn Roosevelt was ready to provide whatever
was asked for from the Walter Reed files. It would be like peel-
ing an onion, layer upon layer, until what was left was Jay's
troubled soul.

Doctor Klingelhofer continued, "—and I do have questions . . ."

Three hours later, Garland or his staff had answered all possible versions of the same three questions: What is depression? Can it be cured like a gunshot wound or a coronary? Can a recovered patient resume duties as president?

Garland and Roosevelt were shrewd men. They knew that no amount of talk could answer any one of these questions to an exhaustive conclusion. There would always be one more way to argue the case. No one can know another's soul. A soul is beyond the reach of law and order. No one could have written the Twenty-fifth Amendment to anticipate all the nagging doubts that can surround a disabled president. Yet Garland and Roosevelt knew that the cabinet could talk and talk and talk and yet at the end of the talk, no matter what else, the cabinet had to decide. There would be no call for checks and balances, no courts, no doctors' counsel, no White House physician, no help from anyone outside the room, and no time for anything but a vote.

Garland meant to rush the cabinet. They couldn't stop him. He'd fired Old Boney last night and refused to replace him today, so that there would be only fourteen, not fifteen, votes and still they couldn't stop him. He could fire each of them unless they voted for him. But Garland wouldn't go that way. He got the ball and threw it.

"I think we've reached a place where we can't go on," Garland declared at a few minutes before 7 P.M. "It's been seventy-two hours since the president declared he was returning. Forty-eight hours since I asked the president to withdraw his intention and resign. Twenty-four hours since I announced my challenge. We've got twenty-four to go. I'm of a mind to get on with it now."

Garland had said what they'd expected, and still the fourteen weary cabinet officers blinked harder and sighed again.

"I'm going to take a walk," Garland continued. "I want you to vote. Mr. Kahn, I'm appointing you foreman."

"Yes, sir," Rocky Kahn said. Kahn was as smart and able as any man in government, and yet here, up against a one hundred percent political process, he felt ill equipped and lost. He asked most sincerely, "Are there guidelines?"

"No," Garland said. "But if you're asking, I'd like a unanimous verdict. Up or down. The country'd appreciate the clarity. So would our allies. And if you're asking, I'd like a vote by hand."

Goldie Klingelhofer raised her eyebrows. Musclebound Attorney General Sawyer Ruslan in his wheelchair, the only lawyer on the cabinet, made a note on his monitor. The women officers Zvlosky, Awad, Thulborn, von Jablonski, Alwyn, and Redwood looked most uncomfortable. Only bulldog Archie Learned smiled at the thrown gauntlet.

Garland had made his point, and continued, "But if you try a secret ballot, then that's your decision. I'll say this, I wouldn't recommend it. My daddy says that hanging an outlaw in private don't pay."

No one smiled, not even Garland. He thought, *Okay, walk the walk,* and then he stepped through to the Roosevelt Room, where Quinn Roosevelt awaited him with a big glass of lemonade.

The Roosevelt Room was empty except for Garland, Roosevelt, and the omnipresent Diana, who'd followed her boss out of the Cabinet Room.

Garland was in a philosophical mood and strolled to the blank fireplace to prop himself on his elbow. Sipping the lemonade, he asked Roosevelt, "How do you think it's going?"

"As we expected. She said. He said. They said. Round and round. They don't like the Walter Reed jargon. Hypomania and like that. But who does?"

Garland hummed. "What do we have from the polls?"

"More than the overnights?" Roosevelt said. He moved over

to a blank monitor and tapped up his security screens—opening windows on most secret information. He quickly set aside what they'd had that morning from the network polls on the challenge—with five for, two against, and three silent. "We've got a flash from our people on the coast at noon their time. Eight hundred and sixty respondents, registered voters. On trust, you beat Jay forty-five to thirty-five."

"How about the coup question? You asked it, yeah?"

" 'Is this a coup d'etat?' you mean?" Roosevelt rolled his right hand out. "Seven say yes. Two say you're Saint Patrick himself."

Garland grinned. The public knew, the public always knew. You don't govern by polls, but don't claim you don't care. What Garland cared about was that the polls were in on this with him. They knew what he was doing, and, if they weren't ready to approve, they weren't screaming uncle.

Garland asked about the cabinet. "You want to give odds?"

"No, but I'll say we've not got old Goldie by the short hairs."

"I don't think she's negative," Garland said. "I think she'd love to get some soup up for poor Teddy and ask him how he feels, but we didn't build that in, did we? She's got to allege out loud that a sob story like Teddy can pop a miracle pill in the morning that gets him to just ripe old grumpy and then he can go out and lead any puppy anywhere."

"She'll vote present on us, you mean?"

"I figure I finessed that dodge," Garland said. "I hope I did. Boy, this is tight, you know."

Roosevelt heard Garland's anxiety and wanted to ease it. "We're doing what we have to, Mr. President."

"Well, sometimes I think we should just go ahead and take him out. Poor Teddy this, poor Teddy that. The guy's a loser. He's a broken little loser, and he's trying to hold on to what he's lost. Take him out and lose him."

Roosevelt sounded the sober note. "We did discuss it."

"But I don't think you believed it," Garland observed. "FA-THER'S DAY. I don't think there was one of you at the table who believed we were going to do it. Hank's the only one of you who took it seriously. I was right to recommend we ready the option. I was right. You don't go into a thing like this unless you're ready to go all the way if you have to."

Roosevelt said, "We all understood—it wasn't only Hank—that it would be dangerous for the country if we weren't ready to cut this off, at some point . . ."

"With the market down eleven percent in two days, you mean, and that blood on the Street you talked about."

"It's worse to see than I figured it'd be," Roosevelt admitted. "Those guys in New York today looked angry at us. We can't let this go on long."

"Rough, it's all rough," Garland judged. "And to have to beg that sad-eyed gang in there. That we have to beg them to save the country from . . . that we have to beg them to dump a man so dead in the water the body's not going to float . . . that we have to—"

"I'm sympathetic."

"I'd just like to . . . I'd like to . . ." Garland was thinking about Sensenbrenner. Would Sensenbrenner take the order to go? He'd taken the order to get ready to go. But go? Maybe not. Could he give the order? No. Not now. *Keep talking. Keep up the attack.*

"You all right, sir?" Roosevelt asked.

"A little tired in the teeth, like my daddy says." Garland drank more lemonade. He felt like the accused chatting with his mouthpiece. As if he were the question. As if the cabinet wanted to convict him. It made him mad to beg. It was a character flaw. He knew about it, and he didn't worry about it. He hated begging—from others, from himself. Begging was slavery and slavery was death, and Garland hated it.

"You know," Garland started again, "those guys did get one thing right with their Twenty-fifth . . ."

"How's that?"

"They made it so you've really got to want it." Garland was trying to cheer himself up. "A herd of walleyed longhorns and gaggle-toothed black bears would be easier to drive than that gang of do-gooders in there . . . I mean, shoot, I haven't talked that fast and loose since I asked Daddy for my first car—a 1965 Corvette Stingray, baby blue."

Quinn Roosevelt liked his boss's sense of humor and laughed to cheer them both up. "Yeah."

"You stay with them. I'm going to stretch my legs."

"Roger that," said Roosevelt.

"And when you send for me, have Rocky and Archie stay on, and have Sonny and Jesus come in here on the double. And Billy Wheat, if we can get him away from that gorgeous troublemaker he married—find him anyway and tell him he can just call in. And Hank, get him back from the TV studio or wherever they've got him talking that terrible French of his. I want Hank here. I want to hear if Hank's still scared I'm going to lose my cool and go for FATHER'S DAY."

"You want to make old Hank sweat?" Roosevelt teased about his rival. "Just go vacant on him again, you know, when you start to repeat yourself."

"You mean Get-Rope Mad?" Garland asked.

Roosevelt laughed again. Get-Rope Mad. Only the son of Lynch Garland could imagine how mad Get-Rope Mad was.

"Jesus is the man we need on our side now. I want to roll right into the House vote tomorrow," Garland ordered, "and I want to hear Jesus giving his leadership their marching orders."

Roosevelt made the note. Garland was calling together most of EXCOM on the double. Everyone but Ben Mica, who'd flown out to Edwards Air Force Base for the shuttle landing Thursday in California. And Sensenbrenner, who'd gone on to the NATO meeting at London.

"I've changed my mind about Friday," Garland said. "I don't like hanging around the White House while the Hill chews it over. I want out of town. If Jay's out of here, then I am, too."

"Sounds right." Roosevelt asked as he scratched a note, "You want to go tonight?"

"Yeah," Garland said, nodding toward the Cabinet Room. "Soon as we can lose them and talk over tomorrow with Jesus, unless . . ."

He let go the thought that the cabinet might vote against him.

"Call Iphy's people and have her ready for me to pick up in One. Houston by way of Detroit. I'll lift off, what? About ten or so our time and get to her about midnight."

Garland enjoyed his notion. "Me and Iphy at home. I think it feels right. Not to be here while the Hill votes. Teddy in Maine, and me at Daddy's. You like it, Q.?"

Roosevelt put the spin on Garland's inspiration. "What matters is that Texas will love it."

Garland, hearing the positive, speculated ahead. "Just a quiet little Inaugural Ball for about two thousand on Saturday night at Daddy's. Pickup. Come runnin' at sundown. A right friendly fandango."

"I'll get an advance team down there with you, sir," Roosevelt said, making more notes. "You want to do television when you get into Houston tonight? Late, it'll be late, but maybe for their morning news, and across to the coast."

"We'll see," Garland said, and then he didn't want to speculate anymore. He wanted to wait out the verdict on his own.

Garland walked out to the Rose Garden. He gave a high sign to Special Agent in Charge Jude Bruno and the rest of his personal bodyguard and then slipped to the side, toward Nixon's giant sequoia, where he stopped with a view of the Washington Monument.

Those thunderstorms were coming in from the west and south. The air was thicker and cooler. The gusts were turning over the leaves on the limbs. The light turned greenish blue. There'd be a deluge here in minutes. But for now there was claw lightning across the river. And those thunderheads were as big as the Rockies. Garland watched the flash, then the flash again. The claws were tantalizing. The gusts flapped his tie and cooled his brow. Another flash, and then a triple crack—*boom!*

A special agent came up on silent feet. "Mr. President. Mr. Roosevelt is calling for you, sir. He says it's good news."

Garland knew he'd won the cabinet.

Those burly cobalt clouds, they were applauding. There were baby twisters out there. The sky smelled like a lake. The claw lightning scratched Virginia. Behind him, a big brave crow dropped off of JFK's magnolia and swooped toward Jefferson's mounds, riding the gusts.

Garland thought, *Breaking news. Overload.*
Time for the Hill.
Climb, crow, climb.

27 Wednesday Evening, Yuma, Arizona

Long John Longfellow and Senator Nan Cannon arrived in Yuma in the late rays of a blazing day that had sent a dust cloud out of the desert like a looming yellow blizzard.

Here, at Yuma, along the salty tail of that magnificent beast called the Colorado River, four great states, California, Baja, Arizona, and Sonora, crunched together at a barren crossroads of hungry canals. Water wasn't beneficial, it was religion for the pampered Imperial Valley to the west, for the desperate Canal Central south of the border.

Long John had often toured out here twenty years back as secretary of defense, from Luke Air Force Base up the Gila River to the Yuma Proving Ground up the Colorado to the old Marine Corps air station beside the terminal to the passel of gunnery, parachute, and air combat ranges over on the California side, but he didn't recall it so hot and stark.

But then again, he knew, he was much older and the desert never aged—naked bluffs, scrub ironwood, mesquite trees, and a parched uniformity that made you rub your hands together and swallow repeatedly to make sure you were still alive.

Downtown Yuma showed the power of money to transform any part of the planet into a hardwired oasis, and Long John quickly turned to his hard-minded business.

He hadn't come to admire the desert, he'd come to kick dust on Yuma County's favorite citizen.

At the brand-new brassy hotel, overlooking the border bridges west, there was a message from Gus Keebler that he would have a car sent round at six-thirty, if that was convenient.

Long John called Nan Cannon's room and said, "He's on defense already, that's why he didn't meet us himself at the airport. This isn't a formal fellow. This is a man who carries pistols to take out the trash. He's being cagey here, because he's not figured out why we're here."

"I don't know why not. I told his boy Friday that we wanted to talk about Garland." Nan Cannon sounded dictatorially annoyed. She and Long John had rested on the seven-hour flight, but they were still jet-lagged and their clocks were off. "I named the subject—the Twenty-fifth. I named you. I named my credit card number." There was a tinkle of ice cubes as Nan admired her vodka tonic. "I couldn't have been more obvious if I'd sent my best teddy to his launderer."

Long John liked Nan Cannon. If he was ten years younger— make that three—and still had his prostate, he would have made a pass at her. No. But he would've laughed harder at her cracks. He found her funny for a seventy-year-old demagogue—just hilarious.

She'd flown from National to Bar Harbor that morning with a briefcase full of facts on both sides of the contest—the Walter Reed files on Jay that the cabinet was using to decide, picked up at the request of the First Lady; and the FTC files on Augustus "Gus" Keebler, billionaire celebrity and big mouth, picked up by her own staff. She'd done all that traveling for the emergency of the Twenty-fifth. Yet the first thing she'd said when she'd been told she was flying out again with Long John for Yuma was, "I didn't bring the right shoes. Good shoes are better than sex, right, old man?"

At the time, Long John had just laughed in dumbstruck admiration.

But now he was ready to parry her double entendre.

"It's hot in here," Long John complained about the severely air-cooled and perfumed suite of faux French furniture. He repeated himself, looking for affection anyway.

"Wash up," Nan recommended. "We've got more'n an hour until Keebler gets his pots and pans clean, and I'm going to spend it in the tub." She laughed. "It *is* hot, John."

"Yes," Long John said, and then he let romance go for the glimpse he got of the big TV monitor in the wall. Muted on the 5 P.M. local news, there was Garland's handsome head in the Cabinet Room. His smile was as big as the Hoover Dam.

Long John didn't have to turn on the volume to recognize why they were interviewing a nodding Rocky Kahn and a shrugging Archie Learned or what the raised eyebrow of Sawyer Rus-

lan in the Roosevelt Room meant about the day's events. Or why
Goldie Klingelhofer was making a speech on the White House
porch. *Talk, talk, Goldie,* Long John thought, *you know you
bought a bad package.* He'd known Goldie since she was in her
last year as the governor of New York and Jack was in his first
year in Maine. She was naturally suspicious. She was not easy.

Yet Garland had pushed past her. It looked like a sweep.
Garland had his challenge. The ninety-six-hour clock was shut
off. The twenty-one-day clock was started up.

Garland wouldn't wait twenty-one hours. He'd go for the
House tomorrow morning. And when he got the House, he'd go
for the Senate. Long John knew he would, because that's exactly
what he'd do. Take the Hill by storm and spin. Fate of the
nation. Faith of the Constitution. Integrity of the presidency.
Give us Garland or give us—fright.

Long John told the hotel operator he wanted a connection
made to Jean's Hart office. The operator gushed, "How do I do
that?"

Long John, in a temperamental mood and not giving much of
a fig that the operator didn't know who he was, said, "It's your
government. Washington, D.C. The Hart Office Building. Senator Jean Motherwell Longfellow. Leader of the Republicans,
what's left. Please!"

Presently Jean's very dexterous assistant Marc, manning the
phones round the clock now, burst, "Yes, sir!" and patched Long
John through to Jean's hotel suite in Miami.

Jean wasn't in—she and Sue had gone to the beauty salon off
the lobby—but Ellen Quick was, and she promised a callback
within moments.

"Please put her on," Long John complained.

Ellen Quick ran to the elevator bank with the cell phone. "Is
Keebler going to see you before his show?" she asked on the
ride down.

"Looks like it. He's sending one of his armored cars. I'm actually looking forward. It's so hot here I want to try one of his famous pickled jalapeño eggs. Might make me sweat. I can't sweat. I could pass away dry as a pinecone."

"Please, Mr. Longfellow," Ellen pleaded. There was footfalling and bell pinging. Within moments Jean was on the phone.

"What's this about jalapeño eggs?" Jean demanded.

"Curiosity," Long John teased. He felt better now, Jean was paying attention. He loved Jean. She was so much like Louisa it hurt sometimes. Didn't Jack know that?

"How are you, then?" she asked.

"Heard from Jack?"

Jean sighed. She was seated in a fantasy beauty salon in Coral Gables and looking at a decor somewhere between the tropics and a sculpture gallery. After three crazy days without more time than to bathe, she was actually feeling pretty and clean and even glamorous. And her mother was on the salon's phone line with opinions in all directions.

Yet now Jean had to think about Jack again.

"He called an hour ago, when he heard the news that Garland had the cabinet. Fourteen to nothing. Or so they claim."

"Where is he?"

"London, he said, at Gatwick. Refueling for Romania. He said his ETA was five A.M. our time—I don't have a clue what time that is with you or me—and that he planned to stop at Bucharest before going into Occupied Moldova."

"How'd he sound?" Long John tried.

"Like a man on a European junket with his mistress, you mean?" Jean laughed nastily. "He sounded tired and—you know, captain's on the bridge."

"I've been fretting about his part, Jeannie. You should know."

"I know," Jean said, not wanting to debate the peril to her Timmy. Jack had lifted off in a Philip Morris Gulfstream V jet

with Toni Albanese, Tim, and Anna Hrbek. Jack hadn't waved
good-bye, but Tim had kissed her and said he loved her, and the
thought of the scene hurt her heart.

"I know," she repeated. She swallowed her anxiety when she
asked, "What're you going to say to Keebler, have you decided?"

"I'm going to scare him."

"Is it going to work with him?" Jean asked.

"Your colleague the distinguished senator from Indiana
thinks he'll serve up fresh corn and fear-mongering. I figure he's
been waiting to hear about EXCOM most of his adult life."

"You think he knows about EXCOM?" Jean was startled.

Long John corrected, "No, no, he doesn't work that way.
Keebler, and men like him, don't really know anything. He
works by selling. He sells you whatever he wants you to buy. The
weaker the product, the better the selling. The less you want it,
the harder he wants you to have it. He's a charlatan's charlatan,
and he likes his snake oil served hot."

"EXCOM's a lot to sell," Jean said.

"Keebler's passed out his paranoid hallucinations for so long,
EXCOM will come to him like a surprise birthday present."

"I think he's disgusting," Jean said, "a misogynistic, cruel,
mean, stupid man—who uses his billions to make sick jokes and
spread outrageous bigotry—and I wish we didn't have to . . ."

"We need him, Jean. He's our demagogue tonight. If I can
hook him. If he's up to a whopper like EXCOM."

Jean said, "He still gives me the creeps."

"What's Garland going to have when he hears Keebler,
then?" Long John added, "You *will* wait up to hear how it goes."

"You sound like Mother!"

"How is she?" Long John asked. He was afraid of Jean's
mother.

"She's on the other line," Jean said, "and she says you should
get your rest."

"Plenty of rest coming on," Long John mocked.

"LJ!"

Long John smiled. Imagine such a healthy girl coming from such a dragon lady as Fiona Motherwell. "Tell me about Rafi. Has he figured out what you want yet?"

"I didn't tell him," said Jean.

"What's he said to you?" Long John asked.

Jean paused with her private thoughts. Then she conceded, "We have a dinner and dance date. Last year's sexiest man alive is taking me dancing. I figure I'll mention EXCOM during a rhumba!"

Long John got off the line and lay down on the bed to watch TV. *Good for Jeannie,* he thought. Rafi Ros-Rosario drove Jack wild with jealousy. At the governors conference last year, Rafi and Jean had danced like professionals, and Jack had turned purple.

The next thing Long John knew, there was banging somewhere overhead, and it was Nan at the door, and he was groggy and careless on his way to the toilet. "Okay!" he cried, as he flipped open the door.

Dressed in Washington chic, black cocktail dress, a cove of pearls, and dainty Italian shoes, Nan swept in with the concierge. "We thought you'd passed out on us."

Long John called from the bathroom, "Takes me half an hour to do my business!"

In another half hour they were being chauffeured in a white Cherokee racing north on Route 95 toward the slumping shoulders of the Chocolate Mountains.

The novelty of the ride was that Keebler had sent along four members of his private motorcycle guard to escort the Cherokee, and Long John already had the feeling he was being dragged onto Keebler's stage set.

The exhibition continued at Keebler's ranchero. Keebler was

the grandest of the Border billionaires, and he'd raised new buildings to match his new wealth. Down the road was his industrial college park, where they'd built a theme park to the R&D enterprise that had started Keebler's wealth—since Gus Keebler, celebrity, was also Gus Keebler, chairman of the board of the big-cap Yuma Corporation (YUMA). This was the man who was rebuilding the border—satellite village by satellite village.

On the drive out, they'd passed a series of satellite villages for Yuma Corporation's workforce. And here, just off the crossroads between the mountains, was Keebler's hacienda: the main house, the ranch house and horse barns, several guest houses—and then, in the soft bowl, the low-slung television studio that Keebler had built for his success on cable.

All of the architecture was the unique Yuma Corporation combination of adobe brick, glass, and luxury that made the whole border look like a chain-link fence of futuristic rancheros—Levittown in Mexico, they mocked.

Because tonight was a television broadcast night, there were the usual six tourist buses brought in from as far away as San Diego, Las Vegas, and Phoenix with tonight's studio audience of twelve dozen.

The lucky winners of the tickets were being feted to an outdoor snack party, with singing cowboys, horse tricks, and nonalcoholic beverages—beer having been banned since the last potshot at Keebler.

Nan Cannon noted the pistol on every man's hip—the routine costume for the audience—and tried to joke, "This is so savage they must be insane."

Long John shrugged. It was also so perfect that it looked as if it had been built in the last twelve minutes. The newspapers called it Fort Keebler. Its precinct stretched tens of thousands of acres into the hills, for Keebler was buying off the Yuma Proving Ground. He might already own the Chocolate Mountains; nobody outside the Defense Department was sure.

Tonight at eight o'clock local time, eleven o'clock New York time, Gus Keebler owned a significant market share of America's late-night attention.

Southwest Cooking with Sheriff Gus Keebler was the reigning phenomenon on the cable.

There was no explaining it except by admitting that America liked to eat good food and the man was a good cook. He was also a reactionary crank, but then so was half of the cable audience. He was also a billionaire who had openly bought himself election to the Yuma County sheriff's office, but then the cable audience also appreciated a politician who could pay for himself.

What made Keebler famous was none of the obvious showbiz palaver, however; it was because he liked to talk about politics while he prepared his recipes; and he was a very good talker.

The rest of Keebler's outsized reputation resulted from his permitting his audience to come pistol-packing in the Arizona Republican style, a quirk that had rocketed him from a notorious Arizona real estate and building magnate to a world-class American demagogue.

Keebler's popularity was also helped by the well-advertised fact that he was the richest native American in modern history— and he was number eighteen overall in the country at last count.

Long John, who enjoyed the weekly show on a monthly basis, was prepared for some version of Keebler's paranoid genius; he was not ready for what he found when he and Nan stepped carefully down two steps into the TV studio.

"Yes, yes, Senator Cannon!" Gus Keebler called out as he raced up from the kitchen set to take Nan Cannon's hand and give a friendly handshake.

"Mr. Secretary!" he addressed Long John, giving a much more relaxed handshake. "Welcome to Yuma County!"

Keebler looked the same in person as on TV, a fifty-six-year-old giant saguaro cactus of a man—tall, broad-shouldered, clean-shaven, long-white-haired, blue-eyed, and burned-skinned—dressed like a prosperous sheriff, with a string tie, lots of turquoise and silver jewelry, and wearing a smile like a smoker's.

Outside the glass wall at the back of the studio was the sinking sun over the Colorado River. Inside the studio Keebler was all manner of graciousness.

"Please, come sit while I finish up here."

"May I call you Nan and John?"

"Do you mind if I finish my tortillas here?"

"Can you join me for supper afterward? . . . Honestly, I have a really great cook over at home. Her name's Rosa Estrada, she learned from her one-hundred-and-six-year-old grandmother down at Lukeville, and can she cook!"

Long John took a seat beside the kitchen table and put up with the palaver until the third round of compliments.

Up till then, the only displays of Keeblerism evident were the two well-known Keebler aphorisms carved into the countertop and kitchen cabinets:

"You don't have to remember the Truth."

"No man opens his door to the sunset."

And then of course over the stove was the carved plaque that had made Keebler famous:

AMERICA NEEDS A NEW CONSTITUTION

Studio aides ran across the set arranging the platters and tidying up around the campfire that was cleverly built beside the kitchen.

The associate's voice came over the loudspeaker. "Gus, we have twenty-one minutes to taping. We're going to bring the audience in. You want your guests for makeup?"

Keebler had his hands in corn flour. He shrugged and looked at Long John.

Then Keebler dropped the sham friendliness and asked the

hard question, "So—you figure you want to go on TV with me tonight. My guests?"

Long John responded bluntly. "Mr. Keebler, we came here because we don't want to go on television."

"Right," Keebler said, staring at Long John.

Long John stared back.

The sheriff's squint was obvious now. His maternal great-grandfather, Yuma County's Sheriff Hooker, had been slaughtered by Apaches in Bell Canyon in 1865. His paternal grandfather, James Lazarus, was turnkey yard boss at the territorial prison. His mother's father, Little Maus, a Quenchan Indian, was a deputy sheriff over in Mexicali. And then there was Gus Keebler himself, sheriff of Yuma County.

"You two done now?" Nan Cannon asked. "Because if you are, I'll make the necessary point that we have business to do. Shy Garland business."

"I'm listening to you," said Keebler.

"No, you aren't," Nan said, "but you'll hear me that Garland is out of control. We have accusations. Lots of them."

"Right," Keebler repeated. He didn't have his famous long-barreled Navy Colt in his hand, he held only a pepper mill, but he was clearly easing into his accustomed role of bully and enforcer.

Long John had come prepared for this flinty know-nothing facade all the while. Keebler's show of welcome had just slowed down the inevitable confrontation.

Long John taunted with rhetoric. "You want the facts? Or you want the truth?"

Keebler came to the front of the counter and leaned against it like a fence post. Except for the logo on the apron—"My Secret Is the Colorado's Sweet Water"—he looked righteous.

"I want you to tell me how you let this country's security get away from you. You were one of my heroes. You and the Great Communicator. But in ten years. Gone. Ten years ago we'd

won—but now—lookit— And the only way to get it back—
lookit—"

"You lookit," Long John cut him off before he started his
spellbinding nuttiness. "I've heard the song too often. Somehow
I believe it less when you say it. You want to worry about what's
gone? You got the time? I don't have that time left me. I keep
fixed on my own."

Keebler tried to get back the conversation. "That's only right
that—"

"What's my own is my Jack and my Jean," Long John declared. "I want the White House for them. And Shy Garland's in
the way. So are you if you keep talking. But I figure you like
being in the way more than you'd like being the top of the next
administration. You're not leaving here"—Long John waved his
walking cane at the glass wall and the searing red sun settling on
the naked clay dunes—"you'll never leave your desert. Never
leave it for anything. No matter how high you climb in the polls.
And why? Got to turn your back when you're president. Turn it a
lot. And you aren't ever going to turn your back again."

"Make a speech, don't you?" Keebler taunted.

"We call it fishing," Long John countered.

"Tryin' to scare me off?" Keebler asked. "Should be advised
that we don't scare off out here."

Long John aimed just to plain scare him. "It's the backshooters you can't scare off, no matter how fancy you talk or how
many pistoleros you ride with." Long John felt casual about his
rhetoric. He knew where he was going and didn't care how he
got there. "World of backshooters and bushwhackers out there
the other side of those hills, and the capital is Washington, D.C.
Backshooters and bushwhackers. You think the couple of shots
they've got off on you make you a politician? Try the Hill. Try
the other side of the river. Try running for any office outside of
jailhouse chef."

Keebler was mad before his hat hit the floor.

"You're not the guest I figured," Keebler said. "Come in here and tell me I best watch my backside. Who the hell are you?"

"A former government official," Long John answered flatly, "and I've just started about watching your backside. And what I've got to say about the acting president of the United States and a gang of public officials calling themselves EXCOM—well, they won't be worrying about which way they come on."

"How's that?" Keebler asked.

Nan Cannon despised Gus Keebler, and she enjoyed herself when she teased, "Oh, John, why don't you give him the ten-minute version?"

Long John tucked his double chins, unflexed his brand-new knees, and agreed with an abrupt nod.

Then he crossed the line between ambitious father and countercoup-master.

For then Long John told the most reckless and explosive demagogue in the country a story so hard to believe that only Gus Keebler would believe it without a single piece of evidence—and only Gus Keebler would repeat it on live television without a pang of conscience.

28 Wednesday Night, Miami, Florida

Jean and Sue arrived at the network studio in their very pricey new dancing gowns—all manner of black, saffron, and rose shades—and they sat happily in the greenroom trying not to crease their silk and taffeta.

The network producer, a tall Jamaican fellow, Joshua Trent,

came in presently to say they would very much like Jean to go on for the second half hour of the show.

"I told you I can only do the first half hour," Jean explained.

"Please, Senators," Trent asked, "we've asked Senator Pickett to come on and he can't make—"

"I'm sorry," Jean said, "I left a dinner party for this, and I can't help you."

Trent looked lost.

Jean didn't intend to give in. She had agreed to do this at the very last moment. And she'd been told she was filling in for Pickett, who was unavailable.

Now Sonny Pickett was coming on, after all.

Jean added firmly, "We have friends waiting for us."

What she didn't explain was that the governor of Florida, Rafael Ros-Rosario, and Sue's natty husband, Jules Swiftsure, were waiting outside in the governor's car. The four had agreed it would be more discreet if the governor wasn't seen hanging out with the putative opposition—including Jules Swiftsure, the chairman of the Florida Republican Party as well as the high roller of the Blackwater Investment Group of Jacksonville.

"I guess I understand," Joshua Trent said, vanishing quickly from the greenroom; however, he was soon quickly back with his boss, the executive coproducer, a sharp-looking young pro named Naomi Alexy.

Naomi Alexy took up the pitch. "We appreciate your plans, but you see, we worry it'll be unbalanced if—"

Jean interrupted, "If Sonny Pickett wants to talk with me on the air, he can phone it in."

Joshua Trent tried, "But please, how can we balance the debate if . . ."

Jean was feeling taken advantage of. Ellen Quick, who'd put off most of the media for days, had begged Jean to do this *Nightline* to keep the groaning National Senatorial Committee chairman Cindy "Cat" Belleau from blowing up. Belleau had been demanding since Tuesday that Jean "display leadership." Of course, Cindy Belleau was also a lackey of the jealous Brownie McDonald, who might or might not be out of his sickbed.

So how did they want Jean to "display leadership"?

Go on live national TV, seven-second delay, and double-talk with Sonny Pickett.

Jean smiled testily at Trent and Alexy, two hardworking pros, and said, "I'm trying to help you. We can do the first thirty minutes. It's late, isn't it? Senator Pickett can fill in for me fairly after I go, I'm sure."

Sue Bueneventura laughed. "Fill in for himself."

The producers left in sighs.

Jean sighed, too. She had so many obstacles ahead of her tonight, it seemed that every bump was a mountain.

And the biggest mountain was Rafi and telling the truth to Rafi and getting Rafi to go along with the deal for Luke Rainey.

Certainly Rafi knew she was here for deal making, but he hadn't rushed her. He was waiting for her to move first.

Everyone was waiting for Jean to move first—her family, the Senate, the network, and Jack!—and what she had to help her was her political intuition and maybe luck.

Joshua Trent soon returned and said it was time to go up to the studio, would Jean and Sue please follow him, adding, "Please watch the cables. They're gummy."

Jean glanced at her expensive shoes. "Oh, great."

A few minutes later, they were up the elevator to the sound stage—the usual filthy chamber of ugly equipment that smelled like cleaning compound and was as overheated as a taxi. Jean despaired for her new dress, and—

Just then the governor of Florida pushed through the sound door from the producer's office, followed close behind by his cue-bald bodyguard. Instantly the atmosphere in the studio changed from sloppy and routine to starstruck. The most powerful man from Jacksonville to Havana had just walked in and taken over the center of attention with his glamour alone.

"Jean, dear, wait," Rafi began, "we have to talk—Sue, you, too—we have to talk before the show . . . your father-in-law's called . . ."

Jean was spun around and took Sue's arm to balance herself. Sue's husband, Jules, hurried into the room as well and gave the sign to his wife that there was important news.

The governor thanked Joshua Trent and the harried Naomi Alexy and asked for a moment with the senators. Everyone on the sound stage stepped back to wait on the presence of Rafi Ros-Rosario.

The governor's overpowering charm was in spite of the fact that he was the elementary Latin lover in a pencil-thin mustache: he looked like a Don Juan tip to toe, five-ten and as tightly wound as a matador, and his voice was deep chocolate and most soothing—but in truth he was a kind, patient, dutiful governor and father.

He was also the smartest politician Jean knew after Long John.

"We knew you wouldn't hear in time," he began to her. "It's Keebler."

Jean blinked.

"Long John Longfellow just called me in the car to alert us about Keebler tonight," he continued. "The Keebler show. It aired the last thirty minutes here. I had my office transmit in a tape of the show. It's dynamite."

Jean, not following entirely about Keebler, did get that Rafi was a little ahead of her about Long John and why she'd come to Miami to see him tonight. "How much do you know?" she asked. "How much did LJ tell you? About Jay and Garland and . . ."

Rafi's smile lit up the sound stage and told Jean that he knew most everything.

"Tell me what LJ said," Jean urged.

"Long John called me a half hour ago," Rafi replied, "right after we dropped you off, to tell me about his meeting with Sheriff Gus Keebler. About tonight's show. About Long John and Nan Cannon going out there to feed Keebler—"

"This is about Keebler or LJ?" Jean asked.

"Both, Jean. It's all on the tape." Rafi took a cassette from his dinner jacket. "Here."

"I don't want to see it, I want to know what Keebler said. What LJ told him to say!"

Rafi rolled his eyes. "Dynamite, just dynamite. He said there's a gang of bushwhackers in the White House called EX-COM. He said they're plotting to steal the presidency. He said Sensenbrenner was in on it with an air cavalry unit ready to attack. He said Garland was a renegade and . . . he called Garland a backshooter."

Jean exhaled. "Shit."

Sue blanched. "Oh, my God."

Jean thought, *Have we gone too far? Have we? No? Giving it to Keebler? Have we gone too far?*

"He actually said 'backshooter'?" Jean asked. "He said 'EX-COM,' too?"

Around them the sound stage was reassembling itself for the broadcast. The sound engineer was telling the line producer he needed to test Jean's and Sue's sound levels. The gofer was staring at Rafi's beautiful dinner clothes. A higher network executive, a handsome young Cuban woman, came running up to Rafi. "Governor, are you a guest this evening, too?"

"No, no," Rafi returned, looking to the camera and speaking

directly to the local producer and, through her, to the executive producers back in the Washington studio. "I'd like a chair, here, off camera. The senators and I are just talking." He batted his black eyelashes. "All right for you?"

"Oh, yes," the local woman swooned.

The studio people went into emergency speed. Chairs arrived for Rafi and Jules. Makeup arrived with touch-ups for Jean's and Sue's hair. The locals had an inspiration and switched backdrops, substituting downtown Miami looking toward Little Havana for downtown Miami looking along Biscayne Boulevard. An aide arrived with a tray of iced tea that Rafi was known to drink when speaking on TV. It was all Rafi's ceremonial due—El Presidente Cubano in his glory.

Meanwhile Jean was quizzing Rafi. "What did LJ say to tell me?"

The governor answered, "He said to tell you that Keebler was yesterday's news. He said that you were tomorrow's news."

Jean smiled a little. *A love letter. Dear LJ.*

Jean said, "Keebler's so sick, he's such a crank, a disgusting, bigoted, and cruel crank. I hate using him, having to use him."

Rafi asked, "How much of it is true?"

Jean nodded. *Damn, this is scary,* she thought.

Sue, leaning close to Jean, took up the argument for her friend. "You know all of it's true, Rafi. You know it's why we came down here. Don't fool around with Jean. We came here for your help, because it's all true."

The potentate in Rafi came out just a flick as he leaned forward, eyes down, and let worry cross his face like a cloud across the face of the sun. He was a strong-minded man, and he'd played politics as hard when he was in Washington as he did now that he was decamped in Florida; however, even for Rafi Ros-Rosario the scheme of EXCOM had gone a step too far. It was the talk of Sensenbrenner. It was too far. A Cuban-born American patriot had deep feelings about juntas. Garland had gone too far.

"I'll know what you tell me," Rafi said to Jean and Sue. "But don't wait for me to believe what's on this tape. Keebler's a lying devil. My papa calls him *el Diablorosa.* I can call him worse."

Jean had charge of her thoughts now. Long John had called Rafi and told him about Keebler in order to set Rafi up for the deal. Rafi was not only primed, he was eager to get on with it. And she felt a little anger in him, too.

Jean began, "Yes, Keebler's a liar, but we had to use him. He was the one who could say it so that no one would believe him, yet the White House would know that . . ."

Jean's full answer had to wait, because the tech aides rushed up to plead with Jean and Sue. Please put the earpieces on. Please, we're on the air—right now! Please sit forward. And watch the camera? And speak naturally? And wait for the host down there in the monitor to address them directly? And could they please put on their earpieces?

Jean and Sue sat side by side, and Rafi and Jules sat off camera within arm's length. The senators looked very far from ordinary politicians, but then, they did look grand.

Jean, smoothing down her earpiece, knew what she wanted to do before the signal came. She wanted to shake Rafi's damned self-confidence that he had figured out the whole thing—regardless of what LJ had told him—and that he could somehow get on top of it and manage it.

Self-confidence was Rafi's weakness. It made him a fabulous romancer and campaigner and leader, but it made him a poor tactician in a real fight—a murderous fight.

The TV show began with the usual bumper tunes and logo promotion.

Fifteen feet in front of Jean was a monitor showing the host in Washington. This evening it was the hot young war correspondent Michelle "Mickey" Plumb—the one who'd been shot down over Turkey.

"Rafi," Jean started, taking out her earpiece, speaking sideways, "we want Luke Rainey to take the vice presidency when we force Garland out, you hear me?"

Rafi responded, "Yes."

"We want Rainey ready to go this weekend. For an announcement Friday, when we move to block the challenge on the Senate floor."

" 'We' means you and Sue and the elephant?"

" 'We' means that we left the president at eleven-thirty this morning," Jean said. "The president is onboard. And so's Connie, if you're asking."

"I deliver Luke Rainey to the president's camp by Friday," he posed, "and what do I get?"

Jean laughed and put her earpiece back on. The deal was struck. Or was it? Rafi was the head of the Florida Democratic machine, and Luke Rainey was its crown jewel in Washington. Rafi had everything to gain by putting Rainey into the vice presidency. And there was the obvious possibility that Rafi would become the dark horse Democrat for the Ought-Four nomination.

Jean decided to stay firm and avoid his tricks to charm her into giving away too much.

"No promises," Jean said without caring if he heard her. "Jack said no promises."

"Jack said, did he?" Rafi teased, with some bite. "How is Jack?"

Jean was immediately distracted by the network chatter in her earpiece. The red light was on. The celebrity hostess—Mickey Plumb—was speaking to Jean.

Rafi asked Jean anyway, "And where is Jack in all this? His

father with Keebler and you with me? Where's the great white elephant's great white hope?"

Jean didn't get to answer.

The network's obsessive voice in her ear overpowered her, and she had to listen to Mickey Plumb's easy first question about the cabinet vote. "Did it surprise you it went so quickly?"

Jean answered, "I was surprised the cabinet didn't ask for more facts, weren't you, Mickey?"

Mickey Plumb wasn't a first-team interviewer, but she was a dexterous thirty-six-year-old yellow-haired china doll with a deep voice, no facial tics, and good timing.

Mickey's second question was troublesome. "How do you feel," she intoned in long vowels, "about Shy Garland becoming president without the people getting to vote? I mean, are you comfortable—"

Jean interrupted by shaking her shoulders and starting out weakly, "President Ford served generously following President Nixon's resignation . . ." but then she heard herself being pompous and dropped her chin, speaking right into the camera on rhetorical attack.

"But if you're asking me does it feel good? No, it doesn't. Does it? We voted three years ago. And the man who got more votes in his party's primaries, the man who got the vast majority of votes in the national polling, he's still with us. He's still our president. And all of a sudden we're being told that maybe he isn't our president. It doesn't feel good. I don't feel good about it."

Mickey Plumb's blush deepened. Jean had hit the oratory target. Mickey Plumb asked Sue for her thoughts.

Sue was all liberal highmindedness in a very pretty Blackwater rage. "I want my president back. He's my president, too. I came in with President Jay. I've worked very happily with him for Florida and for the environment. The president stood right with us to defend the Okefenokee . . ."

Jean relaxed at Sue's genius to paint Jay with the martyr's brush. Only four minutes to go and no Sonny Pickett to answer back.

But then the network gang tried an ambush on Jean and Sue by popping up a new window on the interview screen.

Senator Sonny Pickett, all six feet six inches of majority leader, silver white mane flicked over his giant ears, huge teeth snapping at the screen, lit up America with his predatory smile.

Mickey Plumb remarked ceremoniously, "Senator Pickett, thank you for joining us on such short notice. We've just been discussing the cabinet vote this afternoon . . ."

"Very gratifying, and a tough decision," Sonny Pickett said.

Jean thought, *What a pretty jackass you are, Sonny.*

And then Mickey Plumb made a network news maneuver: without changing the pleasant smile on her neatly featured face, she used the question fed to her earpiece by the line producer, and it was a very hostile question.

". . . and I was about to ask Senators Motherwell and Bueneventura if they'd heard the report this evening—just moving on the news wires in the last hour—that Sheriff Gus Keebler this evening claimed that there's a secret working group at the White House in charge of the challenge against President Jay."

Pickett's smile dimmed, and he squinted like a fox.

Jean cut in before Pickett could breathe twice. "I'm surprised to hear that the White House would want to keep anything secret about the challenge, aren't you, Mickey?"

"This is irresponsible trash," Pickett said.

Mickey Plumb, sensing fireworks, asked Jean and Sue, "Do you senators in Florida know anything about a secret working group called EXCOM?"

Sue said, "What's it called again?"

Pickett was rattled. "I have to insist that we quit this. Gus Keebler's an irresponsible tax-cheat and convicted felon. Why should we discuss anything that—"

Jean asked, "Sonny—my distinguished friend, Senator Pickett—have you ever heard of something called"—Jean emphasized—"EXCOM?"

"Don't be trivial, Jean," Pickett snapped.

"I'm only asking to be reassured, Sonny," Jean said, fully in control of how she was baiting him. "I'm as surprised as you. And you know more about what goes on at the White House than—"

Pickett cracked, "Let's not pretend you're some outside innocent, Senator."

Mickey Plumb tried to interrupt. "I was just asking about a sketchy report about—"

Sue shot at Pickett as well, "Innocence we'll leave to the courtroom, Sonny. We're talking about throwing away a good man, and if there's any truth to the White House plotting against the president, then—"

"You two are nursemaids to a three-legged mule," Pickett replied.

Jean wanted to smile but managed to maintain her handsome pout. Sue gave her best shocked incomprehension glance. Rafi squeezed Jean's hand in approval. Jules blew a kiss to his wife.

The firefight was done, though Mickey Plumb tried hard to get one of the three to salvo again. They pulled in their tongues—Pickett even used the "no comment" line—and let the network drone on until the commercial break.

Jean and Sue pulled off their earpieces and waved to the studio booth and got out of the lights.

Jean said, "Boy, do I need a glass of wine, and it better have bubbles!"

In the short time it took to get to the car, they were cruising slowly down Eighth Street, the famous Calle Occho of Miami's Little Havana.

It was a soft sea night, less than a hundred yards from Biscayne Bay, and the street was filled with cruising cars headed for late suppers and the dance clubs. Rafi's long white car was well known, and more than a few folk waved to their favorite governor. At the curb, Jean felt like spinning right across the sidewalk and into the sexily lit up facade of the hottest nightclub in town, named Mayaimi.

There was a little crowd at the ropes, waiting to be admitted, and there was applause for Rafi.

It was like traveling with a movie star, and Jean teased Rafi, "Have they seen you dance, or do they just like the way you dress?"

"It's show business, isn't it?" Rafi said.

They were soon sashaying across the dance floor to their swishy little flamingo-decorated table. The crowd was rich, thick, and lustful. The dance band was loud with plenty of horns, and the late floor show was just getting to its complicated body-beautiful routines.

Jean was so excited by the change in her surroundings, was so pleased to be away from the tangle of Jack and his betrayal, and Garland and his betrayal, that she wasn't ready for the twist.

Instead of stopping at their little table, or ordering dinner, Rafi urged Jean to drop off her wrap and purse—leaving Sue and Jules behind to enjoy the show—and then he took her by the arm.

They weaved many careful steps through the clattering diners to the partition to the private dining room, where the music was less demanding. One step inside, Jean walked into the arms of the opposition party machine. At the round table were the sixteen big Democratic bosses from the Keys to the Panhandle.

And at the side of the table, in his huge white dinner jacket, sat the Speaker of the House, Congressman Big Luke Rainey, just closing another one of his skillful tall tales.

"Well now," said Jean.

Rafi asked her, "You're not surprised?"

Jean got her breath by leaning into Rafi's shoulder as she watched Rainey shout, "I ain't kiddin' ya!" to the bosses.

Rafi was too clever. He was even cunning, but then, she thought, wasn't that our story together?

Years before Jack, it had been Rafi, not she, who had moved them apart when she was beginning to fall in love with him and torment herself about his wife and children; it had been Rafi, not she, who had counseled her that Jack was a serious suitor who was in love with her and whom she could work well with.

And now it had been Rafi, not she, who had prepared Big Luke Rainey to be vice president even before he was asked.

"Senator Motherwell!" Rainey boomed out as he spotted Jean's keen gaze. He leaped up with the grace of a giant.

The bosses heaved themselves up, too, sixteen men in roomy business suits, all looking a little weary for the rush they'd put on to get here at the governor's call.

Rainey was clearly the most rested of the bunch, with his excellent tan and easy, athlete's motions. He filled the room with the grin that was so goonily generous it had won Rainey the nickname Br'er Luke. They also called him Mickey Mouse's personal congressman, since he was born and raised in Orlando, and his children all worked for Walt Disney. Whatever the reason for his cheer, he was always the providential man in a room, spreading around a genuine delight in life like chocolate-covered snacks. And if very few took him seriously as a leader, everyone liked having him around as a hand-shaker and storyteller.

Jean felt her own smile. "Mr. Speaker, I am pleased."

"Saw you on the television," Rainey boomed. "Terrific, jes' terrific. And you looked so pretty, almost as good as you do here with us. Golly, jes' pretty."

Jean blushed. Why did he remind her of her grandfather? Because he was nice?

And why was she thinking so well of having been set up, first by Jack, then by Long John, then by the networks, then by Rafi, and now probably by Rainey—who no doubt was aware that he had prepared all his life to play golf as the vice president.

Jean told Rafi once more, soft-voiced, "No promises," and then she turned to Rainey. "May I have a moment of your time, Mr. Speaker?"

"Now, come on, Miz Jean, call me Luke, can't ya?"

29 Early Thursday Morning, Air Force One

Thirty-two thousand feet over the Mississippi River valley, Garland was sitting up late in bed and reading over a final draft of the speech he was giving at 2 P.M. to the National Audubon Society conference over in Austin—an event that Roosevelt had come up with spontaneously to provide a platform for Garland's thoughts on the challenge while they waited out the House vote today.

Garland wrote some baseball logic in the speech margin, "You can't get a walk out," in order to explain to the audience why he was insisting the House and Senate take up the challenge as soon as possible. But this seemed obtuse. He crossed it out and reframed it bluntly, "Throw strikes—behind, ahead, throw strikes."

Am I throwing strikes?

Garland glanced at the old baseball he kept on his nightstand. Autographed by Don Drysdale, the great right-hander of the sixties.

I'm throwing strikes. Nothing fancy. Paint the corners. Stay away from their power zone.

And never let those double-crossers on the Hill extend their arms, and pow!

The telephone lit up next to the bed. Garland slipped out of bed and padded across the chamber. His knees ached, too much time on the StairMaster the last few days.

Indeed he'd held tonight's quick EXCOM meeting in the exercise room on the White House's third floor, and while Garland had pounded up a simulated three hundred and twenty floors, he'd heard Jesus Magellan boast that he'd deliver the House to sustain the challenge by tomorrow evening: "In the bank," Jesus had said.

Garland picked up the phone. He knew who it was and said softly, "Yes, Q."

Iphy sat up in a start. In the low green-tinted light her white skin shimmered, and her red hair fell across her bare shoulders like a scarf.

"Shy," she complained, "tell Q. you're married to me first and Texas second and him a distant third, will you."

Garland held the phone away from his mouth. "It's just Q.'s way to say good night with the details."

Iphy wasn't fooled. Exhausted and puffy-eyed, she rolled sideways and got out of bed to pee. "Just get your rest, honey," she said and jumped over to the wc. "Ohhh," she sighed in her gritty way.

They were both exhausted, but Garland felt especially bad for his wife. Picking her up at Detroit had been a fine idea; however, the delays getting out of Andrews—the EXCOM meeting had run long and ragged—had made the rendezvous way too late. Worse, the PTA meeting in Auburn Hills had broken down her good spirits. So many angry voices, so many hostile eyes, all directed at her on the stage, all communicating Michigan's contempt for the challenge. It didn't signify to them that President Jay was unfit. It mattered only that their favorite son was on the rack of history, and the Twenty-fifth Amendment was the tormentor.

"Okay, make it quick," Garland said.

"This is serious, Mr. President," said Roosevelt from the White House. "I knew you'd want to know we've got some trouble kicking up. Dust in the eyes so far."

"Wait," Garland said.

As Iphy came out of the wc, the hem of her nightgown caught on the latch and made a small tearing sound.

"Damn, damn, damn!" she exploded. "Look at it. This is brand-new. I just got it! And now it's—"

"I'm sorry, honey," Garland said.

"Oh, go take your details and shove them!"

Garland moved over to tuck his wife in. There were tears on her pink cheeks. She was so tired she couldn't think or rest. Garland smoothed his hand over her backbone and leaned close to kiss her on the back of the neck. She smelled lush and safe.

"It's okay," Garland told her, knowing it wasn't; and then he padded into the wc and closed the door to give Iphy some respite from the game.

"Yes, Q.," Garland began when he finally picked up.

"EXCOM has come out," Roosevelt said.

"How?"

"On Keebler's cooking show tonight."

Garland exploded, "Shit!"

"I can't be sure of all of it, I've just seen the tape once—but what Keebler said—"

Garland spat, "I don't want to hear Keebler, I don't even want to think about him. Keebler didn't get it. Who gave it to him?"

Roosevelt was stubborn. "You should hear what Keebler said. He said it outright, 'EXCOM.' Just once. 'EXCOM.' Then he said there was a gang of bushwhackers in the White House out to backshoot the country—"

"What a load of bull—"

"He repeated 'backshooters' several times and told his people to watch their backs."

Roosevelt ruffled pages and explained, ". . . I'm looking over a transcript taken by hand off the set . . . He said the White House was in the hands of 'grizzly' backshooters. He said . . . oh, yeah, here it is, listen to this . . ."

Garland muttered, "I'm listening."

"He said the backshooters were ready to turn the cavalry on the people—and, here's the quote, 'they've got an air cavalry, and they're gonna use it on us, so watch your backs' . . ."

Garland didn't think it could get this bad this fast. "He said 'air cavalry'? He said that?"

"He mentioned Sensenbrenner. He called him your spit-and-polish cavalry puppet."

"Shit, shit, shit. Who gave this to him? Somebody had to! He's too loony to work this up himself."

"It gets rougher," Roosevelt reported. "What happened right after Keebler's show was over was that Sonny Pickett went on network opposite Jean Motherwell. *Nightline*. It was Sonny's idea, he didn't clear it with me."

"I told him to stay away from her. I told him I'd handle her when it was time."

Roosevelt argued, "It might have been an ambush match. She

was in Miami, and they didn't tell him about it until airtime. It was nothing until they were asked about Keebler's cracks. 'EX-COM' came out again. Jean Motherwell asked Sonny if it was true there was an executive committee at the White House overseeing the challenge to Jay. And Sonny refused to comment—"

"God, no . . . !" Garland said.

"And then Sensenbrenner's name came up, from the Keebler broadcast, and Sonny said that Sensenbrenner was the most loyal American soldier he'd ever met, and that it was irresponsible to repeat a tax-cheat and felon like Keebler."

"Don't tell me . . . !"

"Then Jean Motherwell baited him and he lost his temper. It's bad. Sonny told her she was a member of the Senate, not a nursemaid to an invalid mule."

"Sonny called Jay a mule?"

"Actually, 'a three-legged mule.' "

Garland grimaced. *Sonny! Can't you keep shut two more days?* Garland tried to control his response. "How bad is it going to get?" he asked.

"I can't tell yet," Roosevelt said, and his voice sounded cautious. "I'm glad you're going to be in Texas. I'll handle the damage control here."

"How bad?" Garland demanded.

"All right, bad," Roosevelt admitted. "I'm moving on it now. The theme is that Keebler is irresponsible."

"Good," Garland said.

"I've called in the big-foot press for breakfast to get our story out. Background. Who, what, when, where of EXCOM, and I'll demand they hold it for the weekend. Then I'm using our friends in New Orleans to put out the denial in the regional press first. Say, a small item that Keebler's show was unusually irresponsible. I'll be calling a full press conference for noon today. I'll let the squaw start it, and I'll come on about ten minutes in and take over. Crisis atmosphere. I'll issue a full denial and accuse Keebler of irresponsibility during a time when every loyal American should remain responsible."

Garland liked the framework but judged, "It won't do it, Q."

"It's a start," Roosevelt argued, "and it'll get Magellan and the House through the day to a vote. I've got a call in to Magellan's legislative aide for a wake-up call on him at five A.M. I'm letting him sleep for now."

Garland slumped forward against the partition. The hum of the aircraft was like a massage, and he let the GE engines rock him with taut vibrations.

It was all falling apart. Garland could see his careful plans crumbling from the edges in. And all he could think for the moment was that he'd been betrayed. Betrayal!

"Who talked?" Garland asked.

"I don't have facts, and I can't use our communications office without spreading around the wrong things . . ."

Garland appreciated the problem. Because EXCOM was a secret handful, it lacked its own staff and access to the White House's vast staff resources. Hell—Hank Lovell was the staff, and the rest of them were chiefs.

So who? Garland ticked off the faces. *Sonny? No. Billy? No. Jesus? Never! Rocky? No. Archie? Ben? No. So . . .*

Garland asked Roosevelt, "What about Sensenbrenner?"

"You think the general leaked?" Roosevelt asked, changing his voice to most sober and surprised. Roosevelt, accustomed to all possible turns of the screw, didn't resist the wild notion that the chairman of the Joint Chiefs would double-cross the president of the United States.

Roosevelt said flatly, "I hadn't looked at that. He's out of the country again. Off to London." Roosevelt prodded, "But he lacks a motive, he lacks everything, doesn't he? Why would he?"

Garland showed his anxiety. "I don't care why. Find out. Call him. Call his boys over there, that Breckenridge, the marine hero. Lean on them. If it's Sensenbrenner, he'll get the message. If it isn't, he'll shake it off."

Roosevelt argued weakly, "You want me to accuse him?"

Garland ordered, "I want you to turn off the leak! Then I want you to stop Keebler. Send out the word we want Keebler off the air. And if any of the networks or big cables try to put him on a talk show, we're punishing. Put it out. Hank and his group make the calls. You tell those big feet, from me. Tell the *Times,* the *Post, USA Today,* the *Journal,* and especially tell Capital Communications. Keebler is done in my town and their town and every town."

Roosevelt didn't want to disagree. He knew silencing a crank phenomenon like Keebler was futile. How do you shut up a gossipmongering billionaire Indian sheriff who could cook?

Roosevelt also knew that accusing Sensenbrenner as a leaker was nutty. But . . .

"Yes, sir," Roosevelt said.

Garland flared up again, "Keebler! We should have buried that creep three years ago when he was on the carpet with the FTC. Buried him. We let him buy his way out. We had him in black and white. Restraint of trade. Felony wire fraud. We had him, and we let him get off with a slap. Justice made the deal and we signed off, because of the primary season. Wrong! Wrong! Always put away a team when they're on the brink. Always—"

"We can handle him, sir," Roosevelt assured.

"Keebler talking about an air cavalry coup! The only thing that could be worse is if he said 'FATHER'S DAY'! What could be worse!"

"They don't have anything hard," Roosevelt tried.

"They've got nothing! I know that! What does Jeannie Motherwell have? And stupid Sonny! And . . . you call Sensenbrenner! You tell him I don't care what it takes, if this leak is from him or his people, he has two minutes to shut it down and lose the leakers. You tell him! And you call Sonny, and you tell him he better zip it up or we're going down together! And you call—"

Garland slammed the wall with his fist. He was panicking. *But of all things. Keebler!*

And Sensenbrenner? Could it be Sensenbrenner who talked?

I never should have trusted Sensenbrenner. He's just not one of us. He doesn't understand . . .

This is Sonny's fault. Sensenbrenner is Sonny's boy, and . . .

And why was Sonny popping off on TV to Jean?

Garland stood up quickly. A nasty idea had just jumped into his sight.

Are Sonny and Sensenbrenner in this together?

And Keebler?

Garland felt his paranoia rising like bile.

He told Roosevelt, "I'm getting off, Q. Ring me back in thirty minutes. And have one of your attack teams ready. I've got to think."

Garland ducked out of the wc, glanced at the sleeping Iphy, grabbed up his pants, shoes, and windbreaker; and, in the quick time it takes a former space shuttle driver to dress in one g, Garland was out through the conference room and up to the flight deck.

The special agent on duty, blue-faced Jude Bruno, followed the president up the stairs. A sleepy steward came close behind. "You need something, sir?" asked Bruno.

"Yeah, I need a cigarette," Garland teased.

Bruno blinked. The steward didn't understand that the president was joking.

Garland tapped on the cabin door, and the first officer opened up with a curious look until he grinned to see Garland. "Come on in, sir."

They were accustomed to visits by Garland. He settled into

the copilot's couch and peered outside. A painfully clear night at thirty-five thousand feet.

"That's the lights of Cairo, Illinois, off starboard, sir," Major Hewlett remarked.

"I'd like to get a lot higher up," said Garland.

" 'Bout twenty-two thousand miles, huh?"

"Yeah," Garland admitted, "and then another quarter million out. Build that lunar base finally. Get it done."

He liked the jolting feel of the engines and the cold assurance of the view. He scanned the flight panel. Certitude. Exactness. Everything the big chips could do to read and write time and space and tell you when and where you are.

Garland pushed deeper into the couch and put on the earphones. He told the communications deck to pipe in the BBC morning shows, one after another, then to range over Europe to find news flashes. Garland ably understood French, Italian, and Spanish. He listened to the daily trials. Bad weather in the North Sea. Factory fire in the Saar Valley. Police report on a terrorist bombing on Corsica.

And then the market news. Tokyo off four percent. Hong Kong, Bangkok—all down. The long bond still sinking. The dollar getting cheaper by the tick.

Garland pressed the button and told the warrant officer, "Give me the White House. Roosevelt."

"Sir?" Roosevelt started. "I've got Leeb, Knudsen, and Gerbino here with me. We're set."

Garland was clear-minded now. He knew what he had to prepare for. Like baseball, use the bench.

"One: I want to know what Sonny knows."

"Wire him?" Roosevelt asked, knowing the answer was that they were going to order the FBI to spy on the Senate majority leader.

"Two," said Garland, "find me a new chairman. Not Breckenridge, not Meriwether, none of Sensenbrenner's people. Not army, not marines. Maybe CINCPAC. Maybe Space Command. I want three names surfaced by Saturday, and put the FBI on them."

"Yes, sir," Roosevelt said, who was impressed by Garland's ruthlessness. Dump Sensenbrenner and shove him into confirmation hearings for the vice presidency without that uniform on, and if he didn't measure up, then . . .

"Three," said Garland, "I want a video call with the president tomorrow evening after the House vote."

Roosevelt said, "You're sure?"

Garland said, "I'm sure."

Roosevelt communicated his nervousness. "We're going to get him, sir. We don't need—"

"Do it," Garland demanded, "and we'll get him when we get him."

"Okay, but—"

"Damn it, do it," Garland ordered angrily.

His thoughts were even angrier. *Do they doubt I'll do it? Don't they know I'll do whatever it takes? I'll get Jay—one way or another.*

30 Thursday, Occupied Moldova

Jack knew that time was the threat. He knew that haste was going to wreck the expedition. But what could he do about it? They had to go fast, they had to take the risks of speed, they had to get Schofield's confession back to Jean before the Senate vote on the challenge.

Did they have to suffer the consequence of haste? In the end, all the mistakes were stupid, all the failure was avoidable, if only there'd been enough time.

At first all the parts seemed to be falling into place: the Philip Morris Gulfstream hopped from Dublin to Bucharest with the professionalism of the highest technology, and they landed at the shabby Otopeni International an hour after dawn in Romania, Thursday morning. The refueling might have warned Jack that they were headed into trouble, because it took four hours to complete, and in the meantime the Morris pilot, Emshwiller, had to argue with the air traffic bosses in order to get his flight plan filed for Chisinau, the capital of Moldova.

"He says it's a mess over there," Emshwiller told Jack. "Nobody's in charge. Only the locals will fly in. And he doesn't think I can get permission to land. Should we call my boss in Paris and try to jump up some channels and . . . ?"

Jack, knowing he was being incautious, said, "Let's push on. They'll let us land. We're private."

They lifted off again in a light rain for the hour jump to Chisinau. Jack slumped back into the cabin and tried to prepare Toni, Tim, and Anna the best he could for the perils.

"NATO's pouring money into Chisinau to prop up the government. We're safe going in there. The field's the best from here to Kiev because of the military. Getting down to Bendery is more a pain than a challenge. I figure we can hire a car—buy a car—and make the drive ourselves. About two to four hours by car, from the reports . . . you see there's a river valley—"

Toni interrupted, "Can't we call Red from where we're going? From Chisinau? I thought once we got into Moldova, we could call him. They have phones, you told me."

"No, no," Jack said, trying one more time to untangle the

misery of Moldova. "Red's in Occupied Moldova, on the Left
Bank of the Dniester. The country's partitioned. From the Pret
to the Dniester used to be Romanian. On the other side of the
Dniester is what they call the Trans Dniester Moldovan Republic, and what we call Occupied Moldova. And Bendery is a no-
man's-land that—"

Exhausted by her bad sleep on the overnight flight, Toni
spoke testily. "Don't tell me any more, just get me to him." She
brushed her curls back and looked much older than her forty
years. "You understand me, Jack?"

"Sure," Jack said.

Maybe it's her children, Jack thought—*maybe she's thinking
she shouldn't have left them like that. But then, she goes away a
lot; she travels to California regularly, so . . .*

Anna Hrbek contributed, "We'll be all right in Moldova, Mrs.
Schofield. There's no real fighting. It's a beautiful country, farms
and vineyards. The gangs are the problem, and they won't
bother us. Months go by without any incidents. The terrorism
was years ago."

Anna Hrbek was a brave young woman, who, now that they
were out of proud America and back in the nightmare of Eastern
Europe, was more comfortable with her prejudices—and very
certain of her cynicism.

"We'll get to Bendery probably by supper time. I know journalists who have been filing stories from Bendery every month.
It's a river port city, and mostly it's just poor. We can stay at the
hotel I've heard about for journalists. The journalists will help
us. And everyone will know where the U.S. Army is."

"What's that mean?" Toni demanded.

"Our people aren't all that popular," Jack said.

Tim liked Anna a deal, but he heard the simplicity in Anna's
explanation and the sharp editing in Jack's version, and he protested, "We're going where the bad guys are. Not just Bendery,

but across the river. The broken-down Trans Dniester Moldovan Republic. Where the old Commies still haven't given up. I looked it up." He pointed to the onboard monitors that were connected to the Americana service by the cell phone net.

"The old Soviet Fourteenth Army," Tim explained, "just sort of camped on the other side of the Dniester and called itself a republic. That was twelve years ago. They've been fighting ever since."

Jack didn't argue back. He knew the politics in Moldova were senseless, and that going in was dangerous. But the naval hero in him told him that the gamble was worth the reward.

If only I were alone, Jack thought, *if only we didn't have to get in and out of there before tomorrow morning . . .*

If only I could get my breath . . .

Emshwiller didn't give the civilian controllers at Chisinau an opportunity to chase him off. On instruments, he came down through the clouds and just told them in French and English he was coming in on private business, let them draw oddball conclusions. This ploy worked in some way, because the civilians didn't bother to call the NATO bosses to make a decision. Emshwiller put them down with precision, parking the Gulfstream beside a NATO Hercules that was guarded by Swedes.

Jack asked Emshwiller to give him eighteen hours. "We'll be ready for takeoff tomorrow morning," Jack promised.

Emshwiller, an old air force driver, rubbed his meaty face and asked his copilot, "You figure a night in lively Chisinau? Is that where we are? Chisinau? You figure they've got a night life?"

"Old university town," Jack answered. "Bound to be one bar that will serve the Marlboro men."

Emshwiller grinned. "I'll call Paris and tell them we're looking for better petrol. He won't know what I'm talking about, but he'll let it go. Your old man, you see, he has pull with my boss."

Jack, glad he had a notoriously hardheaded father like Long John, pounded Emshwiller on the back. A little camaraderie was welcome to provide some momentum.

At 10:30 A.M. in a misty rain, the trouble was not just momentum, however, nor was it just finding a car to make the sixty-mile trip down to Bendery.

The trouble was Toni Albanese. Jack had felt her slipping into a funk all night long, as he tried to talk to her about the trip. She'd just sat in the cabin and nodded dumbly, and pretended to rest, and only sparingly had she spoken with Anna. Otherwise, Jack felt Toni turning away from him and the others.

He told himself it was because of Jean and the cold way things had gone with the confrontation.

He told himself it was the end of an affair, and nothing was going to go well until they stopped seeing each other forever.

Then again, Jack knew it was worse. Toni was fixated on Red Schofield now in a way she'd never been before. Red this, Red that, every remedy was Red. It'll be all right when we get to Red, she'd say; I'll know what to say when we get to Red, she'd imply; I'll rest when we get to Red, she'd add.

Toni didn't specify what would be all right, nor what she would do afterward, she just communicated that Red was her savior.

And why? Jack's intuition was that Toni felt she'd betrayed her family by passing on Red Schofield's warning to Jack. That this was irrational was secondary. Betrayal wasn't a rational act.

She's obsessed with Red Schofield, Jack thought. *It's as if he's all she has to hold on to. Look at the symmetry. He called her to start this, and now—she wants to get to him, to cling to him.*

Clearly Toni was moving away from Jack. She neither welcomed his attention nor glanced his way when there was a chance.

The alienation was physical, too. Most notably, Toni had

taken to lowering the power on her hearing aids, or just turning them off altogether when she didn't care for what Jack was saying.

And the closer they traveled toward Red Schofield, the more pronounced was Toni's rejection, the more she fussed with her ears, the more she retreated into a sullen shell.

Indeed Jack and Toni's break was so rapid that by the time they found a car, Jack let Toni sit in the backseat with Tim, while he and Anna took charge of the drive in a ten-year-old battered Volga sedan.

Chisinau was a Baroque Romanian city that the old Soviet system had poured ten square kilometers of concrete on and then abandoned to rot, and the twelve-year-old war had turned it into a NATO camp, helplessly dependent on foreign aid. There were food lines in a country that exported food; there were bunkers at the intersections; there was a prison compound strung with wire and ringed by guard towers. Since almost no one would visit such a nightmare except journalists—whom NATO didn't care about—it was easy to leave town once they'd cleared the NATO checkpoints. The twenty-dollar bills Jack carried bought anything he asked for.

The crumbling two-lane road took them into a gorgeous river valley that was a sweeping dark green as late spring settled on the plain and lit up the hornbeam and oak forests. There was light traffic, including a public bus and two military convoys of lorries. Within an hour they'd stopped at a cement heap called the Hotel Sfintul Nicolae for lunch and a check on the landscape. From afar the hotel looked substantial, but up close it was closed up except for the roadside eatery. The old hotelier, Talmaci, told them in Romanian that Bendery was a short hour along.

Talmaci added that there was a demonstration today in Bendery, he'd heard it on the radio.

"A big march," said Talmaci, who thought they were all journalists because Anna had shown him her Reuters ID. "Black Sea Cossacks. Marching, marching."

Anna Hrbek translated Talmaci, and Toni asked back, "What's the demonstration for?"

Talmaci scratched his head. "A funeral. By the Black Sea Cossacks. You know, they have big funerals."

Anna pretended she knew who the Black Sea Cossacks were and asked Talmaci, "Who's dead?"

Ignoring the question, Talmaci exploded with xenophobia that would have been laughable in such a sad old man if he wasn't so raw. "You Americans!" He spit on the cats. "Kill our people like dogs, and no one stops you!"

Soon after, they ate salty pork and old rice off of good china that Talmaci was eager to show off. At least the local wine was excellent, and after a glass, Toni's tongue loosened.

"This is a terrible place," she said. "I don't mean poor and hopeless. I mean, why do we have our troops here? What can we do for them? Did you see those prison camps in Chisinau? And what did he mean about marching against the Americans?"

Anna asked Tim, "What do you know about the Black Sea Cossacks?"

Tim looked for the answer in his handheld pc. It was blank, and he toggled for a connection. "Did you bring yours?" he asked Anna.

"I left it on the plane," Anna admitted. "You said we didn't need two."

"Well, what—"

Jack broke in before they fell out. "It's not the hardware, Tim. Look."

Jack flipped out his cell phone and punched for a connection. Nothing.

"We're outside the net," Jack explained. "I noticed it when we landed."

Tim and Anna glanced at each other. Toni asked Jack sharply, "What did you say?" She tapped her ears.

"It means we're cut off and—" Tim said.

Jack declared, "It means we keep going."

No more pampering; he got them back in the car without confiding in them that he was worried. He didn't like the talk of a paramilitary gang called the Black Sea Cossacks. He didn't like a funeral procession. He didn't like Moldova, or the weather, or Toni's negative attitude, or anything about why they were here or where they were going.

Bendery came up piecemeal, starting with rundown cottages and soot-stained chimneys and then moving to ramshackle warehouses and heaps of rusted-out or burned-out vehicles. There was very little trash, though, a sign Jack took as a measure of deprivation. The cotton mills and shoe factories were next along the railbed, and from there the stone streets of old Bendery sloped down toward the big Dniester.

Jack's doubt about Bendery was confirmed right away. The lorry route emerged abruptly on an old fountain square that was jammed with men and women wearing black armbands.

Jack wanted to turn around, or try the exit across the square, but before he could maneuver between the pedestrians, he was too deep inside the back of the pack and trapped.

Atop the stone fountain, several men with bullhorns were leading the crowd in a strange chant that Anna translated simply: "Death to the Germans."

Anna explained, "The Germans are the mythical invader. It's hard to say who they are."

"Bogeymen," Tim said.

Here and there in the crowd were lightly armed fellows wearing black blouses and black breeches and caps with a strange flag on them, and it was easy to suppose they were Black Sea Cossacks.

This fountain square gathering was a satellite demonstration to the main throng gathering below in the vast riverside market square.

"We've got to get across the river," Toni insisted with a strain in her voice.

Anna fell back on her profession. "Let's look for some journalists. We can walk around and ask for the newspaper offices."

Jack liked Anna's plan; then again, panicky as she sounded, Toni was right, too. He looked to Tim for his choice.

"We shouldn't leave the car," Tim said.

Tim's right, Jack thought. *But so're Toni and Anna. And we've got to hurry this* . . .

Suspending his best judgment, Jack told them they were going to find the newspaper offices and get some up-to-the-moment information about this demonstration and about Schofield's battalion.

Here at two o'clock under wet skies, Jack had a hard feeling about leaving the car the moment they passed out of sight of it.

As they moved, Anna asked questions of women with children and old men chewing on cigarette butts. They were directed in a zigzag from the fountain square along the stone street toward Printing House Square.

The streets smelled oddly of kerosene and the barnyard, details Jack knew were routine in a country that had lost most electrical power and petrol supplies.

Everything he saw—the poverty, the bad complexions, the silent babes in arms—told him that Bendery was on the brink of catastrophe. How long it had been like this he couldn't say. But it was clearly a place without law or order, held together by tribal warfare.

At Printing House Square, they had a view down steep stone

steps of the whole of the riverside market square. There were several thousand people spread across a looming dark open area; however, for a crowd they were most subdued. The chief sound was the public address system, for a line of public speakers were addressing the crowd from a platform raised over an old Soviet armored car. A banner draped across the tires read in Romanian, "Friendship of the Black Sea Cossacks."

Anna Hrbek found the offices of the Bendery weekly, *Saint Dimitru's Truth,* a seedy storefront with a taped-up plate-glass window on the square. Inside, Jack went with her to quiz whoever would talk.

The little fellow said his name was Viorel, and he chatted politely with Anna.

"He says it's the Cossacks, like we thought," Anna told Jack. "He says that the city police are part of it. He says the city is seceding from Moldova." Anna added, "It's crazy stuff."

"Ask about Schofield—the Americans, where are they?"

Anna tried three times, twice in Romanian and once in Russian.

Viorel was dumb. Jack gave Anna one hundred dollars in twenties, and she used a copy of the newspaper to cover up the transaction. Viorel took the money and rushed to his accountant's table to write out something. It turned out to be a receipt for a subscription to the newspaper, and across the top was written the message, "Come with me. Please."

Anna asked Jack, "What do we do?"

Again Jack ignored his caution and went along with the scheme. He figured he was making so many mistakes now, he couldn't stop.

The wonder was that they followed Viorel a short distance, across Printing House Square, to a two-story red-roofed printer's shop. The moment they opened the door, they could smell the musty old paper and that strange alcohol base of the inks. Jack thought this was some sort of misdirection, but then Viorel was introducing them to a mousy, pretty little blond woman behind the counter named Christina.

Christina kept glancing at Anna and Toni and blushing. She spoke animatedly with Viorel, and then came over in tiny steps to address Anna in Russian.

Anna translated, "She says she's Red Schofield's friend. She says she doesn't want trouble. She asks if he's going away from her." Anna added, "She thinks we're American officials, which is a way of saying spies."

Toni came forward with many demanding questions—a very healthy American brunette leaning over a wan European blond, and the two of them using ruddy-faced Anna Hrbek as translator.

Jack was now convinced that Toni was out of control. Her eyes showed her fear and desperation. She kept shouting, "What!" in a hoarse voice that was unnerving. Jack wanted to mediate; Jack wanted to comfort her.

Instead he spoke to Tim. "We've got to get going. She doesn't know anything. At most, she's Schofield's girlfriend."

Tim looked over the rundown shop and the small stacks of cards, envelopes, and sheets for sale, and sighed. "It's kind of sad, sir. We send our guys over here to keep the peace, and it's impossible that anybody could, and they . . ." Tim looked at the tiny Christina. "She's so poor."

Jack tried to look with Tim's sympathetic eyes. It didn't come to Jack to feel sorry for Bendery, or Christina, or even Schofield and his troops. He'd seen too much worse in Africa. And he wasn't here to feel anything, he was here to get a job done.

The twist was that the job was already done—that instead of their going to Red Schofield, Red Schofield was coming to them.

The assault came well before Jack was aware. The first indication he got was shouting outside the shop, and then there was clearly the report of automatic weapon fire.

From the front stoop of the shop, Jack and Tim could clearly see down the stone steps to the market square.

The crowd was massing around the speakers, but that wasn't the new threat.

Across the river, against the green-blue of the low hills, there was a low diesel roar and the metal grinding and smoke blowing of first-class armor.

"You see them?" Jack asked Tim.

"Our guys, you mean?" Tim asked.

Jack squinted with his captain's eyesight. At a kilometer, he counted five, six Bradleys and at least twice as many Hummers. And swinging over the hills were two AH-6 Nightfox helicopters.

"Show of force," Jack said to Tim.

The Black Sea Cossacks recognized the threat. But instead of retreating, the crowd swelled, and the speakers on the BMP raised their voices, and the crowd from the fountain square started pouring into the riverside market square.

At the same time, down in the crowd there were two coffins being tossed aloft like rowboats bobbing on pink hands. And then there was more popping gunfire—rifles raised in anger and fired wildly into the gray sky.

The lead Bradley mounted the far end of the bridge and raced across, with two Hummers trailing closely, taking up a firing position at this end of the bridge. The column followed, with dismounts as they came. One scout helicopter swung over the bridge's apron. The whole operation was so textbook, it took less than five minutes, and at the end its smoothness was its strength.

Before the crowd could react, it was facing overwhelming firepower.

Then a command Hummer swung out of the Bradley line and

headed directly toward the BMP. One lone vehicle taking on several thousand hostiles.

Tim, who had been asking Jack a series of technical questions about the operation, said, "They're really pushing it."

"That's the point," Jack said, who anticipated the next step. "You either push it and push it, or you might as well get out."

The command Hummer lurched forward. Two soldiers in body armor stepped out and climbed atop the hood. The big one pointed at the public speakers. The speakers pointed back.

Without any identifiable trigger the situation exploded, with the two flanking Bradleys stuttering their light machine guns in warning bursts, the dismounted troops firing smoke and tear gas in a star pattern, the back of the crowd panicking and breaking away.

"Shit!" Tim said.

"Police action," Jack said.

Jack and Tim were safe from the mess for the moment, yet the crowd was going to flee in all directions, and up the stone steps eventually. Jack pulled Tim with him back inside the printer's shop, and he shut the heavy wooden door firmly.

Tim asked, "But what's going to happen?"

Toni and Anna were at one front window; Christina and Viorel were at the other.

Jack, unnerved by the infectious chaos, shouted, "Get away from there. They're shooting down there!"

They flinched but stood frozen.

"Timmy, close the windows," Jack ordered. "Everyone back. We're going to wait it out here. Anna, tell them we're best here until the shooting stops."

"What is it?" Toni demanded.

A few more bursts of automatic fire, and then there was a steady stuttering from the Bradleys.

"Red Schofield's down there somewhere, Toni," Jack explained. "Those are our guys. We've found them, but we'll have to wait."

"Red? Where? He is? Are you sure?"

"Look, Toni," Jack said loudly to her, "I'm not sure of anything. But I think we've found what we came for, and now what we have to do is wait to get closer to them. They're clearing the square; our guys are scattering the Black Sea Cossacks and everyone else. Tear gas and real bullets. We're going to stay here until . . ."

Toni turned away to the window.

"You've got to listen to me about the windows!" Jack protested. "Will you please . . . There's random fire everywhere. Those rounds penetrate walls."

Toni avoided Jack's reach, stepped up the single stair, and pushed out the front door.

"Toni, get back here!"

What Jack hadn't seen, and what Toni had, was the incredible figure of Red Schofield and a small radioman climbing the stone steps from the market square.

Despite the wafting clouds of tear gas, the popping of automatic weapons, the crisscrossing roars of the diesel engines, Red Schofield was making a display of his godlike power to come and go at will.

He was deliberately walking from the now captured BMP, across the stone square, over the debris of the mob, and even past a few folk who'd fallen by the side, to the stone steps up to Printing House Square and his war bride, Christina.

Only an American commander who had discarded all sense would have made such a walk. It was as aggressive as murder; it was evidence of a crack-up.

Toni knew none of this. She knew only that she'd spotted a man who walked like her Red, and she was right. Under the helmet and armor, Red Schofield strode up two steps at a time, cocking his head left and right, watching for ambush.

Jack got to Toni before she could start the steps. He manhandled her back. "You're not going down there! There's shooting!"

"Get away from me!" She scratched his hand, then slipped sideways, her face a mask of fear.

"You can't do this!" Jack cried. "He's coming up here. Wait! Listen!"

He could have tackled her. He should have done anything.

She didn't get a dozen steps down before she seemed to slip and tumble sideways like a doll. She struck against the rail like a dead thing, a huge bullet wound in her throat, her hands trying to hold back the blood, her voice gone as she heard absolute silence at the last instant.

31 Thursday Afternoon, Capitol Hill

In the posh Speaker's office, just off the floor of the House, Majority Leader Jesus Magellan (D., Calif.) addressed his leadership on the imminent vote on the Twenty-fifth Amendment.

"I don't want any screwing around on this," Magellan said, looking at his unlit cigar.

Magellan had come up through the union hall, and he treated the Democrat-dominated House like a posh UAW confab. "There's screwing around on this, I'm holding 'em to task. I told the president there's no screwing around here."

Magellan got his breath. He'd eaten a full lunch of pasta primavera with half a bottle of superb zinfandel, and he was eager for a smoke as a reward.

"You think about it," he added aimlessly.

He'd borrowed the Speaker's formal office not only because it was convenient, but also because it was one of the few rooms left in the Capitol Building where you could smoke in peace.

There were nine of the leaders and their staffs in the ceremonial chamber, and they had arranged themselves in a loose pecking order at the table and in the wing chairs—whips, caucus, steering, and party. The legislative assistants were spread along the back wall. There were about two dozen pros in all, listening carefully to the floor boss—the man you didn't cross and stay a leader.

"We're suspending rules, the lawyers tell us," Magellan continued, "so that means there's definitely no screwing around. And remember there's gonna be cameras everywhere. They're sneaking them in with their pinky rings. We can't screw around on this! We got three hundred and five members want to screw around, I know it. Not gonna happen—Bud, you tell 'em."

Bud Dimehauser (D., Mo.) was the veteran deputy whip and the most no-nonsense floor manager in Magellan's arsenal.

"We've got forty minutes each side of the aisle to let 'em talk. I'm giving the signal now"—Dimehauser flipped open his communicator—"to alert the members we'll bring it to the floor in an hour. Sixty minutes from now. We'll start with the paeans from the old days and we'll finish with the paeans from the new days—to poor old President Jay."

"Paeans" came out like "pins." Dimehauser was not an eloquent man. So short he looked bitten off by a hungry god, he was also the worst dresser among two hundred members who competed for the Worst Dressed title each year, in his mud brown suit and black knit tie and unwhite shirt. He was also the guy whom everyone feared, a product of his early career as the D.A. who cleaned up the Two Quello Gang in East St. Louis.

Today, Dimehauser's job was to clean up the membership who wanted to say less than nice things about the president they

were about to discard—President Jay—and less than great
things about the president they were about to support—Shy
Garland—and when Bud Dimehauser cleaned you up, you were
very, very clean.

"I told the Michigan bunch they can cry all they want,"
Dimehauser said about the concerns of the Michigan delegation
that they were killing their own favorite son on live TV. "And if
they want to vote last, we'll see what we can do. Say things like
'make the hard choice' or 'good for the country' and like that."

Dimehauser repeated himself in the Magellan style. "Forty
minutes tops to the paeans, got it?"

The staffers scribbled on their pcs. The leadership looked at
their feet.

The majority whip was one hundred light-years and a dozen
tailors from Dimehauser, the stunning and tough-minded Kait-
lin French-Kohn (D., Calif.), who ruled by moneyed enterprise
and the other traits that differentiated Silicon Valley from the
Mississippi valley. French-Kohn always let Dimehauser give out
his usual order of battle, then she would speak up with her high-
toned diplomacy.

Today, her diplomacy was combative. "This isn't an If we win
it, it's a How we win it, Bud." She turned to Magellan. "I'm
concerned there's too much suggestive and even indecent talk. I
mean the cracks to the press about mental illness. No names
necessary, you know it's the same old sound-bite artists on both
sides of the aisle. I've heard indefensibly bigoted remarks about
President Jay. We can't let them go by."

"Whatcha want, Katy?" Magellan asked.

French-Kohn tapped her sharp finger on her bright silver
hair. "I want them persuaded to quit it," she said. "I have a list. I
want them asked and cajoled and urged and—muzzled."

"And if not?" asked the angelic deputy whip, the soft-eyed
Angie Sine (D., N.Y.).

French-Kohn looked at Bud Dimehauser.

Dimehauser demonstrated his D.A. grin. "We unmake their party profile."

"Profile" came out like a punch in the face.

Jesus Magellan wasn't satisfied. Katy was right—there was too much loose talk. Members were popping off at every camera and microphone that popped up. He could turn the radio on right now and hear remarks from coast to coast about depression and healing and forgiveness and the favorite word these days, "Machiavellian."

"Bring in the counsels," Magellan ordered, since it was time to frame the issue in the customary double-talk of law.

The side door opened and three heavyset attorneys, two males and a female, traipsed in, each followed by an aide. These were the general counsels for the Steering and Policy Committee; Magellan called them "Teeny, Meany, and All-Miney."

"Tell 'em," Magellan ordered.

The general counsels began with indirect introductory remarks, and then they came to the point about the Twenty-fifth. "Our recommendation is that, while the vote today doesn't have to be brought to the floor with the force of law, well then, we've still recommended it be brought up under suspension because . . ."

Magellan let the lawyers rattle on with House rules that were meaningless if you had the votes, which he did, and no use whatsoever if you didn't.

He leaned over the Speaker's desk and tapped on the phone panel, and nothing happened.

Shit, Magellan thought, *what's with this damn thing? Doesn't Rainey have anything that works the first time?*

Magellan eventually made the connection to his office and told them to put through to Garland.

While the attorneys droned on, Magellan plopped down in

Luke Rainey's gigantic swivel chair—Rainey, at two hundred and forty pounds, was twice the size of Magellan—and touched the switch.

Shy Garland's image appeared in the tiny box screen on the phone panel.

"Mr. President," Magellan began, "we're just wrapping up here with my people, and I figured you wanted to say something before we moved out."

Garland was in his father's study at the family house in River Oaks. "Maybe," Garland said. "Hold on."

Garland was dressed in his cowboy clothes after a late morning ride, and he was sipping on a Coca-Cola Classic—Garland's only known vice—and watching the cable news about himself and the cascading stock and bond markets.

Garland put down the Coke. "I want to talk to you, not them. Where are you?"

Magellan nodded at the room in front of him. "Locked and loaded in the Speaker's."

"Where's he?" Garland asked.

Magellan shrugged. Last he'd heard, Luke Rainey was on his way in, the Speaker's usual prerogative to stay above partisanship by arriving late to every big showdown. "I figure he's taking a late lunch. You know, he always makes it in time for the TV votes. Maybe he's on the golf course again, I don't know . . ."

Garland didn't make much that his majority leader wasn't sure where the Speaker of the House was less than an hour before the vote. Garland did make much of what he'd discovered last night about the possible betrayal by Sonny Pickett and Sensenbrenner.

"I don't have anything new to say," Garland said. "I do have something for you."

Magellan heard trouble, but still he wanted Garland to goose his troops. "You know, it'd help if you just said—"

"Okay, okay, put me on the screen."

Magellan didn't know how to work Rainey's video-conferencing system and had to ask for help from the aides.

Presently Garland's folksy image shimmered on the big box screen that hung in the corner over the conference table.

The general counsels stopped talking and fell into their triple chins.

Garland could see them on the overview camera. *What a crew,* he thought. Dimehauser looked like a franchise gangster, and Katy French, gorgeous like a cat, looked as if she'd pull out his fingernails as happily as shake his hand.

Garland, in a blunt and cranky mood, passed along his temperament. "Yeah, well, good afternoon, ladies and gentlemen," he said tentatively.

The leadership picked up on their president's unease and shifted around like truants.

Dimehauser took the lead. "Mr. President, we've got it in the bag. I've been on the horn all morning. My state bosses are in line. The delegations are all with us. Except Michigan, but you gotta figure they're iffy here."

Gentle Angie Sine tried, "Everyone wants to do the right thing, Mr. President. It's hard to say good-bye to President Jay. We don't want to hurt him."

Dimehauser said, "We just hurt three hundred and five of them to our side. In the bag."

Garland liked Dimehauser a deal and wished he had three hundred and four more of him. "I'll bet you do."

Garland watched French-Kohn cross her excellent legs, and he asked her, "Katy, what's Rose say today?"

House Minority Leader Westy Rose (R., S.C.) changed his mind twice a day as a matter of policy.

"He told me he's releasing to their consciences," Katy French-Kohn replied. "And if you believe that—"

"Yes," Garland said. He'd long figured that the House Republicans would vote against him out of fundamental orneriness—though not all of them. The southerners would likely want to go his way, and there were more than a few votes in Keebler's backyard, the Arizona and California republics.

"Anything else?" Garland asked, sounding as distracted as he felt.

The leadership shifted their shoulders and eyes again. What was wrong with the president? He was never this curt. He always had nice things to say about Katy French's triplets or Bud Dimehauser's famous poker game. And no wisecracks with Magellan at all?

The leadership got the message: something was wrong. The president was fretful. Trouble out there.

Magellan had his aides get everyone out of the room as soon as possible. In the delay, Katy French-Kohn passed a note to Magellan.

What about Keebler? she'd written.

Magellan balled the note up in his hand. Yeah, what about Keebler? Should he ask? His office was taking heavy faxes on Keebler's nuttiness. On Keebler's crack about bushwhackers in the White House—about EXCOM. Nobody believed him. But then, everybody didn't have to believe Keebler for them to listen to him. The guy was a highly credible nut. California was too damned close to the Arizona republic. *We should do something about Gus Keebler. He's a pain. He's dangerous.*

"We can talk now," Magellan said.

"Who's there?" Garland said.

"Just my team," Magellan said, holding his hand out to his chief of staff, publicist, executive assistant, and two counsels, who had remained at the conference table. "You want them out, too?"

Garland eased forward in his father's chair and sipped the

Coke again. Then he flipped off the video line. He was about to work Magellan over, and he didn't want him reading his eyes.

"I was wrong about Sensenbrenner," Garland began bluntly. "I should have listened to you, Jesus. I should have gone your way with the vice presidency. Q. and I talked about it. But, you know, we listened to Sonny about getting the military on board."

Magellan was stunned and felt his face flush. Garland admit he'd made a mistake? Garland reverse his course? It didn't happen. Except—

"I can't reposition us now," Garland continued, "since we've committed to Sensenbrenner. But I want you to know, I'm making him emphasize he's not staying on the ticket next summer. Q. will bury him until then. No tours, no speeches. Just lock him up in the Naval Observatory. You get me?"

"Yes, sir," Magellan answered. "But . . . what . . . ?"

"I wish you were with me on this one," Garland said. "Sensenbrenner—what was I thinking? How could I let Sonny talk me into him?"

"Yeah," Magellan said. He was worried. Was Garland spinning him around for some purpose? Speaking against Sensenbrenner in order to get Magellan to make a mistake? What kind of mistake? Magellan had nothing to hide.

Garland leaned close to the speakerphone and came to his point. "Jesus, who gave Keebler the word on EXCOM?"

Magellan panicked. "You think I did? You think it was from my people?"

"Who did it?" Garland repeated.

"It wasn't me!" Magellan claimed. He was sweating. His staffers didn't know what was being said, but they lowered their heads to see their absolute boss getting worked over by his absolute boss.

Garland knew what he was doing and where he was going. Nothing over the plate. Now, high smoke.

"Do I want everyone on your staff interrogated?" Garland asked. "Do I use Q.'s people to do the interrogation? What do I do about the leak? There's a leak. Keebler got his stuff on a leak. I want it plugged. And no one's out of this. So what do I do?"

"It wasn't my people," Magellan said, feeling better already, since if it was a member of his team, he could handle it himself and still claim innocence. Magellan tried to redirect Garland's suspicion, "But what if it was Sensenbrenner? You think it was him?"

Garland told half a truth. "I don't know what to make of the general. He's done everything we've asked for years. The man's a heavy lifter. And on Tuesday, he was first-rate. I thought we had us a real plus . . . and now . . ."

"It doesn't add up," Magellan said, deciding to back away from his thought, "that he would double-cross us."

"I know," Garland said. "But who else knows about EX-COM? Who knows about FATHER'S DAY?"

Magellan understood where this was going now. Garland didn't distrust him; Garland didn't distrust Sensenbrenner. Garland was pointing a finger at Sonny Pickett—at his best pal, his oldest crony, his bosom pol.

Magellan thought, *Should I stick up for Sonny?*

Magellan said nothing.

Garland was pleased with the way he'd handled Magellan, and he tapped the video line back on and looked over Magellan's damp brow.

"I want the challenge sustained by seven P.M.," Garland said. "Put out the word now that it's as good as done—maybe you can stop the market from this damned sell-off. Have you seen the price of Telephone?"

Magellan, who'd invested his fortune into his UAW options from Caterpillar, Cummins, and Chrysler, sighed back and said, "We'll deliver, sir. It's a done deal. And I think we'll be all right with Sensenbrenner. We'll take him by the hand and show him where to sit for the next fourteen months, until the convention."

"I'd hoped you'd see it my way, thanks," Garland said, and then he got off the line and took the little make-believe walk off the mound and to the dugout, feeling lucky.

32 Thursday, Occupied Cairo

After the working supper in the big operations room at the American Embassy, Sensenbrenner told the NATO commander that he was driving down to Old Cairo and the City of the Dead.

"Tonight, sir?" asked the Italian general, Fazio. "We haven't got the situation stabilized just yet. It seems early. And what you say, fluid."

Sensenbrenner looked at the map of the city on the table. "Fluid" was another word for out of control. There were national flags pinned all around the city to denote the disposition of guard units. The riot today had spread from the Old City Wall in Gamaliya right down Port Said Street as far as Old Cairo on the river. There were still fires burning in the shopping districts, and they could still hear automatic gunfire from Tahrir Square.

Two American flags were at the American university off the square—two American infantry companies taking casualties from snipers and fire cinders. Another American flag was at Manyal Palace, where an American security team with light armor was trying to hold the bridges. Below the Zeinhom Gardens, there was a power blackout.

"We're expendable, you and me, General," Sensenbrenner

said. Trim little Fazio was an old forty-three-year-old and around his dark, sunken eyes he looked ten years older. He was way overworked holding together four brigades from seven NATO members. There was little more Sensenbrenner could do for him tonight but sympathize. "I'll take my team and two command cars."

"But what can you do out there?"

"I won't ask what we're doing in here." Sensenbrenner looked over his immediate staff—the adept Lieutenant Yudron; the new man from Intelligence named Alfi (an Arabic speaker); and then his team leader, Sergeant Sandoval—and shrugged off his negative thoughts. They were ready to go. So was he. And what he could do out here was look into the face of horror and ask himself, *Have we lost already?*

Sauve qui peut?

"I'll be back by the midnight briefing," Sensenbrenner told Fazio, "and let's hope we have good news on the water pressure by then."

Fazio threw his hands up in the Roman way. "Only backfires will stop it. I've told them!"

Sensenbrenner checked in at the ambassador's office down the hall. The embassy was a fortress now, and the ambassador both worked and lived in his suite. Sensenbrenner tapped on the open door, and the ambassador's wife called a welcome.

He said, "I need a word, if I can."

"Of course, General," she said, blanking the videophone for a moment, "please, go on in, he's on the line with Washington."

Georgia Ketcham was her husband's senior aide since they'd sent half the embassy personnel staff out with the evacuation of the foreign compound. The Ketchams, in their midforties, were as professional as any military type. Ambassador Ketcham was at the one bank of windows that was sealed up, and he was on the phone.

"How can I help you, General?" Bob Ketcham said. He was

still in his combat fatigues after a day of visiting the hospitals. "You're not going out, are you?"

"Bob, I want you to tell your boss that we need those gunboats they've held back on downriver. It's time to partition the city, what we discussed early in the week. Was it Tuesday? I need firepower to cover the bridges."

"Shit," Bob Ketcham said. "You think it's going that badly?"

Sensenbrenner glanced at Ketcham's pitted face. The man was wasted, ashen, panicky, and he was pretending he was still an ambassador. The earthquake had cracked more than the Nile. The old Egyptian Republic was finished. Ketcham was beaten, but the pro in him, the career fireman for the world's disasters, couldn't give up.

"I'll be back by midnight. You're on with State?" Sensenbrenner asked about the phone call. "Tell them I'm looking at evacuation of the American university."

"But no, no. What will that look like?" Ketcham started. "We can't bug out. The city will collapse."

"The city collapsed two years ago," Sensenbrenner said. "And it wasn't anything we did, Bob. It was 7.6 on the Richter scale. You didn't do it. You can't fix it."

"Okay, okay," Ketcham said.

Sensenbrenner led his team to the first floor, to the service exit ramp. The command car was the lightly armored Hummer variation favored for city duty, with screens to fend off rocks and the big cowcatcher on the front fender. Yudron made certain the SATCOM was brought over from the car, and Sandoval insisted that a second Hummer mounted with twin light machine guns, slaved to the gunner, be brought up to take the lead.

Sandoval's bodyguard team also wore extra ammo pouches, and everyone was fully armored and on helmet mikes. The high-end tech stuff they left behind, since there was nothing out there to read, and heat signatures tonight were futile.

The convoy didn't go directly south; it swung up to Tahrir Square to call on the American task force commander, a strict and taciturn Tennessean named Kirk Unruh. Unruh's two infantry companies were deployed at the barricades, with sandbag redoubts at the approaches.

The square was dominated by a roaring hotel fire that lit up the sky and poured hot, black chunks down on the troops.

Sensenbrenner walked from the vehicle to Unruh's Ops in a rain of orange cinders.

"Sir!" Unruh greeted his commander. "Great of you to come out for us, sir!"

Unruh's staff inched closer to hear the conference and to watch Sensenbrenner. He was more than the chairman of the Chiefs now; he was the man who was going to be vice president, the man who was going to save them from peacekeeping in hell.

"He'll bring us home" was the scuttlebutt.

"You're holding here till morning!" Sensenbrenner said. "We can't pull you out. We can't reinforce! I'm having gunboats brought up. Maybe tomorrow, by noon. Got it?"

"Sir!" Unruh shouted. "We'll button up."

It was the smell that made them shout. The tank farm to the north of the city was on fire, spreading poisonous fumes that raced the heart and made you scared.

"No water pressure!" Sensenbrenner said of the fires. "We're working on it!"

"Yes, sir! Thank you, sir!"

A large chunk of a building landed in the square. A team with extinguishers attacked it before it threw coals on the redoubts. The wind blew a horde of cinders like fireflies across their boots. Unruh glanced toward the Tahrir Bridge. He had no escape routes. He had to hold. Where at West Point had they taught him how to hold off a burning city and an enemy of beggars armed with rocks?

Sensenbrenner saluted Unruh's gung ho desperation and got back to his vehicle. They drove down a highway of burning roofs that kept the landscape illuminated with a swaying glow. There was no opposition; this part of the city was either abandoned or paralyzed.

Sensenbrenner sat in the command vehicle feeling calm and resigned. He'd lost Cairo. Two years and twenty billion dollars, maybe more, and he'd lost the city, the region, the state. Now he had to go along with the NATO plan to relocate sixteen million people. It was a radical idea, but there was no other way. Planning had already worked up the blueprint to raise a network of satellite cities in the eastern desert behind the Muqattam Hills, then later the western desert beyond Memphis. Start all over again. A thousand-year-old city to be leveled and rebuilt.

Sensenbrenner watched a line of refugees cross in front of the headlights. A whole extended family: ancients, parents, children, burros—who knew where they were going? No panic, no noise whatsoever, they were just walking in a city of smoke.

Sensenbrenner told the driver to turn off at the old Roman fortress. "Do you know the way to the City of the Dead?" he asked. "The Southern Cemetery?"

The driver laughed nervously. "Yes, sir. You want we should go that way? It's kind of narrow over there for this baby."

Sensenbrenner leaned around to Yudron. "I want to try and find the boy."

"Sir, it's late, we could come tomorrow."

"If he's there, he's there," Sensenbrenner answered.

Yudron knew the problem. It was the legless beggar boy who'd run under the car on Tuesday. The embassy had bought the information Sensenbrenner wanted. The beggar boy's address. Or at least where he could be found—at the mausoleum of the Khalil-el-Mafouz family, in the Southern Cemetery.

Yudron decided to go along with the general's strange interest. "Listen to me," he told the driver. "I'll guide you. Turn here."

The streets narrowed quickly. The smoke thinned. The driver banged over rubbish. The stone walls were like a maze. They crossed the railbed and plunged back into the alleys. And then the driver lost his way and stopped at a black lump in the road, a dead horse covered only with parasites—the city's dogs had already been eaten.

Sensenbrenner and his team moved out securely. They knew where they were going because of the guides they'd brought along, two street boys named Ragheb and Nehro.

Presently they were in the silence of the tombs. They shut off their torches and used the moon and starlight. The terrain was more extraordinary than anything manmade Sensenbrenner had ever seen—the colorless vision of blockish mausoleums, the dark profiles of prayer towers, the small heaps of automobile parts and rags.

The boys Ragheb and Nehro ducked into one mausoleum and emerged with the three old women who lived there.

Some of these tombs were five hundred years old; they provided sound shelter and a good place to hide your food.

In a city of sixteen million, there was food enough each day to feed nine million.

"Here, Khan, this way," the boys told the Arabic-speaking officer from Intelligence, Captain Alfi. Alfi questioned the old women on his own.

"Sir, I don't like this," Alfi told Sensenbrenner. "They say he lives with a gang. That's a way of saying that he's with people with weapons. I don't like it. Not in the dark."

"Are we close?" Sensenbrenner asked. He snapped out his small sketch pad. The moonlight on the marble mausoleums. The dry air. The lines were so sharp they seemed diamond-cut.

He was also surrounded by hundreds of eyes watching him from hiding.

Sensenbrenner started to sketch. Just five lines on paper, and then he put his sketch pad into his pouch.

I've failed. I've let them down. They're doomed. They always were.

What could I ever have done?

Why all the casualties, then? Three hundred and ninety American soldiers in two years. For what?

"I want to go on," Sensenbrenner said.

Above the tombs now was the profile of the Muhammad Ali Mosque, a mile away, but in this air it seemed so close it was as if it were within reach.

The tomb of the Khalil-el-Mafouz family was intact in the midst of several crumbled tombs. No more than a marble box, it was covered with graffiti from several centuries—crude drawings of ships and mosques and odd flowers.

On a wooden bench just outside the tomb, three of the legless boys were asleep like toy bears leaning against one another. Their precious carts were tied together, and the rope was tied to their wrists.

Ominously there was a tall, bearded, wasted man in a turban and rags standing in the doorway, just standing there. He watched the Sensenbrenner team approach in steady steps. The tall man's face didn't change, but his eyes grew larger as he recognized the men were in uniform.

Still, the tall man didn't move. This was his house. He was the beggars' keeper.

Lieutenant Alfi told the tall man in Arabic to light a lamp. The man was dumb.

Around the edges of the field, small figures were darting into hiding.

Sandoval, spooked by the feel of hundreds of eyes, ordered

his team to light up their torches, and the whole little dirty square blinked bright with white light.

The boys Ragheb and Nehro ducked into the family tomb to please their masters by finding the beggar boy.

"I'm going in," Sensenbrenner told Yudron and Alfi. He hesitated, though, listening to the scraping sounds around him. It was as if thousands of beggars were dragging their bare feet across the dust, as if millions were shifting away from the unnatural brightness brought by the Americans. Sensenbrenner asked Yudron, "You don't think this was a good idea, do you?"

Yudron the professional nodded. "We're in good shape, sir. I've got communications fine." Yudron tapped his helmet mike. He didn't say that the marble field was breaking up his radio link with the command vehicle, and from there he was linked back to the embassy. "You want to go in, it's fine, sir."

Sensenbrenner moved past the tall man into the tomb's doorway.

Sandoval stepped in front of his general, using his body like a moving shield. Sandoval didn't choose this zone from any other zone; they were all secure if you made them secure.

Inside the stink was human waste. A piece of the slab roof was missing. The light from the torches outside reflected off the marble walls and lit up the chamber in shadows.

The boys Ragheb and Nehro gestured to the stack of sarcophagi along the side wall.

Sensenbrenner bent down to peek into the bottom sarcophagus. Three little figures were laid out up against one another, since, without legs, they could be stored like sacks.

Children. My God. Why do they have to suffer like this? They have nothing, not even legs, and some not even arms, and some not even faces.

Sensenbrenner didn't know what he wanted to do. *Just to see the boy? To touch him? To rescue him? How?*

Only poor boys care about poor boys and girls, he thought.

"Captain Alfi, come in here," Sensenbrenner ordered.

Alfi ducked in. The chamber was crowded now, and Sandoval had to back out to give his officers room.

Sensenbrenner said, "Tell these children I want to take them to the hospital."

Alfi's face couldn't conceal his horror at the sight of the legless children in the sarcophagus. "All of them, sir?" he managed.

"Yes! Make arrangements. Pay the fellow out there. What you have to do, do it! And which one is Nader?"

Nehro pointed. The boy Sensenbrenner wanted to see was named Nader. He was at the end of the row of children.

"I want to help you," Sensenbrenner told Nader. He urged Alfi to translate. "Please, we're going to America. We'll get you legs. For you and all your friends."

Alfi passed on the news and told Sensenbrenner, "I told him. I don't think he understands us, sir. He might not be able to understand. They're not just cripples, sir. You see—they were probably abandoned so young they don't have much language."

"Tell him again," Sensenbrenner ordered.

Nader's wounded eyes showed great fear. He had few teeth. He spoke to Alfi in excited mumbles. And then, pulling himself up out of the sarcophagus like a spider, he dropped down on the straw and dust and hand-walked himself to the wall.

Nader tapped on the wall.

"There's more of them in there," Alfi said.

The wall was false, and there were cutouts. Nader was pulling at something in the wall.

Sensenbrenner said, "What is it?"

The other boys had crawled out of the sarcophagus and were scampering to escape, but the exit was blocked by Sandoval.

Nader's long arms pulled out a child. Sensenbrenner guessed

the child was no more than four. Tiny, thin, filthy, here was a child with all four limbs.

Nader mumbled to Alfi. Nader's eyes were bright with encouragement. Nader repeated himself.

"He says it's his brother, sir. His little brother."

Sensenbrenner couldn't weep. It wasn't in him anymore. But then he did feel tears as he bent down to show Nader he understood.

Alfi lit up his torch to help the general see.

What Sensenbrenner saw was a pistol. Underneath the child's rags was a pistol. As if he'd been sleeping with it. The treasured possession, a pistol, hidden under Nader's brother.

Sensenbrenner didn't understand. He never saw what happened. At one moment he was reaching out for Nader's brother.

The next moment there was a *tphut*, and he smelled nitrates, and he felt the dull sharpness he'd felt before, and he reached below his body armor, and he found the wet stain in his groin, and he rocked back on his heels.

Lieutenant Alfi didn't understand right away either. He'd heard the *tphut*, but what was it? He'd smelled the nitrates. He saw the screaming children.

Little Nader had his baby brother in his arms and was screaming.

Sergeant Sandoval came in at the gun flash. He had his weapon drawn but didn't know where to shoot.

"Sergeant," Sensenbrenner said, "I'm hit."

"Where, sir!"

"It's nothing," Sensenbrenner said.

"Sir! Sir!"

Sensenbrenner tasted his teeth. *What's happening? I'm on my back. What's wrong? It's not serious. What's that screaming? The boys are screaming? No. Tell them to stop.*

"Sergeant, it's not bad," Sensenbrenner said.

Sandoval ripped open the general's vest and blouse, and he was yelling, "Lieutenant! He's down."

Sensenbrenner shuddered. It wasn't good that he was so cold. And the light was bright. Too bright.

He thought, *No, not now. I'm not ready.*

The general plunged into shock. He didn't die right away. His team of Yudron, Sandoval, and Alfi did everything they could think to stabilize the trauma, but this was a gut shot—the bullet shattered inside—and the wound was dragging the man's life away like a creature carrying off its kill. Still they might have got him out of the Southern Cemetery to die at the hospital if not for the fact that they couldn't get communication with the embassy operations room.

The American Embassy was off the air, and with it all the satellite uplinks. For at approximately 2200 hours a suicide terrorist had rammed a Volga sedan through the checkpoint and into the service entrance of the American Embassy before detonating four hundred pounds of C-4.

The explosion broke the superstructure on the southern side and tore down the bottom two floors of the building. Missing and presumed dead in the catastrophe was the NATO commander for the city, the Italian general, Niccolo Fazio.

It took all night to sort out the personnel who had survived in the upper stories of the building. It wasn't until near dawn that Ambassador Bob Ketcham and his wife Georgia were brought down to the street level.

By that time the unconfirmed report was that a NATO general was down. The flash went out on the SATCOMs at the airport.

The reply came back: What general? Who? More than one? Who?

33 Thursday, Occupied Moldova

Jack stood on the tarmac with Red Schofield. It was raining heavily now, and the dark was seamless away from the airport lights. It was after twenty hundred hours. The field had refused to clear the Gulfstream's takeoff. Emshwiller was taking responsibility; he was lifting off, no more waiting on the bribes to work. They were going home.

Inside the aircraft, Tim and Anna waited on fate. Outside, two grown men in ponchos, Jack and Red Schofield, were watching the Gulfstream warm up, listening to the engines hiss and whine, waiting on their own silence.

What was left to say? Jack had wept and blamed himself. Schofield had wept and blamed himself. Toni had died anyway—gone swiftly with bleeding they couldn't stop, gone painfully as she choked to death.

After she was dead, and after Jack had screamed at Schofield for the stupidity of his assault on the Bendery demonstration—"You're a butcher, that's what you've become!"—and after Schofield had screamed back at Jack for the stupidity of bringing Toni into Moldova—"I told you to leave her out of it! I told you all!"—and after they'd repeated themselves too many times for sense, Toni was still dead.

The following eight hours of getting her body cleaned and tucked into a body bag and transported back up to Chisinau had slid past Jack like the weather.

And now he stood on the tarmac, and he still hadn't asked Schofield for what he'd come to Moldova for. He still hadn't asked for the statement about FATHER'S DAY.

Jack was thinking, *I don't care. It doesn't matter. I don't care* . . .

Finally in the rain the two men couldn't find a way to go on in their anger and fear without words, so each of them broke down in his own way.

Jack said, "What has to be done, I can do it. For Toni, for the children, I can do it. You know, I lost my first wife. Something stupid like this. Her plane went down. A Cessna 170, a little thing like mine. One night she was flying in great weather, and the next moment she was down in the woods and dead. With her dad. Broken necks. Not a mark, you know how it looks, like they were sleeping. Not like Toni."

Schofield said, "Not like Toni. Not like Mac."

Schofield had been thinking of his dead brother Mac all day, and it was always the same three unanswerable questions: Why didn't I take care of her? What about the children? What kind of brother am I?

Jack changed the subject just as unpredictably as he'd veered to Allison's death. "I guess we know what has to be done."

Schofield said, "I can't come along. I can't come back with you. And I don't give a damn what happens."

"Neither do I."

Now that they were done lying to each other, Jack Longfellow and Red Schofield were ready to begin again with their duty at hand: Jack to get Schofield's statement about FATHER'S DAY; Schofield to give up the truth about Sensenbrenner.

Jack glanced at the Hummer waiting on the colonel. There were two of Schofield's soldiers slumped against the fender, the rain popping off their helmets. The big one was Sergeant Tom Owen. The little one was Corporal Ky. Their posture was defeat. The battalion was in mourning for the colonel's beloved Toni. They'd never met her, only ever seen her dead, but they knew their colonel was heartbroken, and they were, too. All the problems of being stuck in hell with hostiles on both sides of the river—all that was nothing to them now, as they fixed their grief on the dead woman.

Jack saw their grief. *That's what we look like,* he thought. *Stupid guys in the rain. Stupid. Tough. Stupid. Losers.*

Jack said, "It isn't over."

"No, it isn't," Schofield said, and he had a deal of murder in his eyes when he glanced at the Gulfstream, and in the Gulfstream's cabin was Toni's dead body, cold and white inside the body bag.

Jack, having made one step away from Toni's death and toward his duty, fell back again. He couldn't pull away from his guilt. He'd never solved the guilt he felt for Allison's death. Now he was going to shoulder the guilt for Toni's death the rest of his life. He picked up the burden. It was too heavy. He tightened up.

"I brought her along," Jack said, repeating his self-blame for the fiftieth time. "If I hadn't brought her along, if . . ."

"I made the call," Schofield said, repeating his self-blame. "I didn't have to. I . . ."

They'd said this so often before that they didn't even finish their sentences. They were stuck.

Try again.

They were looking past each other now. The airfield didn't exist, Chisinau didn't exist, the pretense that NATO was in charge didn't exist, not even the storm existed. They were both in a prison where they wanted to suffer for what they'd done.

The prison's name was revenge.

"It isn't enough anymore to say what's happened," Jack said, and this time he was moving past Toni—he was closing in on his target. "No more talk. We do it, or we don't. We get Garland and Sensenbrenner, or we don't."

Schofield understood most of Jack Longfellow now—after

he'd seen his savage grief over Toni's body. He didn't like the man as much as he'd figured—he thought him overbearing and obtuse. At the same time he knew the governor of Maine was a sailor, and he could trust the part of the man who'd gone into Walvis Bay to bring out the tankers. He could count on the soldier part of Longfellow. And he could count on the man's father.

Long John Longfellow's a stand-up guy, Schofield thought. *If he sends his son to me, I should . . .*

Schofield's caution made him test himself again: this was a guy who could drop into Walvis Bay and run for the presidency all in the same lifetime, Schofield figured.

Also, this was the guy whom Long John Longfellow had brought up to be president.

Schofield the good soldier took his conscience in his hands and marched on to his own doom. "Okay, Governor, what do we do about it?"

"We get them," Jack said. "We get the guys responsible."

"We're responsible," Schofield said.

Jack let his poncho hood fall away. "Yeah, we are," he said. He liked the rain—it was chill and hard as ice, and it hurt; and he let it blind him a moment. "But we didn't start it. Garland started it."

"You said that already," Schofield replied.

Now that they were finally moving together, they were two elephant bulls going at each other as much as going ahead. Men like this were never complicated about their decisions. They saw what they wanted—they went after it. Neither knew how to back off from a goal, and they might have been locked up together anyway. Not a team, more two men who were not enemies. And what brought them together was that they hated what they'd done; they hated what had been done to them—to the least of them; and their hatred and disgust and rage transformed their motives. It was as if they were laying claim to a carte blanche.

They weren't doing it all at once. In the manner of bosses, they were talking their way to the next level of violence.

"I want to get the guys responsible," Jack muttered.

"You want me to write it down?" Schofield asked.

"It's a start," Jack said.

Schofield left Jack abruptly and walked to his Hummer, ducking into his command seat and fetching out his portfolio. Schofield was a few minutes in writing, and he didn't bother turning on more than the panel lights. When he was done, he strode back to Jack with his head down and handed over the folded-up sheet—a single sheet of yellow foolscap—enclosed in a cellophane food bag.

Jack put it in his bloodstained Marlboro parka without comment.

The truth was that Jack didn't care about Schofield's statement just now. What did it matter? Now that he had it in his pocket—two hundred and twelve exact words about Fort Chaffee and Sensenbrenner and FATHER'S DAY—he didn't care.

He was thinking, *Why should I care? Take it back to Joe Friar? Let Friar call up Roosevelt and read it to him? Watch while Roosevelt squirms and makes a deal? Wait by the side while Garland backs off? For what? Would any of that make it better?*

Jack thought, *I got Toni killed. Schofield got her killed. Garland got her killed. Garland turned us all into Toni's killers.*

Jack's anger was pushing him to go too far to strike back at Garland. He knew that. He went further.

"We get them," Jack repeated his threat one last time.

Schofield heard Jack Longfellow's wrath. He listened to his own rage when he asked, "How's that?"

34 Thursday Evening, Somes Sound

Doctor Connie Jay closed the press conference with her vivid, even-tempered authority at just after 7:30 P.M.

She walked away from the microphone area immediately and started down the long drive of the old Rockefeller place. Halfway along, she took the arm of the president's portly chief of staff, Joe Friar, and the two started talking carefully about events.

Up behind them the TV lights were popping out like supernovas, the correspondents and hangers-on were trampling the iris and tulip beds, the camera crews were scurrying to haul the setups for the tapings and grab the best spots for their correspondents.

There were easily two hundred people moving in all directions between the microphone area at the head of the drive and the satellite-mounted vans across the road.

Another quarter mile down the slope, on Route 102, two dozen folk were busy setting up hot suppers for the crews. It was going to be a long night on presidential watch, and the network folk were settling down to the wait in their lawn chairs and their minivans until the graveyard shift arrived after the late news hour.

Meanwhile, the location producers in the big trucks were on the phones back to the studios. The tapes were rolling. The editors were arguing. And no one was certain which way this huge story was going to jump next.

An hour before, the House of Representatives had sustained Shy Garland's challenge of the president by an overwhelming majority of three hundred and ninety-nine to twenty-six, with thirty not voting. The press conference from the basement of the Capitol had featured Majority Leader Jesus Magellan, who had said it was a somber day in the history of the Republic.

Also, thirty minutes before, Press Secretary Little Crow had read a statement from the White House that Acting President Garland was gratified by the House's decision and that the House had looked carefully at his decision and chosen to back him up. And from Lynch Garland's estate in Houston, Iphigenia Petropoulos's spokesperson issued a brief comment that the Garlands' prayers went out to President Jay.

At the same time, on the international desks, there was the now five-hour-old story out of Cairo about a terrorist car bombing at the American Embassy—though there were still too few details to expand the coverage, and the networks would have to wait until correspondents were able to get to the site.

And now, just concluded, there was the First Lady's reply to the House vote.

The location producers and studio producers reached a compromise on how to play the story.

All else remaining equal, a longish sound bite of the First Lady's remarks would be the leader for the news summaries at the top of the hour.

"We're not resigning, we've no plans to resign, we'll never resign," she'd said straight into the camera's eye, "and those who're calling for our resignation with a single orchestrated voice are going to have to shout louder, and we're not listening anyway."

On the drive, the First Lady was reviewing her statement with Joe Friar.

"I wanted to make it clear," she said, "but I might've sounded too severe. I should've eased up or something."

Friar replied, "You did it right as it can be done. They expected it, and you satisfied them. A no is a no when you say it like that. Everyone got the message."

The cell phone on Friar's hip lit up, and he excused himself and turned away to take the call.

The First Lady stopped at the sharp edge of the big shade cast by the pines. It was a glorious June evening, the golden treasure of the sun on the sheer blue horizon, the sea air freshening from the east, the ground feeders hopping across the undergrowth.

For all the beauty of the setting, Connie Jay looked down at her patent leather shoes and frowned. Her feet hurt, her elbow was sore again, and she was unhappy with how harshly she'd answered the media's questions. She didn't like her figure on television. She looked angry even when she wasn't—and much too nonnegotiable for a politician's spouse, especially for a First Lady.

Friar turned back. "It's the White House calling—Q., I mean. Garland wants a video call with the president at our convenience."

The First Lady asked, "Comments?"

Friar was succinct. "They want us to surrender. This is Garland's idea of mercy: let us deny we're quitting on the air, and then offer us one more chance to walk away—'with our heads up,' he'll probably say. Roosevelt's running the timing of this with the latest polls in his hand. He thinks if you've got the poll numbers, you've got the policy. He can't help himself—he thinks polls are solutions."

The First Lady responded immediately. "Here's what we want. No video call. We don't have the equipment, and I don't want a lot of people on the call anyway. I just want the president and the vice president, and tell them we'll signal when. Comments?"

Friar obeyed and then held the cell phone at the ready. "Done."

"I suppose we're going to have to tell Garland again that we're not quitting," Connie Jay said. She crossed her arms. Her dark suit was like battle fatigues, and her pretty face had the set of a combatant. "We'll call the networks. We'll do the Sunday shows from here. And *Sixty Minutes*—get their camera in here tomorrow. We'll tape it so they can leak out teasers all weekend. And tell the major papers we want their first teams in here Sunday at noon."

"Yes, yes," Friar said.

"And then give me fifteen minutes to call Jean, and then get Garland's call up to us in the bedroom. I'm going to ask the president if I can sit in with Garland. You stay off the line, but in touch. Comments?"

Friar was delighted. At last they were going to fight in public. For five days the president had refused all interviews, and now the First Lady was going to feed the press.

"I'll be downstairs on the intercom," Friar said, "and good luck with Garland."

"He thinks he's playing rough," she said.

"He's nervous," Friar said. "It's the Macbeth thing they're talking about on the news shows. Garland doesn't want the head on his hands. He's hoping we'll give it to him. And since we won't, you can put it to him—if you want."

"I want to make him understand, finally, completely, unambiguously, that we're not quitting, and he's not winning anything. Will he get it? In plain talk. Will he understand?"

Friar shook his head in sympathy and rushed off to his duty, feeling that maybe it was possible to pull this off—maybe if the First Lady helped the president stand up to Garland, and if the

Longfellows could carry out their plan, and if Jack Longfellow brought back Colonel Schofield's confession—and if they could get to Sunday, and if—

The First Lady strode into the house and found her press officer, Adam, at the front phone bank. She gave him a summary of her orders to Friar. She also remembered to ask for the children to be picked up from their supper date down the road.

"I'll want to see little Ted when he gets in," she said, and then in the same breath she switched from mothering a five-year-old to state business, "and get Senator Motherwell for me."

Upstairs, the First Lady crossed quickly to the deck door and peeked out on the president. He was in the green Adirondack chair, wrapped comfortably in his brand-new red windbreaker, and reading his Bible. She decided not to disturb him before she talked with Jean.

On Capitol Hill, Jean took the call at her office in the Hart Building. She was working at her electronics desk in the back of the suite, with the pcs and monitors, overlooking the inner courtyard, and she came alert when Adam's voice came on her line.

"Did you get to see the press conference?" Connie Jay asked.

Jean sighed from exhaustion. "I did, but I didn't listen, I was on the line."

Jean and Connie Jay had talked on and off all day, since Jean had arrived in Washington back from Miami. And Jean expected to be on the phone right up until her flight up to Maine tonight.

Connie Jay reviewed her remarks and then told Jean about Garland's request for a call.

Jean sighed several times as she listened. The results were all on Garland's side. He had the cabinet and now the House, and from what Jean had learned all day, he probably had the Senate. She was on callback with her leadership, and Sue Bueneventura and Nan Cannon were down the hall working their way through the members. The results were less promising than Jean had expected. Brownie McDonald was probably going over to Garland and taking Cindy Belleau and many others with him.

But the Republicans weren't the bad news for the president—it was his own party. Jean had dialed through the eight senators Friar had said were leaning their way.

The two Michigan senators, Sangmeister and Klink, were solid with the president, but the other six from Friar's list—Torkildsen, Molinari, Kanjorski, Bonilla, LaFollette, Talent—were very short of certain. The strongest they'd go along with was they wouldn't announce they were voting against and were willing to entertain joining a filibuster.

Jean could add and subtract. She needed forty-one votes to tie up the Senate. At most she had twenty-five: seventeen Republicans and eight Democrats.

Jean didn't want to talk about defeat just now.

"I agree that Garland won't understand you," Jean finally remarked to Connie Jay. "He thinks you're holding out for something. He can't help himself."

The First Lady said, "That's what Joe says of Roosevelt. 'He can't help himself.' It's like we're dealing with predators."

"I had the same feeling last night," Jean said, "when I was sitting with Rafi and his bosses." Jean didn't want to talk over Miami again—she'd reported at length already—however, she'd come away from the nightclub sometime early in the morning with the feeling that she'd been used by powerful and ruthless politicians. "I know we need them, but that Florida machine isn't something I can ever be comfortable working with, and it makes me glad to be a Republican. And Luke Rainey, he's at home with them. For all that people laugh at him as the best golfer on the Hill, he's got a go-for-the-kill part like them."

Connie Jay wouldn't doubt herself now. She'd agreed to the Rainey deal, she was staying with the Rainey deal.

"We made the right choice," the First Lady insisted. "And now that the House has voted, we can call Rainey tomorrow."

Jean agreed, "Yes, it's time the president called Rainey."

Connie Jay cradled the phone against her cheek and bent her head slightly to look out on her husband. She felt as overburdened as he looked with his slumped shoulders and too-thin cheeks.

Then Connie Jay asked Jean the question most on their minds all day, "Nothing from Jack and Timmy?"

"No, but . . ." Jean decided to reveal her worry. "Long John says that Jack wouldn't call in anyway. That he'll maintain silence until he gets to you in person. Some sort of naval or military thing, you know."

"Yes, it is," the First Lady agreed. " 'Eyes Only' or whatever."

"Jack's coming back, I know it, with Timmy." Jean snapped her teeth together. "And they're bringing what we want. I know that, too. I can feel it."

Actually, Jean felt cold and frightened, and she couldn't stop imagining a phone call similar to the one Jack had received once before, when his Allison was killed in the plane crash.

Long John was sympathetic to her but was also demanding she have faith. He was back at the Georgetown house now, waiting to fly up to Maine late this evening with Jean, and he'd told her earlier in the day, "Jack's silent because he's got it and he's coming home. That's it, Jean. It was always this way with him."

Jean was not comforted, nor did she hide her distress from Connie Jay.

"I think something's gone wrong," Jean said.

"It's hard to wait like this," Connie Jay said. "I'm sorry you have to take so much on yourself, I am. Jean, I love you."

"Thanks," Jean answered, "and I love you. Call me after Garland."

Connie Jay glanced at her face in the dresser mirror, told herself to cheer up, and strolled out to the president.

"Ted, here I am."

The president looked up with one of his sweet smiles. How he loved his wife; how crazed he'd been without her; how much he needed her now if he was going to outlast the demands outside and the demons inside.

"How did the press conference go?" he asked. "Were they listening to your answers?"

"I don't think so. I said what had to be said. It must've worked, because Shy Garland called right after. He wants to talk with you."

The president settled back in his chair and glanced across the cobalt Sound to the brown cliffs and then up toward monumental Cadillac Mountain. His eyes followed two gulls circling down to the shore and then to the lawn by the quay.

"What do we say to him, after all this?" the president asked. He still hadn't shut his Bible, and his gaze, coming all the way down from the gulls, caught the line at the tip of his finger. "I suppose," he continued, "he'll want me to listen to his case one more time."

"We tell him," Connie Jay reminded her husband matter-of-factly, "that when he fails to sustain the challenge, he resigns in favor of Luke Rainey."

"Is he?" he asked.

"Is he what, dear?"

"Resigning?" the president asked.

The First Lady was aware that her husband's energy and focus were not right. She couldn't know if it was the stress or the pharmacotherapy. As a physician, if he'd not just emerged from months under comprehensive care at Walter Reed, she would have looked at the possibility that he needed a physical examination.

Something's wrong down deep with him, she thought. *I'm losing him. His memory? His attention span? His eyesight?*

Is he looking at the Bible right now? Or is he daydreaming?

Yet the option of a checkup or an overnight stay at the clinic wasn't available. The press would figure it out and pound him in the papers tomorrow. Besides, she had the Walter Reed man, Futter, who seemed satisfied that the president was dealing with extraordinary circumstances with an admirable calm.

Futter might call it calm. She called it depression. And in her dark moments since yesterday, she couldn't understand why the Walter Reed team had declared her husband recovered. The symptoms were everywhere she looked. His sleeplessness, his loss of appetite, his disinterest in pleasure or laughter, his inappropriate silences, his self-reproach about trivial details and indifference to large events.

Either way she argued it to herself—if he was lapsing back into a major depressive episode or he was still emerging from one—his conduct veered sharply between the warmth of a loving husband and the cool silence of the man she'd left on the second floor of the White House last autumn.

"I'll have the call up here now," she said. "We'll make it quick. Do you mind if I sit in?"

"No, please do, please." He tried to make light. "You know you always spook Shy. He's not a confident man around women like you."

"Oh?" Connie Jay tried.

"You know," the president said, "women he hasn't married yet."

Connie smiled and took back her dark thoughts for the moment. He'd made a joke! And it was an old joke between them about Shy Garland's notorious libido. It was even welcome, since it addressed the sexlessness of their separation. There was still no spontaneous intimacy between them, and sex would have been a miracle given his distractions and his distance, and yet there were twenty-two years of marriage, and four pregnancies, and three births, and three adoptions, and all those cruel campaigns.

Perhaps he is coming out of it, she thought. *Some rest, a little luck, and he'll come back to me.*

Friar was downstairs in the makeshift office in the dining room. "Joe," she spoke into the cordless, "we're ready for the call."

"Good," Friar said. "Wait a moment, and just put the phone down and tap Intercom. Are you outside on the deck? It's okay, we'll adjust the levels from here."

Friar was sweating with all the balancing he was doing between the presidents and their teams; and he had less than a skeleton staff—just a handful of the First Lady's people, and the president's secretary. It wasn't nearly enough, and it made him angry for the president. That a man who'd given his honest best to his office should be deserted by everyone, that there was no one who even called to help. All the calls just wanted him to quit.

Friar punched on the White House. "We're ready here," he told Roosevelt. "You are I are to stay off the line. Don't screw around, Q."

Roosevelt was in his hardwired chamber in the West Wing of the White House. He could watch Garland take the call in Houston on video while he listened in on the call from Maine. He had no intention of following Friar's order.

"Your call, Joe," Roosevelt said, and he smiled when he pointed to his attack team sitting at his conference table, waiting to process the tapes of the call and use whatever they could to feed the national press.

There was a click. Connie Jay put the cordless on the arm of the chair and sat down on the Adirondack opposite the president's.

"I love you," she whispered to her husband.

The president nodded down at the small blue cordless. "Shy, I'm listening now. It's a lovely evening on the water here. I can see a nest of great blue herons, and there were deer on the paths above me a half hour ago. And the sunshine is brightening the cliffs across from me. That's Parkman Mountain, I think. It's as if God were painting the hillsides for us. It's really more beautiful than I can say."

"I'm glad to hear you're relaxing, Mr. President," Garland replied gently.

Garland was in his father's study, on an open video line to the White House and a voice-only line to Somes Sound, leaning forward, elbows on his knees, hands together, features showing impatience. He'd changed from his riding clothes into a dinner jacket, intending to catch up with Iphy later at a dinner party for him across the road. His shirt was so white it glimmered in the video.

Garland continued, "I hope you've had a chance to think about our conversation on Tuesday evening. And I hope you've looked at what's happened since then."

"Yes, Shy," the president said. "I've been kept up to date."

Garland didn't like Jay's tone. He sounded too peaceful for this sort of conflict. Was he indifferent? Or was there something wrong?

Garland looked into the monitor to signal his puzzlement to Roosevelt with an open right palm.

Roosevelt signaled back with the same gesture. Neither man could read the president's mood.

Garland said, "We need you to move on the resignation, Mr. President. We need it tonight. The House vote was clear. Did you get a chance to see Majority Leader Magellan's comments afterward? He said that 'the will of the House' was as clear as any he'd seen in many years. It's time to listen to your own party. For the good of the country, it's time to listen. Drawing out this question is purposeless and even . . . unwise. Have you seen the markets today? They want to respond positively. Everyone does. We have responsibilities, you and I. We must heed them."

Garland leaned farther into the monitor. What else could he try? A heater under the chin? The man was knocked down. Why wasn't he out?

Get the ball and throw it, Garland thought.

"Mr. President, letting this play itself out is a waste of our resources. You got sick, you resigned. The end of the story."

Connie Jay watched her husband tilt his head and blink quickly. He wasn't going to respond to Garland's creepy provocation.

The First Lady broke in, "Shy, you haven't provided anything new here, have you? You told the president the other night about your responsibilities. We are more than informed of your responsibilities. It's our responsibilities that seem to bother you."

Garland flicked his eyes to Roosevelt.

Roosevelt made a fist.

"Mrs. Jay, it's good to have your help—"

"Was there anything new, Shy?" Connie Jay asked. "Because we don't think there is."

The First Lady's temper showed only in the sharp way she bit off her sentences.

Garland tried, "We'll be going to the Senate tomorrow, you understand, and then the resignation won't—"

"There isn't anything new from you or Majority Leader Magellan or Majority Leader Pickett, is there?" Connie Jay asserted. "Thank you for calling. We'll call you if we want more from you."

"But, Mr. President—" Garland started.

Connie Jay reached out and tapped off the cordless. She punched Intercom. "Joe, did you hear him?"

"Yes, ma'am," Friar answered from his seat, bent over in a tight ball, kneading his neck of the tension. "And you should know, my equipment indicates that Roosevelt was on the line. Someone else was. We were being recorded."

"Comments?" Connie Jay asked.

"About what we expected," Friar said. "It's Garland's style to close the deal early."

"He's a creep, Joe," she said.

"He plays rough," Friar admitted.

"What'll he try now?" she asked.

Friar loosed his tongue and speculated with jargon: "He'll probably call Sonny Pickett and yell at him about the latest poll numbers. Our wire services are reporting a spot poll out of San Francisco that says three out of five approve of the speed of the challenge. Sixty percent's the kind of number that Roosevelt worries about, and he'll worry Garland, and he'll worry Pickett. All night, they'll go round and round."

Friar's instincts were better than he could know, for at that moment Garland, stung by Connie Jay's disdain, was complaining to Roosevelt that Sonny Pickett better deliver tomorrow or he was going looking for a new majority leader right after he chose a new chairman of the Joint Chiefs.

Yet Connie Jay wouldn't have cared. She had her head down, watching the tide change as she questioned Joe Friar closely. "So you think they're going to fight among themselves until tomorrow? Nothing more dangerous tonight?" she asked.

Friar wanted to be decisive. "That's about right. Never not dangerous, but not tonight. They're queasy."

"EXCOM, Joe, what about EXCOM?" she asked. "Are they going to use it tonight?"

It was the critical question, and Friar gave his best answer: "Not tonight, Mrs. Jay." He needed to explain the more. "Garland thinks he's going to win in the Senate tomorrow. He thinks

we're finished. That's why he was trying to close the deal tonight. You see, the president understands Garland very well. He
thinks the presidency is a triumph. And his way of being president is to show off. He was trying to close the deal before his
friends on the Hill close it for him. Garland would say he was
trying to strike us out looking."

"They're creeps," Connie Jay said, and it did make her feel
better.

Friar raised his pitch. "Mr. President?"

"Yes, Joe," the president responded.

"You were great letting him go on, just letting him run at the
mouth. It was great to hear. You know how it makes Garland
crazy when you don't answer his questions."

"Thanks, Joe."

Connie Jay punched off. "Joe sounds upbeat."

"You're the one who deserves thanks," the president said, and
with that he opened his Bible to the passage he'd marked.
Catching himself at his own strange defensiveness, he said, "You
put our side right. There isn't any more to say to Garland. If we
have more, we can call him. He certainly didn't sound like a man
who's won, did he? But then, you've never thought Shy sounded
as confident as he carries on."

Connie Jay was puzzled by her husband's remarks. Not because he was off the mark about Garland, rather because he was
penetrating and apt. Was he getting better, after all? But what
about the aloofness?

Connie Jay said, "I'm going to talk with Joe about doing the
weekend shows. I think we're going to have something to say,
don't you? About Luke Rainey joining us. And about this EX-
COM business that Shy and Roosevelt dreamed up—with Sonny
Pickett and Jesus Magellan and Lew Sensenbrenner. Don't you
imagine the public and press will want to hear more about
EXCOM?"

The First Lady injected her full contempt for Shy Garland.

The president heard his wife's scorn and automatically tried his old habit of seeking to heal.

"You know, EXCOM is chiefly a product of thorough staff work. I know it's gone off, but I'm sure Shy started out doing his job as he sees it. Lew Sensenbrenner wouldn't ever do anything to hurt the country, and Sonny Pickett is . . ."

Connie Jay watched her husband rationalize and asked herself again what was wrong with him.

Can he take this heat? Are we forcing him? Am I any different than the rest of them? Is he strong enough? The damned people won't let him go; his damned staff won't let him go. And now I won't let him go.

But we can't quit!

We do have responsibilities!

If I take Ted to the hospital, we're finished!

Damned Garland!

Connie Jay's forty-nine years of self-discipline couldn't contain her anger in all directions, and she focused it on the president's weakness.

"What are you talking about, Ted!" she demanded. "Listen to what you're saying. Staff work! They're trying to steal the office! Ted, they've plotted to kill you!"

The president's features dimmed; he glanced at his wife, then glanced at his hands, then stared into the Times Roman typeface of the Revised Standard Version.

"All right," he said, "all right. They're wrong."

Connie Jay put her hand on the president's shoulder and leaned over to kiss him on the cheek. "Ted, I shouldn't have snapped. We'll get through this. I shouldn't fuss at you. You're doing everything you can to fight them."

"No, there's always more to do," said the president. "You're right, we have to fight Garland. You remember, during the campaign, you always had to remind me to strike back at him. Sometimes I do miss his attacks."

Miss his attacks! she thought. *What! What's wrong here?*

"We're all tired, Ted," she said. "We have to help each other as much as we can think to."

I need my diary, he thought. *I need to write this down for the children. Connie doesn't understand. Joe doesn't. This is my failure. I chose Garland because I thought he was the best man for the job, and I was wrong. And then I got sick and chose again to let Garland do a job he wasn't suited to. I failed. I did. Not Shy, not Roosevelt, not any of them at the White House, or on the Hill. I failed. I've brought on my own destruction. I'm the plotter. I'm the assassin.*

The president wanted to tame the moment, and so he changed the subject to the future. "Wait till the Sunday shows. We'll get the upper hand then. Yes, there's reason to hope there."

He was thinking of his confession.

The First Lady, pushing aside her doubts about her husband, was thinking of strategy. "I'll be downstairs with Joe. I'm sure there's about fifty calls coming in to tell me how I shouldn't have frowned into the camera." She brushed her hair off her face and turned into the wind. "Do you need anything? Do you want supper sent up, or will you eat with us in the kitchen?" She kissed her husband on the crown and tried not to worry how thin his shoulders were. "Do you want me to send Helen and little Ted up to kiss you good night?" She straightened the collar of his windbreaker. "You should get to sleep early tonight, Ted. You sat up half the night last night, and we'll need you fresh tomorrow. Jean and Long John expect to be here early in the morning. And Jack Longfellow, we hope."

"Is Jack Longfellow back?" asked the president.

"Not yet." She waited to see if he was going to ask for details about Schofield—about what might save his presidency. When nothing happened, she tried, "You know, it will be a long day tomorrow if we're going to stop the Senate."

The president, not answering the point about the Senate, said he wanted only some fish soup sent up.

The First Lady, believing she'd handled the crisis for the moment, raced down the stairs, reviewing her exchange with Shy Garland. After three years of tolerating him as her husband's vice president, it was time to admit that the man was a creep. She should've called him a creep to his pretty face. She could tell the story on *60 Minutes* how she'd forced herself not to call Garland a creep. "Creep," she said aloud. Hit him as hard as a blade, she thought, right between those lying eyes.

Am I taking this personally? Damned right I'm taking it personally. Somebody in this house has to take it personally. Somebody has to fight back hard. "Creep," she repeated.

President Jay stayed in his Adirondack chair well into the magnificent rosy dusk. He read his Bible and stared at Parkman and Norumbega mountains. In time he was happy to see his youngest daughter, Helen, and his youngest son, little Ted, when they ran through on their way to bed. And he sent his bowl of fish soup back empty.

Mostly he continued to read his Bible and watch the gulls lift and sink on the drafts.

Later, they would discover that he'd been going over the same passages repeatedly for days, especially those from Paul's two letters to the Corinthians, such as:

"We are afflicted in every way but not crushed; perplexed, but not driven to despair; persecuted, but not forsaken; struck down, but not destroyed; always carrying in the body the death of Jesus, so that the life of Jesus may also be manifested in our bodies . . ."

As the sun settled into the tree line, the breeze strengthened and the evening opened to the sky—first to burning Venus and a slender moon, and then to the burst of starlight from the Milky Way spilling across the roof of the world.

At the old Rockefeller place, the lights were no less necessary. Out front on the driveway, the TV crews and international press corps were under blue light waiting for the next briefing by Adam LeMarche. In the two-car garage, the Secret Service teams were busy chatting with the Somesville command center. And in the dining area and kitchen, the First Lady and her staff were working with Joe Friar to return calls and make plans.

Soon it was past ten o'clock, and Connie Jay told Calcavecchia's team to get the minivans ready for a trip to the airport. Jean, Sue, Nan Cannon, and Long John Longfellow were coming in from Washington within the hour, and the First Lady wanted to greet them and review the evening's events.

The First Lady was feeling more buoyant than she had for months. Yes, she knew these were the worst moments of the crisis, but yes, too, she was doing something to fight back; she was helping again and not sitting by like a deserter. She climbed into the back of the minivan and pulled up a cell phone to call back Joe Friar, whom she'd just left.

"Joe, I'm thinking we need more communications equipment in. We're out of lines now. And I want video, too, like Jean's got at her house. One of those kitchen table screens. We should've moved on this earlier. Can you find someone to install it tonight? For the morning?"

She glanced at the TV trucks lined up like a gypsy caravan along Route 102. "There must be somebody here who could help us. Don't we have friends on the networks, somebody?"

Friar answered, "We've got lots of friends, Mrs. Jay. It'll be done by dawn."

Friar got off the line and started humming to himself. He was thinking what a champion Connie was. How he'd missed her moxie. No White House staff, no sixty-eight senators and three hundred representatives, could equal the weight one hard-minded First Lady could throw into a Constitutional battle. And what he liked most about Connie Jay was that she had a potent temper and a clean sense of justice.

Yes, yes, yes, he thought. *When we've got Connie Jay and Jean Motherwell, who needs the Twenty-fifth in the first place?*

Friar was in such a good mood that he closed himself off from the news wires for the next few moments as he punched through to his telecommunications pals.

He wasn't paying mind. He wasn't even watching the eight windows on his monitor, when the night turned menacing.

It came on the AP wire first on the window on the lower right corner.

"Cairo. Chairman of the Joint Chiefs General Lucius S. Sensenbrenner was shot dead tonight in an accident during a mission of mercy . . ."

Friar read the words without sharp focus. Then newsreaders started breaking into the other seven windows. Friar flipped open the radio lines on his earphones. News stations in New York and Boston and Detroit and Toronto and as far away as Chicago started picking up the wire. Soon Friar could hear the same AP line read on every fifty-thousand-watt frequency east of the Mississippi.

Chairman of the Joint Chiefs Lucius S. Sensenbrenner. Dead at fifty-six. Shot in Cairo's poorest neighborhood by a four-year-old child. While on a mission of mercy. Not related to the car bombing of the American Embassy nor the death of Italian general and NATO commandant Niccolo Fazio. Recently advanced as vice president designate by Acting President Garland . . . Shock in every capital . . .

Once he shook off his own shock, Joe Friar did two things at once. He called the First Lady's car on his cordless, and he churned upstairs to the president's bedroom.

"Joe, I'm here," Connie Jay answered.

He told her, "Sensenbrenner's dead. Killed in Cairo by a child. Sometime this afternoon, our time."

"My dear God," she said. She was on the tarmac at Bar Harbor. The minivan door was open. The Secret Service had coffee for her. She looked into Calcavecchia's eyes.

Calcavecchia started toward her the instant he saw her fright.

Friar said, "I'm going to tell the president."

"I'll be home as soon as possible," she said. "My God, my God. Sensenbrenner. You're certain? My God. Wait—" she said to Calcavecchia's inquiry. She waved Calcavecchia off. She told Friar, "I'll . . . has anyone called yet? Has Jean?"

"It's just on the wire. My board is lighting up downstairs. Let me . . ."

Joe rapped on the bedroom door. No answer, and he pushed it open. The bed was turned down. There was opera low on the sound system. Puccini's *Girl of the Golden West*. Friar crossed to the sliding doors out onto the deck. The reading lamp was on beside the Adirondacks. The president wasn't anywhere to be seen.

Friar felt the cold of the night air. And something else. His neck prickled. He crossed to the stairs down to the yard. He squinted toward the water and descended the steps quickly.

"Can I help you, sir?" asked the special agent at the base of the steps.

"Where's the president?" Friar asked.

The agent's name was Rolly Fitzpatrick, one of Agent-in-Charge Kleczka's. He leveled his eyes toward the quay. "He's walking along the shoreline. He says he likes the lap of the waves."

"Where?" Friar said.

"There," Fitzpatrick said, but he jumped a little at the alarm in Friar's voice. "I just saw him cross in front of the light on the dock. There. The green light."

Friar slipped and skidded on the sea-damp grass as he and Fitzpatrick padded down onto the wharf.

Friar couldn't get his breath. His question came out as an exhale. "Where?"

Fitzpatrick called out, "Mr. President?" He walked to the motorcraft. *He's sitting at the wheel. He's there. Everything's okay.* "Mr. President?" Fitzpatrick sprang down into the motorcraft. He used his flashlight. Nothing. "Mr. President?" Fitzpatrick asked the darkness and the sea.

Friar was shaking so badly he dropped the cordless on the deck, and it splashed into the water.

Fitzpatrick spoke into his headset. Kleczka came back immediately. The alert was instantaneous. "Peacepipe" was missing. The president didn't answer. "Peacepipe" was missing.

Friar found him. He was hanging half off the floating raft. The hem of his brand-new red windbreaker had saved him from drowning by catching on the ladder. He couldn't have been in the water more than moments, because his flannel shirt was still dry above the chest.

The Secret Service team tried CPR reflexively and then, when it was clear there was no water in his lungs and his heart was beating, carried him back up to his room. No one mentioned suicide. The Walter Reed doctor Futter gave the first word on diagnosis, and it stood up to Connie Jay's opinion when she arrived fifteen minutes later. Still no one mentioned suicide.

The president was paralyzed on the left side of his body with a cerebral stroke. He was breathing on his own. He was alert. He was in no pain. He was as silent as Maine granite.

35 Friday Dawn, Air Force One

Texas dawn was lustrous red out the starboard side port as the big plane leveled off at thirty thousand feet with a ceremonial rock in clear-air turbulence.

Inside the president's quarters, the coffee was rich and hot on the conference table, the overhead TV monitors were aglow with all the network morning shows from the East Coast, and the aides were in and out of the conference room to deliver the latest summaries from the National Security Council, the CIA and the SecDef, the Arab League, and NATO on the ongoing crisis—though they all communicated the same event in the same stark language.

Lucius S. Sensenbrenner was dead.

The chairman of the Joint Chiefs had been shot by a four-year-old orphan boy.

Sensenbrenner had died of his wounds in the back streets of Cairo.

Cairo was rioting out of control now that America's great military hero was dead.

America was in mourning for the top soldier.

All these summaries were directed at the head of the conference table, where Shy Garland and his wife were seated with telephones cradled against their cheeks. They were also both addressing the large video conference monitor on the credenza.

The dour oval face of Quinn Roosevelt was in the monitor,

and he looked as exhausted as he sounded. He had reason. He'd been on duty all night—repeating over and over the same immutable news that Sensenbrenner was dead in Cairo.

Also, for most of the same night, Roosevelt had been arguing with Garland and Iphy, and he'd lost every point.

First, at 10 P.M., when Roosevelt had reported the news to them at their River Oaks dinner party, Roosevelt recommended they remain in Houston through the weekend and not rush back to Washington. "We can let the Pentagon handle this, sir— they've got the plans for it—while we concentrate on the humanitarian side. Get relief into the city. Start the evacuation. Advance our plans to relocate the population."

Garland had rejected the advice and declared he was coming back in the morning to take command of the first crisis of his presidency.

"It's my bad luck, and I'm going to handle it personally," Garland had said. "We've got a weakling president we're about to turn out, a dying secretary of state, an invalid attorney general, and now a shot-dead hero—I've got to show we're still breathing. Full press conference. Address the nation. Foreign policy watershed. Tomorrow night at eight P.M. Call the networks."

Second, past midnight in Houston, after they'd endured the first barrage of demands from the press and their nervous minions, Roosevelt argued that the Senate vote on the challenge scheduled for tomorrow should proceed without interruption. "I know it sounds rough, sir," Roosevelt had said, "but the Senate's never more spooked than in a foreign policy crisis—they'll go for the strong hand by acclamation."

Garland had rejected the advice and declared that the Senate vote was off until after the state funeral for Sensenbrenner.

"I want everything inside the Beltway to stop," Garland had said. "I want every head of state who can walk to attend.

I want every NATO brass hat on the globe to be there. Lying in state Sunday in the Capitol Rotunda. A conqueror's triumph down Pennsylvania Avenue, then across the Fourteenth Street Bridge. The drums beating. The pipers, I want pipers. And the horse-drawn caisson. And the riderless horse. And all the services and the academies—the full West Point corps— the veterans of Walvis Bay and Cairo, all of them, marching in the procession. I want Monday declared a national day of mourning—no banks, no schools, no government. Shut the country down. We're burying our hero at Arlington."

And then, at first light, while they were driving to the airport, Roosevelt had argued that NATO should be left to get the remains out of Cairo and back to America, and they could greet them at Dover AFB.

Garland had declared that Iphy was going to Rome on Air Force One to bring the body home as soon as possible. "She's taking Sensenbrenner's widow—and I want his children there, too; I think they're all in the army—and I want the airport at Rome secure. Whatever it takes. None of that anti-American crap. You tell the Italians. Have Rocky Kahn call them and say we want the full show laid on for the transfer of the body onto Air Force One. They'll get it. They lost a general, too. And have the Italian prime minister put through to me . . ."

And now airborne for Washington, after settling down to business before the seat belts sign had flashed off, Garland and Iphy were arguing with Roosevelt once more.

The problem this time was EXCOM.

"I want a meeting at late supper after my press conference," Garland said, "and I want Sonny cut out."

Roosevelt snapped back, "I can't recommend that, sir. Senator Pickett isn't a problem. He won't understand why he's being cut out. We need him. He's one of our best people on the Hill.

He's ready to deliver on the challenge, and then he's ready to deliver on the delayed budget vote, and . . ."

Garland said nothing to Roosevelt; instead he muttered into the open line on the cordless, "Get me Senator Wheat."

Roosevelt wanted to put his head in his hands; he forced himself erect in his seat with a strong stretch of his back muscles. His could feel his white shirt sticking to his back. He'd eaten two pieces of bland Sicilian pizza in thirteen hours. He'd not spoken directly to his wife in two days.

". . . My people have checked everything on Senator Pickett, sir," Roosevelt began again, remarking upon the surveillance his attack teams had used on Sonny Pickett. "He wasn't the source for any leak. We don't think it came from inside. We think Keebler got it from outside."

"Have you finished?" Garland asked. "Pickett's done," he repeated. "Sensenbrenner was his brainstorm. And his brainstorm just blew up. He's out. You make the call."

"But, sir . . ."

The warrant officer up on the communications deck signaled to the president that Senator Wheat was on the line from Chevy Chase.

Garland spoke into the receiver. "Billy, I need to see you when I get in. We're pulling the plug on the vote today. Yeah, the Sensenbrenner thing. We'll talk about it. Ten o'clock in my private office."

Garland punched the macro key to return to the open line to the Federal Reserve. He asked for the bond quotes from London. He checked the time on the digital clock. Three hours to go before futures opened in Chicago. "Shit," he said.

Roosevelt held his place and waited on his boss. Underlining his humiliation was the fact that this conversation was being watched by upwards of twenty of his staff, who were the stony faces in the windows of his video monitor.

Roosevelt was sturdy enough to try once more. "Sir, perhaps

we can discuss this with Senator Wheat and make a final deter-
mination at that time . . ."

Garland was nasty in reply. "You don't get it, or you don't
want to get it? Or are you saying you want to turn this over to
someone there who does get it?"

Iphy spoke up to the monitor. "Q., I'll make the call, if that's
how I can help. Maybe I could ask Sonny to escort me to Rome.
How would that be? We'll talk about it when I get in. Can you
meet me at Andrews? About three hours?"

"I want Sonny to stay right here where I can watch him,"
Garland said into the monitor while addressing his wife five
feet away, "and if I want you to take along any escorts, I'll
speak up."

Iphy tossed her red locks, made a good decision not to
brighten her smile, and then relented on a point not even she
could hope to alter.

Roosevelt retreated evenly. "Yes, sir. I'll call the senator. Are
there any directions I should give him?"

"You're such a fan of his, ask him," Garland said.

Garland put his open receiver down and took up his coffee
serving. There was no use asking for more doom from the bond
vigilantes. Overnight in Asia, the long bond had cracked like a
pencil at the news of Sensenbrenner's death. Garland didn't
have to check on the markets in Europe this morning—he knew
what Victoria Falls looked like.

The coffee was so hot it bit his upper lip. He'd had a glass of
champagne last night before Roosevelt called with the news of
Sensenbrenner. Now he needed about sixty minutes on the
StairMaster to shake it off. He sipped again. Sixty minutes on
the StairMaster and six minutes on Iphy. Who did she think she
was? Interfering like that? He glanced at the weather map on
one of the network shows. High pressure from the Panhandle to
the Great Lakes. Low pressure off the Outer Banks. Squalls in
Nova Scotia. What was the weather in Rome?

Garland yelled at an aide, "Get me up weather across the Atlantic to the Med. Now!"

At the White House, Roosevelt in the monitor continued to sit in obedient silence at his desk.

Garland was drifting. Garland felt furious in all directions. What kind of help was he getting? This was a nightmare. What was Sensenbrenner doing in Cairo? Didn't he have any sense of what his job was? He was the goddamned vice president if he'd lived out the month. How did he get shot by a four-year-old? What did it say about America to have him shot by a baby? And what did Roosevelt know about the goddamned Senate. Fire them all. Fire Iphy, too. Backshooters! What did Keebler know about backshooters? Clean house!

"Get out!" Garland yelled at Roosevelt in the monitor. Then he was on his feet and yelling at the five aides huddled at the foot of the cabin. "Get out! I know he's dead. How many ways can you tell me. Get out. Shut it off! No more calls! I know he's dead!"

Iphy waited for the aides to recover from the outburst before she slipped across to her husband. The jumbo jet rocked again in turbulence. She didn't speak; she put her slim form against his side. "We know it's bad, Shy, dear, we know. You've worked so hard. It's not fair."

Quinn Roosevelt continued to sit in his chair in the West Wing. His skin was paste. He could have been asleep with his eyes open. He couldn't think clearly. He watched Iphy comfort his boss.

Roosevelt thought, *What can I say to him I haven't already said? It's no one's fault? We can't panic now? We can't break up a winning team? Sensenbrenner's dead because a child shot him with a pistol, and it has nothing to do with us?*

Roosevelt said, "Sir, we'll be moving on the funeral preparations. It'll be what you say. A national day of mourning. The challenge can wait. We'll still be here a week from now. I'll call

Senator Pickett right away and tell him to cancel the Senate session for the day."

Quinn Roosevelt finally got off the line. The bank of video monitors behind him, which had been blank while Garland was on his main screen, popped on with the stony faces of his attack teams over in the Executive Office Building. In front of his desk his primary team of Leeb, Knudsen, and Gerbino was standing at ease, each of them wearing his mike headset and holding his cordless pc on his hip, ready to punch.

Roosevelt patted down his tie and began in his distinctive tone of displeasure: "You heard the president. Air Force One will be outbound for Rome with Mrs. Garland and Mrs. Sensenbrenner. There's a state funeral on Monday. There's a prime-time press conference tonight from the East Room. And there's a meeting of EXCOM tonight. I'll take EXCOM. You do the rest."

Roosevelt put his feet into his loafers and yanked himself from his seat. He needed a walk in the grass. He needed a piece of cheesecake. He needed eight hours of sleep. His assistant opened the door into the Oval Office. Roosevelt took small steps on the thick carpet. The drapes were drawn, so the morning light only leaked around the edges of the large windows. He sat in front of the bust of FDR on the coffee table.

"Okay," he said to the bust. "Okay. Okay. It's my job. Okay."

And then he took his cell phone out of his pocket and told the White House operator to get Senator Pickett on the line.

This is bad decision-making, he thought. *This is asking for it. This is turning a crisis into a catastrophe.*

"Q., what's up?" Pickett, who answered himself, came on the line. "What a day already, yeah? Can you believe how bad it's going. Jesus, look at how they're hollering—and did you hear? Four years old. It's unbelievable. I tell you, I've been thinking about Lew Sensenbrenner, and he was a great man. He really was. This isn't just hot air from me now, this is you and me, and Lew Sensenbrenner was good people."

Roosevelt began finally, "Senator, we've had a change in plans. It's been decided that we are going on without your participation, and the president has asked me to suggest you consider taking a break from your chores."

Pickett's voice was sober. "Speak it plain, Q."

"I have, sir."

"Why's he doing this? Is it because Sensenbrenner got killed? Is he blaming me for that?"

"Sir, there have been several unexplained breaches of confidentiality."

"Hell, Q., you know I didn't leak shit. Why would I do that?"

"I understand, sir," Roosevelt said.

"This is bullshit," Pickett said. "Why he has to have someone to blame . . ." Pickett paused and found his conversational tone again. "All right, you tell the president that I'm obeying orders. I'll stay in line. I'd like to be with you these last few days, but I understand. And tell the president I will deliver the Senate next week. As soon as we get past this Sensenbrenner problem. I'll be here for you, Q. Tell him that. I'm on his side, whether he trusts me or not."

"Yes, sir, I will tell him just as you say." Roosevelt was feeling better. Pickett was a first-rate politician. Never say never.

"And Q.," Pickett added, "tell the president to watch his back. There really is somebody out there who's working against us somehow. I do believe that. Watch your backs. We all should."

"I will report your good and judicious counsel, sir," Roosevelt answered, "and sir, I agree with you. Something is working against us. It's my problem but I haven't been able to solve it. So far."

36 Friday Morning, Somes Sound

Jack slouched in the copilot's seat alongside Emshwiller for the landing at Bar Harbor. It was five hours from Chisinau to London, and, after a sluggish refueling at Gatwick, it was eight hours from London to Maine. Jack had sat awake for the first few and last few hours of the flight. Now he was empty of every emotion but cold regret.

The Gulfstream dropped through the cloud layer ten miles out, and soon Jack was able to fix on the skull's head of Swan's Island and the green giant profile of Mount Desert, then there was the slender canyon of Somes Sound. The sea was slate, the wind was strong from the west, the tide was out, and it was going to storm later, rain squalls spinning counterclockwise down from Nova Scotia.

Jack's mood was so black that he felt a sharp relief to see that the island wasn't on fire, the fishing fleets at Bass and Southwest harbors were intact, a gleaming Coast Guard cutter was on quiet patrol off Great Cranberry Island.

The president's fine, he thought. *Connie's fine. Dad and Jean and Lil and Lou are fine. I'm the one who's not. And Toni. What do I do about Toni? About the coroner? About her babies—God, her babies—*

Emshwiller identified his equipment to the field once more and told them he was proceeding straight in. The field came back with the winds and the active runways. As they banked over Frenchman Bay, Jack forced himself to stare at Hancock Point.

Two days ago she was alive down there, getting dressed for the office. And then Dad called. And then she volunteered. And I let her. And she's dead.

The Gulfstream banked over the water, gained the trees, then settled smoothly in heavy air, flaps down, power up and down, the ryegrass field racing past in a blue line. The parking lot of private airplanes stretched wing to wing from the shrubs to the taxiway, with the multiple-engine and jet aircraft deployed closest to the airfield office. The Maine National Guard helicopter, an old Blackhawk, was tied down near the auxiliary hangar. Emshwiller taxied back in and parked alongside the president's plane—a Gulfstream V that looked to be the exact twin of Emshwiller's.

Jack was immediately alert to spot the First Lady's man, Calcavecchia, who came trotting out of the field office. Jack glanced to the other side of the fence to see the Secret Service minivan and two cruisers pulled up with their lights on.

What's wrong? What's worse than Toni?

Jack unbuckled, patted Emshwiller on the shoulder, and pushed back into the cabin. Tim Seward and Anna Hrbek were just waking up, and they looked to Jack for instruction. If he'd had more time, Jack would have comforted them—Toni's death had battered their faith in a better tomorrow—but Jack wasn't slowing down even for them; and he ordered, "We're going to have a lot of questions from Customs. You let me handle it."

Tim wiped his face and glanced back at the body bag laid out behind the last seats. It wasn't a nightmare. "I still can't accept it," he muttered.

Anna Hrbek took Tim's hand and opened her lips to speak at length; but then the reporter in her offered only, "We're safe now, Tim," and she sat back in dejection.

Jack knelt down beside Toni's body. He couldn't touch her anymore. She wasn't here. This was the remains.

The copilot popped the hatch to lower the stairs and let in the moist Maine air. The sudden power shutoff settled a rushing silence on the cabin. The ordeal was done, they were home, and each of them, Jack, Tim, and Anna, felt the failure.

Within moments there was pounding on the steps and Calcavecchia pushed inside. "Sir, Governor, sir. You've got to come with me, sir. The First Lady needs you."

Jack said, "I can't just yet. We've got trouble here." Jack let Calcavecchia register the body bag first and then Tim's and Anna's sober postures. "Mrs. Schofield was killed overseas. At a place called Bendery. Random gunfire that caught her."

Calcavecchia's eyes showed he'd seen body bags before. "Yes, sir," he said. He punched off the light on his headset.

"I've got to deal with Customs and her family and—"

"Governor, please," Calcavecchia said. "My people can take care of Customs—"

"No, no," Jack said, "I want to handle it. The funeral home, and we've got to talk to her family and . . ."

Calcavecchia's expression was shadowy and his tone was dogged. "I'm sorry for this, but . . . sir, the First Lady needs to see you right away. I'm not pushing this aside, I understand you've got it bad here, but . . ." He tapped his cell phone on his belt. "They're expecting you. Your wife's there, Senator Motherwell, and your father . . . we've got to go now, sir. It's a hurry-up. Major hurry-up."

Jack objected, "I can't just leave her like this."

Calcavecchia asked if he could see Jack outside. His eyes locked on Jack's, and he wouldn't back off. He was also forceful in the way he led Jack down the steps and out several yards from the aircraft. The sky was grainy gray now, the wind backing, with droplets in Jack's face.

"Sir, the president collapsed again last night . . . he went into the water somehow." Calcavecchia spoke in bursts of information. "Off the dock there at his house. They got to him before he went under, but they say he's hurt. Paralyzed a little. I didn't see it. Larry Kleczka got him out of the water and says he's kind of paralyzed down the side. The doctor you brought from Walter Reed says some sort of small stroke. The First Lady had him put in their bedroom, and she doesn't want us to move him to the hospital. We're not allowed to move him. You see?"

Jack didn't respond and kept looking away, back to the aircraft and Toni.

Calcavecchia's face flamed with frustration. "Sir . . . I don't know, but it's my job, you see . . . ? The First Lady says he's safer at home. I don't know what she means. We should get him to the hospital, shouldn't we? Why shouldn't the president be safe at the hospital? Is something going on we don't know about?"

"Take it slow, Mike," Jack said.

Calcavecchia swallowed and then rubbed his hands together. "Your wife, Senator Motherwell, and your dad—I mean, Secretary Longfellow—they flew up late last night, and they've been with the First Lady all night. Larry Kleczka and I've been waiting for you. We need your help, sir. We're thinking we maybe should get the president to a hospital, and, you know, we need you to help us with the First Lady. The fact is she's not talking to us. She told Larry she wouldn't make a decision until you got back. Senator Motherwell, she told me that you'll make the right decision."

Jack glanced to the president's plane. "Where's my dad in all this?"

Calcavecchia's shadows deepened. "Last night, he was on the phone, you know, about General Sensenbrenner and all, you know, and I didn't see him after that. I think he went back to your house. I've been here since before dawn waiting for you."

Jack heard what Calcavecchia said, but it didn't make sense to him for a moment. He could see Calcavecchia's worry; and he could hear that even for bad news, this was worse. Jack thought, *Sensenbrenner?*

"What about Sensenbrenner?" he asked.

"He's dead—you know, did'ja hear? You didn't hear? He was killed yesterday in Cairo."

"Yesterday in Cairo?" Jack repeated blankly.

"Yes, sir, by a child, they said—an accident, they said, he was trying to rescue children, and a pistol went off. Weird, you know."

Jack asked, "When did this happen?"

"Yesterday. Last night," Calcavecchia corrected. "Though I think it happened sometime yesterday afternoon, our time—we didn't hear about it until late last night."

"Before the president collapsed?"

"About that time, yes, sir." Calcavecchia realized that Jack was assembling the sequence of events. "Certainly not after," he said. "Because I was down here with the First Lady waiting for your wife and dad to come in, and that's when we got the call from Mr. Friar that General Sensenbrenner was dead, and right after that—just a few minutes—the call came again from Mr. Friar that the president's down."

The president's down, Jack thought. The words triggered Jack's imagination. *The president's down.*

Is that how we do it? Jack thought. *Is that what we should do? Is that how we get Garland?*

It was a premature idea. He didn't have the facts.

Still, Jack thought, *the president's down.*

Jack didn't have time to think his idea through now, he just had time to give orders and react. He called Emshwiller and the copilot outside and told them he needed them to wait here with their equipment. He told Calcavecchia to get his men in here to deal with Customs about Toni's body. He told Tim and Anna what to do, what to say, and where to wait for Customs and the coroner. He told Tim especially, "Stay by the phone, we'll need you today, your mother and me."

Jack considered going inside the aircraft once more to say good-bye to Toni, but he decided that was irrational and would probably drag him back down. Instead he walked briskly to the Secret Service vehicles. Jack knew all the state troopers at the cars by sight or first name, and he returned each of their taciturn nods with the same. The governor was back, they understood, and something big was happening—time to button up.

"You drive me, Mike," Jack told Calcavecchia, and then he climbed into the front seat of the minivan. He had to check his idea. "Swing me around to the president's plane a moment, will you?" Jack asked. "I want to take a look."

Calcavecchia puzzled but didn't comment. He eased the minivan around the fuel storage tanks and onto the taxiway, then backed up to the overhang of the president's parked Gulfstream V. "It looks fine to me," Calcavecchia said. "We've had your troopers guarding it since we landed. Some problem?"

Jack looked from the president's plane to Philip Morris's. Except for some of the electronics and the midair refueling capacity, they were the same equipment. And Schofield had taken a good look at the inside of the Gulfstream cabin and flight deck.

"Some problem, Governor?" Calcavecchia repeated.

"None," Jack said.

Jack thought, *It's far-fetched, but—it'd work. If Jean set it up—it might.*

Jack ordered Calcavecchia to take him to the president. On the fifteen-minute drive, Jack weighed all his doubts against his expectations. He asked himself how desperate he was feeling. He asked himself how far he would go. He had the motive. He had the weapon. He had the opportunity—if the president would give it to him.

But a small stroke? What's a small stroke?

The TV trucks were lined like a chain-link fence all through the village of Somesville. Even at this early hour, the Higgins general store was open to serve the demands of the media crowd. Jack watched the weary faces of the reporters and crews as they sipped coffee, ate doughnuts, smoked cigarettes, and shivered in the drizzle—all of them with the gloomy looks of professionals getting set for another day of doing their jobs. The semis, the vans, the sedans and motorbikes, the campsites filled up with RVs—it was as if a circus had come to town, as if the greatest show on earth was arrayed around the big top of the old Rockefeller place to watch the last act of President Teddy Jay.

Jack had Calcavecchia stop at the general store long enough for him to get a copy of the *Bangor Daily News*. He had time only to scan the heads. The hydra-headed story was all in big type:

Jay Will Not Resign—First Lady Rebuts Garland
House Supports Garland, 399–26
Senate Vote Crucial—Motherwell Comments
Cairo Embassy Destroyed—City Abandoned
Global Financial Markets Shaken

Below the fold in the state news columns, there was a headline that Senator Nash had rejected Governor Longfellow's savings plan. Jack smiled at Bonnie Nash's name. His favorite adversary seemed faraway and a long time ago, and he felt comforted by her mention.

Out at the turnoff, the state police cruiser leading them forced aside the final obstacle of a semi unloading more equipment. Hall Quarry Road was a stream of heavy electrical cable from the generators. At the old Rockefeller drive, Calcavecchia took the turnoff sharply, halting only an instant at the checkpoint to show his ID and tell them to call the house, the governor was coming in.

As they pulled ahead, Calcavecchia asked Jack, "Sir, can you tell me why we took a look at the president's plane?"

"No, I can't," Jack said.

Calcavecchia's frown told Jack that he'd alienated the man. Jack let it go. For what he had in mind, he couldn't get close to the Secret Service.

The house was a fortress now, with Secret Service agents and state troopers posted at the corners and along the drive. The Fisheries cutter was midchannel in the Sound. Jack figured that if the reporters had just used their intuition, instead of waiting on press releases, they could have spotted that the president's party had circled the wagons for a severe cause.

There was an AT&T van pulled up in front of the front porch, and the troopers were watching two Mainers haul large crates.

Jack got out of the car beside the van, and the state police watch commander, a Bangor man named DePalma, hurried up to the governor to report all was well.

Jack pulled DePalma aside from Calcavecchia. "What happened last night with the president?"

"We don't know, sir," DePalma said, nodding toward the Secret Service agent on the drive. "They've taken care of the inside of the perimeter. But I know they did have something on last night." DePalma added details that were not conclusive but most suggested that there'd been an accident by the water.

When the steward opened the front door, Joe Friar was standing there in a dull white shirt and black suspenders, looking as if he'd been beaten. "I'm relieved you're back," Friar started, his hand out wearily. "Did you get what you went for?"

"I did," Jack said, but he didn't hand over the paper right away. He wanted news first. The hall smelled of coffee and frying eggs. Jack could hear the two children and their nanny in the kitchen getting ready for school. The TV monitor in the living room was on low volume with the morning news shows. It was odd to see the president's grim portrait flashed over Friar's shoulder. And then there was a clip of Garland in a dinner jacket and Iphy Petropoulos in a gown both parading out of a house in Houston.

Jack asked, "What about the president? Mike said a small stroke, and he's paralyzed. Is that right?"

"Mike told you about the president?" Friar asked, avoiding the question with obvious discomfort.

"And he told me about Sensenbrenner," Jack said. "We were flying all night, and missed the news. You realize—with Sensenbrenner gone, what I brought back is nearly useless. Without Sensenbrenner, there's no link to Garland and EXCOM. Joe, do you understand me?"

"May I have it?" Friar asked. He reached out without energy.

"Joe, what's going on?" Jack asked. "How bad's the president? What's a small stroke?"

"The president and the First Lady want to see you right now," Friar said.

Jack realized that Friar was lying. "Is the president dying, Joe?" Jack asked. "Is the First Lady hiding that he's dying? Is that why the news blackout? There's a wall of cameras out there about a quarter mile. How can you keep news like a stroke from them? Tell me."

Friar sidestepped the point: "The First Lady says we're waiting for you, and for the statement from Schofield. Please, just let me take it to her."

Jack reached into his parka for Schofield's statement and handed it over, still in the plastic food bag. As he straightened the lapel, Jack touched a dark spot on the hem. He'd changed out of the Marlboro parka he'd had on yesterday that had been stained through with Toni's blood. This wasn't blood, but it made Jack angry all over again.

"I need the truth," Jack demanded. "Toni Albanese is dead,

Joe—she died for that paper. Yesterday, in Bendery, she was shot in the throat. Just like that—she was alive, then she was dead. For that paper and for the president. You hear me? She said we couldn't get Schofield unless she went along, and she was right . . . right, right, right"—Jack paused to keep himself from hitting Friar in the face—"because after she died, Schofield just handed it over without argument." Jack lowered his voice to emphasize his fury. "What's happened to the president? Tell me."

Friar cringed and sagged. He wouldn't give up to Jack no matter the threat.

Just then Jack heard a familiar ninety-horsepower motor from the direction of the water, and he stepped past Friar to get into the hall far enough to see through the dining-room picture window. It was his father and wife coming hard across the Sound in his Boston Whaler, with Jean at the wheel. Jack didn't ask permission of the agents, he stepped down through the mudroom and went onto the lawn and then down to the wharf.

It was a much harsher day on the water than on land, with the wind gusting down the Sound and the downdraft off Northumbega and Parkman mountains. The mist was icy; the air tasted like iron. Long John's white hair was frayed in the wet wind, and Jean looked drenched in her best trench coat. A bow wave struck high enough to slosh Jean's boots. Jean backed the engine and glided toward the floating raft. Jack raised his hand for Jean to toss him the line. Just then, Jean saw the grief in Jack's gaze and demanded over the idling of the motor, "No! Is it Tim? Jack, where's my Tim?"

Jean's puffy eyes and plain face showed she hadn't been awake long. Indeed she'd slept sitting up, first next to Long John on the Philip Morris plane up from National, and then next to Connie Jay in the upstairs parlor at the old Rockefeller place. At dawn she'd forced herself awake to dash over to her house to change for the day—and just as she'd gotten out of the shower, she got the call from the Secret Service that Jack had landed at Bar Harbor.

Now her thought was terror. *It's bad news. It's—*

"No, no!" Jack called over the engine. "Tim's fine—he's at the plane with Anna." He knelt down to tie off the line. "It's not Tim . . ."

Long John slapped his knees. He'd had only one fixed worry for two days, and now it was eased. Jack was fine.

". . . it's Toni," Jack continued. The boat banged once against the planks and Jack kicked it off muscularly. "She was killed yesterday in Bendery. Nobody's fault, everybody's fault. A ricocheted round in her neck, and she died . . . She died trying to run to Schofield. Down these steps during a riot. We brought her body back and it's still on the plane. Tim stayed to deal with Customs. Her family doesn't know yet."

Jean could hear her husband's fury and guilt. "My God, dear, dear God," she said, her eyes brimming with tears.

Long John leaned aside and made a rough sound of depleted despair.

"I told you she shouldn't go," Jack said, but then he remembered that if anyone was worth blaming here, it was himself, and he added, "Okay, I'm sorry, okay . . ." Jack kept talking as he helped his father and wife up out of the boat. He repeated every detail he'd already communicated about Toni's death and added nothing they didn't know about the catastrophes of Jay and Sensenbrenner. And when he had said everything about Toni twice, and when he was beginning a third time to tell how he and Schofield and Tim and Anna had wrapped Toni's body and brought it home, he was interrupted by the momentum of events.

"Governor!" called out Joe Friar from the rail of the second-story deck. Forty yards away, Friar still looked tired and frustrated. "We need you now, Governor! Senator Motherwell! Mr. Secretary! Please!" Friar beckoned. "The president and First Lady need to see you!"

Behind Friar, at the drapes, was the pale, stern face of the First Lady. Below Friar, in the dining-room window, Larry Kleczka and Mike Calcavecchia were standing with their arms crossed and their jaws fixed.

Jean could see Connie Jay's sad eyes even from this distance. Jean had spent all night trying to console the inconsolable. "They want us, now," Jean told Jack. "And there's something you've got to know about the president."

"Help me get up there," Long John asked, waving his walking stick at the step above them.

Jack took his father's arm as he asked Jean, "You mean what I don't know is that the president's dying, is that it? I could tell Friar was lying to me. What is it? How bad a stroke?"

"It's not a stroke," Jean said. She took Long John's other arm, and together with Jack she eased him up the ramp from the raft. Jean declared, "I think he tried to kill himself. Last night. I think so, don't you, LJ?"

Long John nodded. "Yes, yes, tell him, Jean."

Jean cleared her throat. They were at the flagstone path. Friar was watching. She spoke in haste. "They got him out of the water in time, because he collapsed before he could go in. Back there, on the ladder of the raft. But from the story I got, he was clearly trying to do away with himself. Just go swimming and not come back."

Jack was not stunned. Jay was a genuinely crushed man, totally unfit for office, and suicide was just a grotesque part of the risk of the circumstances. "Was there a note?" Jack asked.

"I haven't seen it. I think so," Jean explained. "I sat with Connie for most of the night while we waited for you and watched over the president. There were things she said and didn't say that make me think there's a note. She knows it was suicide. She knows how sick he is. We agreed to wait for you before we talked again."

"Right," Jack said. His idea was growing into a plan of action and a battle order. He did reach for some reassurance and some facts. "Dad," Jack said, "you always say that in this business, we fight because we fight. And we fight to finish." Jack knew the answer, but he asked anyway, "We finish this one, together, right?"

Long John gripped his son's arm. Everything he'd worked toward was in this boy, along with a great deal he hadn't counted on, such as cunning. "Yes, Jack." And then he switched over to his judgmental voice. "Will the president finish with us is the question. Whatever we do, we still do report to him."

Halfway across the lawn, Jack asked, "Dad, did you get to see Keebler? Did you put the line about EXCOM across?"

"Wednesday night," Long John answered. "It was on television within hours. In fact, Jean was on television, on *Nightline*, talking to Sonny Pickett about EXCOM within hours. We've no information what damage we did, but Garland's been quiet in Houston since then, and I think he's headed back this morning. That's the latest on the television, that Garland's en route to the White House. The Sensenbrenner crisis. They're paralyzed down there. I talked to Ez Kahn this morning, and he thinks there's real panic at the Pentagon. I'll know more when I talk to him later."

Jack liked what he'd heard, and he turned to Jean's news. "You did *Nightline* with Sonny Pickett? From Miami? Good, good. Did you get Rafi and Rainey to come along with us?"

At the edge of the lawn, Jean spoke conditionally. "I think so, this time, yes, Jack. I don't know what they'd say if they knew what we do about last night, but yesterday they were with us. It was a strange situation—me and the whole Florida machine in the back room of a nightclub, but they made the deal you thought they would."

Jack spoke to both Jean and Long John. "Good, you did real good, thanks."

"What are you thinking?" Jean asked.

"A way to finish," Long John answered for Jack.

Jack and Jean struggled carefully to help Long John up the slippery steps to the second-story deck. The three of them knitted together as they reached Friar.

Jack snapped, "You lied to me about the president."

Friar shrugged; he'd lost control last night and wasn't going to get it back—not between temperaments such as those of the Jays and the Longfellows. He wiped his wet lenses. He couldn't feel his fingertips. "Schofield's statement makes me sick at heart," Friar said. "To see that Sensenbrenner went along with such an outrage. To hear the praise for him on the news, and to see what he's done."

"That isn't an excuse for lying to me," Jack fired back, and then he shoved past him.

As Jack approached the First Lady at the open sliding door, he found he was ready to go on the attack. These lying Jays. These weakling Jays. What was he fighting for if they were going to run away? What had Toni thrown herself away for? Who was in charge if the Jays weren't in charge?

"I'm here to see the president and speak my mind," Jack told the First Lady. The cold smell of the open air rushed off of Jack's large form and overwhelmed the soft warm interior of the room.

Connie Jay blinked at Jack's aggression and stepped back, twisting her mouth in concern. "That's all we ask, Jack, and"— she let her eyes dart into the room behind—"we're glad you're back."

Jean squeezed through the door between Jack and Connie

Jay. She could see Jack's rage, and she tried to signal him without words that he should be considerate and remember all their problems before he started with his demands.

The president sat stiffly in the big armchair, dressed in a red-checkered wool shirt and voluminous corduroy trousers. His face was vivid and too thin, but he didn't look as weak as Jack had expected. They'd brought in the emergency equipment such as the oxygen tent and the life-support monitors, but none of the machinery was hooked up. There were vomit bags under the book stands. Jack glanced again at the president. What did a suicide look like? He was alive and soft featured, as if he'd had the best sleep in the house. Yes, the left jaw seemed stiffened, and there was a bruise on his temple and a raw abrasion on his throat from a fall, but he wasn't acting like a man who wanted to die. His dark eyes clearly were focused. He watched Jack stride into the room to the edge of the hook rug; and he watched Jean sit at the edge of the loveseat and Long John settle beside her.

The First Lady yanked the drapes closed to leave the chamber in a dull gray southern light. "Jack," she started again, "the news about Mrs. Schofield is awful and sad, and I'm—we're—very sorry for her family. You must have had a terrible time—"

Jack interrupted, "She was trying to help, wasn't she?" He emphasized his change of pace. "And now we're going to help, too, or are we, Mr. President?"

The president hardly reacted—perhaps a roll of his right shoulder—as his wife stepped closer to him in protection. Connie Jay had the yellow foolscap of Schofield's statement in her cardigan pocket. She involuntarily touched it as Jack pointed at it.

"But that isn't going to do it, is it, Mr. President?" Jack asked. He took a strong step toward the armchair. The president's face remained alert and passive. "I told Joe and now I'm telling you. That doesn't do it. Schofield signed that last night. It names

Sensenbrenner and the vice chairman, Breckenridge, and a colonel named Johnny Jones of the Joint Staff. It doesn't mention Garland or Roosevelt or anyone at the White House or on the Hill. Just the principals of FATHER'S DAY."

The First Lady tried to stop Jack's assault. "We understand there're problems with it."

"No, you don't," Jack said, and again he directed his anger at the president. "Because you still think you can work this out with Garland. You've thought that since we saw you at Mount Vernon on Tuesday. You think it's between you and Garland and the Constitution and something called your 'responsibilities.' Hey! It's not! You can't work this out with Garland! Sensenbrenner's dead. Right, Joe? He's dead and so's what his presence could have done for us?"

Joe Friar had his head down and his hands jammed in his pockets. "Yes, Governor, he's dead."

"Dead is right. It's amazing but it's apparently true. Dead by a gunshot, the paper says. By a four-year-old. Right," Jack continued. "And with Sensenbrenner gone, there's no link between Garland and EXCOM. Sensenbrenner was the only vulnerability Garland had. With him gone, Garland's clean. You know the way it works at your level. You talk about responsibilities but you're not responsible for anything you do! You mislead about your responsibility. You misrepresent your responsibility. You invent your responsibility. And no one can blame you. You know that the only person who can stop Garland is you or someone at your level. And Sensenbrenner was the man at your level. But he's gone, and you're frightened. You finally want to quit. But you can't, can you? Because this has gone past you and Garland. You look at the reporters out there. You read the headlines this morning. We're in trouble. And you know we are, and you know you caused it—"

Connie Jay interrupted, "You don't know what you're talking about."

"I know a lot," Jack shot back. "I know Toni Albanese died miserably because of you"—Jack threw his fist out at both the president and the First Lady—"and I know you tried to quit. With your stroke!" He shot a look at Joe Friar. "Your stroke in the Sound."

Connie Jay stared at Jean, and Jean stared back. *I'm with Jack,* Jean thought. *I'm staying with Jack.*

"And I know," Jack continued, "we're not going to get out of this trouble by making deals with Garland and his EXCOM pals—who are the damned government, Mr. President—EX-COM is the damned government you left behind as a caretaker while you took care of yourself. EXCOM is Sonny Pickett and probably Jesus Magellan and probably more of your party's whole godawful leadership on the Hill and in the cabinet. Who isn't EXCOM of that gang you left in charge of the White House while you faced your personal crisis for five months of hand-holding?"

The president waved his right hand across his chest. He wanted to talk, but nothing was coming out. And then he managed, "Yes, Governor."

His voice was a croak, but it was speech. Jack shot back, "You can talk? Good, good, you can talk."

Connie Jay was still trying to shield her husband. "What do you want from us?"

"I want you to do what I say," Jack returned. "We're all in this, and we're going to get out of it my way. Are you listening to me, Connie, or are you worrying about your suicide watch?"

"You can't know how it is for us," the First Lady said. "I'm not going to stand here and listen to you tell me what we should have done and how we should have thought and what we must do. It isn't for you to tell us any of that. You can't know what it's like to be in the White House. You can't come in here and tell Ted what he's done wrong. You see what they've done to him. You see how they want to destroy him."

Connie Jay took a breath. She'd listened to her own words and didn't like what she'd heard. She was very smart, and she recovered from her self-pity with, "Okay, okay, wait . . . Jack, I'm sorry. You're trying to help. I just needed to say that. I shouldn't have."

"No, you shouldn't have," Jack returned bluntly. "It wasn't what they've done, Connie. It's what you and the president have done, and what you've done is you've failed. You too, Joe. What you should have done is kept winning. From the first day in office, from the first hour, you had to keep winning. And you didn't. You got off onto something called governing and policy making. You know, what I think is, to hell with your governing. Your job was to win and win and win. You're only one-third of the government—you have to win every day to hold up your part. And you tried governing. Goddamn governing with scheming little EXCOMs in every agency and on every congressional committee."

The First Lady looked as if she was going to argue back. She started, "Jack, it's really just not fair of you to preach to us now."

"Connie, you want to fight Garland? You want to be right, or do you want to win?"

Jack was now so wound up he didn't care where he was. He was the governor who mistrusted government, the heir apparent who disapproved of the inheritance.

"I want us to help my husband," Connie Jay answered.

"That's beating Garland—so say it!"

Connie Jay nodded. "All right, Jack."

"Good, because we're going to beat Garland with his own weapon," Jack said. "With his own damned weapon. Beat him bad! Because not until we beat him into the ground are we going to win. No deals, no exchanges, no trade-offs. We win or we lose. And I say we win."

Jack stared angrily at the president. "I'm not asking your

permission. You're not president another moment unless you do what I say. You tried to leave us last night. Now you're going to fight the way I say."

Jack knew exactly what he wanted, and the first thing was that he wanted the president and First Lady to stop withholding the truth about last night.

Jack addressed Connie Jay. "We need what he wrote you last night before he went into the water. The letter, the note, whatever it is. Give it to Jean. Now."

Connie Jay asked, "Why?"

"Do it," Jack said.

"I can't," she said. Her face was a beautiful mask of piety. "It's private. It's not mine to give."

"Mr. President, I want the note for Jean, now," Jack said. "Answer me. You can answer me."

The president had his head down, listening but not responding to his shame, but at Jack's remark he bobbed his head. He felt as if he were already gone, as if he were listening in on what history was saying about his significance. But then he deliberately raised his good right hand and gestured for his wife to act.

Connie Jay understood him, and she stepped to the dresser and took the president's diary—the plain black cloth binder—out of the top drawer and moved toward Jean. "It's not a suicide note," she said. "It's his diary, and he left it open to this page." Connie Jay showed Jean what she meant by "this page" when she pulled the diary open as if it weighed fifty pounds. And then Connie Jay carefully tore out the page and handed it to Jean.

Jean shook her head in sympathy. To leave your wife a goodbye in your diary. Was it loving or cowardly? Jean didn't want to decide.

"We need the statement from Schofield, too," Jack said. "Please, give it to Jean."

"I need to know what's going on here," Connie Jay replied, though she had her hand on the sheet in her pocket.

"It's called a honey trap," Jack said, "and that paper's part of the honey, and Garland is his own trap. Now we're ready to begin."

Jack checked his father's face. " 'Honey trap' is the right term, Dad—the right spook word?"

Long John Longfellow gave his son all the approval necessary. " 'Honey trap' is exactly the right word."

"Everyone has an assignment," Jack said, "and once we begin, we're going to have to move fast without arguing about it. This isn't the White House and isn't going to be. Joe"—Jack turned to Friar—"we're going to need statements put out this morning and maybe all day. Have you got a team that can do it? And have you got the equipment?"

Friar shrugged at the irony of his predicament. From a White House staff of twelve hundred, he was down to about half a dozen, counting stewards. "I could use a pro or two," he said.

Jack said, "Put out a statement that the president will have a major address tomorrow at noon. Get that on the wire as soon as you hear that Garland's landed in Washington. Give it first to the cable networks." Jack ignored Friar's doubtful glare. "I need it now, Joe."

Friar looked at the First Lady. When she nodded, he asked Jack, "The president will have a personal statement? Will he take questions?"

"Yes, a full press conference. Noon, here, rain or shine. Tell them it's a major statement and let them run with it."

Friar asked, "Are we talking about a resignation?"

"We're not resigning like that," Connie Jay said.

"There's no good way to resign," Jack reminded them. "And we've got a deal of fighting before then." He asked Friar, "Those crates I saw coming in from the telephone van. That's video equipment?"

"Yes, we got it looking to do the Sunday shows," Friar explained, "before things got away from us."

"Get it set up now, in the big window room downstairs, looking out on the Sound."

"We're going to make video calls?" Friar asked.

"Just one to the Pentagon," Jack said. He turned to Jean. "Have you got your cell phone on you?" Jean tapped her trench coat pocket. "Get Ellen Quick," Jack said, "and have her conference you with Tim at the plane at the field. Dad . . ."

Long John brought his hands up on his walking stick, waiting on his assignment, which turned out to be to offer more approval.

". . . we bring them all here. Every one of them, right, except Rainey, who we'll keep on the margin. We push Garland's mug into it. Right? And you can help us make the calls to the Pentagon, right? You know how the go code will work?"

Long John had guessed as much, and he agreed. "A honey trap. It can be done."

"Better yet, Dad, we're going to do it."

Jean thought, *Do what?* But she wasn't rested enough to think fast yet and so held herself back, waiting for her orders.

Jack aimed to give the president his assignment first. He squatted down before the armchair in order to make sure he was in the man's line of sight. He wanted to sound considerate. It came out contentious. "I want you dressed and ready to make video calls right away. You're calling the Pentagon. You understand me?"

After a brief delay, the president croaked, "Yes, Governor," and then nodded.

Jack asked Connie Jay, "Is his speech any better than that? He doesn't sound like himself. Can you give him something to give him energy? It's the drugs that're making him like that, is that it?"

"No, I'm not sure," Connie Jay said. She leaned across the

president's chair and embraced her husband. "I need to tell him," she said to the president. And then to Jack, she said, "Whatever is causing it is localized. There are risks keeping him here. We both know it, and we discussed waiting for you. Now . . . I don't know what can be done, but there are people I can talk with at Walter Reed."

"We need another day," Jack returned. "We've got to have one more day. Can you do that?"

The president didn't hesitate. He put his hand on his wife's hand. "Yes, Jack," he pronounced deliberately. "One more day."

"Do you know what I'm going to do?" Jack asked him.

The president moved his mouth but the words didn't come out right away.

Jack discarded this pretense that the president wasn't well enough to think and answer for himself. "We're going to bring Schofield in here. Here. We're going to give the go code for FATHER'S DAY. I need you to give the order on the video-phone. Can you do that? Speak for yourself and answer for yourself? Or can we do something that will help you do it?"

The president's eyes registered the dimensions of Jack's honey trap. He replied softly, the croak underneath the whisper, "I'm tired, Jack. I'm tired, is all."

Jack pressed, "Did you try to go into the water last night?"

"Yes and no," the president said. He wasn't convincing that he could hold a conversation, but he was sincere. "I thought about it. I might have. I failed that, too."

"No, Ted," Connie Jay objected.

Jack wanted to give the man some respect. "You ready to stick it out another day? I want to know."

The president's eyes were watery. It might have been his medication; it might have been the gravity he heard in Jack's voice; it might have been plain exhaustion.

Jack suddenly worried Teddy Jay was going to collapse. He

rushed to close the bargain. "We're going to get Shy Garland. You hear me? And you should know that getting the guy in the White House is tough."

The president rolled his head to his usable right side. "I've failed everyone, Jack."

Jack wouldn't wait for more confession. "Get him dressed, Connie," Jack said to the First Lady. "We'll make the call as soon as Jean and I get back."

"Where are you going?" Connie Jay asked; she looked to Jean protectively, as if Jack was about to abduct her. "I mean, can't you tell me?"

Jack answered, "Of course—a press statement, from your front drive, in the rain, thirty minutes or so. Jean, you ready?" Jack went to the door first and looked back at the president to the left, and his father to the right. "Dad," Jack said, not entirely sure of how to handle the president's disability. Was the man competent? Was he reliable? "Would you explain to the president what I've got in mind? My recommendations?"

"I'll make your report in full," Long John answered. He pulled himself up with his walking stick and reached down to usher Jean up. "Stay with him, Jean," he said to her, "he's going very fast."

"Are we going along," Jean asked, "with this honey trap?"

Long John said, "You're the real honey, you know?"

Jack said, "Get ready for the call, Dad, we'll be back in an hour."

Jack led Jean out of the president's bedroom, and by the time they reached the downstairs hall, they were both on their cell phones, in conference with Ellen Quick and Tim Seward. "I need a statement for Jean, under four hundred words, calling for a full Senate investigation of Sensenbrenner's death," Jack said.

"Get ahold of the wire services right now," Jean told Ellen Quick, "Reuters especially, because I want it going out for Europe's evening news. Tell them I'm going to go on cable in thirty minutes."

Jack answered, "Oh-seven-twelve. We'll make the eight o'clock summaries in the East and they'll have us for rush-hour news out west. Let me get the area set up for us. I want to make it obvious that we're ready for trouble."

Jack punched off, leaving the statement to Jean, and ducked outside the front door to call over the troopers' watch commander, DePalma.

"I want a detail of troopers, well turned-out, with sidearms, up around the podium at the press area. Also, pull four cruisers up there, lights on. With the shields showing on the vehicles. And get me a shotgun."

DePalma said, "Yes, sir. What's up?"

"Television," Jack said. "I'll want the shotgun for a prop, so empty it. Got it?" And then Jack turned to Jean. "Let's talk this through."

Husband and wife darted into the hall restroom. Jack sat on the edge of the toilet while Jean did her own face again.

"If you were going to ask me," Jean started, "I can tell you I see what you're up to and I think it's fine so far. Very risky, but so far, all right."

"You know what we want. Full investigation. Press the security issue. And I'm going to speak after you," Jack said, "to underline my point about security. The two points we want to get across is that we're concerned with security of the country and security of the president. Those two points have to be linked. You do the country. I do the president."

Jean brushed her cheeks. There wasn't going to be time for TV makeup. "What you can do is change your shirt, and now get out of here so I can have some peace a moment."

As Jack stood, he brushed against Jean and spontaneously bent down to kiss her on the back of the head. He didn't have

anything to say about his kiss, and Jean pretended to ignore it, so
he kept going out the door. He continued on to the dining area,
where Friar was on the headset in front of his big pc monitor.
"Joe, I want the cameras ready to roll in fifteen minutes for Jean.
Call them in their trailers, now. I don't want them to have time
to talk back, just time enough to react. If you make the call,
they'll get the connection between the president and Sensenbrenner."

"What do I say is the senator's topic?"

"Tell them Jean's going to speak about Sensenbrenner. Ellen
Quick's already made the call to their bosses, so this will shake
up the ones who are awake and terrify those who aren't."

"Fifteen minutes is tight," Friar said. He punched a macro
that, the first time, came up empty. He muttered, "What I really
miss is the operators I have on my staff at the White House. You
know, kids who can really handle this equipment. I'm lost here
when it doesn't work." Friar tried the macro again, and this time
it put him on a conference line with the network producers
sitting in the RVs in Somesville. He identified himself and told
them he was calling on behalf of Senator Motherwell. "She's
coming up with a statement about General Sensenbrenner's
death," he explained to the conference line. "After consultation
with the president, that's right."

Friar held the Mute button and asked Jack, "They want to
know if the statement's ready for release ahead of time."

"No, and say I'll have a statement after hers. And emphasize
for background that Jean and I stand in lockstep with the president of the United States."

Friar nodded and, blowing out his cheeks, asked, "Can you
tell me how far you're going to go, Governor? What I heard
you say upstairs to the president—are you going to call the
Pentagon?"

"The press conference first, Joe. Jean's going to put a major obstacle to the Senate challenge. I figure Garland's already weighing if he should call the challenge vote off today. This will decide it for him."

"A full Senate investigation of Sensenbrenner's death?" Friar asked. "That would stop all forms of government as we know it for the summer. Shot by a four-year-old in a Cairo alley or something. The Southern City of the Dead. It's bizarre."

"It will do, and what I think about his death is that he was the best general we had and he still couldn't hold up his end without responsible leadership from your end. And you failed him, didn't you, Joe?"

"You're tough on us, Governor."

"Just starting this morning."

Friar opened his mouth and then decided not to argue. He did say, "What do I do with the reaction to the senator's press conference? They're going to want a statement from the man."

"Tell them to call their member of Congress, and if they are a member of Congress, tell them to call their consciences, and I'm serious."

"I know you are," Friar said.

Jack wasn't ready for kind words. He was still too angry and too aggressive. He looked across the room to see Adam LeMarche directing the technicians with the video conference equipment. He thought, *Okay, it'll work, okay—if the president can just rally himself for one more performance, okay.*

Jack thought just a moment about Toni, and then he telephoned Lilly back at the house. She answered immediately. "Yes, Daddy, Jean said you were back. Daddy—"

Jack didn't have much time, so he asked her to bring over a clean shirt and tie for him in the truck, and to tell the troopers on duty to drive her over. He didn't mention Toni's death. He wanted to do that in person later.

Jack found Jean standing beside the front door, her left arm across her waist, her head bent as she talked on the cell phone. She looked magnificently in charge and most confident as she told Ellen Quick not to bother with the fax, just read the paragraph again, she'd memorize it. Jean also spoke to her son. "Tim, do you like it? All right."

Jack was impressed with her voice, as well—relaxed, sonorous, projecting, the voice of a leader of the Senate.

Jack and Jean were surrounded now by the coming and going of staffers, stewards, troopers, agents, telephone technicians, and even the cooks looking for any additional breakfast orders. Still, the two of them paused long enough to take account of each other.

"We can do this," Jack told her.

"You take my arm," Jean said, "and where's your clean shirt?"

The rain was a steady cold drizzle now in one of those grim, gusty June mornings that was indistinguishable from October except for the color of the foliage and the quality of the light leaking through the overcast. Jack and Jean took a big umbrella from the troopers and chose to walk up the drive rather than ride so they could continue to consult with Ellen Quick and Tim on Jean's statement. Jack wanted Jean to mention Garland by name. Jean wanted to stay with mention of Sonny Pickett. They compromised by talking about "the Garland administration and its friends on the Hill."

The press area was ablaze in TV lights. The crews were repositioning the podium under a small tarp held up by clothespins on a quarter-inch line. The light banks were swaying badly in the rain, and so they'd brought a semi up the road to serve as a windbreak. The working press crowded closer together for the storm. The crews were dressed in voluminous green ponchos, but the reporters and press personnel were arrayed in such a colorful variety of raingear and boots that the mass of them resembled a grammar school at recess. Everyone was up to the ankles in the mud of the trampled flower beds. The only group that looked comfortable with conditions was the state police, who'd run four big General Motors cruisers up behind the microphone area. Sixteen officers in long slickers were deployed around the sides of the press area, and four big troopers stood to the right of the podium, arms folded, eyes locked straight ahead. No camera angle could leave out the stern, plain faces under the broad-brimmed gray hats.

It was 7:55 A.M., and the TV monitor bank in the truck was showing all the morning shows proceeding with the standard fare. This morning, of course, the topic from the top was Sensenbrenner's death, and the anarchy in Cairo that had killed him. Jean's promised statement was a tantalizing addition to the story, and carrying her live was an attractive option to the cable networks. This was, after all, the ranking Republican in the country. And wasn't that her husband the governor, talking there with the teenage girl? His daughter?

"Thanks," Jack said to Lilly, who'd run up from a cruiser. There wasn't time to change his shirt but he'd do what Jean said anyway. He took Lilly's hand and they ducked into the back of another cruiser. "Lilly, Toni Albanese's dead," Jack started.

"I know, Dad, Tim called me," Lilly said. "And I'm sorry for her and for you."

"Yeah." Jack pulled on the shirt. He was thinking about Allison again, how much Lilly looked like her mother in the morning—moved alike, thought alike. It was as if Allison was haunting him. He reached for the tie.

Jean was at the microphone and already speaking when Jack got back to her.

". . . General Sensenbrenner was a most honored and decorated officer of the greatest military force ever put in the field." Jean spoke into the wall of lights. "And I want you to know that I have spoken with many on my side of the aisle, and our sympathies and respect go to his wife and family on this terrible, terrible news to our country . . ."

Jack stood at Jean's left and threw his shoulders out. He'd counted on her ability to control a press audience, and he was more than satisfied. Everything Jean knew about public relations was going into the clarity of her statement. The measured voice. The knowledgeable smile. The level gaze into the camera. And then a recitation of events that resembled a short story. The honored dead. The sympathy of the country. The grief of the Senate. The gravity of the loss. The demands of state business. All this in four hundred and forty words, ending with her clear charge:

"General Sensenbrenner was always available to me and my office, and what I learned from him was that all losses can be turned into gains. We've lost him and we've got to investigate his death. Not only because he was a good man, not only because he was a statesman, but because it's our job to know why our highest-ranking soldier was lost to us. Why did he die? Why? No business before the Senate is more critical. We can't and won't go on until we know how he died, and why he died."

The reporters in front started shouting questions the moment Jean lowered her gaze.

Jack took the shotgun from the sergeant, a sixteen-gauge pump, and tucked it under his arm like a duck hunter. He hopped up to the microphone and eased half a step in front of Jean. His size and the weapon demanded the camera's attention.

"I'm Jack Longfellow, governor of Maine—some of you old fellows know me, most of you know my dad—and the senator and I want to thank you for your attention this morning, on this balmy Maine morning, and I want you to know that I'm stepping up security on this island right now."

Jack knew that the moment he said "balmy Maine morning" the network producers in the trucks would lose focus and interest. Fine. He didn't want himself televised. He wanted to interrupt Jean in such a way that there wouldn't be questions on her statement.

The reporters kept shouting at Jean. Jack shouted them down. The shotgun served the same use as a gavel.

"I'm not going to explain any more than this . . ."

The reporters in front were sinking in the muck; the fellows toward the rear of the mass had turned away from Jack to hunt for coffee. The camera crews were worried about the rain popping through the tarps. A big generator truck fired up with a low roar. The cordless microphone started crackling and weakening.

Jack raised his arm, hand open, and raised his voice to its fullest timbre—a booming wave of sound:

". . . that there's been a lot of nasty talk about threats to the president this past week. In my state. Against my president . . ."

A few of the reporters in front began to comprehend Jack's remarks, and some of them pulled their PDAs out of the waterproof pouches; others flipped their minicorders on.

"That talk ends here, this morning. You know the Secret Service won't comment. I will. It's my state, and nothing happens here that I don't know about and don't take responsibility for."

Jack's manners were so rough and direct that the photographers started whirring and clicking just for the icon of the man with the jawline in the rain. The shotgun. The huge body. The war hero talking tough. The sandy-haired gargantuan husband of the Republican leader. *Click, whirr, click.*

The local reporters, who knew their governor well, pushed their faces out from under the hoods and umbrellas and asked one another open questions. What's that about threats? What kind of responsibility?

And has he said "EXCOM" yet?

Jack was thinking of Sensenbrenner's remarks from the East

Room on Tuesday as he closed his own remarks. "Anyone out there who thinks the president's safety is different here on the coast of Maine than it is in the White House, I'm guaranteeing it's not."

Jack looked up into the lights. Had he made the point? The eyes of the reporters were as distracted as before. There was only the drumbeat of the rain on the canopy. He let the water hit his face and the anger show in his mouth.

"And about this talk of 'EXCOM' I hear of," Jack added. "This 'EXCOM' . . ."

The TV camera lights were on again. By now every news organization in the world knew that whenever the pols used the acronym EXCOM, they had best pay heed; and this pol was hefting a shotgun.

". . . I don't know what others might mean by it when they use it on television, but I know what I mean. EXCOM is a lie. And whoever uses it to explain anything is a liar. I don't even know what it means. EXCOM? What's that mean to you? EX-COM? Sounds like a ball team I wouldn't pay to see lose."

Jack thought, *Are you listening, Shy? Reach for the sky, Shy. Start crying for help, Shy.*

Jack stepped back to Jean and took her by the arm. "We're done here," he told her.

"What do we do now?" Jean asked.

"The president makes a video call about a coup," Jack said. "We listen in."

37 Friday Morning, the Pentagon

General Breckenridge was balanced at the edge of his chair at the conference table in the Tank. This was the Friday morning roundup with the war lords and iron majors, but Breckenridge was going through the motions of the meeting. The parts shortages in the Pacific command, the new communication system at Fort McPherson, and again and again the updates from the National Security Council on the catastrophe in Cairo. Archie Learned and Ben Mica had gone to the Situation Room at the White House, and they were firing off directives every few minutes. Around the table the business of the building carried on relentlessly with the three-star deputies of the services along with three deputy warlords from SOUTHCOM, CENTCOM, and SACEUR, and behind them the majors, lieutenant colonels, and commanders from the J-directorates—everyone trying to move their packages with tight talkers, tighter point papers, all the right tabs for the implementers. Johnny Jones was at the door, clicking in the next speaker with his "More meat . . ." Each step in the process was normative as the digital displays on the walls showed it was morning again in the Puzzle Palace, 0840.

Breckenridge wasn't normative, and he found he couldn't hear very clearly. Each time one of the iron majors spoke up, all Breckenridge could hear was "The boss is dead . . . the boss is dead . . ."

Breckenridge knew he was in shock over Sensenbrenner's death. He'd felt this sort of shock before, and he knew he needed time. But he didn't have the time. The weight of Atlas had just fallen on him, and he wanted to scream for mercy. He needed help. Where was Meriwether, where was Catedral, where was Izsak? The confirmation that Sensenbrenner was KIA had come in eleven hours before, and the recall for the service chiefs had gone out eight hours before, just after midnight here in Washington. They were coming from western time zones, and the travel time was mostly an equipment challenge. Still, they had to get back to the building. They had to help him get Sensenbrenner's body back to Arlington.

We can't hold the city, Breckenridge thought. *We can't get the remains out. I promised him. I can't get him out. Cairo's broken down. God—get him out—I have to think about evacuating our people. I can't get him out if I can't get our people out. Gunboats, he wanted gunboats on the Nile. Disaster.*

Johnny Jones was suddenly at Breckenridge's side. "Sir, we have to take a call in the chairman's office. Sir?"

Breckenridge slowly fixed on Jones's manner. Jones was a huge, aggressive figure, long armed and clear eyed, and he never showed opinion in his face. But his lips were wet, his hands were balled up. He tapped his earpiece.

Breckenridge leaned back. "What is it, Johnny?"

"A call from the president, sir."

Breckenridge glanced at his pc monitor with windows on his directorates and commands. If there ever was a room for a secure call from the White House, this was it. So?

"Is it about Cairo?" Breckenridge asked, getting up heavily. "There's nothing new there, is there?"

"No, sir, I don't think it's Cairo." Jones pressed his earpiece closer for an incoming call from his staff. "I think we better take it—it's President Jay."

Breckenridge told Myers, army deputy, to take charge of the meeting, and he strode in big steps out of the Tank into the very busy anteroom and even busier hall. All the D Ring faces were grim and downcast. Breckenridge had seen grave details with better morale. The building would survive Sensenbrenner's death, but this was a blow like none since those first damaging weeks of the Walvis Bay crisis.

The video screen behind Sensenbrenner's desk was lit up with the face of the watch officer from the NMCC. Sensenbrenner's inner office was such a long, deep room, with so much hardwired gear in it—Sensenbrenner had favored up-to-date gadgetry—that Breckenridge didn't have to sit to take the call; he was on screen from any angle, and he could view from any stance. He stood beside the big globe and told the officer, "This is Breckenridge, vice chairman; what is the status of the link, Major?"

"It's a commercial line, sir, normal and all. It's a regular phone call. From Somesville, Maine. It's the president. And Secretary Longfellow is with him. They said to put you on. And Colonel Jones. They're waiting for our callback. They said they wanted a video line to you, sir. And they said immediately."

"Make it so," Breckenridge ordered.

The small monitor on Sensenbrenner's desk lit up with the image of President Jay, seated in a chair. The president held his right hand up in front of his face as he worked his fingers in an impatient fashion. The president's suit jacket was too big for his shoulders and it rode up around his white collar.

The first thing that happened was that the president's eyes focused on the ribbons and medals on Breckenridge's large chest.

Breckenridge snapped to attention, speaking as he released his salute. "Mr. President, this is General Breckenridge, vice chairman of the Joint Chiefs. I am in the chairman's office at the Pentagon."

Jones was also at attention and delivered, "This is Colonel Jones, Mr. President, director of the Joint Staff."

"Yes, I know," said the president.

Long John Longfellow was seated just off the screen beside the president. The First Lady was standing behind her husband. Neither was going to wait long before intervening.

"I have reliable information," the president said. He garbled the four syllables of "information." The president started again. "I have proof that you . . ."

"Sir?" Breckenridge asked. He was confused by the president's brittle pronunciation, however his own thoughts were clear. *God, God, God, he knows everything.*

"The designator is FATHER'S DAY," the president said.

"Yes, sir," Breckenridge tried. *Should I confess? What do I say? I was ordered. No. Let it happen. The boss is dead. Let it all happen.* Breckenridge added, "I am very familiar with the operation, sir. How can I help you?"

"You've . . ." The president slumped in his chair, and his coat balled up behind him like a shroud. There was Pan-Cake makeup on his shirt collar. The fallen left side of his face, out of the light till now, came more into focus on the screen.

Breckenridge, sensing something wrong, asked, "Sir, I didn't hear you."

Long John Longfellow's voice broke into the call. "You can quit the double-talk."

With a single button, the image expanded to include more of the room around the president. A picture window. A rainy day along the water. Cliff sides. The president sunk in a straight-backed armchair. The tree trunk of the former secretary of defense. The tall beauty of the First Lady.

"The president called you this morning," Long John said, "and you're going to come to attention and ask him for your orders. Do it."

Breckenridge knew Secretary Longfellow through several advisory groups over the past years. He also knew him to be as surly and inflexible a SecDef as the building had endured in its sixty years. A politician's politician. A World War Two volunteer who distrusted staff officers by definition. An attacker. Still, Breckenridge held back. He said nothing.

Long John saw the hesitation in Breckenridge's eyes and unloaded on him.

"I've seen evidence of your FATHER'S DAY," Long John continued, eyes locked on the screen in front of the president, "and what I've seen makes me ashamed. Ashamed. I'm not going to talk about the dead men you've shamed. How about the six hundred thousand we've got left to hold it together? You know how hard we've worked these last ten years to hold on to our force structure. You know how the jackasses in the Congress and the administration have tricked us and abused us. And what you have done is given them incontestable proof that the greatest threat to the Constitution is the force sworn to defend the Constitution. Shame on you. Shame. Can there be any harder word to say to a general sworn to give his life for duty and country? Shame . . . Now"—Long John banged his walking stick down in his fury—"you don't explain anything, you don't answer back, you don't do anything but obey the president of the United States. Soldier, look at me."

Breckenridge found his courage. Right down there next to his despair. *God in heaven. Mary, dear Mother of God. I'm guilty.*

"I'm going to make a short speech, soldier," Long John said, "and it goes like this. All the bellyaching, all the finger pointing, all the blame shifting I've outlasted for fifty years—since I first arrived in Washington—can't push aside this disgrace. General Sensenbrenner is dead, and that's merciful, because I'd want him tried and condemned and hanged. God's mercy to let him go like that. God's mercy. That's my speech, soldier. Now, pray God you do what you're told and do it right."

"Sir," Breckenridge said, "I understand you, sir."

The president spoke up again, "The designator is FATHER'S

DAY. The go code is . . ." The president, without moving his head, glanced in the direction of Long John Longfellow. ". . . 'Happy Father's Day.' "

Breckenridge's jaw tightened, so that when he started to speak, "But sir," he had to clear his throat to continue, "that's meant to target you." He perceived the paradox and exclaimed in confusion, "I can't do that, sir! Do you see what you're saying? It's an operation meant to target you. What are you asking me? Let me explain, sir!"

"The go code is 'Happy Father's Day,' " the president repeated, crisply this time. He rephrased the sentence. "I have the go code."

Johnny Jones hadn't flinched from his stance, but now he spoke to his boss sideways without shifting his stance. "Sir, we can resign."

"I heard that, Jones," Long John declared, "and I'm recommending you shut up. General, that man is a fool."

"I apologize, sir," Breckenridge said.

"The hell you do," Long John said. "I want this conversation written down. Both of you. Write this conversation down and sign it and send it to the president today. Acknowledge."

"Yes, sir," Breckenridge and Jones returned.

The First Lady contributed. "My husband has given you the correct command, isn't that true, General Breckenridge?"

"Yes, but . . . he's not . . . the president." Breckenridge wanted to raise his arm and point. Didn't they understand how mixed up this was? What was he supposed to do? What was the guideline for taking orders from two presidents at the same time?

Breckenridge wasn't given time to call a meeting, or to call the Hill. Instead he tried to explain himself. "My order from General Sensenbrenner was that he was to give the go code."

Long John said, "This is your commander in chief."

"Sir!" Breckenridge returned.

"No, Mr. Longfellow, give me a chance to speak," the First Lady said. Her eyes were icy. "General, you plotted my husband's murder. You ordered grown men and women to organize an assassination of the president of the United States. You've conspired with members of the administration and Congress. You're a disgrace and a coward. And now you tell us that my husband is not your commander in chief. And you also tell us that a dead man gave you an order? What kind of marine are you?"

"I'm a marine, Mrs. Jay, just a marine. And I'm appealing to you—do you understand that you're ordering the operation down on you? How can I send the strike force at you?"

The First Lady had the last word. "What I understand from any number of explanations," she said, "is that my husband is your commander, and he wants this order carried out by dawn tomorrow morning."

"But . . ." Breckenridge broke off. They wanted it to come down on them. Why? Why had it been drawn up in the first place? Sensenbrenner hadn't told him or anyone. What was EX-COM? Why did he have to take the fall? What sort of twist was this? *The boss is dead,* he thought. *It's all gone. Cairo's gone, the boss is gone, I'm—*

Long John gave out the last details. "The *Teddy Roosevelt* is in the North Atlantic. You put a blanket on us here. Acknowledge."

"Yes, sir."

"I don't like your cut, soldier. I don't like the way you answer the president or the way you're cleaning up after Sensenbrenner. I don't like you, I don't trust you, I don't care about you after this call ends. Acknowledge."

"Yes, sir," Breckenridge said.

"You're still a marine," Long John said. "As long as you're a

member of the corps, I expect you will do your duty. Acknowledge."

"Yes, sir."

"If you're thinking of alerting the White House or anyone
else," Long John said, "don't do it. You're finished now. Salute
your president and carry out your order and then fade away. It's
what you've got left to do. Fade away in disgrace. It's your duty.'"

38 Friday Morning, the Senate Chamber

Senators Cannon and Bueneventura were lunching on decaf-
feinated coffee and raisin bagels while seated on a leather sofa in
the outsized vice president's office just off the Senate chamber;
both were also chewing into the receivers on their cell phones to
Jean Motherwell.

Jean was lunching on fruit cocktail and iced tea while seated
on the port sofa of the president's Gulfstream V—Air Force
One-Half—and she was about an hour out of National, coming
down from Maine.

It was just after noontime, and the news wires on the PDAs
and pcs were flashing with waves of bad reports. Chief among
them was that the New York Stock Exchange was down sixteen
percent. There was also the false report that the president of the
Exchange was said to be considering closing the market at 1 P.M.
The Washington headlines included the fact that Iphigenia Petropoulos had departed with Mrs. Emily Sensenbrenner on Air

Force One for Rome to bring General Sensenbrenner's remains home.

What was not a headline on the wires, but was certainly well known on the Hill, was that there was a roll call in progress in the Senate, and it was the fourth roll call in four hours, none of them so far achieving a quorum for business—despite instructions to the sergeant at arms. The Democratic leadership and the whole of the Garland wing of the party were absent. The Republican leadership was spread out between the Motherwell supporters and the Brownie McDonald supporters. The nonaligned were wandering the cloakroom and the hall in a daze of gossip for the two overwhelming rumors of the morning.

The first rumor was that Majority Leader Sonny Pickett had been jettisoned by the White House in a feud with Shy Garland.

The second rumor was that the White House had offered a deal to Jean Motherwell to be the new Sonny Pickett in a bipartisan alliance with Shy Garland.

What was strangely true was that both rumors were accurate. All over the Hill, the ninety-nine senators (Brownie McDonald was still hospitalized) were now talking through the details of another of those unprecedented Senate maneuvers wherein the minority leader might very well become the administration's power broker on the Hill.

Jean, who'd been on the line to Jack back at Somesville, came back on the call with Nan Cannon and Sue Bueneventura.

They were discussing Jean's invitation to the White House for supper. Jack had claimed that Garland would call Jean within an hour of this morning's announcement, and he'd been right within thirty minutes. The White House had called for Jean about nine-thirty.

"Now Jack says he wants you two to go with me," Jean told Nan Cannon and Sue Bueneventura. "He says he thinks the three of us will intimidate the EXCOM gang because they have nothing to offer us."

"Dinner at Shy and Iphy's?" Nan Cannon returned. "I suppose it's dear that Jack doesn't want you to go into the wolf's lair alone?"

Sue Bueneventura remarked, "We can ease up on that, Nan."

Jean let Nan's crack about her relationship with Jack go. Toni Albanese had been like a storm cloud in her marriage, and now that she was dead, there was no letup in sight, just rain.

Sue Bueneventura changed the topic, her index finger on her lips as she tried to swallow her bite of bagel. "Jeannie, are we going to make a deal with Garland or not?"

"Yes, we are," Jean answered. "But right now I want you to make certain that Sonny Pickett is in hiding. How's the latest roll call?"

Nan Cannon's legislative assistant held up his fingers to indicate ten, twenty, thirty and five members answering the call on the floor.

"We can go at them again," Nan Cannon told Jean and Sue. "Sonny's not going to show up today. And Brownie's going to stay in hiding."

Nan Cannon had enjoyed the telephone call she made that morning to the assistant minority leader at his Walter Reed hospital room to tell him that, since Sensenbrenner was dead, so was Brownie McDonald's love affair with Shy Garland and Sonny Pickett.

Nan Cannon told Jean, "I'll take this one. Sue, you finish your coffee."

Nan Cannon kept her cell phone in her suit pocket as she made her way down to the well of the Senate by way of the wc off the vice president's office. For sixteen years she'd been going through the same ritual when she aimed to speak on the floor: good shoes, good jewelry, and good posture before she strolled in to her colleagues.

"Madame President, I want to be recognized," Nan Cannon called out in her feisty voice as she reached the well. The presiding senator this morning was Merry Mars-Grassley (R., Kansas), who was going to do what Nan Cannon wanted and do it as meekly as the Wabash Cannonball conducted herself roughly.

The collection of senators and aides on the majority side of the aisle continued talking among themselves with darted looks across to Nan Cannon's entrance. The carpet was thick, the air was laced with tobacco smoke, the single consistent sound was the frequent ping of the PDAs signaling incoming E-mail.

Nan Cannon, taking the microphone from the gentle Senator Frost, went on to state the obvious, that the pressing business before the Senate this morning was a call from the minority leader for an investigation into the circumstances and facts surrounding the death of General of the Army Lucius S. Sensenbrenner.

Nan Cannon added that, after consultation with her leader, Senator Motherwell, it was most appropriate to assign the task to a Senate and House select committee in which she, as ranking minority member on the Foreign Relations Committee, would be a primary participant.

"I'm sure the majority leader, my distinguished friend Senator Pickett, would offer his swift approval were he present at this time. To repeat the remarks of my distinguished friend from Maine and minority leader, Senator Motherwell, no business before this body is more crucial to the nation. Madame President, we need a quorum. You will please *again* instruct the sergeant at arms to provide us a quorum immediately. The means are at hand."

Merry Mars-Grassley looked to Billy Wheat, assistant majority leader, seated at his desk on the far end of the front row. Billy Wheat was on his cell phone at the moment, a letdown in decorum that showed Nan Cannon she should press her assault.

"Madame President, what is the delay?" Nan Cannon asked,

and this time she turned stagily toward the Democratic side of the aisle. "Have my distinguished colleagues in the majority looked around this morning? Have my distinguished colleagues noticed that the markets are sinking as low as federally subsidized corn?" Nan Cannon rotated to the press section of the gallery.

"Where is my distinguished Majority Leader Senator Pickett? Where is the distinguished majority?"

Nan Cannon had accomplished her exercise for the fifth time this morning—to make a demand upon the Senate and House for a select committee, to call for a quorum, to mock Sonny Pickett and the administration, and then to deliver a theatrical barb once more.

"Madame President, I ask for a call of the roll," she said, and, handing the microphone to Senator Frost, she strode off the floor by way of the clerks.

"There'll sooner be an entitlement program in Hades than a quorum today, boys and girls," she said, no smile in the Cannon fashion, and then she returned her good shoes and jewelry and posture to the vice president's office and Sue Bueneventura.

"You couldn't see," Nan Cannon reported to her cell phone, which had remained open so that Jean could overhear the proceedings, "that Billy Wheat was scratching his ankles again. That awful habit of reaching under his socks to scratch. Oh, just like a tomcat."

Sue was on her phone, too. "What's going on, Jean, really? Why is Sonny Pickett hiding? I thought he was a ringleader of EXCOM. Why are we going to the White House tonight? What do we want?"

Jean looked up the cabin of the Gulfstream. Tim was on the line with the office to issue an expanded press release clarifying her call for a select committee. Ellen Quick was on the line with the networks to set up Jean's interview schedule in the TV studios around Washington. Jean was going to spend the afternoon nodding her head into the camera and speaking somberly about the crisis in the military and the government following Sensenbrenner's death.

"What I want," Jean answered Sue diplomatically, "is for you and Nan to stay on the floor until supper time, and turn over the quorum calls to Merry while you're with me at the White House. I want you to ask for a roll call every ninety minutes. I want you to hold the well so that Sonny Pickett or Billy Wheat won't dare try to move other business. This is filibuster by other means, and I want you to make clear to them that we're going to stand on this line all night. That's what I want."

Jean punched a button and Jack came back on the line. He was at the Sargent funeral home in Ellsworth now, and his voice was low and careful. He'd just called Toni's parents in California, and he was about to call Schofield's parents—Toni's in-laws—at Belfast. The children had to be told, and Jack didn't know how to think about such a tragedy. He just knew it had to be done.

"Jack, are you okay?" Jean asked.

"Yeah," Jack said. "Are Nan and Sue clear on what they have to do?"

"Jack, I want you to get some sleep," Jean said. "I'll need your advice tonight, and you're in bad shape."

"It's this place," Jack said, referring to the funeral parlor. "It's where I brought Allison, too. It's all jumbled up in my head. I won't ever want to bring anyone here again, except I know I will."

Jean knew to force Jack to concentrate on the business at hand. "I do the interviews, right, Jack? I tell the networks that Sensenbrenner died for his country, right? I build him up to the Eisenhower who might have been, right?"

"Yes," Jack agreed.

"I demand we know why he was in Cairo during an insurrection when we needed him at home. Right, Jack? I suggest that we need to look into the decision making that went on from Tuesday at the White House to Thursday at Cairo. I say that we need to know what Sensenbrenner's mind was when he died, because he might have known something we need to know about the nation's security— Jack, are you listening to me?"

Jack said, "Thanks, Jean. I'm sorry. It's this place. The smell of the flowers. How quiet it is. And, you know, what I'm asking you to do tonight and tomorrow. Jean, I don't want to bring you here. Jean?"

Jean decided she'd take control for both of them. "It's twelve-thirty, Jack. The president's asleep. LJ's asleep. You should be asleep, too. But since you're not going to nap until you collapse, then listen to me. Tell me where Schofield is right now."

Jack answered grimly, no fire in him at all just now, an exhausted man who was depending on his wife to hold him up on a cell phone call. "He's got his orders, Jean. God help us all, Schofield's got his orders and he's not stopping."

39 Friday, Occupied Moldova

Schofield called his captains to the Operations tent late afternoon, around 1815 hours local time. It was raining steadily, with thunderclaps and a wall of wind from the west, a black ugly night ahead on the Left Bank of the Dniester. Fruit trees were down all across the collective farms, and the brave souls were out trying to save several ancient apple trees.

The battalion mess had sent over several canteens of black tea
and a pile of hot meat sandwiches. Everyone knew to eat first
and fast, sipping the tea in gulps from Styrofoam cups, shaking
the weather from their ponchos. Nobody smoked anymore, nobody even chewed gum—five self-disciplined gunsmiths, five
months in the field.

Brauchli, Engelmann, Incavagglia, and Wesson had a notion
of the topic, and they settled with their heads down.

"We've got the go for that operation from last Sunday," Schofield said, seated sideways on his camp stool, eyes straight ahead.
The lantern twisted with the drafts. The shadows on the walls
were like puppets prancing around the tables of electronics. "I
doubt you're in the dark what's going on. You might have heard
on the radio that President Jay's gone to Maine. That was the
governor of Maine here yesterday."

Schofield could hear them hold their breathing a pause. Was
the boss okay? With his brother's wife dead like that? What's
wrong with the old man?

Schofield emphasized, "You probably know there's something
on back home. I can't explain it. There it is."

The battalion's top sergeant stood at the tent flap, wearing his
pot and poncho. Tom Owen, thirty-six, was so much more at the
center of the regiment than any of the officers that he didn't
need permission to participate in confabs. "No call to talk it to
death, sir," Tom Owen told Schofield. "We none of us didn't
figure it was going to stop with Sunday. Or with yesterday."

The four captains nodded with their heads down, bobbing
their shoulders, working their swollen hands. Thirty-three-year-
old men accept responsibility honestly, though it ages them prematurely. What did they know about the presidency? They'd
been born under Nixon. They'd won their appointments to the
academy under Reagan. They'd served in an army like musical
chairs—each time the band stopped playing, there was one less

place at the table. No, it wasn't going to stop with last Sunday, or with the action in Bendery.

"I don't want to let this happen as if it was an exercise. This is not an exercise." Schofield was staring now at the Mercator projection map pinned on the side of the table. "General Sensenbrenner's dead. The man who gave us the operation is dead. You've heard it on the radio. I'm telling you what I've heard on the radio."

Tom Owen crossed his arms and asked, "The go came anyway?"

"Twenty-five minutes ago," Schofield answered. He patted his waterproof pouch that contained his written orders for Operation FATHER'S DAY—signed by Breckenridge, initialed by Jones. "I asked for confirmation. I got it."

"The Seventeens coming in with this weather?" Tom Owen asked, jerking his large head back toward the storm. "Those boys are going to earn their flight pay hittin' our LZ tonight."

Schofield reached down to retie his left boot. "Here's what I want. This time, total effort, one hundred and twelve from each company." He looked to Brauchli. "I want you to take charge of the rear guard here—I'll leave you Dog Company and our extras. Cello will take your Able and go lead on the LZ. I don't want contact here." He emphasized to Brauchli, who was his most veteran company commander—the man who'd probably get the battalion someday if Schofield had any say. "Especially if the Blackies provoke you. Ring the wagons and hunker down, understand?"

Brauchli showed no disappointment in remaining behind. His mission was to hold the laager indefinitely. Schofield was leaving him the greenest troops.

Schofield looked to Incavagglia. "Charlie Company is second wave this time." He glanced to Wesson. "You give the cooks rifles and fill out your Dog for here." He told Engelmann,

"Baker's the ready reserve. Charlie's second wave. Got it? Able and Charlie down. Baker lays off. Dog stays here. We'll take our two Nightfoxes and as many Hummers as we can carry on the extra Seventeens they give us. Three companies, two choppers, half-dozen Hummers."

The captains shifted in their seats. Six C-17s to onload and to off-load. A logistics nightmare. Whatever can screw the pooch was going to screw the pooch.

"Sir," Tom Owen asked. "No Ospreys this time? We go straight in on the Seventeens? And we come straight out?"

Schofield said, "No Ospreys. Hot LZ. One-way."

Tom Owen didn't react because he never reacted when he knew it was pointless.

Schofield continued, "I want you to understand what I understand. This is not a drill. This is an operation to capture the president of the United States. You're not coming back here anytime soon. What stays behind stays behind. Dog is rear guard and holds the fort. Questions?"

The four captains had nothing to say. What difference would it make? They'd known since they'd hit the mock-up at Fort Chaffee that they were going. Until it happened, it was all so much talk anyway. Red Schofield was a hard boss. Who knew what the truth of it was? The brass hats were sending in the Seventeens. Let the brass hats worry about what-it-all-means.

What-it-all-means was an old army joke. You were a fool to waste sleep thinking about it.

Each of the four captains had upwards of one hundred and seventy soldiers to worry about—one hundred for the go, sixty or so for the bunker. Equipment, personalities, needs, desires. Tell them what? Take them onto the Seventeens tonight to do what?

Schofield signaled Cello to bring in the company lieutenants who doubled up as the battle staff. They'd been over at communications making lists. Moving five hundred human beings onto long-range intratheater heavy-cargo transports required many lists. The captains yanked out their notebooks.

"We have map overlays for each of you," Cello said.

Incavagglia took the transparency and raised it to the lantern light. "What is this? Some coast somewhere?"

Cello spoke in the orthodox manner. "It's the target."

The captains grunted in complaint and bent over the master documents with their outlays. The target was the target.

Schofield walked over to Tom Owen. "Briefing for your NCOs in thirty minutes. You take the pathfinders. You're with me. Questions."

"I didn't figure it would come to this," Tom Owen said.

Schofield said, "Here's what I want from you . . ."

The two of them were at the open flap. The rain was blowing sideways. The regiment's Broadway was a mud river. Schofield's Hummer was twenty feet away, door open. Already there was equipment moving up from the motor pool. The rendezvous was set for twenty hundred and thirty hours. A night landing and takeoff on a secondary field.

"What I want . . ." Schofield said again.

Tom Owen was thinking as a Top was paid to think. Feed the soldiers. Hot food. Everybody shaves. The rear guard gets the letters. By noon tomorrow the Black Cossacks would know the battalion was gone. After that, disaster or not. Before that: LBEs. Gore-Tex parkas and boots. NATO camouflage suits. M16s. Smith & Wesson .357 revolvers. Beretta 9mm automatic pistols. Ruger Mini-14s. Pump-action 16-gauge shotguns. Stun grenades. SAWs. LAWs. Claymores. Lots of bullets. Feed the men hot food again. More bullets.

"What I want is that I'm the shooter," Schofield said. It didn't sound right, but he'd said it. "You're with me, Sergeant. I'm the shooter. You're the backup. I don't want you more than a step away from me. As close as Ky. You stay with me."

Tom Owen breathed out of his mouth to make vapor. It was something a dead man couldn't do. He answered his colonel, "Yes, sir."

Can I do this? Schofield thought. *Does he think we can do it? Shoot the president?*

"We do the job," Schofield said.

40 Friday Evening, the White House

It was a serene, temperate evening on the Potomac, but the lights at the White House were dimmed and there wasn't any spark in the eyes of the marine guard or in the faces of the executive staff. The weight of Sensenbrenner's death was still settling on the administration, and with that weight came a workload that was now 'round the clock. The West Wing was ablaze with Quinn Roosevelt's attack teams attached to their monitors in order to reach out to the layered network of partisans throughout the country and the world. Across the park, behind the swaying white oaks and American boxwoods and giant willow oaks, the Old Executive Office Building was blazing with the energy of the White House propaganda machine as it reached into every home in America.

Everywhere the message was the same, as fashioned by Roosevelt. The great patriot Sensenbrenner was dead. The state funeral would begin as soon as his body reached Washington. Attendance was mandatory.

Everywhere, too, the goal was the same. We must bury Sensenbrenner and move on. We must bury Sensenbrenner and get the country back on course. We must bury Sensenbrenner and make Garland the one and only president.

The White House staff knew much more than the information its propaganda machine cranked out—knew that Quinn Roosevelt was tolerating no fence sitting or backsliding. The word had gone out to the Democratic Party members that loyalty to President Garland was now the only acceptable display. No more rhetorical pronouncements that President Jay was an old, dear colleague who was hard to leave behind. No more coy silence on the issue, either—you were to declare you were for Garland and then shut up.

Certainly the party was warned that there would be a crippling price for those who did not fall in behind the Garland banner. There were no exceptions. Already there was the strong rumor out that Sonny Pickett had crossed Garland somehow and that the majority leader was as dead as Sensenbrenner until further notice.

But what to make of this new rumor out of the Florida machine that Speaker Rainey was going over to Jay's camp? No one in the White House was sure. This was dangerous ground. The Roosevelt line was that if any network or newspaper called to ask, you were to mention Sensenbrenner's funeral plans. If the reporters persisted, you were to joke that Rainey played golf every day of the week he was in town up the River Road at either Burning Tree or the Congressional country club, give the clubhouse a call and ask for him.

Jean Motherwell was the one person in Washington who didn't need to track Luke Rainey down at a clubhouse, because she knew exactly where he was. He was in her pocket. She'd talked to him twice that afternoon in between her television interviews. The first time he'd been in a bunker on the eighth hole at Burning Tree; the second time he'd been on a dogleg approach and puzzling over his choice of clubs to get around a tree. Both times he'd made himself clear to Jean that he was not taking calls from Quinn Roosevelt, that he was on board with President Jay.

"I like our side—we've got the better legs, and yours and the First Lady's aren't bad neither, Senator Jean, yes'm," Rainey had said. "And just between you, me, and the 'gators, I can't stomach that little dropping Quinn Roosevelt anyway."

Jean was talking with Rainey once more as the presidential limousine sent for her pulled up to the North Entrance of the White House. Nan Cannon and Sue Bueneventura were listening in on the speakerphone.

"You know I'm here with Nan and Sue," Jean told Rainey, "and you know they've spent the day trying to get a quorum out of Billy Wheat. And now they want me to ask you—where do you think Sonny Pickett's been hiding?"

Rainey laughed from the bottom of a barrel of apples. He was at dinner in Old Town Alexandria with his golfing partners, Gershwin Metz and John Zavarello. Rainey was a good old boy with as big an appetite for gossip as he had for thirty-six holes a day.

"You know, Senator Jean, I can swear to you he's not under our table. That's the only place I'm sure of."

Jean wanted to sound more playful but it wasn't possible just now; she felt too threatened by events, too vulnerable to fate. "I think he's hiding from his duties, Mr. Speaker. I think he owes us an explanation, and he owes the American people an accounting. Where is he? The country's in a crisis. Where's the majority leader?"

Rainey laughed from the barrel again. "I thought it was me who's never to be found, isn't that right? Mr. Speaker-on-the-Links they call me, isn't that right?"

Jean heard some fire in Rainey's wit. He was changing somehow. He was acting more dignified despite his trademark self-mocking style.

Nan Cannon contributed, "They're all jealous of your handicap, Luke. Ask yourself, how many of them would have given up the Pro Tour for a desk job on the Hill called Congress?"

Sue added, "I'd rather tee it up with you than anyone else in Florida except my daddy."

"God bless you, Senator Nan," Rainey returned. "And I love you two arms full, Senator Suzie."

"We'll call you after we finish at the White House," Jean told Rainey. "I think we're about to find out exactly where Sonny Pickett's hiding, because I think we're about to have supper with the much-denied EXCOM."

"Call me anytime," Rainey flirted, "long as you call me out of the rain."

Jean got off the call with much puzzlement about Luke Rainey. *I wonder if we've made a deal we didn't count on,* she thought. *I wonder if he's what we think he is. I wonder what Rafi makes of him now that he's the only option out there.*

What happens after tomorrow? President Rainey?

Jean didn't have more time to brood about Raincy, because she was quickly into North Entrance Hall and handing over her wrap to the stewards. The three senators linked arms and strode the cross hall. The surprise was that they weren't heading to the family dining room on the first floor, or to the family quarters on the second floor, but rather up to the third floor. There, stewards were waiting to conduct them to the Billiards Room.

"An odd place for supper," Jean said.

"This is a trick," Nan Cannon warned.

"I don't know why," Sue joked. "Maybe Sonny Pickett's under the pool table."

Nan laughed in her froggy voice, and Jean tried to match her light mood by giggling. It didn't work. This was dangerous territory. They were strolling into the lion's den.

Tonight the den was smoky with Jesus Magellan's cigar. There was a hot and cold buffet laid out on the side table, and a female steward to serve, but otherwise there was no indication this was a dinner invitation.

"I'm glad you're on time," Garland began as soon as Jean cleared the archway entrance. "We've got lots to discuss, Jeannie." He made a show of looking at her again, this time down to her ankles, and then he spoke as if they were alone in the room. "You look good, Jeannie."

Jean glanced side to side. Jesus Magellan, Billy Wheat, Archie Learned, Rocky Kahn, Quinn Roosevelt, Hank Lovell. No Pickett.

The only White House female present beside the steward was the omnipresent Diana the scribe, seated in the corner beneath a photograph of FDR at the racetrack.

Jean spoke as bluntly as had Garland. "Good evening to you, Mr. President. This is EXCOM, is that correct?" She looked down at Quinn Roosevelt, who was seated forward in his chair, his chin resting on his hand. "We're brought into secret doings at last, is that correct, Mr. Roosevelt?"

"Good evening, Senator Motherwell," said Roosevelt. "I'm pleased you were able to come down from Maine on such short notice."

"From the president and First Lady's," Jean elaborated.

"And how is the president?" Roosevelt asked.

Jean knew from the way he asked that he knew nothing. *Q.'s in the dark,* she thought, *Q.'s unarmed tonight. Jack's right. We can do this.* Ignoring Roosevelt, she pushed her lips together and grinned at Garland. "The president didn't say, Mr. President, but I suppose he sends his respectful regards to the lot of you."

Garland took his double-breasted suit coat off and dropped it on a chair. He'd been shooting pool by himself. Now he nodded to Billy Wheat to rack up the balls.

Nan Cannon dropped her clutch bag on a chair and rubbed her hands together. "Don't worry about us, gentlemen, we'll serve ourselves. Sue, you want the chili?" Nan Cannon dipped her finger and tasted the sauce. "Wow—they left in the kick. And what's this? Pumpkin corn bread? Jean, can I get you a plate of the pasta salad?"

"Thanks," Jean said. The men were not going to move. They weren't even going to acknowledge that the women had arrived in cocktail clothes for a soiree while they were all loosening their business clothes and settling down with beer and finger food. Hank Lovell was the only one who looked focused, with his notebook monitor screen up and ready to type. Archie Learned and Rocky Kahn were leaning back in their chairs in their shirtsleeves, their bright silk ties unknotted. Rocky Kahn was toying with the TV remote, flipping all possible baseball games through the windows on the overhead monitor. The volume came up for a long home-run hit at Camden Yards.

"Birds are up four–zip in the second," Rocky Kahn told Garland. "That new kid from Guatemala."

"I knew we should've gone," Garland said as he banged away at the cue ball.

Jean took the plate from Nan Cannon and put it over the corner pocket near the door while she balanced the glass of iced tea on the side table. She had a flicker of pity for the boyishness of this performance—Shy with the cue stick like a lance, his courtiers dawdling around the round table—but then she reminded herself that she was all grown up and so were they, and that the mysteries of life also included hitting back so hard the enemy buckled.

"Let's get to an understanding," Jean said. "I brought Nan

and Sue with me tonight because we've all had a crummy day trying to find Sonny Pickett and move the pile on the Senate floor. We want a quorum, Mr. President. We want to move the question of a Select Committee to investigate Sensenbrenner. We wanted it this morning when I told the networks, we wanted it all day while your party evaded its responsibilities, and we want it tonight, right now."

Garland banged again and sent the six ball against the edge of Jean's plate with a clank.

Jean thought, *Now make the bastards sweat.*

"What I want is Sonny Pickett," she said.

"Us, too," called Nan Cannon, sipping her vodka tonic.

Garland said, "What you'll get is an offer to join forces, Jeannie. Why don't you sit down and have a bite of the pasta and listen to Q.'s presentation. It can't hurt. You know now that Sonny's not here. He's not coming late, either. We want to talk with you. And with Nan and Sue." Garland waved his hand in Nan Cannon's direction without turning toward her. "It is our responsibility. That's why we're here. And why I asked you tonight."

"You asked me because you're in trouble with the challenge," Jean pushed back. She wasn't going to sit. She wasn't going to go along with any of Garland's wishes—and she particularly wasn't going to let Quinn Roosevelt start up his snake-oil salesman patter about the good of the country and what was in it for Jean's Republicans. "And if I can't get Sonny Pickett to answer my call, I'm going to take it to *Nightline* tonight and hope he shows up. And then I'm going to send Nan and Sue into the well tomorrow morning and hold the Senate open for business until July fourth. Nothing gets past us until we get the Sensenbrenner investigation. Not the budget. Not the challenge. Nothing."

Jean was supreme over the pool table. Billy Wheat's mouth had fallen open to drink from his beer, but he left it hanging there, amazed. This was throwing a hay bale into a president's face. Jesus Magellan blew smoke and felt sweat on his temples. *Bad news*, he was thinking, *bad news because we haven't got anyone to go up against her on Nightline.* The cabinet officers, Learned and Kahn, just sat by, waiting to be given an order.

Garland flicked his glance at Quinn Roosevelt, who took a breath.

Roosevelt tried, "I think you should listen to our case, Senator. Responsibility goes both ways."

Jean knew she was winning by the gentleness in Roosevelt's voice.

Roosevelt stood up by the end window and gestured with a slight bow toward Jean. "We want to help each other," he continued. "You need to satisfy your call for an investigation. We need to get on with the business of government. We believe the challenge must be the first building block. Everything else will follow in order of preference, and we've gathered here to bring you into the process of planning preference."

"Oh, Mr. Roosevelt," Sue Bueneventura spoke up, "you say that so nicely. I wish you'd been there for us when your party fought the EPA funding in February." Sue was eating her chili with a serving spoon in large bites, and her voice was hollowed out by the fire in the peppers. "We could have used some say in preference."

Roosevelt bowed to Sue Bueneventura's clever point. "There are a lot of ends to this meeting," he said, "and certainly one can be a coming together about our legislative ambitions."

Nan Cannon, chewing a butter-heaped muffin, her feet up on the cross slat of her chair, addressed Hank Lovell. "Are you going to draw up a contract, Mr. Lovell? Party of the first part— that would be EXCOM—and party of the second part—that would be my leader. We sign before we go home, and then Monday morning, coolly and boldly, we set aside our quorum call and proceed to vote on the Twenty-fifth. Sound like a deal for you?"

Hank Lovell knew he was being mocked and wiped the sweat from his lip. "Senator Cannon, I'm only taking notes."

Jean had made her point. She was dealing from strength, and they knew it, so it was time to confuse them the more and make demands.

"What is the deal, Mr. President?" Jean asked Garland. "From you."

Garland shot his cuff and lined up a shot. He talked into the green felt. "Following Sensenbrenner's funeral on Monday, we get the challenge. On Tuesday, I announce that you get the vice presidency."

Jean had been prepared for almost anything; however, this deal was a new level of practical cynicism to her. Not even Jack had thought it through this far.

"A bipartisan government," Roosevelt picked up for his boss. "A national reconciliation. You are the leader of your party in all but name. You give up your Senate seat in exchange for the vice presidency. You're free to get off the ticket next summer. You will want to, no doubt, if and when your husband runs, or you do."

Jean decided to eat to show she was listening. They were desperate men. Jack had been right about them. To offer her the vice presidency was to prove beyond question that they were capable of FATHER'S DAY. Anything was possible with them. Garland would not stop until he had the presidency. Or until he was stopped.

Jean thought, *Does he take my deal?*

Nan Cannon asked the logical question. "What's in it for Jean and my party—to let her help you out of the mess you made?"

Roosevelt answered, "Our responsibilities are mutual. Let's admit the country's in a crisis. We're going to bury Sensenbrenner and hit a low in the polls on morale and confidence about the future. We need a tonic. We need Senator Motherwell."

Nan Cannon returned, "And only Jean can desert Teddy Jay and make it seem like a patriotic decision. Her best friend's husband and her duty, the profound choice between love and duty."

Roosevelt bowed to Nan Cannon's concise rhetoric.

Jean put her plate down. "We want to talk, Mr. President," she said to Garland. "The two of us. Without the baseball games."

Garland nodded. "Fine, Jean, that's fine. In my office downstairs." His handsome face was more plastic now. He had hope. He was thinking she might be ready to deal. He waved his hands and his lackeys started to move around. Only Jesus Magellan remained seated, and his frown showed what he thought of Garland's offer. From second choice for the VP, he had just slipped to third.

Jean was stalling while she decided on her next maneuver. She had to get Garland alone to make her offer. But first, what she also wanted to do was call Jack about the vice presidency deal. It was so outlandish a twist. Shy Garland was out of control. She needed LJ's counsel, too. Yet Jack had warned her that a cell call out of the White House would be monitored by Roosevelt's people, and she was not to call until she got back to the car.

Jean decided to compromise on her instinct to consult by sending Nan and Sue scurrying with the news of the deal. She took up her clutch bag and told Nan and Sue, "I think I'll be going home in another car. This snack's at an end. Why don't you get on back to the Hill and relieve Merry and make some calls. We'll want to consult with all our leadership."

Nan and Sue understood that what Jean meant by "leadership" included the conspirators in Maine as well as President Jay. They gathered up their clutches; Nan finished her vodka tonic in a head-back gulp; Sue touched her jewelry; and they joined Jean at the exit through the archway. The escape from the cigar fumes was a pleasure. Presently the three senators were striding together down the hall behind the steward. The men of EXCOM dawdled behind in mumbled consultation. Jean walked her friends all the way to the elevator for a proper send-off.

"Call Jack and Long John," she said to Sue Bueneventura. "Tell them I'll try to call later. I might not get to it until we're airborne."

Sue kissed Jean's cheek. "I love you," she said. Nan Cannon hugged Jean. "The bastard," she said of Garland, "the total bastard. To bribe my leader. The bastard."

Then they were gone, and Jean was on her own in the hands of EXCOM. She marched back to the Billiards Room in time to see Garland gesturing sternly at Jesus Magellan and Billy Wheat. *Poor Billy,* she thought, *he's at sea without Sonny, and Sonny's been banished. I wonder why? Crossed Shy? Or maybe because Shy needed a fall guy. That's like Shy. To blame while he reloads.*

"Mr. President, I'm ready," Jean called into the archway.

Garland had his suit coat back on, and he came out of the room in a rush of perfectly tailored blue pin-striped worsted wool. He took Jean's arm and pulled her close to his considerable muscles while his men looked on. "I'm glad we're going to get to talk together," he said in an intimate tone. "It's been too long since we said what we thought to each other."

"Always the smoothie," Jean said.

"You liked it once," said Garland.

Jean let Garland lead her to the stairs. EXCOM was not invited—not even Roosevelt was coming along—and the others turned off toward the elevator. Jean suspected they'd wait in the West Wing for a late debriefing. She had other plans for them, and she kept her step in line with Garland's. The second-floor hall was flawless and silent, though it was lined with anonymous staffers and Garland was followed by the usual bodyguard and military officers. The navy commander with the football sat on the chair outside Garland's office.

Garland and Jean parted as they cleared the door. The only person following them in was Diana the scribe.

"We can call for some espresso," Garland said, looking back at the steward. "Or don't you prefer cappuccino?"

"That'd be nice," Jean said, crossing the bare wood floor and taking a seat beside the TV monitor. Jean hadn't been in here before, but it looked like the other offices of Garland's she'd visited over the years. Always the rustic appointments, like a bunkhouse, like a rancher's study. Her distinct memory was that he liked sex on a bedroll on a naked floor. She had, too, once upon a time.

Over the mantel was the now famous NASA photograph of Major Garland in a white spacesuit, hanging on a tether from the shuttle *Enterprise* two hundred miles over the Gulf of Mexico and brave Texas.

Shy, Shy, Shy, she thought, *you're such a nice obvious little boy to have become such a . . . ?*

"We can be comfortable with each other," Garland said, leaning against the mantel. "You wouldn't have come down here unless you were persuaded a little. I know that much. You and me, Jeannie, we'd make history. The first Father and Mother, the first bipartisan presidency, and you'd be the most powerful woman in history."

Jean looked at Diana, who was standing still, pen in hand, eyes on her paper, waiting to write Jean's reply. Jean understood the use of Diana—no audiotape was safe, but history required an ear—however, she didn't have to tolerate what was clearly to Garland's advantage.

"I want this private," Jean said.

"Oh, okay," Garland said, waving once. Diana backed out the door like a retainer. "Better for you?"

Jean teased, "I wanted to be alone with you when you told me we'll make history. It's a line you never tried to my ears. It's something Cleopatra might've heard more than once, don't you think?"

"Any way you want to put it," Garland said. He smiled beautifully at Jean's jest about Antony and Cleopatra. "I've been thinking that perhaps it was fate that threw us together like this again. That Teddy Jay had to fail, that I had to reach for Sensenbrenner to satisfy the wolves, that we had to come to this crisis so that you and I could get together again. We started together on the Hill, we can carry on together down here."

"My terms are mine to name?" Jean asked. "I get EPA to name, I get Justice to name—we clean house, fire the whole cabinet that deserted Teddy Jay, and I have approval of the new cabinet, of the budget revisions in conference, of the Defense Appropriations Act? I rewrite New Reconstruction?"

"Whatever you want, I mean it."

"Not even Cleopatra had that."

Garland spoke eagerly. "You know I'm making concessions to you. You know I can't break the logjam you've thrown up—not right off, anyway. Sonny Pickett is finished with me. He double-crossed me with Sensenbrenner. It was his idea, and somehow it fell apart. Someone talked out of school. Then Sensenbrenner went and got himself shot. I'm holding Sonny responsible as a lesson to the rest of those double-crossing social climbers on the Hill. Like Jesus, like Billy—they've got to learn this job's for me, no one else."

"Presuming the electorate agrees next year?" Jean asked.

Garland was having such a good time that he displayed his grandiosity in the way of a peacock, turning slightly, arching his back, throwing his long arms out. "They've already approved. Haven't you seen my polls?"

The steward came in with the cappuccino and pastry service. Jean waited to sip twice. The scene was coming together fast and neat. Jean was ready to hit Garland with the coup de maître. *How did I ever love you, Shy?* she thought.

"I'll answer your offer," she said. "I came here tonight to make an offer of my own. I came with a message from President Jay."

Garland moved quickly to her side and squatted at her feet. He looked directly into her face. "He's quitting?"

Jean knew about Garland's intuition. He was very good at guessing ahead. She counted on his thinking too fast to spot the trap.

"It's worse, Shy," Jean said. "He wants to resign. And he wants to resign to you. Here's why."

Jean had a choice to make. Did she reach into her clutch and show Garland Schofield's testimony? Or did she show him the torn out page of the president's diary with his suicide note?

Which would convince Garland that he'd won? To admit that President Jay was intimidated by EXCOM and wanted to surrender? Or to admit that President Jay was unfit to continue another day?

Jack had left the choice to Jean—to make at the last moment. Use the Lady of the plot, or the Tiger of the suicide? What Jack hadn't known when he'd fashioned the deal was that Garland would preempt the game and offer her the vice presidency. How did that change the deal?

Jean chose by feel.

"The president tried to kill himself last night, Shy." She brought out the suicide note. "I'm telling you the truth as I know it, and this is the note he left for Connie, in his diary. He gave it to Connie this morning, and she gave it to me. I came here to tell you that the president is finished. He wants to resign. But he knows that he must resign to you. No explanation. My message is that he wants to resign to you. In person."

Garland touched his lip. He stared at Jean's knee but he was thinking about history and eternity. He took the paper and read aloud from the first sentence, " 'No man is more important than his responsibilities. I'm not. I must be responsible. I must take responsibility for my own choices. I want to stay with you. My responsibility is to the Constitution. No one will believe any of us unless we keep faith with our oaths. I love you.' "

Garland raised his eyebrows and then sighed. He recognized the responsibility argument that he'd used on Jay, and here it was transformed into a suicide note.

"When was this?" he asked.

"Thursday night, last night, right after he heard about Sensenbrenner."

Garland asked, "When did he tell you he wants to quit?"

"This morning."

"Before or after you called for the investigation?"

"Before," Jean said.

"You sandbagged me," Garland said.

"I did what's best for my party and country."

"You're the same as me."

"No, Shy, I'm not. I'm the minority leader."

Garland shook off the disagreement. "When does he want to quit?"

Jean was back on safe ground—all artifice. "As soon as possible," she said. Here was the moment of maximum sales. She had to get him to agree to coming to Maine tomorrow morning. But should she say it? She deflected. "Connie wants to put him in the clinic immediately. You see, there's some paralysis on the left side."

"Jesus," said Garland.

"That's right, Shy, he's falling apart, and my thinking is we want to get this done before the press figures out the suicide. The country's shaken enough. That might crack it open. And,

Shy, we both know they'll come looking for someone to blame for driving him into Somes Sound and paralysis. Or worse yet."

"That's how he tried to do it, in the water? What a death. Drowning. The burning lungs. The blackness. The fear. The coldness."

Jean waited. Garland had thought about suicide. What did that mean—he was brave? Or he was just thorough about his job. To have the power to destroy the world is to have the power to destroy yourself.

How nervy is he? she thought.

"Does my offering you the vice presidency change the deal?" Garland asked. He stood quickly, stepping so close to Jean that his shins brushed her skirt hem. He looked down at her like a merciful conqueror. His words were affectionate. "Can you come with me? If we go. How will we go?" Garland asked.

Jean thought, *He's hooked.*

"We can take the president's plane back," Jean said. "The president recommended it. That's part of his message. Come in quietly and take his resignation. Then make the announcement."

Garland reached for his monitor and tapped on a video window, making the call to the Oval Office. There appeared a tiny shot of the room, like a miniature architect's photo. "Q., I want you right away. Everybody else, go on home. Jesus, I'll call you. Billy, stay in touch with Q. about tomorrow. Rocky, Archie, I want business as usual out there, but get Sensenbrenner's body home safely. I don't care how you get it out of Cairo. Get it home. And Hank, I want you up here, too. Move it."

Garland tapped off and turned back to Jean. "The Secret Service won't like us both being together outside of here," he said. "Two presidents spooks them as it is."

"I'm the messenger," Jean said. "President Jay is taking a chance. Perhaps he's taking more of a chance than we ever could."

"Giving up, you mean?" Garland asked.

Jean wanted to answer him honestly. Despite the fact that she was tricking him, she wanted to speak the truth as she saw it. "Trusting the Constitution regardless is what I mean," Jean said.

Garland spun around and tapped his monitor again for the deputy chief of communications, one of Roosevelt's attack team boys. "What time is it in Rome? Yeah, that late? Leave a message for my wife, then, will you. I don't want her wakened. Tell her that—"

Garland broke off and looked at Jean. "I guess telling Iphy you and I are going to run the country isn't the best news to wake up to?"

Garland finished to the monitor: "Tell her that I love her and will call her with good news before noon her time."

Suddenly Roosevelt pushed through the office door with Hank Lovell on his heels. "Mr. President?" Roosevelt said; he was breathless, and his tidy round body was on overdrive. "Have we got a deal?"

Garland put his hand on Jean's shoulder and stood as close to her as a husband. "We're going to Maine in the morning to take Jay's resignation, and then Jean and I are going to face the cameras. Full press conference from where—from your house, Jean? You're right across the water, aren't you?"

"Yes, Jack's house backs on the president's," Jean said.

"I suppose we'll need to tell Jack you're going to be vice president," Garland remarked. "And ask for his house for the swearing-in. Good. Good." Garland looked to Roosevelt again. "From Jean and Jack's house. I'll take the swearing-in there. Use the local judge. Same as LBJ did coming from Dallas. We're back here tomorrow by noon."

Roosevelt's face darkened and brightened with the news. His lips vanished in his teeth, and then he said, "No, I don't think—"

Garland cut him off. "We're going, Q. We've got the deal and we're going."

"But, sir, if he wants to resign, then—"

"We've got to end the Twenty-fifth now! It's smothering the country. I've got to get the job done."

"Yes, sir," Roosevelt tried.

"Set it up and put your teams on the release for tomorrow. And keep that funeral coming. It'll be my first public show. I'll give the eulogy at the cathedral and lead the mourners with Jean."

Roosevelt said, "It's my job to say that I don't like you and Jay getting together outside of the White House. Why do you have to go to him? Can't he come here?"

In the pause, Jean was sure Garland was deciding what to say of the suicide.

Garland made the heroic decision. "No, he can't. He's ill, and it's the decent thing for me to go to him. Going to the mountain, Q. Now. Hank, I'll want a letter of resignation prepared by my departure."

"Yes, sir." Lovell nodded deeply. "Like Nixon's, you mean?"

"The same," Garland said. "Q., get your men working on shaking the bodywatchers off right away. The senator and I are dining alone. Jean's staying the night at the White House. Tell them any suggestive thing you want. Make it deliberately ambiguous, with Iphy out of the country. Distract them. Make a crack about old flames talking over the fate of the nation. Feed them romance. Make it salacious. We've got to get in to Jay without the press alert to it."

"I don't like sneaking," Roosevelt said.

"Get on it, now," Garland declared. He squeezed Jean's shoulder. "The senator and I will have a proper meal in my quarters. I'm famished again. Send in the steward. The cars for Andrews should be ready in four hours. What do you figure, Jean? Liftoff for Maine by three A.M.?"

Jean couldn't resist her instinct to raise her hand up and cover Garland's hand warmly; she pressed his fingers as a wife would communicate support. "Yes, Mr. President," she said. "We'll be on the ground by dawn."

Roosevelt and Lovell tried to argue again. The Secret Service. The press. The timing. The haste—why the haste?

Garland would have none of it and ordered them out. He took Jean's hand in his own and led her to the connecting door to his dressing room. The light was low, and when the steward came in Garland ordered him to put the dinner before the window overlooking the lawn and the lights of the Washington Monument.

"Jeannie, there's no chance we could actually make the press think we're having an affair, is there?"

Jean was ready for the question. It was ten-thirty. Four and a half hours to takeoff. Whatever it took to get him to Maine, she was prepared to do. She felt nothing but duty now. He was a condemned president. She was his last seduction. And what would it matter?

She kissed him on the cheek and breathed against his shoulder. "We're both tired, Shy, and have a long night ahead of us. Let's dine quietly and talk. The other is for another time. I think that's best, don't you? Tomorrow's to be the most demanding day of our lives."

"Another time?" Garland put his arms around Jean and gave her a hug. "You and me? You're kidding?"

A honey trap, she thought. *Jack's right, I'm the honey, and a man is a man is a man is a man.*

"Shy," she whispered, "relax."

Garland did relax his arms around her, and then he went further. He pulled back a little—enough separation for him to be able to look down upon her glowing face.

"Jeannie?" he began.

Jean knew she'd gone too far.

He knows, she thought, *he's figured it out. He knows I'm here to bait him. He's going to—*

"No, never mind," Garland said. He lowered his head again.

Jean pushed up on her toes and came as close to kissing the president as she could without actually biting his lips.

Garland thought, *It's just not possible.*

His kiss was not an old friend's, and he enjoyed how she tasted. She tasted of victory.

4 1 Early Saturday, Mount Desert Island

Jack waited for Jean's call until midnight at the house, and when it didn't come, he decided to drive up to the summit of Cadillac Mountain. On good days it was an arduous trip, weaving over the ridges and along sharp drops; in tonight's soup it was a challenge Jack took scrupulously.

At the summit, there were no stars, and the sea breeze was strengthening again, with more squalls out to sea and back to the west, closing in on the coast. Poor driving, worse sailing weather, stupid flying weather, but that wouldn't stop anyone tonight.

Jack got out of the Cherokee and roamed along the paths. He headed to one of the easier-to-reach redoubts over the lights of Bar Harbor. Far below, like a toy set, the streets were fuzzy yellow with the fog blowing in. Jack's face was rinsed with saltwater. He couldn't see anything out in Frenchman Bay. It was blacker still to the south and back east. He might as well have been at sea level for the visibility.

Yet somewhere out there to the north was a light infantry

battalion in heavy air transport C-17s, topped off by a tanker and circling in descending spirals in preparation for the run in to the coast.

Also, somewhere way up there above the storm system was the total blanket of security his father had demanded from Breckenridge—the immeasurable power of a supercarrier battle group with all its predator names of combat air patrol equipment: Hawkeyes, Tomcats, Hornets, Phantoms, Intruders, Sea Dragons, Sea Stallions. Higher still would be the AWACS and J-STARS air-traffic-control aircraft circling like gods. And over all of it would be the eye of the cosmos in a spy satellite that could record everything in real time down to the heat register of Jack's Cherokee.

Finally, back there to the southwest on the high-altitude route was the president's Gulfstream inbound from Andrews, on the J55 line to the Hamptons and then the Providence and then the Boston beacons before it passed over to the Kennebunk and St. John beacons to find Mount Desert in any weather.

No, not yet. Jack checked the time: 0126 hours, Saturday, June 14. If Jean had closed her deal, if she'd convinced Garland to dash for Jay's surrender, then they wouldn't be launching for at least an hour. Would Garland cut it fine? Aim to pop in here at dawn to get Jay's resignation before breakfast? And then . . . ?

I don't know, Jack thought. *But if . . .*

If, if, if, Jack thought. *How's it going, Jean? Did he bite?*

The only certainty Jack had so far was that call from Nan and Sue at nine-thirty. They'd told him of the EXCOM game in the Billiards Room and of the bribe of the vice presidency to Jean. What a deal. Jack was astonished at Garland's recklessness. To bribe Jean. To make her the vice betrayer for the president betrayer. Of all the marks already against Garland— Toni, Sensenbrenner, Jay—Jack was now convinced that bribing Jean as if she were for sale was the one that sealed Garland's end. He was a bad judge of womankind as well as a petty tyrant and high traitor. Snapping him in two was justice . . .

Jack let it go. No more moralism. Do the job. Garland's trick would make Jean's trick simpler. Jack had figured Garland would be suspicious of a trip outside the White House—that Garland's staff wouldn't want the two presidents together. But now that Garland had offered Jean a plot of his own, maybe he wouldn't spot Jack's.

You want the big job, Shy? Come on, Shy. Bite. Bite it all. Go for it, Shy. Come on.

Jack squatted down on the rock face and flipped up his cell phone to call his father. That afternoon before the weather closed Jack had directed Long John to fly to National in the Philip Morris Gulfstream. One punch and his father answered on Jean's little white cell phone.

"I'm on Cadillac," Jack said. "Where are you?"

"In the kitchen, toasting cheese on rye bread."

"Sounds good," Jack allowed.

Long John asked, "What's the weather?"

"Dirty," Jack said.

"Get your rest," Long John said.

"I'm thinking about Jean with that cretin," Jack said.

"He's the acting president, too," Long John said.

"Aren't you going to tell me not to worry?"

"No." Long John sighed. "I'm worried, you should be. We've both of us spent nights like this before. It's the same each time. The worst imaginable feels real until something actually happens."

"I wish I could joke about it."

"Rainey's joking," Long John said. "I just got off the phone with him. He says he's teeing off before seven at Burning Tree, to get in thirty-six holes, and if I want him, he'll be right in the middle of the fairway."

"I'll call as soon as I know, Dad. You just keep Jean's phone in your pocket."

"I know what to do about the call, Jack. What I have to figure out is how to catch up with Rainey if he's buried in some bunker."

"He does like his golf, doesn't he?" Jack said. "You'd think a man in his situation would want to sit around and save his energy—not do thirty-six in the heat. He's different than I figured. He's got heart to talk easy, with what he knows."

Long John made the paternal point. "It's how you'll talk when it's your turn."

"Dad, after Toni, I don't know if—"

"You keep your own counsel about your heart," Long John warned. "We have a dark night of the soul in front of us."

"If anything happens to Jean—it'll be on me, you know."

"You want my permission to take the risk?" Long John asked. "It's late in the game for you to ask my permission."

Jack hesitated. He could tell from Long John's edgy tone that his father was about to get angry at Jack for weakening.

"Okay, Dad. It's just the size of the risk is hitting me slowly. I was in a rage this morning. I'm tired now, and it's scaring me."

"You stay scared," Long John said.

"But is it right? Have I done the right thing?"

"You feel unutterable anxiety, is that right?" Long John asked.

"Yes."

"So did John Adams. He wrote it down. Right before they went past the point of no return with the Crown. 'Unutterable anxiety.' Respect the men and women out there to feel the same as you and John Adams and still do their jobs."

"I want to trust them," Jack said.

"Then trust them. What do you think the president's doing tonight in his room, his body deserting him when he needs it, perhaps dying, with the First Lady sitting beside him to watch him breathe? With two of their babies asleep in a house that might not hold up. How scared are they? And what about all those boys out there with Schofield? Our boys, with mothers and fathers and sweethearts and wives—and plenty of children all around."

"Yeah," Jack admitted, "I hadn't thought about Schofield and them this way. Scared, too, I suppose. Coming on to infamy or worse."

"How about their unutterable anxiety? Respect them all and don't doubt them. It's a wonderful country if you trust it to do the job."

"Yes, sir," Jack said to his father.

Long John was almost done backing up his son; he reached deep into paternal vigor and offered a roundabout compliment. "What did you feel before you jumped into Walvis Bay?" he asked.

"Terror," Jack said.

"Get some rest, Jack."

Jack tucked the cell phone into his windbreaker, pulled his hood up over his rain cap, shoved his hands in his pockets, and walked back to the Cherokee. His mind was numb with worry. He gazed up to the clouds, where he imagined the spy satellite hung like the Holy Ghost, watching him breathe and radiate heat. Someday soon a commander could speak an order to the sky and it would be transmitted around the world instantly.

Get some rest, Jack, he thought. *Right here in the car. Relax.*

He also thought, *Allison. Toni. Jean. I'm sorry.*

42 Saturday Dawn, Mount Desert Island

Stretching and twisting up the port airstair, Schofield made his way to the flight deck of his command C-17 to chat one last time with the flight leader, an air force MAC driver named Wilshire.

Fourteen hours into the mission, Schofield was used to the rattling drone of the ship and the rank recirculated air. He was also used to the fact that Wilshire and his copilot Bluebell Lee did little more than watch full-color television monitors called MFDs. The ship was fly-by-wire with a computer-generated flight plan passed down from the satellites. The aircraft even talked to the crew in a gentle mechanical voice that reported routine and extraordinary events throughout the systems. With airborne refueling, the C-17 could stay aloft indefinitely, circling the earth and waiting for orders to swoop.

The only true interest inside this tireless robot was the takeoff or landing, when there was something out there to hit.

Schofield slipped into Bluebell Lee's copilot's seat and addressed Wilshire with dry lips. "We've talked it over, my XO and me." Schofield sipped from his water bottle. "And we need to get our Pathfinders down fast."

Schofield pointed into the blackness of the night sky, stars and a crescent moon above the storm clouds to the west. "We've decided we want to go straight in on the shrubs and make our LZ on the primary. No pass for look-see."

Wilshire punched up an MFD monitor over their heads that showed several distinct views of the Bar Harbor–Hancock County Airport recorded in the last hour by a satellite. He windowed up both radar imaging and infrared, using sideways and overhead glances. Schofield glimpsed the familiar landmarks from the previous hour. Parked National Guard helicopter under low-angle lights. One state police cruiser with its engine running. Runway lights and power plant. The heat signature of the underground tank farm. A parking lot of cooled engines. A north-south runway. Approach from Frenchman Bay. The trident-shaped headlands of Sorrento, Hancock, and Lamoine. The boot-shaped Lamoine Beach. The Jordan River. The tree line.

Wilshire tapped more keys and twisted his mouth in thought. "Can do it, sure," he said, "but it's not my favorite. Here's why. With this load, we need about nine hundred meters to stop once we touch wheels. And you want me to put you right on top of the targets, so you're giving up most of the runway. Nine hundred meters is about all that's down there from the trees to the targets, and I don't know about the damn treetops." He gestured toward Polaris, meaning the satellites. "I don't trust those birds for giving me an accurate size of those trees."

Schofield argued, "You told me you take down trees like a cowcatcher."

"I was bragging," said Wilshire. He was thirty-one, a captain with the Seventeenth MAS, a bony and jaunty cowboy from the Idaho Panhandle, and he felt as confident of his equipment as of himself. It was the trees that he didn't believe in. Down at the South Carolina field, they were always showing bird nests in the landing gear. "We take on the wrong white pine, we don't bounce with seventy-five kilotons of load. And they've got big firs. It's Maine, isn't it? Big, big firs."

Schofield pointed at the MFD's image of the LZ. "One pass of this ship will wake up those state troopers. And they've got a radio dispatcher I can't get to. I've got to get my Pathfinders to them before they start thinking. Maybe three minutes from when they hear us. I need the primary approach. I need the edge."

"What about the rest of the flight?" Wilshire asked.

There were five C-17s behind them—two loaded with infantry companies, three more loaded with vehicles, lots of bullets, and the battalion's two critical thermal-imaging Nightfoxes.

"They lay off seaward until we're down," Schofield said of the flight. "Once you lift off, they'll know it's doable."

"So—if we get down, it works," Wilshire summarized. "But if we don't, what about them?"

"They keep coming," Schofield said.

"Roger that," Wilshire said. Schofield had just told them that there was no abort. This was more of the unusual part of the profile of this mission that both puzzled and pleased Wilshire. If this was a black exercise, it was most streamlined. There was no wiring diagram above them. He and Schofield made the calls—and mostly it was Schofield. The colonel was his own command and control. No one over his shoulder but the satellites and the weather.

"I'll find us skinny firs to slip between," Wilshire returned.

"Set us down, Captain, and we'll thank you kindly."

Schofield climbed down to the cargo hold. There was a crowd at the head again. He'd had the troops drinking water with electrolytes all night to buck their energy. Now there were one hundred and twelve men in the hold in various states of wakefulness. Tip-up seats were not for sleeping, so the men had rested by slumping forward. There'd been edgy talking the first hours, but since the midway point most of the men had just stared at the blue light in silence.

Mario Cello had set up an operations table at his seat, and Cello's team were gathered over their folding portfolios. These three lieutenants were the heavy thinkers of the outfit, Cello's worrywarts—and Schofield needed to satisfy them.

"He came around to us," Schofield reported on Wilshire. "We take it all at once."

"What'd he say about the trees?" asked one of the lieutenants.

"He said he'll find us thin ones to fly between."

The ship banged in clear air turbulence again, making the lieutenants laugh.

Cello didn't look up because he was already past the tree problem and still working on the big challenge—getting inside the Gulfstream with the president without alerting the crew.

"We've been doing some guessing about the target," Cello said. "And you're not going to like this."

Just because Task Force Schofield was going to own the field, the communications channels, and the backup didn't mean capturing the plane was straight.

"Look at this, sir," Cello said. "I've changed my mind. The G-V's just not a big enough fuselage for us to use ordnance on its emergency exits like before. It's only seven and a half feet wide and six feet high. No reinforcement—heck, sir, there's not even any jamming gear on her, she's a luxury aircraft. We think we'd crumple her."

"How do we get in, then?" Schofield asked.

"We don't," Cello said. "I'm guessing now, but won't they do like before? Remember how the heavy pilot's reaction to a blown tire was to shut her down? Those Eighty-ninth MAC guys don't take chances with that supercargo, and rolling on a blown tire is a chance. So—if that's true again, why rush in? If we stop her, won't they shut down and open her up for a visual inspection and wait for a tow?"

"You mean, shoot out the tires again? And wait for them to open up? Send out the vehicle as if we were the welcoming committee?"

"It's simpleminded, I know."

Schofield looked at the drawings Cello had made of the

Gulfstream V—the same aircraft that Governor Longfellow had flown to Moldova. A luxury craft. Ninety-six and a half feet long from nose to tip. Twenty-five feet three inches high from wheel to top of the tail. A ninety-foot ten-inch wingspan. Crew of two in a six-foot ten-inch cockpit. A nine-foot seven-inch crew compartment behind the flight deck. A thirty-five-foot four-inch passenger cabin of rich chairs and couches. Two hundred and twenty-four cubic feet in the baggage hold aft. Two BMW/Rolls-Royce BR710 jet engines. Maximum passenger load of nineteen. No armor. No extra weight for air defense. Survival capsule? Probably not. Jamming gear from SAM threat? Negative.

He asked, "What if they smell us and try to take off?"

Cello bobbed his chin. "Then we have no choice."

Schofield spent the last thirty minutes in his seat writing out the last of his letter to Toni's children. If it came to it, they'd find it and send it on. Mac and Toni's babies. His responsibility. The two best reasons he could figure for surviving this operation. In prison or not, just survive it.

Probably not, Schofield thought. *The man who shot the president.*

He had the .22 in his Beretta holster. It was cleaned and loaded. He didn't touch it, because his old superstition was that you shouldn't touch a weapon unless you were going to use it. If he didn't touch it, then . . .

The loadmaster gave the signal to stand up.

Seats stowed, packs and weapons checked, everyone braced the walls the best they could for a hard landing—face to the rear. The trick was standing while crouching to ride the bumps. Already the ship was banging like a car without shocks and they weren't close yet, just riding at zero meters above the waves on a dirty night of gusts and rain showers and ground fog. Wilshire plowed on as if he were driving a bus on an interstate in a quake.

The ship banked port, then leveled off. Lights out, jump light on, the loadmaster marched to the port paratroop door.

"Five minutes, Colonel," he shouted, holding up his fingers and squeezing his headset to his ears to listen to the flight deck.

Schofield didn't care to listen to the pilots. They'd do the job. Schofield was paired with Corporal Ky and the manpack transceiver. He gave Ky a thumbs-up. Ky returned the same and mouthed the words as he was saying, "All green lights, sir."

Schofield glanced to starboard, to the Pathfinder leader Tom Owen. He was focused on the loadmaster. Everyone had their pairing and their assignment. Schofield was going out with Tom Owen and the Pathfinders as soon as the loadmaster opened up the paratroop doors at the rear. The bulk of the company would go out the rear loading ramp once it struck the runway.

Wilshire's brilliant robot picked up the Petit Manan light in the Gulf of Maine. He ordered the ship down to the waves and increased power to three hundred and fifty knots. The MFDs told Wilshire he was five miles to the headland at Schoodic Point. The buffeting was rhythmic. Bluebell Lee hooted as they passed the lighthouse within two hundred meters. Outside, the Atlantic was as black as a cave. But from inside on the MFDs the world was bright and even transparent with night vision and infrared signatures. The master warning caution annunciator was popping with voice and audio alerts, and Wilshire shut down the beeps and whistles. Trust the ship and the extravagant miracles of GE and Honeywell and Teledyne and Allied Signal and General Dynamics. The talking ship reminded the pilots to watch the information flashing on the Hud and MFDs. They were too busy to think; they responded to the numbers. A Chris-Craft couldn't have come in harder on those choppy seas. The ship was meant to land anywhere, anytime—over water or under fire—and it closed on the coast like a fat seagull.

Schoodic Point passed in an infrared heap of smashing rollers out of the North Atlantic. Wilshire throttled back and brought her to a new heading in on Frenchman Bay. They were going straight up the main channel. Egg Rock Light. The ship talked. Rum Key. The pilots sat still. Bald Rock. Wheels down. Four Pratt & Whitney turbofans fought the drag.

Landmarks for the three points of land dead ahead. Wilshire began the turn over Hancock Point. He eased her about and goosed her nose up. They made landfall over Raccoon Cove. The birches. The Siberian stone pines. The firs. Nose higher. Bumping underneath. The five-thousand-foot airstrip. North-to-south runway. No lights. None necessary. Cold LZ. Flaps down. Nose up again. Airspeed dropping to one hundred and fifteen knots. Rudder over. The talking airplane. Settle. Allied Signal wheels. Contact.

The C-17 hit without a bounce and stuck on the concrete, racing forward with the negative g load. Thrust reversal screamed to stop her. The wing ribs and bulkheads expanded as the full weight settled. There was that vertiginous moment when the whole mass might continue into the earth—and then she recoiled and settled forward. Ground speed dropping. Six hundred meters. Seven hundred. Eight-fifty. Carbon brakes.

Wilshire made hard over on the three-point turn, whipping round the wingtips and tail plane. He braked again at the edge of the concrete.

Green light.

"Go!" cried the loadmaster, popping the paratroop door. "Go-go-go-go-go."

Schofield stayed on Ky's flank. The rain was blowing sideways from the south. They high-stepped over the hundred wet yards from slick concrete to slicker grass to the gleaming puddles on the macadam. There were three objectives: the state police cruiser in the upper parking lot, the National Guard helicopter and crew on the tarmac between the two open-door hangars, and the graveyard-watch Guardsman in the field office.

The state police cruiser was the threat with its radio. Night vision goggles showed Schofield the car like a burning green box. Owen's hand signal was a silhouette against a flame.

Schofield, out of breath, stopped and waved Ky to take a knee beneath the wing of a tied-down Cessna 172. Schofield grabbed the horn and clicked Cello. "Cargo, this is Sky King. Tell me they're out of the ship, Mario. Tell me they're moving onto the road. Roger. Over."

Schofield watched Tom Owen at seventy yards. The state troopers were alert. A small one got out of the car and held up his hand. Tom Owen's team took both troopers without stopping, and the second team veered toward the helicopter. Pathfinders were spreading out in the rental parking lot to open up the Avis and Hertz and National cars. They needed them for transport—no car alarms this time; they had the keys from the rental offices.

The easiest objective was the airfield office. The Guardsman met them at the door with a Hello, who are you people?

"This is Sky King. Get that bird up, Mario! Roger. Over," Schofield ordered Cello.

Wilshire started rolling his aircraft to the launch point before his ramp was up. Takeoff with a zero payload was six hundred and seventy meters, and Wilshire aimed to use just that last measure of the runway. No mistakes now, in the dark and wet. The ship made a one-hundred-eighty-degree turn in a tight thirty-five meters and then launched in a roar of the externally blown flap system like a locomotive blasting off on four orange plumes.

The second C-17 with Charlie Company was on the final approach over Raccoon Cove.

Schofield ordered Cello to get his company moving across the quarter-mile grassy field that bordered Route 3, the north-south road onto Mount Desert Island.

The time was 0335 hours. They had an hour to get all strike elements down and deployed before the Secret Service's C-130 would be coming down.

Schofield planted his weight and breathed. His headquarters team was formed up and took over communications with Able Company's three platoons. The EW/GCI unit they'd hauled on a hand dolly was cranked up beneath the Cessna's wingspan, and they threw a tarp over the wing to shield the operators.

Charlie Company's C-17 sounded like an avalanche cascading over the tree line.

Schofield thought, *How could they not hear it? But then, who's out there but Longfellow's state police and maybe the local cops on a drive-by.*

Schofield called Cello. "Talk to me, Mario."

"Sky King, this is Cargo. Everything's copacetic here. Roger. Over," Cello said. He was jogging over muddy ruts with his RTO. Cello reported that Able's advance squads owned the intersection of 3 and 230, that Able had cut the road onto the island, that Able was waiting for Charlie's vehicles to forward base. Cello said this was an exercise in a rainstorm. No bogeys. No lights. A few fishermen's cars on the road. The dead of a dead night. Cello continued to answer his boss's demands. And here came the Seventeens. Charlie Company down and unloaded, then the Seventeen launched in H plus twenty minutes. Hummers down and unloaded and aircraft launched in H plus thirty-one minutes. Nightfox helicopters and Hummers down and unloaded and the Seventeen launched in H plus forty-seven minutes. Baker Company well off seaward for ready reserve. No breaks, no glitches—no screwing the pooch to be found. The headquarters team ran the LZ in the dark as if it was home port.

By H plus fifty minutes the reports were in from the big town of Ellsworth, six miles up the road, that Charlie Company's First Platoon owned the automated switches on Main Street and the cell tower on Watts Hill—no shutdown, just control in case they had to cut the outside lines—and they were in position to hit the police station at Town Hall.

At the same time, Charlie's Second and Third Platoon had deployed forward in the Hummers and the airport rentals as far as the Town Hill intersection. No contact. Probe all the way to Somesville. The television trucks along Route 102 were dark.

"Mario, button them up," Schofield ordered Cello. "Tell Incavagglia, button them up like slugs. Roger. Over."

The EW/GCI picked up the advance C-130's transponder on the J573 jet route as soon as it passed the Kennebunk beacon. The Secret Service liked to have its equipment on the ground well before the president. The Office of Protective Research was routine and fussy. But tonight, the usual tech and transport teams were coming in just before the president—maybe forty minutes ahead of the president's Gulfstream out there on the J55 route to Boston. The C-130 didn't expect the field to be lit up, since Bar Harbor was usually an uncontrolled field after dark.

Ten miles out, the 89th MAC pilot called the fixed-base operator at Bangor to chatter about ID, ETA, and weather. Schofield didn't listen in. The Bangor tower responded. All was in order. Coming out of the storm, the C-130's turboprops sounded like an electric beater as it made Bartlett Island, then the Western Bay, then started its slow bank over the Narrows. The pilot lit up the runway lights.

Schofield looked at his watch. Able's Second Platoon was the strike team. They waited until the aircraft was down and rolling back to the taxiway before they showed themselves from their hidey-holes—jogging alongside the rear door like two dark tails in the green glow of Schofield's night vision. The crew feathered the turboprops beside the rental office building, near the parked executive jets. The forward hatchway popped open and raised up like a carport door.

Schofield couldn't see the detail of the strike from his vantage.

Within five minutes the call came from Cello. "Secure here, sir. One casualty. On the way to the battalion aid station. Roger. Over."

Schofield hadn't heard gunfire. He didn't have time to think about it. The headquarters team reported picking up the transponder of the Gulfstream, now locked on the St. John's beacon. The president was fifty miles out.

At this moment, Schofield's instinct was to hit Somesville and Ellsworth now—to take them all down and lock them all up, to whack them as hard as he whacked Bendery and anything that moved in Occupied Moldova—to bring the peacekeeping home.

No, no, he thought, *this isn't the time. No. It won't work yet. Panic's a weapon. Use it later.*

At H plus seventy-five minutes there was first sunlight on the horizon somewhere out there beyond the storm. Dawn was scheduled at 0451 hours. This morning there were only thunder bursts from far away. Temperature about 40 degrees. Twenty minutes past low tide. Precipitation over an inch in twenty-four hours. Barometric pressure at 29.85. Variable winds, with gusts at twenty-five miles per hour. The end of the night. The end of the storm?

"Sky King, this is Bravo One-Three—ETA three minutes, sir," Tom Owen called from the field office. "He's reported in, and we gave him what he wants. Roger. Over."

"We don't show any escorts here on our scope," Schofield replied. He was standing over the shoulder of the EW/GCI techs. "So if he had any chase aircraft out of McGuire, they're gone now."

Cello called from the C-130, "Sky King—we've got the limousine ready to roll. Roger. Over."

Charlie Company's Incavagglia reported in from the intersection on the island. "No sweat, sir," he summarized. Inky was point on the strike force leader against Mount Desert Island and the Coast Guard station at Southwest Harbor, and he was as wired as a TOW 2.

Schofield called Tom Owen, "Get your people moving."

Schofield called Cello, "This is Sky King. I want both shots on the tires. Both at once. Acknowledge."

Cello asked, "Two rounds each, sir?"

"Make it happen," Schofield told Cello, and then he and Ky moved forward to their hidey-hole underneath a Beechcraft prop parked off the taxiway.

Tom Owen joined them. They all threw off their ponchos. The rain soaked their body armor. There was nothing to say, so they watched their watches.

It wasn't dark anymore. The Gulfstream was a gray-white bird. The MAC pilot turned on the field's remote-controlled lights. He made the turn over the bay and came in gently. He needed all of one thousand meters to land, and he took it, north to south, flaps up, power up, carbon brakes, the *whoosh* of a Winnebago going by, the squeal of a Rolls-Royce overdrive.

Schofield let his hand fall to the holster.

The Gulfstream turned one hundred and eighty degrees and accelerated to thirty-five miles per hour to the taxiway.

Cello's sharpshooters hit the Goodyear tires, making two puffs. Then two more puffs.

The Gulfstream rolled on another few hundred meters and then, just when it should have turned right to cross the field, it began to hobble on its two broken front tires. Landing lights flashing, parking lights flashing, the Gulfstream slowed.

Cello started the limousine out to the runway.

The rain was lighter.

Schofield asked Ky, "What's our luck?"

"Green lights, yes, sir."

Schofield tasted his teeth.

43 Saturday Morning, Mount Desert Island

Garland felt the aircraft shiver, and he looked up from his monitor in the aft salon area. Quinn Roosevelt was in the forward area with six of his attack team members, and they were already popping their belts and reaching for their coats and pcs. But back here Garland was alone with Jean Motherwell and his scribe Diana.

The second bump made Garland pay attention. The high-performance driver inside the politician could still feel an aircraft in trouble.

The cabin lights surged and dimmed, and then a shudder raced through the airframe as the front tires failed even while the mass hurled forward at thirty miles per hour.

Garland tapped his desk. *Blown tire,* he thought. *Gear's holding. Shutdown.*

He told Diana, "All crash landings are lucky to talk about."

Special Agent in Charge Jude Bruno came out of his seat in the conference area amidships and locked his gaze on his president. Bruno popped the window shade. What he saw was the dull gray concrete of an airfield in an ordinary rainstorm—no longer nighttime. The runway lights were green and blue. He squatted a little to look closer. He saw the limousine's lights coming out.

Quinn Roosevelt saw the same limousine from his portal and wondered how the advance team had gotten so damned considerate all of a sudden. How did they know to send out the limousine before . . . ?

The captain came on the intercom and addressed Garland as a colleague. "Good morning, sir. Sorry about that. We're sagging here like a little swayback pony. We'll shut down and get a tow in."

Garland leaned sideways to speak to Jean. "A wake-up call, Jean. The front tires blew out. Do you think it means anything that we landed on our face?"

Jean opened her eyes. She knew what it was. She thought, *What do I do now?*

"Jean, you okay?" Garland asked. "It's just the tire. It happens every day in every airport. They'll send out the car. I remember once—"

Jean tried, "Okay, Shy."

Garland reached across to touch her cold hand. "We're both tired," he said like a lover.

The night had gone so quickly for Jean that she felt she'd outflown her exhaustion, and yet now it pounced on her shoulders like a house cat.

Forward, the copilot opened the flight deck door to reveal the Honeywell flight-control system lit up like a video game. The steward was well out of his tip-up seat in the crew galley, and he took the order from the copilot to release the airlock and open up.

Jude Bruno took another peek to the starboard side. *Where was that limousine now?*

Garland was feeling rosy with Jean after a night of her articulate attention just short of bed, and he spoke lovingly. "We're going to get wet a bit, have you got your raincoat handy?"

The wrong sounds were the only warning. Garland heard them and felt them—a strange snorting, a metallic crack, a thudding footfall—and then he was out of his seat and jumping toward Bruno.

The next wrong sound—a shout of "Go!"—told Garland a fact, and the animal in him organized the chaos into the threat.

No, he thought, *how? What? What! Sensenbrenner? The hit?*

Jude Bruno twisted around in front of Garland, his arms out like a goblin's. "Cover!" yelled Bruno.

Suddenly two fully armored soldiers were headfirst through the doorway and rolling over the steward and copilot to firing positions on the floor.

Roosevelt was trapped in his seat by a screaming staffer. The three agents in front of Jude Bruno cleared their weapons and shouted, "Down! Down!" at the staffers between them and the invaders.

The first four-man fire team leaped into the crew galley door like a taxi squad, their M16s across their chests, their heads down, their helmets like rams, smashing down everyone on either side of the aisle.

One agent got off a single stupid round into the ceiling before he was barreled over and butted aside. A second fire team came through the hatchway and kept bulling onward with another wall of body armor and Kevlar helmets and M16s.

There was an incoherent curse from the cockpit, and then the staffers started screaming again.

The troopers were wordlessly noisy with scratching and snapping sounds as their arms and legs moved their body armor and metal.

Now two thousand pounds of soldiers filled the aisle from the crew galley to the aft salon. Several of the troopers had just tackled the three agents and bashed them to silence. A third fire team pushed into the hatchway to give cover.

By then Jude Bruno, seeing he couldn't get a shot, had jumped on top of Garland like a manhole cover.

In the confusion Garland both protected his face from Bruno's elbows and yelled to Jean, "Get down!" He did loose one arm to reach out for her, but he couldn't get Bruno's weight off his shoulder.

Jean sat and breathed. She'd wondered if they would hurt her, and now she saw they didn't have to shoot. They were so big and violent. It was hopeless. She was nothing to them. They swarmed over the plane and pushed the passengers into the carpet. She knew she was in shock. Time didn't matter to her. The men standing over her smelled like LJ's gun oil.

A big trooper put his boot on Jude Bruno.

"Keep your hands on the floor, sir. We're Uncle Sugar. Just up easy. Keep your hands on the floor." Bruno wouldn't move. "Do it!" the trooper yelled.

The other soldiers were hauling the passengers out the door into the rain. There was whimpering and crying though general meekness.

The one passenger the soldiers treated with respect was the navy commander who carried the football, the nuclear codes, and he departed the aircraft in good order.

Quinn Roosevelt was handled like a sack. He didn't protest; he knew what was going to happen, and yet he couldn't accept it.

Jean realized her eyes were closed. She was frozen, and she had to move.

"My name is Master Sergeant Owen, sir." Tom Owen addressed Garland. "This is a strike element of the First Battalion of the Fourteenth, Tenth Mountain, and I'm asking you to get up into your seat, now, sir."

A trooper eased Garland back into his couch seat.

Jean opened her eyes. The Secret Service guards were gone, and she faced the dark gaze of giant soldiers. The aircraft was dim gray and tomblike.

Garland was walled off from Jean and everyone else by the breadth of the body armor. He addressed Tom Owen. "I want your CO, Sergeant. And I want my chief of staff brought back to me immediately."

"My people can't do that, sir," Tom Owen said. "And we need for you to stay here where it's surest for now."

Garland heard the "surest for now" as a death sentence, and he tensed as a healthy animal should—the flight-or-fight instinct taking over his brain. This was a brave man. He pushed aside four million years of instinct and spoke clearly.

"Diana, are you here?"

Diana had been removed with the staffers.

"Jean? Are you there?"

"I'm here, Mr. President," Jean said.

Garland's gravity overcame his panic, and he told Jean, "It's five twenty-two in the morning at or near Mount Desert Island. Saturday, June fourteenth. I am authorizing you to carry out my orders in the event of my death. Do you understand me?"

"Yes," Jean said.

"Your investigation of General Sensenbrenner will turn up a black operation—designator FATHER'S DAY. I want you to find it, Jean, and take it to my successor and tell him to bury it."

Jean was impressed—in truth, shaken. Shy Garland was the president of the United States, and he knew he was going to die because of this fact, and yet he continued to do his duty as he saw it.

"Repeat that back to me," Garland said.

"I understand, Mr. President," Jean said.

Schofield entered the aircraft in a limber hop and came down the aisle.

Jean wasn't surprised by the professional posture, nor by the way the soldiers backed away from their CO. She did expect to hear Schofield speak. Here, after all, was the man who was death, and death was a conversationalist.

Death didn't speak this morning. He took a pistol from his holster and raised it to Garland's eye level.

Garland watched the pistol come out and said, "I am your commander in chief, and I order you to put down your weapons."

Schofield clicked the safety.

Tom Owen stepped from behind Garland and, in an easy, cruel motion, hooked his hand and yanked him forward across the tabletop.

Schofield moved the gun barrel for the armpit.

Jean demanded, "Colonel Schofield, no!"

Schofield stopped his body and retracted the tendons and muscles in his trigger finger. Smoothly he put the .22 back in the holster.

Jean watched the gun go away and then moved her gaze sideways to where they'd slammed Garland's head down.

Garland turned his face toward her. His eyes said, *Judas*.

44 Saturday Morning,
Somes Sound

The rain eased; the island was entombed in a weighty ground fog.

Jack watched the fog roll up like a billowing sheet. Seated

across from Joe Friar at the dining-room table, he was ready for almost anything to emerge from the fog, and when he heard the thumping off the cliff sides, he knew to look up and wait for the first Nightfox helicopter to dart over the Sound like a black bee.

"Tell Kleczka and Calcavecchia," Jack told Friar, "that they can't show their weapons. That chopper can see right into the house, and we can't provoke them."

Friar picked up the intercom receiver again. He'd been through this once already—five minutes before—but it was good logic to make certain.

"I want you to stay with the president," Friar told Special Agent Kleczka, who was upstairs with President Jay and the First Lady. "And I want Calcavecchia's people to remain in the garage."

Friar nodded into the receiver. "Uh-huh, yeah . . ."

Behind Friar, the First Lady's chief of staff, Adam LeMarche, turned in his chair to look to Jack for assurance. The other staffers were at their stations in the kitchen, the mudroom, and the basement. They'd been trained to stand by no matter what the threat; they knew to remain silent and wait for orders.

"No, you've got to stay out of the windows," Friar told Kleczka. "Yes, I know that's an army helicopter out there." Friar emphasized, "You must stay with the president. They're our boys. Yes. We know what it is. Yes."

Jack watched the Nightfox bob in the foggy downdrafts. Visibility was a guessing game after fifty yards. Mostly Jack stared at the Chain Gun that was slaved to the copilot gunner's hand. The helicopter slid from one end of the Sound to the other, moving laterally in and out of the soup.

The Fisheries boat in the Sound was helpless. Jack hadn't told the state police what was coming, just as Friar had not told the Secret Service what was coming; and now that the strike was here, there was no credible explanation.

Friar punched off the intercom. "We're sure we've done it right?" he asked Jack.

"We couldn't have controlled it," Jack said. He kept his hands folded and on the table. He was thirsty and wished he'd brought out some orange juice beforehand. "We've both seen how they work."

"But just to sit here, with Kleczka's and Calcavecchia's guns in the house? I didn't know it would feel like this. We've been stupid."

"That helicopter out there can finish this house," Jack said, "and anything on the island. What are we going to tell them? 'This is a coup, fellas, so relax'?"

There was a *pop-crack* from the distance. Friar's intercom light made him pick up on the First Lady.

"Yes, we heard it," Friar told her. "Yes, it's them. Jack's sure, I'm sure. Yes, they're coming now. I don't know. I don't. No—there's no way we can be sure. No . . ."

Never an American coup, Jack thought. *Never a junta. Never a GI shooter. Never a never.*

Friar told the First Lady, "We'll know when they get here. I don't know if they're bringing Garland. I don't know—I'm sorry—I know. Tell the president that Kleczka has to remain in the room. Okay, you tell Larry. Make him understand, that helicopter out there will fire on the house if it's fired upon. Thanks . . ."

Jack's cell phone flashed, and he picked up instantly. *Let it be Jean.* There was nothing but breaking-up hissing. He tried the macro for Lilly at the house. Nothing but more hissing. He tried the macro for Augusta. Nothing. The phone was dead.

"They've hit the cell tower," Jack said. "Have you got lines out on your network?"

"Shit," Friar said, leaning over to punch on his network. "No, wait. No." Adam LeMarche rolled his head around and gestured that his screens were down. "Everything's gone but the two-way," Friar told Jack.

Jack threw his hands open in defeat—*Idiot!*—because now there was no way to call his father. Schofield was cutting the throat of the island with siege tactics, and then he was going to send fire teams to take the house.

A louder rumble followed by a crack and then a burnt orange flash on the opposite shore made Jack look sideways.

"That was probably the Coast Guard cutter," Jack told Friar. "They've probably put a TOW into her. Maybe the whole station at Southwest is gone by now."

"Oh, Christ, Jack. The casualties, Jack."

"We knew there'd be casualties."

"But there's no real resistance. There's nothing on this island that can stop them. Nothing in Maine. And so why—"

"What's in Moldova or the Yucatán or Kashmir, Joe?"

"But we're . . ." Joe Friar saw his own absurdity and cursed the facts. "Shit, Jack, just shit, there's nothing to stop them from killing all of us."

"Correct."

Jack started to mention Walvis Bay, but he was tired of war stories. The slaughter there had been unbelievable. When continental armed forces take on a mission, they take on the continent, they don't wait, they don't negotiate, they don't know how to stop.

Jack said in his exhaustion, "God, Joe, please don't let Jean be gone, that's not much to ask."

Friar said, "I wish there was more I could tell you, Jack. We called them down on us."

"It was me," Jack said.

The gun pops were closer now—a string of firecrackers and then two low booms.

"Is that the TV trailers?" Friar asked.

"I counted how many guns there were between the field and here," Jack said, "and I came up with just the state police's forty-eight—sidearms and shotguns—not counting Kleczka's and Calcavecchia's teams. Just forty-eight."

"What do you mean, just forty-eight?"

Jack explained, "The guns are all gone by now. He's taking out the TV and radio trucks. It's how they do it. No media allowed. Just like overseas."

"Shit, Jack."

The dull explosion from the Sound jolted the windows of the house. The Fisheries boat was hit and dead in the water; there was a crackling noise of the superstructure breaking up a hundred yards out.

This last demonstration was too much for the Secret Service, and with a crash Calcavecchia pushed through the mudroom door and raced into the long hallway—his Uzi in his left hand, his coat off, his eyes wet with fury. He screamed at Friar, "What the hell is this? You've got to tell me! We've got to move them. This is crazy!" Calcavecchia pointed the Uzi like a long left arm. "You said you know about this!"

Simultaneously Friar was yelling back, "Don't do it, Mike! If you show yourself, they'll fire on the house."

"Who are they?" Calcavecchia cried.

Friar and Calcavecchia continued their argument at full volume, "God damn you, Friar!" and "Shit, Mike!" and much chair kicking. Adam LeMarche and the other staffers watched with the first of their real panic.

Jack heard rifle fire from the quarry side. It was time to take a look—Schofield would be coming, and there was little to be proved by sitting here like victims. Pulling on his rain jacket, Jack told Calcavecchia, "You trust me, Mike—Mike! Mike! Tell your guys to come up here and give up their guns, now! Mike!" Jack continued to the front door.

Calcavecchia raced up behind him. "You tell me, sir, is this whatever-the-hell-it-is coming at the president?"

Outside on the front porch, Jack didn't have to answer, because there was a Hummer coming out of the ground fog and down the drive, with a squad of armored soldiers walking a patrol alongside. The Nightfox that had hit Southwest Harbor's Coast Guard station came in over Acadia Mountain and hovered high over Route 102.

The ground fog wasn't a concern to the strike force or anyone except perhaps to those who were hiding from the soldiers.

Jack knew that going out now was what had killed Toni, but he had to go, there wasn't a way not to go, so he held his hands wide apart and obviously empty and walked down into the drive. "Put your weapon down, Mike," Jack told Calcavecchia over his shoulder, "and get your people up here to do the same. Do it, Mike."

"What the hell's this?" Calcavecchia exhaled mightily. "Damn it, Governor! I can't!"

"Mike! Those choppers have Chain Guns! That's recon for a battalion!" Jack turned back. "Mike, they're going to shoot! This isn't anything you can handle! Mike—look at them. You were army. Look at them!"

Calcavecchia growled in disgust and threw his Uzi away—and then deliberately made the two-way radio call on his headset to his team.

The point men came up at a trot and moved past Jack to the front porch, kicking the Uzi away and bracketing the doorway. Calcavecchia couldn't solve the situation—what was he supposed to do now that he was overrun? The squad was ignoring him, and when the rest of the Secret Service team came out, they gave up their weapons and moved to Calcavecchia.

By then Jack had reached the command vehicle. A blocky lieutenant got out and tucked away his pistol; a specialist came around to look under Jack's coat. "I want your colonel on the horn," Jack told them. "I'm Governor Longfellow—your briefing probably mentioned me."

"Sir!" the lieutenant barked as he yanked the receiver from the manpack. "Can you tell us what's going on, sir?"

"What'd Operations tell you?" Jack asked.

"Not much, sir." The young man shook his muscles and spoke into the radio sharply with his command and signal procedures. A series of grunts, a nod or two, and the lieutenant spoke to Jack. "They're on the way in."

The lieutenant had many more questions but managed only a weak one before he went forward to his men. "We've heard that's the president inside the house, sir?"

Jack didn't answer. He did watch the crest of the incline. The fog was shifting around, and the sea breeze was working to clear the lawn. The black Lincoln limousine appeared at the head of the drive, trailed by another Hummer, and they both accelerated down the drive to Jack's position.

This is it. Jean?

Schofield hopped from the command vehicle and took the same conqueror's walk he'd taken at Bendery—a cocky professional with that rolling motion from all the weight he was hefting. The corporal in the backseat reached to help out a passenger in a flak jacket and helmet.

Shy Garland, prisoner of war, stood blinking at the old Rockefeller place and Jack Longfellow.

The navy commander with the national security codes got out behind Garland and stood waiting on his captured commander in chief.

The limousine driver opened up the back door and Jean's long legs poked out. Jack didn't react to her until Garland glanced at Jean's legs, too, and then Jack leaned toward his wife with the respect due the minority leader.

Jean wasn't about to let Jack treat her as just another ally, and she walked directly into his chest and made him embrace her.

"Jack, it was terrifying—I couldn't think, it was so terrifying—I couldn't think . . ." She knocked her fist on his biceps. "You didn't tell me that Schofield was going to kill him. You didn't tell me! He was going to shoot him right there—"

"I didn't know how far he'd go," Jack tried.

"You should have told me," Jean insisted. "Jack, I stopped him! If I hadn't been there, he would've shot him."

Jack nodded. "It was Sensenbrenner's plan."

"Jack, are you listening to me—Schofield's an assassin."

Jack didn't respond that Schofield was a soldier—that the killer in him was by order from his commanders and always subordinated to the mission. Why argue with Jean? Instead Jack closed his arms around her. "I'm glad you're here."

Garland had no simple way of comprehending what he'd witnessed so far this morning. The flak jacket made him struggle to find his balance. He went from staring at Jack Longfellow to staring at Jean Motherwell to studying the broad shingled house—the disarmed special agents in a congregation of the helpless, the young soldiers chewing gum and watching the perimeter, the buzzing helicopters on both sides of the estate.

"You knew about this," Garland called over to Jack, but then he stopped himself. He was feeling thick tongued. Stripped of all his resources and left with sweaty body armor, he registered that perhaps the way to get through this was to say as little as possible. Later, when he had Q. and his staff back, he'd reorganize. If he got to later. For now, it looked like he was in trouble.

They're going to have to pull me, he thought. *I'm not giving up the ball.*

Garland did organize his feelings in just this adolescent fashion. The great right-hander, when up against defeat, did think about another day and another starting assignment. Simple base-

ball metaphor was one of Garland's strengths, and he held on to
it. Whatever else, he was not going to take this as more than a
blip in his lifetime stats.

"Mr. Acting President," Jack began, and he kept his voice so
low it wasn't clear at first, "the president wants to see you immediately."

Jack touched Jean's elbow in a courtly fashion. "He's asked
for you, too, Senator. Right now."

"Okay," Jean said, rocking her shoulders back, "how is he?"

"I haven't seen him," Jack told Jean.

Jean knew this meant the president wasn't dead, not much
else—and she was so reduced by the attack that a president who
wasn't dead was enough to satisfy her. Jean didn't know how else
to think of a morning spent with men like Schofield. The man
was predation. She'd never understood why Jack was both fascinated by and afraid of the armed forces. Now she had a notion.
Schofield was as merciless as history. And he was immortal.

Jack rearranged himself between his wife and Garland, and
then he turned the screw: "The president wants your resignation
this morning. The president wants you to know that he's directed Joe Friar and Adam LeMarche to take control of Mr.
Roosevelt's and Mr. Lovell's staffs, and that they are terminated
at the White House. Now. This morning. Immediately."

Garland didn't want to reply to Jack. He pretended the noise
of the Nightfoxes was a distraction. *Only the skipper gives the
hook. Turn the ball over in your hand. Look at the scoreboard.*

"I want you to tell me you understand what I'm saying," Jack
continued. "No staff work on this. Just you and me. Say you
understand me."

Garland looked around. *Where's Q.? Why haven't they
brought Q. along?* "I think you've overstepped yourself, Jack,"
Garland said. "Don't you?"

Jean contributed to Jack, "He confessed the whole thing to

me when he thought he was going to be shot. I heard it clearly, and he knows I did because he made me answer him back."

"That won't come to much," Garland responded matter-of-factly. He felt better now. What did they have? Nothing but a lot of talk. And what did he have? He had the polls. The polls knew he was running a coup against Jay. The polls had known it all week—and the polls didn't mind. The polls cheered him on!

"Have you looked at your role in this, Jean?" Garland said. "You lied to get me up here with that incredible suicide note. You think I won't sort this out once I get back to Washington? You tried to kill the president—look at it—you tried to get me killed, and all of you were in on it. That's the fact."

Jack recognized that to argue with Garland would lead to a rage. He took Jean's arm. "Let's go up now."

Schofield stood off by himself on the front steps. As Jack went by, he told Schofield, "We'll need a SATCOM—did you bring one?"

"Yes, sir," Schofield said.

"You come up, too. The president wants to see you."

"Yes, sir." Schofield didn't know whether to salute the governor or not, so in his measured way he shrugged in deference and then relaxed in having orders to obey—wagging the fingers of his right hand at Corporal Ky for the horn.

Garland watched Jack's exchange with Schofield but he didn't comment. *Sold out,* he thought, *how? Sonny Pickett! How?*

Garland was steadily recovering himself. After the momentary presumption that the colonel was going to shoot him, he'd already regained his sense of sovereignty. He would have preferred to get back his communication with Roosevelt and the White House; however, he could wait for that as he waited out whatever Jay had to say.

What could Jay say that signified?

The fact was that Garland was the acting president of the United States until and unless the Twenty-fifth Amendment took it away from him.

The hook, Garland thought again, *they want me to give myself the hook. And I'm not going to give up the ball . . .*

Joe Friar had gone up to the president. In the foyer, Adam LeMarche asked Jack what he wanted done with the useless communications equipment—were they going to get it back on line? Jack, looking over the shaken staff and the two soldiers standing at the ready with their assault rifles pointed down, spoke gently to the aides. "We're going to confer with the president, and then we're going to be shutting down here. Get together your papers. Get ready to move." Jack took the hands of the president's secretary, Marthe, and told her things were going to work out for the best.

Marthe was resolute and, glancing at Garland, returned, "Just work them out, Governor."

Upstairs, Jack came upon Larry Kleczka looking disoriented. There were two more soldiers at the ready standing at the bedroom door.

"Jesus, Governor!" Larry Kleczka said to Jack. "Will you get these people out of here? I don't care who they are! You've got to!"

Jack was finished with worrying about the edgy Secret Service—since Kleczka's basic problem was that he was outgunned. "Get your people together. This is a battalion. Our battalion. Look at them."

The steward opened up the door prematurely, since Connie Jay hadn't gotten the president ready. She was trying to sit him up in the overstuffed armchair by fitting pillows on either side and propping his useless forearm across his lap.

The president was missing. His tall elegance, his bony agility, his clear features—all were gone completely and not coming back. What sat here now was a ghost wearing a plaid flannel shirt, voluminous taupe corduroys, untied black sports shoes.

He's dying, Jack thought. *He's blue already.*

Jean saw much the same thing; however, her response was to move to Connie's side in order to touch the widow, to embrace her best friend and pull her back from the pyre. "I'm so sorry," Jean whispered, "we have to get him to the hospital, Connie, we have to . . ."

The First Lady held Jean with one long arm and placed her free hand on her husband's neck as if she could animate him.

Joe Friar stood bent-backed in his rumpled brown suit.

Garland weighed each detail and rearranged himself. The president was doomed; the suicide note was genuine; the battle axis was here; the counterattack was now; Sonny Pickett had sold him out to a bunch of losers—he saw all this instantaneously.

"Give me a chair here with the president, Friar," Garland ordered. He uncinched the flak jacket and dropped it to the floor; he tossed the helmet behind at the empty doorway; he walked straight on to Jay, deliberately touching the president's shoes with his heavy steps; he came to his full six feet and smoothed down his blue silk tie. "The chair, Friar!" Garland barked.

Joe Friar obeyed dutifully.

"We're going to push aside what brought us here today, Mr. President," Garland began as he sat. "We're not going to address your incompetence in last year's budget or election, we'll leave out your marriage troubles, we'll go past your collapse, your leaving me without a new budget on January seventh—we'll even overlook your agreeing to go on mind-altering drugs at Walter Reed, your library of therapist's reports, those news leaks about your improving condition and your bold treatment—all that we're leaving behind us. And your spontaneously surprising performance in Miami—skipped. And your walk into the Oval

Office last Monday as if we were holding your coat—not worth thinking about. Nor is your sending Jean to me like Mata Hari last night. Nor this exercise at dawn. Gone. *Poof!*"

There was clatter at the doorway, and Schofield appeared with two soldiers behind him bearing the gift of the SATCOM radio telephone.

Garland hardly paused, leaning forward to stare into the president's moist black eyes. "We've come to here, Mr. President. To this crisis. To the facts of the crisis. I am the commander in chief. And you are a moral bankrupt and a physical coward and a liar. By not resigning, you are a cheat. By not defending the Constitution with your life, you're a coward. By not upholding the letter and the spirit of the Constitution, you are a criminal liar."

Garland summarized by ticking off his points. "Cheat. Coward. Liar. And now this morning you've tried to steal the presidency from me. So—thief and traitor."

Jack wanted the president to raise his head—just that—a single demonstration that he wasn't a legal figment. Yet Jay held himself so still it wasn't possible to see him breathing beneath the folds of the flannel.

In despair Jack flicked to the soldiers to put the SATCOM on top of the dressing table. The corporal ran the wire of the antenna out to the hallway window and pointed the little canopy into the fog.

"Have you got the resignation ready, Friar?" Garland asked without turning his gaze from Jay's throat. "Answer me. The resignation. Who's got it? The one that was meant for me. I had one prepared for you, so where's the one you prepared for me? Give it to me."

Joe Friar asked the First Lady, "What do you want me to do, Mrs. Jay?"

"What she wants you to do," said Garland, "is obey your

president. I wouldn't need you at all except that Q.'s gone
AWOL on me, and he has the resignation we brought along.
Now let me see it."

Jean addressed Garland. "You've lost your head, Shy. I wasn't
sure, I thought maybe this was a fantastic game for you—but
now I think you've lost your decency."

"And what are you going to do about it, Jeannie—make a
speech on the floor? Tell them the truth? You and the truth
belong together. It's your best friend, and you think it's reliable?
Use it, then. See what it gets you. It's not reliable, Jean, it's
fickle—it jumps from side to side. And you, with your dignity
and your trickery and your big brave thunder-headed husband,
are not fast enough to jump with it. No one is."

Garland tapped his foot, kicking the president's shoe suffi-
ciently to make his point that he was ready to walk over the man.

"The resignation, Friar, and if you can't do it, get Q. in here,"
Garland said. "I want Q. anyway, so fetch him, Friar. You're still
on payroll. Fetch Q. if you can't handle your job."

The president moved his jaw. It so startled them all that they
spooked one another—Jean and Jack jerking their heads, the
First Lady contracting her hand, Friar jolting forward—even
Garland was caught midbreath.

The president moved his lips. No sound. The First Lady bent
down and performed the same service as a cardinal might have a
thousand years before at the deathbed watch of the pope.

"He wants you to make the call," she said in translation. She
looked at Jack. "He wants you to call your dad, Jack."

"Yes, fine," Jack said. He told the corporal beside Schofield,
"It's a Washington number. How does this work?"

Corporal Ky answered, "Just like a cell phone, sir—that's
what it is, sort of. The antenna's got the satellite. You just punch
in the numbers."

"Do it for him," the other soldier said, a master sergeant

whom Jack recognized from Bendery, from the airfield at Chisinau. Tom Owen, the battalion Top.

The president was moving his lips again. The First Lady translated. "He says you're right," she said to Garland. "He says you've done your duty. He says—he says he's sorry."

"What?" Garland demanded. "Sorry for what? Sorry because he's an irresponsible stick of the man I helped get elected. Sorry because he let the country down. Sorry because he . . ." Garland thought, *What's the use?* "Just sign the paper. Friar? Put it down here."

The president spoke. Connie Jay glanced down. Friar stepped up with the single sheet of White House stationery and laid it flat on the arm of the chair.

Garland snapped it up. It was the minimum necessary to satisfy the law—patterned after the Nixon resignation. It was addressed to the president pro tempore of the Senate and the Speaker of the House and read simply, "I hereby resign the office of the presidency."

Garland flipped it back down. "Connie, take his hand and help him sign it." Garland was done with rhetoric, he wanted action. "Jean, you're the witness. What time is it? All right. It's ten after seven. We'll need a photographer. Jean, pay attention. I still need a vice president, Jean. I know what you did last night. I know why I'm here. I'm not holding it against you. It was a little raw there an hour ago, but that's part of it—"

Jean shook her head. "You're the best I've ever seen, Shy," she said.

"You, too, dreamboat." Garland rolled his head back. "You know, Jack, I like your wife. I guess I always have. You're a lucky fellow. She belongs in the White House. Last night, I was fairly certain I needed her, but now I know I do."

Jack kept his head down, since he knew this wasn't his territory.

"Don't do that, Shy," Jean warned Garland. "Jack isn't made like you and me." Jean swallowed the fact that she'd lied to herself this badly about Garland all these years. He wasn't a hero; he was a very beautiful, very eloquent, very charismatic rascal. Jean declared, "He's not a real politician like you and me, Shy."

Garland grinned. He felt lighthearted. He'd arranged the news to fit his needs. There was still the detail of the resignation, however, and he started crabbing again. "Friar, are you going to call Q. or what? I need to get this done."

The president's lifeless left hand lay at the edge of the paper.

"Connie, listen—it won't work, stalling me anymore," Garland said. "Yes, if you could somehow get through the next three weeks, then maybe . . ."

Garland pointed at Jean as if she were his best student. "Tell her, Jean—I need your help here. Yes, you might make the headlines shake with your revelations about EXCOM, you might crack the markets worse than they're already cracked and scare the usual suspects, but still it would take three more weeks of hammering to stop the Senate vote, and you haven't got the time. Look at the president. He hasn't got three days. Say it, Jeannie. I've won. We've won. The country's won."

Jean sighed. "All I see is a dead loss, Shy."

"Help him sign, Connie," Garland ordered. "Make his mark for him."

The First Lady kept her face close to her husband's lips. "Joe, perhaps you'd best help me."

Friar asked, "Is that what the president wants, ma'am?"

"Stupid!" Garland exploded, and he jumped up so quickly the chair flew backward. "Connie, sign the damned paper! And get me Q.! I want communication with the White House now! I want the photographers up here, now! What have I got to say to make you people move it?"

The clever animal of Shy Garland turned on the trio of Schofield, Owen, and Ky. "Colonel, get your people out of here, and
bring my bodyguards immediately." Garland saw the hesitation
in Schofield's face and he spoke to it. "I know why you're here,
Colonel. Hellfire, I brought you here. If you want to know, I
think what you did this morning was outstanding—all the way
around, a credit to you. And to Sensenbrenner. Okay? You're
working for me, and you always have been. Now just get moving
again. I want my bodyguards. Get me Jude Bruno right now on
your radio. He'll bring Q. up here. Questions?"

What happened next was as inevitable as the full force of the
Twenty-fifth Amendment.

Schofield and Tom Owen stood at the ready, their hands on
their weapons across their breasts, their eyes fixed on the center
of the room.

Jean, tucked up behind the First Lady, felt her body quiver
with hunger and a two-day lack of sleep. She'd been scared for
so long now that she didn't care—she just felt blank—and she
fixed her eyes on Jack's silent darkness.

Jack had the SATCOM receiver in his hand, and he was
watching the First Lady's face—her long nose, the way her
mouth opened beside the president's eyes. Did he see what was
happening? He couldn't get in charge of his own premonition.
He'd lit the fuse, and now it was detonating in slow motion, and
what could he do to stop it?

The president's eyes were his lone alert feature. In them
there was a resigned mortality. There was also plain anger.

The president moved his lips.

The First Lady raised up from her husband and spoke directly to the back of the room. "Colonel Schofield, the president
says to do your duty."

Garland had warning. He was a bold man, and he knew that
the final rational act is to get mad at death. He heard Tom Owen

move, and he spun back as if facing a thief, shouting, "Hey—come on—"

Tom Owen swung his weapon like a staff and bashed the inside of Garland's left knee.

Garland tried to hang on to Tom Owen's mass but missed his hold and fell to his hands and knees. Starting to rise up, Garland barked, "Fuck you," to Tom Owen.

The next blow sliced Garland's head at the neck and slammed him against the foot of the bed frame so hard that he didn't bounce, he just collapsed like a quilt.

Schofield drew the .22. Tom Owen took Garland's hair and yanked the body over and laid it facedown on the hook rug. Schofield knelt down and pulled the suit coat up. He placed the barrel against the armpit and fired three times, *tphut, tphut, tphut.*

Schofield paused to let the body settle, then raised the barrel and fired two more bullets into the base of the brain, *tphut, tphut.*

The gunsmoke made a twister in the middle of the room.

Jean couldn't breathe.

Connie Jay told Friar, "Help me!" and Friar moved up to take the president's left hand. The two bent over the president to fit the pen in his fingers. They dragged his fingers over the paper to make the scratches that had to stand for his signature.

Friar took the paper up. "Okay," he said, "it'll do."

The First Lady ordered Jack, "For God's sake, make the call."

Jack jammed the receiver against his ear. Was the connection made already? It wasn't ringing. Was his father there?

Jean ordered, "Jack, hurry!"

"Dad?" Jack started.

4 5 Saturday Morning, Burning Tree Country Club, Potomac, Maryland

Long John wasn't sure enough of the golf cart to drive it by himself, so he drafted his town car driver, the Mauritian Creole, Parsifal.

Maryland's humidity was already crawling over the carpet of Kentucky grass; the sunshine wasn't warm, it was like a barbecue pit; the grasshoppers and honeybees ruled the fairways, while the sparrows and buntings patrolled the deep rough.

The choicest foursomes had been out for ninety minutes, since full sunup, and Long John had to guess which charging crew of middle-aged warriors was Rainey's. He just missed him at the fifth tee, and might have missed him altogether if Parsifal hadn't gotten them lost so that they chanced upon the Speaker at the sixth green.

Rainey was dressed in a loose-fitting Disney golf blouse and was wearing his trademark golf cap in the shape of Donald Duck's bill. He leaned on his putter while watching a partner hole out.

From the near distance, Long John could see no certain sign that Rainey had prepared himself. No press contingent, no staff whatsoever, just his three partners and their caddies and the lone bodyguard due the Speaker of the House.

Parsifal rolled the cart silently up the walkway and parked it near the weeping willow. The green was seven feet above them, and Long John struggled out. He used his cane in the soft grass to gain traction for the last push.

"Mr. Speaker, here!" Long John called. Rainey was just above him, looking the other way. "I need a hand, here!"

The breeze off the green smelled of luxuriant summer. Long John's eyes stung with sweat, and he put his head down to find his strength. A right hand came down to take Long John by the elbow and lift him up. Long John tottered on the mushy grass and tried to breathe evenly.

"Good morning, Mr. Secretary," said Dean Bonaparte—the just cashiered secretary of the treasury—a big, craggy man who was also former chair of Bankers Trust. "I'm sorry we weren't quicker to see you coming up."

Luke Rainey hurried over with the other two golfers— Rainey's best friend, the lobbyist and ex-congressman John Zavarello, and Rainey's lawyer, Gershwin Metz.

The four same stood around Long John like Boy Scouts waiting on their good deed for the morning.

Long John planted his cane, wiped the sweat from his mouth, and spoke out. "Mr. Speaker, I've had a telephone call from my son within the half hour. The acting president is dead. The president has resigned his office. The president's message to you is that, as per the Twenty-fifth Amendment and the Statutory Succession Laws of nineteen forty-seven, you are to assume the duties of the office immediately." Long John breathed hard and offered his wet hand. "Congratulations, Mr. President."

Rainey's broad, pleasant face changed forever. His grip was as wet as Long John's.

"Thank you," Rainey said automatically; then: "Shy Garland is dead?" he asked.

"Yes, sir," Long John said.

Metz and Zavarello, two of the roughest operators in town, exhaled in gasps and wavered. Dean Bonaparte asked, "How, in God's name?"

Long John had heard five shots on the open line. He answered, "I wasn't present," and successfully maintained compartmentalization for Rainey and his colleagues.

Rainey knew enough to ask, "It's certain, then?"

Long John tried, "We'll want to get started back, Mr. President. There's the swearing-in. And I saw Mr. Justice Dain's car in the parking lot."

"My God, Mr. Secretary," Rainey said. "I didn't know—I didn't—did you know Shy Garland was going to die?"

It was a sober but unhelpful question. Long John glanced away to break the tension, and when he did he spotted a strange sight. Across several fairways from the direction of the clubhouse was a long snake of figures coming hard at the sixth green. The leading figures were young men in suits, carrying small briefcases, and they were running full-out—that would be the Secret Service.

The trailing figures were men and women in jeans and polo shirts, carrying cameras and boxes—that would be the press.

Rainey saw them, too, and stepped up to Long John. "How did they find out so soon?"

"They know everything—that's my experience," Long John answered. "We can't keep a secret more than the time it takes to say it. We're only the passers-on, anyway."

"What?" the president asked.

Long John didn't want to explain anymore. Besides, if he was going to counsel a president, it was going to be Jack, and it was going to be next year.

"My dear God," the president said. He was standing flat-footed, his putter balanced across both hands, watching the mob race over the roasting grass toward him. "What do we do now?"

he asked Long John as well as his friends. "Should we just wait here? What do you think?"

"I think I should get out of the sun," Long John said.

"You can't stay?" the president said. "I could use some help, here, Mr. Secretary."

"Sir, you've got the best help there is. And we'll see each other again soon enough, I think."

"When?"

"New Hampshire, I suspect. Next February."

Rainey gave the politician's smile of all's well.

The new president wasn't trying hard to hold Long John Longfellow to his side, he was just passing time while awaiting the inevitable; for history was coming at him—the leaping, sprinting, falling, cascading human beings coming on in a stampede over the bunkers, across the traps, up the slopes, headlong for the sixth green.

Long John turned away and started down to the golf cart and Parsifal. He'd done his job, and it was time to get on back to Georgetown and take a nap. Maybe then he'd pack his bag again and get out to National.

Good idea, he thought. *Up to Bangor today. Get a ride down to the island eventually. Try to beat the crowds going to look at the scene of the deeds.*

"After all," he reminded the willow tree, "tomorrow's Father's Day. My day."